THE FALCON'S FLIGHT

NATALIA RICHARDS

A NOVEL OF ANNE BOLEYN

BOOK 2

The Falcon's Flight

A Novel of Anne Boleyn: Book 2

Copyright © 2020 Natalia Richards
ISBN-13: 978-84-946498-9-9

This is a work of fiction. Names, characters, businesses, places, events and incidents are either the products of the author's imagination or used in a fictitious manner. Any resemblance to actual persons, living or dead, or actual events is purely coincidental.

M

MadeGlobal Publishing
For more information on
MadeGlobal Publishing, visit
our website
www.madeglobal.com

To my partner, Michael, who shared my
adventures in the Loire

To Anne,

When I see the brunette in order,
young, of good figure, descendant of the gods
and that her voice, her fingers and the spinette
lead a gentle and melodious sound,
I have pleasure, both from ears and from eyes,
more than the saints in their immortal glory
and as much as them I become glorious
as soon as I believe I am a little
                              loved by her

Clément Marot

England

Bruges
Calais
Amiens
Paris
Argentan
Gien
Amboise · Blois
Dijon
Méjières en Brenne
Chamblet
Cognac
Lyon

France
Montélimar
Nîmes · Avignon
Marseille · Hyères

The Journey

*'One of these hours shall open the gate
Of blissful life, or relentless fate.'*

The Low Countries
and Northern France,
October 1514

Still he would not speak. Sighing, I urged my horse on and retreated into my thoughts as we cantered through the meadow grass. I felt homesick. My year at the court of Margaret of Savoy, as one of her *demoiselles*, had proved happy, but now – what? What lay ahead? At just fourteen years of age, far from my home in Kent, in England, I was about to join a new household at the French court of King Louis. At least I would see my older sister, Mary, who had already arrived there.

At our first resting place, the man dismounted, sat alone on the ground some distance away, unwrapped a piece of bread and cheese, and bit into an apple. He scowled as he spat out a rotten piece. A second man, Gervais, offered me a piece of the strong-smelling cheese from a scrap of cloth. He ate with his mouth open, his thick, black hair tumbling over his eyes, and pointed with his knife.

'Ignore him,' mumbled Gervais, his mouth full, 'he is in a foul humour with your father or uncle. I know not which and care less. Apparently, this assignment to bring you to

Paris proved sudden and unprepared for. Bernart there agreed to be paid in advance for food, candles, accommodation, and horses, but the money did not materialise in time. He is paying out of his own purse.' He shrugged. 'So what? He pays now and gets it back later. I care not so long as my own time is paid for. Now, later – it is all the same to me.'

I glanced up and saw Madame Dupont pull her cloak about her. I then looked back at Bernart as he bit on a cork from a bottle with his yellow teeth, spat it out, and drank deeply. He stared insolently as he wiped his dribbling mouth, and I quickly looked away. Hateful man. It was not my fault – I had not wanted to make this tedious journey to Paris with these strangers. Why on earth had Father sent someone so loathsome to accompany me?

I tossed my little dog, Bonny, a lump of bread which she caught with a quick snap of her jaw. The talk turned to the fate of Princess Mary, sister to King Henry of England.

'Jesus, Mary, and Joseph, what a prospect awaits her,' said Gervais, wiping his knife clean on his coat. 'Well, they say old Louis will not live to smell the flowers of spring, for the caterpillar has eaten most of the cabbage!' Madame Dupont glared at him.

'That is what comes of being a Princess of England, a Tudor,' she sighed. 'The poor lamb is bartered throughout Europe and sold to the highest bidder – and she only eighteen years old. Why, old Louis is thrice her age.'

'Spoiled bitch, more like,' said Bernart. 'She demands and gets whatever she wants.'

'King Louis,' she continued, 'has sent over the artist Jean de Paris to supervise her wardrobe, imagine how splendid it will be.'

Bernart spat on the ground. 'A year's pay to design a few paltry hats and gowns. What sort of man's work do you call that?'

I bit into my apple and wondered what would be my own fate. I could not expect a high marriage like a princess, but my family would still make the best match they could. But not yet, for I was still too young; and besides, my sister, being the eldest, must marry first.

Having rested, we continued our journey towards Paris along the flat, straight tracks that skirted Brussels, and on through the softly undulating Hainault countryside, to the great Fôret de Raismes. When we trotted out into the light, we then cantered on, following the River Scheldt across the verdant valley, to Valenciennes. Jan, the youngest of the three men accompanying me on my journey, insisted on singing French songs, although he could not hold a tune. He offered to teach me one, but the surly Bernart sharply forbade him with a scowl. Gervais shrugged and winked as he trotted ahead, making me smile. He carried Bonny on the pommel of his saddle, and the little dog's ears pricked to the rustle of possible rabbits.

The journey was slow, for it had started to rain, and the long, muddy tracks stretched endlessly before us. Bird nets tied high on poles stood empty, and I felt glad that the migrating birds had evaded them. I sighed. Nothing relieved the monotony unless we chanced upon a small settlement, and then the people would only venture forth from their hovels and stare in curiosity, wiping their hands on their greasy aprons, to watch our party pass. I noticed that now the women did not wear the stiff white coifs I had seen in the Low Countries, but a linen cloth wrapped around their heads covering their hair and set low upon their brow. Brown-skinned and barefoot, what appeared to be shoes they slung about their necks, and when they called out to our party, the greeting sounded strange and guttural.

As we rode deeper into France, the landscape changed to one of ancient churches, tumbling grey stone abbeys, and abandoned fortified châteaux. I asked Gervais why the little churches we saw were built like forts.

'Too many questions,' said Bernart, kicking his horse on.

'Soldiers!' shouted Gervais, turning his head back to me.

'Thieves from every army have raped this land as they rode through. For centuries mercenaries have plundered whatever they wanted here – grain, cattle, women – even now there is a suspicion of strangers. The villagers had to use the churches as a defence. That is why they are built so.'

I stared at the dwindling smoke rising from the scattered dwellings, and thought how different the houses appeared from those in the Low Countries. Here they were built of timber and covered in twisted, creeping foliage and vines. They were not tall, narrow and neat, but dilapidated, rutted, and in poor repair and the muddy market places were littered with sewage and offal.

We journeyed on through Picardy, across the marshy land, to the crowded, fortified town of Amiens, arriving just as it began to rain again. Bonny gave an excited yelp, for amidst the noise and bustle of pilgrims she could smell the chickens roasting on spits in an open shop front.

'That is the cathedral of Notre Dame St Marie,' pointed Gervais, steering his horse to avoid the bustling, crowded stalls. 'The townspeople wanted to build something special to house a fragment of the head of St John. It is their most precious relic brought back by crusading knights.'

I stared up at the startling sight, just as I had when I visited Canterbury on my journey to Dover. How long ago that journey now seemed.

'But it is *beautiful!*' I cried, staring at the magnificent carvings on the doorway, and the great rose window. 'Madame Dupont, do look!'

The woman half smiled in an uninterested way as I let the raindrops patter down onto my upturned face.

Turning towards the inn, opposite the west door of the cathedral, we halted outside a broken, creaking sign bearing the words '*L'Ange*' – 'The Angel'. Bernart took off his cap and wiped his sweating brow.

'Jesu,' he said under his breath, staring up at the sign. 'Another louse-infested hole.' He waited until Madame

Dupont moved out of earshot.

'Only three more days of this hell,' he muttered, 'and then we shall be in the stinking stews of Paris. Then I go back to Calais, where I see my wife and sleep in my *own* God-damned bed.'

Gervais dismounted and held his arms out to me.

'Ignore his foul mouth. Are you looking forward to seeing your sister?'

'Oh, yes, Monsieur!' I replied as he lifted me down.

'Well,' he said, 'it is six days since we left Mechelen and I can tell you, it seems like a lifetime ago to my old bones!' Bernart slapped his horse's rump as an eager boy led her away.

'Mind the horses are groomed and wisped down properly,' he growled, as we entered the inn. 'And give them a good feed! None of your mould-riddled grain!'

*   *

'How much longer before we reach Paris?'

Bernart made no reply. I frowned. If I had a mind to tell my father or uncle how disagreeable he was, he might not get paid at all. Bonny shivered and blinked against the rain as the horses' hooves made great, squelching noises in the muddy track. Gervais and Jan remained silent, concentrating on keeping their horses from stumbling.

After several hours, the rain stopped, and a watery October sun made for a more cheerful journey. Through forests and high ferns, we cantered on, making good progress until late afternoon when Bonny pricked up her ears and barked. A split second later a horn blew and from out of the distant woods burst a great mounted crowd of gorgeously apparelled men and women shouting '*Voici aller!*' The huntsmen released the baying hounds – great rough-coated beasts – from their leashes and the dogs leapt forward with a cry. Bonny barked with excitement as a body of riders, clothed in green, javelins poised, galloped close behind them.

'Keep that animal fast!' hissed Bernart, turning to

Gervais, as my little dog struggled to jump down. 'The damned thing will be killed.'

As the riders galloped forward, leaping streams and ditches, I saw at the front, richly dressed in blue and silver, a man carrying the Royal Standard of France. Bernart tightened the reins as his horse jittered about on the spot, unsettled by the blaring of the horn and the barking dogs.

'They seek the stag,' he said, narrowing his eyes. I watched as the riders disappeared far into the distance, and the sound of the hounds grew faint. We rode on, but shortly after, Madame Dupont's horse threw a shoe. Bernart cursed as he picked up the mare's hoof and glanced about.

'Froissy is straight ahead,' he muttered, 'we can get the shoe replaced there. Let us hope, unlike Blessed Mary and Joseph, there is room at the inn.' As Madame Dupont mounted the spare horse, Gervaise led her hobbling horse behind them.

When we came upon Froissy and entered a small, crowded dwelling that appeared to be a hostelry, suspicious eyes turned to stare.

'Ah, Messieurs, Madame!' cried an old man rising from his bench. 'Did you see the *rose d'Angleterre?*'

'Aye,' said a woman, throwing pieces of coarse bread down on to the table. 'What was she wearing? I could not see for they flew at such a speed!' Her eyes widened with excitement beneath her unruly red hair.

'Was the handsome François with them?' A young girl pushed to the front, forearms covered with flour.

The dialect of these people sounded strange and harsh as Bernart pulled Jan to his side.

'What is she saying? You understand peasant talk, what does she say?'

The woman thrust a cup of ale into my guide's hand, which he gruffly acknowledged, and then downed in one go. 'I know not what you are talking about woman, or what you are saying. Tell them Jan,' he said, his words muffled by the cup.

'We need a horseshoe fixing,' explained Jan, matching the strange accent and staring around at the company. 'A horseshoe?' He was not sure if they had understood.

A fat woman came forward, wiping her red, chapped hands on a greasy cloth. 'Who asks?' she said, suspiciously, eyeing my coat with its fur collar.

'He does.' Jan cocked his head towards Bernart.

'Your horses are very fine creatures, sir,' said a young gentleman, turning back from the window. 'Did you lose the shoe hunting?'

Bernart untied the neck of his coat. 'No, we did not, now can you fix the shoe or not? These women need rest. If you have rooms here we will be on our way at first light.'

'Gerard can fix the shoe.' The woman flicked her eyes towards a man in the corner, 'and there are rooms. But where are you heading?'

Jan, seeing Bernart's mounting irritation, quickly stepped forward. 'Paris. We have come from the court in Mechelen, in the Low Countries, and are to deliver this girl to the court in Paris to join the new princess's household.'

From the low muttering, it appeared obvious that no-one had heard of Mechelen.

'Why wait till Paris?' The woman poured out more ale. 'The court is at Beauvais, and that is where the hunt is heading.'

'Beauvais?' asked Jan, staring at Bernart. 'But the royal couple and court are progressing from Abbeville straight to Paris for the coronation at Saint-Denis. Surely they have reached Chantilly by now?'

'The king is ailing,' said a man, thrusting his cup forward to be refilled. 'They say his buxom new wife is wearing him out already – they are not going anywhere until he can bear to be moved, and that could be several days.' The crowd started jeering and laughing. 'To amuse themselves,' he said, 'the courtiers are out hunting – hundreds of men, women and boys. That is all they ever do. They ride, destroy the crops and return to their beds half-drunk with wine. They say the nobles keep five hundred falcons between them just to bring down kite and heron. The meat is not even palatable!' The laughing turned to nodding and swearing.

'They are all at Beauvais, you say?' said Bernart, rubbing his unshaven chin. 'That is – what – two, three leagues from here?'

'Aye,' said the woman, who appeared to be the landlady. 'You can rest here and leave at dawn. The child and her companion look as if they need a wash and a good meal.'

Bernart finished his ale and smiled for the first time in over a week.

'Well, what could be better?' he asked of Gervais. 'We shall ride over to Beauvais, deliver our charge, and ride straight back to Calais.'

'But,' said Gervais, 'were we not paid to ride as far as Paris?'

Bernart stared at him. 'And since we have *not* been paid, *I* say we go to Beauvais.'

Chapter One

'I count the bright days only'

Beauvais, Northern France

The ill-lit chamber smelt of musty herbs and dog piss. I stood in my green gown, my hair falling loose beneath a black, velvet cap; outside, birds twittered and fought in the bushes and the shrill noise cut across the silence. A loud barking noise, immediately followed by a blood-curdling yelp, filled the air as the woman walked over and pulled the window shut with a slam, dropping its latch.

'Really, one cannot hear oneself think in here. It is quite intolerable.'

As the woman turned to me, I saw she was dressed in a black gown and wore her hair gathered into a hood with long lappets. She had dark hair, a sallow face with fine brows, and eyes brown and birdlike. I had the distinct feeling that those beady eyes were scrutinising every crease in my gown.

'Now – welcome to the French court, Mistress *Boleyn*.'

Her voice sounded pleasing, and I liked the way she pronounced my name, for it sounded far more sophisticated than plain Bullen.

'My name is Françoise de Maillé, Madame d'Aumont, and I am the *première dame d'honneur* at this court. You are Anne, the sister of Marie, are you not?'

'Indeed, my lady,' I said brightly. Somewhere a chapel

bell sounded the hour.

'We have informed your father that you have joined the court here at the Bishop's Palace, in Beauvais. We did not expect King Louis to fall ill and *le grand echal des logis* has had to house people as best he could, some outside the walls, some in villages. Most inconvenient. In the meantime, new gowns will be made for you, ready for the coronation. The king suffers badly with gout, but on recovering, the court will continue its journey to the Abbey of Saint-Denis for his wife's crowning. You understand?' I nodded, glad that I had paid heed to my French lessons at Mechelen.

'Now, if there is anything you require, you must come to me and only me, and you must report any gossip you hear, particularly if it concerns our dear princess. It is our job as her ladies to serve her by protecting her from foolish talk. Is that not so?'

'Indeed, my lady.'

She appeared satisfied and congratulated my understanding of French.

'The princess,' she continued, 'after much fuss and bother, has been allowed to keep some of her ladies. Lady Elizabeth Grey, daughter of the Marquis of Dorset, Mary Fiennes your cousin, Ann Jernygham, Florence Hastings, Joan Bourchier and your sister Marie. You have been brought over here as an interpreter and companion to the princess, when and if required.' My eyes widened. This position was even better than I hoped for. She then asked me if I had any questions.

'Madame, I am very honoured to be here, but why were those ladies dismissed?'

Madame d'Aumont arched a brow. 'My dear, far too many people flocked to the princess's court in the hope of advancement. We had to be selective. Fortunately, we have a frugal king who does not wish to waste the people's taxes on unnecessary baggage.'

My expression must have appeared unconvinced, for

she sighed. 'Very well, let me speak frankly to you. Lady Guildford turned out to be a complete busybody, irritating the king at every turn. Each time he tried to be alone with his wife, she would appear like some nurse. It was monstrous. The princess is not a child, and the king could not be intimate with her with three of them in the chamber. You will, therefore, serve, but *not* interfere.'

I wanted to giggle, but my face remained serious as she explained that here there would be no more formal schooling, as there had been under the Regent's care.

'This book,' she said, holding a tome up, 'is the Catechism of Perseverance, a book of religious instruction that all French girls are given at the age of twelve. You must study it carefully, and so I will insist that you obtain a copy.'

She went on to inform me of domestic matters, the order of the princess's household, and how many logs, candles, and wine I might be entitled to. I would be expected to dine with the other *demoiselles*, in the great chamber, on whatever meat was provided that day – beef, mutton, rabbit, and so forth. On fast days, I would be served salt salmon, flounders, eels and the fish of the day. My heart sank, for I hated salted fish.

She straightened her back with pride and smoothed down her black gown. 'Now,' she said, 'my position allows me exclusive privileges. I alone, and no other, may bring the first dish to the princess during mealtimes and banquets. Thus, I am seen – and treated – with the highest regard. I do not know how the Regent took *her* meals, but here at the French court, they are a very public and overly relaxed affair.'

Standing there she looked like an angry crow, its feathers ruffled, reminding me of my grandmother, Dame Margot. She explained that the princess did not rise before nine, but when she had woken, her ladies dressed her and then she proceeded to a private Mass. On her return, she visited the king, ate with him, and discussed whatever might amuse him. The rest of the morning might be given to visitors and ambassadors. During that time, I would be called upon to act as a translator. Attendance at dinner, served promptly at eleven-thirty, must be punctual. In the afternoon, the ladies and maids might watch tennis or archery, place small bets on their champions and hand out the prizes. At the end of the day, there would be a ball, a masque or dinner. Old Louis liked to move about, but when visiting Paris, he might stay at the Bastille de Saint-Antoine, the castle of the Louvre, or, his preferred palace, the Hôtel des Tournelles. God only knew why, she said, since it was a stinking, dilapidated pile, freezing in winter and stifling in summer.

At that moment, the door burst open, accompanied by shrieks of laughter, and a group of young ladies tumbled in, their beautiful gowns a dizzy array of colour. On seeing Madame d'Aumont, they hurriedly sank to the rushes, faces red and flustered, all giggling ceased.

'Fie, ladies! What means this rude intrusion?' Madame d'Aumont clapped her hands loudly as the girls scrambled to their feet, eyes lowered. None dared look up. 'Such noise and haste do not become you. What are you doing in here?' She shooed all of them back out of the chamber, then paused. 'Wait! A moment, *demoiselle*, please, I have someone here who wishes to see you.' One of the girls stopped as Madame d'Aumont turned back to me. 'I have said what I wished to say for the present, but when you are finished, please return to my chambers before your presentation to the princess.'

The door closed behind her, and I stared at the girl before me.

'Mary?' I whispered. She raised her head. 'Mary, oh, Mary!' We immediately flew into each other's arms.

'Nan!'

'Dearest Mary, I feared I would never see you or mother again when we heard news of the storm and your dreadful voyage across the sea!' I clung onto my sister and breathed in the familiar, rosewater perfume.

'Why, Nan, I thought not to see you until Paris! What a stroke of good fortune. I want to hear everything from when you last wrote. Oh, I have *so* much to tell you!' She then held me so tightly I almost stopped breathing, and I pushed her away, laughing. 'The voyage to Calais proved a nightmare, Nan, I can tell you, and I felt *so* sick I thought I might die from constant retching. You should have seen us – we arrived on the beach looking like half-drowned ship rats! Duchess Agnes collapsed, and it took two men to carry her off the ship. I almost laughed out loud seeing them struggle with her weight, and she crying and wailing in case they dropped her! But we have all survived. Oh, little sister, let me look at you.' She held me at arm's length. 'Why, your hair has grown so long!'

'But I have a pimple!' I moaned, 'nothing will rid me of it.'

'No, you look charming! Oh, I have never seen such a glorious sight as the arrival of Princess Mary at Abbeville – how I wish you had arrived here in time.' She took my hands and spun me around.

'Tell me, Mary, are our parents here?' I asked eagerly, as we hurried over to the window seat. 'What about Grandfather? Where are King Louis and his princess?'

Mary laughed as my words tumbled out.

'Oh, Mary, I too suffered a frightful journey, with a most disagreeable ma –'

'Wait, one thing at a time, Nan.'

I sat admiring my sister in her cornflower-blue gown. Her brown eyes shone brightly, and beneath her cap, her light, nut-brown hair lay thick around her smooth shoulders. Her skin, clear and bright, showed not a blemish, and she had stained her lips with a faint tint of red. She put her hand to my face. 'You are not ill-favoured,' she said softly, 'for you have the most beautiful, dark eyes.' She planted a kiss on my forehead. 'Oh, Nan, this is such a happy turn of events. Uncle Howard and Father were determined that both *Boleyn* girls – how different that pronunciation sounds – should be here at court together.'

'Oh, Mary, they have been so good to us and we will not let them down, will we?' She knew what I referred to, for her wayward behaviour at home had caused great distress. 'Anyway, where are our parents?'

Mary smiled. 'They have returned to England. Is that not the most perfect thing?' She rose up, threw out her arms and spun around. 'Gone, gone, gone! No more disapproving looks from Father or Mother, or fat Duchess Agnes with her long, suspicious nose poked into everything. She proved such misery during her stay here. It has been awful for me having them spy on my every move and watch who I talked to. You know how I like to tease.'

I felt alarmed. 'Are you still in love with *him*?' I asked, referring to the sordid affair that had resulted in my taking her place at the court of Margaret of Savoy.

She put her finger up to my lips. 'No, Nan – all that is forgotten, as if it never happened, and you must promise to never, ever speak of it again. I am sorry, I truly am, but I cannot undo what is done. I have changed, I have, and I will never be foolish again, I promise. Besides, I do not want another beating – look, I still have the scar.'

She lifted her gown but I did not want to look at the red weal made by the birch cane, knowing it was I who had caused her to be discovered with her lover. I turned guiltily away, for she still had no idea who had betrayed her. Well, here, I hoped, we would enjoy a new beginning for both of us - a fresh start.

'I am a different woman now,' she said, dropping her skirts with a rustle.

I appeared unconvinced, and it showed.

'I am *serious*,' she protested, stamping her foot, 'all is forgotten. Now, dearest, I am only in love with France, and you will be too!'

'Oh, Mary, I want to see our parents, for it has been so long and I miss Mother.'

'Well, you cannot, you goose. As soon as the princess

married old Louis, all the noble lords – including our Bullen and Howard relations – having completed their commission were packed off back to England. Even the lower nobility, which did not please them one bit, as many hoped to stay and gain further honour.'

'All of them?' I asked.

'A few have stayed.'

'Well, what of George – is our little brother well? I long to see him, and he never writes a word.'

'He is well and running Dame Margot into the ground with his pranks.'

I smiled, knowing how Grandmother tolerated no disturbance to her rest. 'Father,' continued Mary, 'has promised to take him to court this coming Christmas to watch his first masque. However, it is the lions and leopards at the Tower he wants to see. He talks of nothing else. Anyway, where is your little dog?' She glanced about.

'You will see her later. She is adorable.'

'Well, take care, Nan, you must not let her out of your sight for a moment, for there is always a fight between the hunting hounds and the ladies' lap dogs. Since every courtier seems to own a dog, the dining hall is like a menagerie!'

My eyes widened. 'Mary, what is the princess like? They say she is the most beautiful girl in Christendom.'

'Well, she is not quite how you imagine – and neither is King Louis. But come, Madame d'Aumont has arranged for your introduction to the princess at three o'clock this afternoon, so we must make you presentable.'

＊　＊

Back in the bedchamber, I watched as Mary flung various gowns across the bed.

'No – no good – useless. Nan, all of these are crushed, and this one has a soiled hem and a tear! What *have* you been doing?' She held up a saffron-coloured gown as I shivered in my chemise, my arms folded across my flat chest. The logs in the fireplace had not long been lit, and I felt frozen. 'Well, this will have to do,' said Mary, as she beckoned for the chamberer to assist me to step into a gown the colour of autumn leaves.

The girl fastened up the laces as best she could, her fingers ice-cold, and lifted out my long hair.

'You must look your best for the princess – and *smile*,' said Mary, picking up a hairbrush and vigorously brushing my hair. 'The most important thing is to impress King Louis. Remember, if he does not like you, he will send you home.'

'I heard that King Louis is a very pious king,' I said, over my shoulder.

Mary moved round to appraise me, her head tipped to one side. 'Mmm … he is, but you have to remember there are two rival courts here. François, his mother Madame Louise, and his sister on one side, and King Louis and Princess Mary Tudor on the other.' She then lent forward and whispered in my ear. 'King Louis is pious because he is half-dead and near to his judgement, and François is young and reckless. He is just waiting to leap up onto old Louis' throne.'

Trying not to appear shocked, I placed a pearl cap upon my hair and fastened a golden girdle about my waist. Finally, the two of us stood together, admiring ourselves in the burnished brass mirror.

'You look lovely, Nan,' said Mary, generously, 'but we must arrange for you to obtain some new gowns – oh, and neck chains. They are *so* fashionable here in France; everyone wears several around their neck and bosom. Now, quickly, Madame d'Aumont awaits us and then – the princess.'

Passing through several guarded chambers, we arrived outside a large wooden door guarded by two gentlemen-at-arms. A group of maids, beautifully dressed in matching gowns of gold and cream brocade, stood simpering and chattering in excited whispers.

'What is the matter,' I whispered to Mary, 'why are they all in such a flutter?'

She pulled me to one side. 'Charles Brandon, the Duke of Suffolk, is in there with King Louis to discuss the coming tournament and every girl is in love with him. Look, Elizabeth Grey is almost swooning.'

I stared at the girl with the inflamed cheeks, appearing to all the world as if she had just been slapped. She seemed the most attractive of the girls, apart from my sister, with hazel brown hair and slanting, green eyes. As I stood admiring her, the door opened, and all the girls jumped back as Madame d'Aumont appeared.

'Mistresses Marie and Anne Boleyn – enter and take your places by the window.'

The tittering girls parted.

As Mary and I walked into the stifling, airless chamber, I saw a man lying in a large, gilded bed and sitting beside him, a young woman stroking his yellowing hand. Next to her rested a lute. She smiled as she kissed the man's heavily ringed fingers, and he gazed up at her, totally transfixed. I followed my sister as she curtsied low, three times, and then took my place with her beneath the stained glass window. I peered discreetly up. The gentleman in bed must be King Louis. Another handsome gentleman I recognised stood to one side, magnificently dressed, his bonnet in his hand. Gazing at the princess, he gave a faint smile of appreciation as if studying a fine mare. Who else could this be but Charles Brandon? As I glimpsed the tableau before me, I felt surprised, for I had expected to see a very beautiful young woman and a truly revolting old man – but that was not the case.

Madame d'Aumont moved forward and whispered into the princess's ear. She raised her head to listen and then said 'Oh, how delightful,' in a soft, lilting voice. Madame d'Aumont beckoned to me.

'Come closer, child, do not be afraid,' said the king, sitting up a little as his wife plumped up the bolster to make him more comfortable.

I walked forward and sank low as the princess rose to her

feet, hands folded on her gown of copper-coloured velvet, its great sleeves trimmed with ermine and pearls. My gown felt very plain in comparison.

'Sire, and most gracious lady,' began Madame d'Aumont, 'this is Mistress Anne Boleyn, a fluent speaker of French, who has just arrived from the Court of Savoy, in Mechelen. She is the sister of Marie, here, and is to be of whatever assistance you desire.'

'Welcome, Mistress Boleyn,' said the princess, her voice as sweet as a chapel bell. 'I know well your mother and father, and I am so pleased that you are here to serve me.' She then turned to her husband. 'I am very grateful, sire, that you have allowed the girl to join my household. If she proves such an ornament as her sister, I shall be well content, and not able to stop myself from kissing you every minute of every day.' She glanced across to the Duke of Suffolk. 'Why, my lord, Anne here will have studied with your daughter Ann, at the Regent's court. How does the little girl?'

I looked up. 'She is very well, my lady.'

I expected the duke to ask me about his daughter, but his eyes were on the princess. He said nothing as if he had not seen me at all.

'Why, how charming, how charming!' lisped the king, his eyes lighting up. 'Stand up, little maid so that we may see you.'

When I arose, I saw an old man with large, watery eyes who smiled at me so kindly I could not help but smile back. His sparse, shoulder-length hair appeared brown beneath his fur-lined nightcap, and pearls dangled from his large, heavy-lobed ears. His face was rather sallow, with a sloping nose and a heavy bottom lip, but it was such a lively, kind face that he made me feel quite at ease. He had a ready smile, which showed a lack of teeth, but he certainly was not the hideous monster that he had been made out to be. Not quite. I then peeped from under my lashes at King Henry's sister. I saw a slender young woman, of middle height, with a high, round forehead, a wide nose, and small, pale, blue-grey eyes. I could not see her hair, for now married, she wore it hidden beneath a black velvet hood, but what little showed appeared to be a rich, auburn red. When she smiled, she showed her even teeth.

The king then beckoned to me with his misshapen, bony finger, chuckling as he did so. 'Well, well, come from the Regent Margaret's court at Savoy, have we? Tell me, little mouse, what does Madame Regent say to me having snatched away this lovely prize, eh?' He looked up at his wife with a wink and kissed her hand.

I felt quite unafraid and smiled brightly. 'Your Grace, the Regent acknowledges that you are a mighty king rich in years, experience and understanding, and beloved by your people. It is only fitting that such a great king should have won the heart of the most beautiful princess in all of Christendom.'

The Duke of Suffolk bristled, for he knew as well as I Margaret's true opinion of the hated Louis. She had set her heart on the princess marrying her nephew and ward, Prince Charles, and had been utterly devastated by this new alliance between King Henry and King Louis.

'Goody, good, good!' The king clapped his hands and wriggled about like an excited child. '*I* am no callow youth.' He turned to the princess. 'No, my wife needs a man of vigour, not a pale boy!' He looked back at me. 'Sit here. Come, come, my clever little blackbird.'

I glanced at the princess as she nodded encouragingly, and carefully perched on the edge of the bed.

'What a pretty speech from one so young, is that not so dearest?' he asked, gazing adoringly up at his wife. 'But tell me, was Madame Regent not a little vexed, eh?' he said in a wheedling tone. 'Not just a little? Taking this fine diamond right from under her nose, plucking it away like a wily fox stealing a chicken? Ha, they could not outfox me!' As he chortled to himself and ended up coughing, I smelt his foul breath, mixed with some sort of herb lozenge and tried not to sit back.

'Sire.' The Duke of Suffolk gave a little cough. 'Sire,' he began again louder, over the sound of the king's hawking. 'I have matters I wish to discuss with you, along with Sir Edward Neville and Sir William Sydney. They are without, waiting for an audience.'

The king, with a wave of his hand, bid the duke kneel beside his bed and leant forward to embrace him most heartily. 'Yes, yes, yes, all in good time, my dear Suffolk, all in good time, but first, I have such a great love welling up in my heart – see my eyes are moist – that I must express to your king that I love him as a brother for sending me his youngest sister, this most priceless of jewels. I command you to tell your master that never did a woman show such dignity, wisdom and honour to me, as she has.'

Suffolk bowed his head and Louis allowed him to rise again.

'Now, I will sleep a little while, the ladies will away, and when I am up, I will speak with you again.' He fell back against the crimson bolster.

'My dear husband,' said the princess, 'I shall sing gently to you while you sleep, and when you awake, I shall be here to take your hand again.' She smiled and blew a kiss, her voice charm itself.

'See what a treasure I have?' cooed Louis, 'Oh, that I was thirty years younger. I would not use my bed for slumber!'

The Duke of Suffolk looked as if he was about to choke, and in an instant, Madame d'Aumont hurried Mary and me out of the chamber.

•   •

That evening we sat on the rushes by the flickering firelight in our chamber, Mary languidly stroking my little dog. I told her about the Regent and the friends I had made, about Mechelen and all that I had seen. She, in turn, described the entry of the princess into Abbeville. I sat transfixed as she told me how Mary Tudor had worn cloth of gold, trimmed with ermine and ablaze with jewels. Led by our uncle, Thomas Howard, Earl of Surrey, and other English and French nobles, she had worn her beautiful long hair loose, under a coronet of sapphires and rubies. In the evening, a magnificent banquet had been held with three days of dancing and feasting, and our mother had worn a new gown of pale green damask. Father had stood proudly with the other nobles, and Dame Agnes had dozed through the entire entertainment. However, much later, there had been a mishap, for in the town a fire had raged, and the alarm bells could not be rung for fear of disturbing the royal couple's sleep. Tragically, it resulted in some deaths, but these were quickly dismissed as unfortunate trifles. Mary then told me how the first royal row occurred only a day after the wedding.

'All the princess's ladies were dismissed,' she said, tickling Bonny, 'and you could hear her wailing from every chamber. King Louis hobbled off in a fury, and the princess wrote frantically to Wolsey to let her at least keep Mother Guildford. You should have seen the letter. I've seen her usual neat script, but this showed the writing of a lunatic, all covered with tears and half off the paper in great scrawling letters. I would have been ashamed to send it.'

I thought of my sister's careless missives and smiled. 'I know, Mary, I heard about it from Madame d'Aumont, who told me the king had his reasons, but it still must have been a shock, so alone in a strange country.' I knew how that felt.

'Well,' said Mary, 'thank goodness Grandfather Howard insisted that we should be amongst the remaining ladies. Mother said he cares not a pin for Wolsey's wishes and takes every opportunity to irritate him. I am very happy, for I did not fancy being bundled back to England. *I* intend to enjoy myself.'

She stretched out her arms, and I noticed her lovely,

blossoming figure through the transparent chemise.

'Well, Mary,' I said, 'I had just become used to one court and its ways, and now I will have to learn another's.'

My sister put Bonny aside and began to describe the French court. 'I have not been here long, Nan, but I *have* learnt that you must remember who is who,' she said, poking the dwindling logs on the fire. I watched as the flames leapt a little and lit up Mary's face. 'People take great offence if they think they have been slighted – something easily done at this court.'

I asked if the princess might be difficult to serve, but she told me that Mary Tudor had proved great fun, for she liked to be gay and loved jokes and pranks. Generous and kind, she had even sent gifts back to England for those ladies who had been dismissed by Louis. Every man swore he had fallen in love with her, although she could sulk if not indulged, for she had been utterly spoilt. Naturally, she wanted girls of her own age about her, and how lucky for us that she did. She loved the French court and was very attentive to her decrepit husband, which, considering all the wailing and weeping when her betrothal had first been announced, was a joke. I would find her a breath of fresh air after serving the old maid of Savoy.

'Margaret is not old!' I cried, indignantly, but she only laughed. 'Why should Mary Tudor not be attentive to her husband?'

Mary pursed her lips and toyed with her long hair.

'Go on,' I said, suspiciously, 'you are hiding something. I know that look.'

'She is playing a waiting game,' she whispered.

'Waiting for what?'

'Waiting for whom. She intends marrying the Duke of Suffolk if ...' – and here her voice fell very low – 'old Louis dies. She is *besotted.*'

'But he is not a prince,' I said, 'and her brother would never allow it.' I thought of Madame Regent who had also been fond of him herself, but she knew she could never marry a commoner, even if he were made a duke. What a scandal that affair had caused, her reputation almost ruined.

'Listen,' said Mary, 'there is something you must be very clear about. Uncle Howard is causing much mischief around Suffolk – you know how they hate each other – telling King Henry that Suffolk is only over here to press his suit with the princess should anything untoward happen to old Louis. Suffolk is in a state of terror over the situation, particularly since his letters to Wolsey have been intercepted. Of course, he thoroughly denies any such designs on the princess.'

I opened my mouth to speak, but Mary continued. 'There is much intrigue about and as two of the princess's ladies – and do not repeat this – we have been told to watch out for her, for she is wished ill.'

'By whom?' I asked, surprised that she knew so much in so short a time.

'Shush,' said Mary, 'by Louise of Savoy. Duchess Agnes told me. You know how Grandfather Howard cannot control his own wife's tongue. She knows everything, I can tell you, and I had to sit listening to it all on the journey here, droning on for hours about every little detail of the court.'

'Mary,' I pressed, 'who is this Louise of Savoy?'

Her eyes narrowed. 'The mother of François, the Duc d'Angoulême, the next in line to rule after Louis. They say she is not loved by anyone except her son and daughter. I have not seen her yet, but I gather she is just as you would imagine – dark like a black spider, although not yet forty years old. Her husband died ten years ago, yet her closest confidant, Antoinette de Polignac, Dame de Combronde, had once been her husband's mistress. The two became very close friends.'

'Friends? I asked incredulously.

Mary nodded. 'Louise hates the fact that Princess Mary has just married King Louis. She despises the princess so much that she has placed spies in her chambers, under

Madame d'Aumont, so that every word she says can be reported back to her.'

I recalled Madame d'Aumont's words. Were *we* those spies?

Mary continued. 'Louise is terrified that Louis might get a son on the princess, for she wants her own son to become king.'

I tucked my knees under my chin and watched Bonny dreaming and twitching in the firelight. 'Go on,' I said, intrigued.

'Just be careful. Duchess Agnes says Madame Louise is spiteful and bears terrible grudges. We are all warned not to irritate her in any way, or her precious son on whom she truly dotes.'

'She sounds wicked.'

'No, she is not wicked, sweetheart, she is rather religious and on rising likes to read a psalm 'to perfume her day.' But she is resentful of others' good fortune'.

'Is she here at Beauvais?'

Mary shook her head, and I felt relieved to hear that she resided forty leagues away at her court at Romorantin, south of Amboise, pretending to be ill. Everyone knew that she was really in a fit of pique over the coronation, raging and cursing. However, she had been strongly advised to attend the crowning.

'Mary, you have become very worldly since I last saw you.'

'Well, you are not to repeat anything I tell you. Do you hear? *Anything.*'

She then went on to describe Claude, Duchess of Angoulême, King Louis' daughter and the wife of François. She was only fourteen, and they had not been married long.

'Ah, yes, the ugly one,' I stated, remembering the gossip I had heard at Mechelen.

'Yes,' said Mary, with a grimace, 'for she walks with a limp, is fat, crook-backed and has a squint. If she does not produce a son soon, I expect she will be packed off to a convent.' There was a pause as Mary stared at my horrified face, before bursting into peals of laughter. 'Oh, Nan, I am only teasing! Poor little Claude might be deformed, but she will not be tossed aside. Why, having King Louis' daughter married to François is *exactly* what Madame Louise wished for, since through Claude, Brittany and the crown of France come to her son, François, by Salic law.'

Although I thought Claude sounded the most hideous creature alive, Mary said it was not so, for she possessed the sweetest of souls. François admired her greatly, but being a man of great appetites, he visited his mistresses as often as possible. However, whenever he occupied the same château, he always shared her bed for he desperately needed a son. I was curious as to what Mary thought of François, and she told me he was spoilt and in love with his sister.

His sister? What sort of a family had I come to serve? She told me that one could not help but like him, for he never stopped smiling, although he had been overindulged since boyhood. He said that in life one should be greeted by a beautiful woman, a beautiful horse, and a beautiful hound and that a court without ladies was more suited to a Turk than a Christian king.'

'Is he handsome?' I asked, curious.

She said no, for she preferred English looks, fair and ruddy coloured, whereas François was tall, dark and swarthy with a cleft chin, a long nose, and eyes like brown hazelnuts which he rolled up to heaven in an odd sort of way when he spoke. His face was smooth-skinned with no beard. However, his easy manner with women was charming, and he could not resist fair, whole-some looking girls, girls who were naturally warm-natured, generous and adventurous. I stared at Mary and then quickly dismissed the alarming thought that flashed through my mind.

'What do you think of him compared to our king?' I asked.

She cocked her head to one side. 'Oh, of the two, I think

our English king is far more attractive. He has wonderful golden hair and fair skin, and being a king makes him even more irresistible. One day, you will find out that power is just as attractive as good looks.'

'Like François? He has power,' I offered.

She shook her head. 'No, I told you, his nose is far too long, and anyway,' she whispered, 'he is not king yet.'

I told Mary that I had met our great King Henry at Lille, and did not like him at all. He had slighted our mother, and besides, what sort of man callously marries his lovely sister to a feeble old man like King Louis? We spoke of François' sister, Marguerite, and Mary explained how she was twenty-two, tall and slender, with light-brown hair, violet eyes and a long nose like her brother. Handsome rather than beautiful, she possessed a heart of pure gold. After the fire at Abbeville, she alone had given money to the grieving families. Grandfather Howard described her as the wisest and frankest woman he had ever met, the pearl of the Valois, for she translated Greek, Latin, Hebrew, Italian and Spanish. She knew something of everything, but could only speak French.

'A lofty mind then,' I mused.

'Yes, indeed. You will not remember, Nan, but there were discussions years ago to marry her to Prince Arthur, but the old King Henry preferred a Spanish alliance with Katherine of Aragon. Then her loving brother, François, forced her to marry Charles, Duc d'Alençon, who they say is jealous, morose and stupid. Still, next to François, he *is* the most important man in the kingdom. That is some consolation.'

But was it? Here was yet another example of a poor woman trapped in a dismal match.

'Anyway,' she said, 'she has her court at Argentan, in lower Normandy, and we must endear ourselves to her as well as to her brother and their mother. The three of them together are called 'the Trinity' – a very formidable trio, and you must *never* forget it.'

I yawned, for it was very late, and moved over to curl up

with my head on Mary's knees. She stroked my hair as we watched the flames dying down in the fireplace.

'There are three social casts at the court,' said Mary. 'The pious and virtuous band around Claude, the lettered and intelligent girls around Marguerite, and the libertines around Louise. She uses them to fascinate her son and distract him from affairs of state.'

'*What?*' I was alarmed.

'Do not worry, Nan,' said Mary, yawning too, 'I doubt we will have anything to do with anyone much except Princess Mary, for it is to her court that we are to attend. It is her and her husband we must please.'

I closed my eyes but then twisted around to look up at my sister's face. 'Mary, you are pleased I am here, are you not?'

She leant down and put her arms around me, enveloping me in their perfumed plumpness. 'Silly girl, of course I am pleased, you and I are going to have the best of times without the interference of old matrons and busybodies. I shall look after you like any devoted sister; I will truly. Now come, I think we should retire, for it is almost dawn.'

Back in our bed, I lay thinking about all Mary had said. Here in France, things did not seem as simple as they had been in Mechelen, but at least now I knew something about the people I might serve. Of all of them, I felt that Louise of Savoy was the most fascinating and dangerous as, from what Mary had told me, she would let nothing get in the way of her precious son becoming king.

●   ●

Madame d'Aumont stood in the *grande salle* and cleared her throat.

'Finally, *demoiselles,* it is of the utmost importance that you memorise your places on the day the princess makes her entry into Paris.' She squinted down at the parchment in her hand, holding it at arm's length, for her eyesight was not good. 'Now, according to this plan, I will ride first with various ladies, followed by Mary Fiennes and Ann Jernygham. Eliza Grey will ride next, followed lastly by the two Boleyn girls.'

I was disappointed. I wanted to ride at the front, not at the back.

'The princess,' she said, 'will enter Paris for her coronation through the Porte Saint-Denis and will stop at each of the eight designated places en route to Notre Dame de Paris. She, and therefore you, will be on display to the public from ten in the morning until five o'clock in the evening.'

We stood, hands folded on our gowns, as she continued. 'Now, *le grand-maître des cérémonies* is allowing no more than thirty minutes to be spent at each pageant. The princess will remain in her chariot, and you will move forward, then halt on either side of her. You will sit quietly on your mules as decreed by *le grand ecuyer*, Monsieur Galeas – and I do not want to hear any tittering. Signor da Vinci has spent a great deal of time designing the brilliant presentations, but no matter how ludicrous they might seem in portraying the king as a virile young god, please remember your manners.'

My sister let out a snigger.

'My meaning precisely,' muttered Madame d'Aumont, rolling up the plan. 'Now, is there anything you are unclear about?'

I spoke up, my face eager and bright. 'Madame, do I have to ride at the back? I would much rather ride at the front.'

Madame d'Aumont appeared mildly confused. 'And why do you think you merit a higher place, Mademoiselle Boleyn?'

I knew from the sound of her voice that I had made a grave mistake but, ever bold, thought it best to press on. 'Because my grandfather Howard is highly thought of, Madame, and I would surely be better placed at the front.'

The other girls began to titter.

'Why, of course!' replied the *dame d'honneur*. 'Better still, perhaps you might like to ride with the princess herself in her royal chariot. Do you think that might suffice?'

I shook my head, aware of the sarcasm in her voice.

'One day, *demoiselle*, when you are Queen of the Fairies, you can do as you please. Until then, *le grand ecuyer* decides where you will be placed. By the Holy Mass, you have much to learn.'

● ●

Within a few days, King Louis felt well enough to commence the journey to the royal abbey of Saint-Denis, about a league north of Paris. It was an extraordinary sight that clattered out of the courtyard of the Bishop's Palace, onto the main track to Chantilly. King Louis and his wife rode matching white palfreys caparisoned in pale blue velvet cloth over which lay scattered silver porcupines surmounted by crowns – the device of the French King – and red Tudor roses.

Mary Tudor appeared surprisingly happy. Her large, red velvet bonnet sat tilted jauntily to one side, and in her red riding gown, she appeared very stylish.

On the other side of King Louis rode François and I was able to see him for the first time as he chatted to the Duke of Suffolk, Dorset and the other gentlemen. He might not have been good looking, but he appeared magnificently dressed, his coat studded with diamonds. Although his legs were rather thin, he sat his horse well and appeared at ease and relaxed. Next to François rode a handsome woman in green velvet, great white plumes flowing from her Venetian bonnet. It was obvious from their similar noses and slanting eyes that this was his sister, Marguerite, the Duchess d'Alençon.

A chilly wind blew and the track ahead lay muddy and wet as we trotted into the open countryside. The mules' hooves squelched and threw up clods of earth, and soon their blue saddlecloths and smooth flanks were splattered and soiled. I asked my sister about the Hôtel de Tournelles.

'Apparently, King Louis holds his court there when he

is in the city,' she said. 'They say it is a huge, rambling old
place in much need of repair, with over five thousand people
housed there and twelve large galleries. We will see it soon
enough. Oh, I cannot wait to see Paris!' she added, kicking
her mule on, 'for I hear it is the liveliest place on earth,
crowded with markets open every day, where you can buy
anything you want – damask, lawn, jewels, fine cheese from
Champagne or Brie, and exquisite pastries – quite superior
to those in England.'

Just to be contrary, I told her how I had heard that Paris
was an overcrowded den of vice to be avoided at all cost, full
of thieves and drunkards.

She laughed at my serious face. 'Nan, what *have* they
been telling you at Mechelen! Jesu, they make everything
sound so dull. I bet nobody there has ever even been to Paris.'

'Neither have you, Mary,' I pointed out, strands of hair
whipping across my face in the wind.

'Yes, well, I know people who come from Paris,' she
replied, defensively, 'and they have told me all about the fairs
and street markets. Anyway, our father likes it and says it is
very, very exciting indeed.'

I pretended to be unimpressed. Margaret of Savoy
had, indeed, told me that Paris was debauched and that
the lascivious courtiers strolling around its streets were all
effeminate. But I did not tell Mary that the girls at Mechelen
had also described everything in Paris as quite thrilling.

'If it is so wonderful,' I asked, 'why doesn't the king or
François live permanently in Paris? Madame d'Aumont said
they spend all their time at their châteaux in the Loire valley.
You see, you do not know everything, Mary.'

As I preened, she frowned easy prey to my teasing. 'That
is because there is nothing permanent about the French
court,' she countered, 'for it is on constant progress, moving
from château to château. They hunt in the vast forests of
Orléans, Blois, and Amboise and only come to Paris for state
occasions and business, usually in the winter. One can hardly

hunt in the middle of a town, can one?'

'Well, as it happens, you can,' I replied, haughtily. 'Once a boar hunt was held in Mechelen's great market place for Prince Charles.'

'Well, there's a thing.' Mary dug her heels into her mule in annoyance. 'Why must you always persist in contradicting everything I say? This is France, now, and things are done differently here. You wait and see.'

●　●

On Sunday, the fifth day of November, the court left the palace and proceeded to the royal abbey of Saint-Denis for the coronation of the princess. The girl appeared magnificent as she sat in her chariot, wearing a gown of silver-coloured velvet, trimmed with ermine, enjoying the admiration. At the entrance to the abbey, we helped her step down, laying out her heavy train on the blue carpet, accompanied by a peal of bells. When I looked up, I saw François towering over a small, plain girl beside him. She appeared beautifully dressed in a red velvet robe scattered with the golden lilies of France and the silver ermines of Brittany, but no amount of ermine and diamonds could hide the fact that she was standing badly as if in some discomfort. She also appeared desperately sad, and I assumed this must be Claude. On François' other side stood a tall, dark, slightly built woman. François kissed her hand with what appeared to be adoration as she gazed fondly at him, her lips tightly pressed. She could not take her eyes off him, and I knew that this must be the terrifying Louise of Savoy, Comtesse d'Angoulême. As Princess Mary approached, I watched as Louise and her daughter, Marguerite, swept low. On rising, I saw that the comtesse's expression had turned cold as she lightly kissed the princess on both cheeks. François then led the girl towards the north and south transept, and onto the high altar. Her ladies followed next, then her maids, including my sister and myself, and then a great company of French nobles and ladies behind.

Meanwhile, King Louis himself watched, concealed rather badly in an upper alcove, heavily wrapped in furs. Hidden away, he would not steal this moment from his wife or take away her glory.

François led the princess to the altar where she was anointed and enthroned in splendour by the Bishop of Bayeaux. The new Queen of France then moved to a stage to the left of the high altar, where she sat on a chair of state beneath a golden canopy, glittering with *fleurs-de-lis*. But something was not right. Alarmed, I nudged my sister as I stared at the queen's strained face, but Mary ignored me, her head bent in her prayer book. I looked back at the pale girl, swaying as if she might faint at any moment. I then caught the eye of Madame d'Aumont. She stared at me quizzically but then turning to see the queen's ashen face, quickly signalled to François, who by chance appeared to be staring in our direction – at my sister. Instantly, he leant forward, whispered something to the wilting princess, and then carefully lifted the heavy crown from her head. Her hand flew to her temples, and she sighed, relieved, as François smiled and tipped his head towards me in acknowledgement. I smiled back but then immediately noticed the frozen face of Louise of Savoy, brows arched, staring straight at me as if perplexed in some way. François, meanwhile, held the crown gallantly aloft above the queen's head throughout the long ceremony, showing no sign of discomfort, as if holding a mere feather in his hands.

●   ●

As I took my place at one of the lower tables between my sister and Eliza Grey, I felt relieved to reach the warmth of the *grande salle* with its blazing fires and heavy tapestries. Crowded with guests, all talking at once, the musicians played a lively tune as the dishes were brought forward to the tables.

I nudged Mary. 'Look at her sitting there. Why is she so sad?'

She turned around. 'Claude's mother,' she said, 'was buried in the vault at Saint-Denis, not a year hence, and she still misses her. Now that her father, King Louis, has taken a new wife, it naturally upsets her, for she sees him giving the new queen those honours that were once her mother's. Is that not so, Eliza?'

Eliza Grey leant forward. 'Aye, and there is worse,' she said, above the noise, 'apparently King Louis has given her mother's jewels to his new wife. Claude felt hurt to see the new queen flaunting a fine brooch that she had given to her mother on her saint's day. And did you see her trying to catch François's eye in the church? As usual, he was not looking at her. The poor girl is treated very badly.' Unfortunately, I knew exactly who had caught his attention.

'By François?' I asked of Eliza.

'No, François is not cruel to her – by Louise of Savoy,' she replied. 'Is that not true, Ann?'

Ann Jernygham covered her mouth with her hand. 'She dislikes her,' she said, 'although in public she pretends to care for her 'dear' daughter-in-law. In private, she dismisses her as feeble bodied and useless, not part of her dazzling trio. She also doubts that she can give her darling boy a son. Everyone bullies Claude. Look at her – it's pathetic. She stares so lovingly at François, but he only has eyes for his mother and sister – or, of course, any pretty face.'

As Claude sat on the dais, next to the smiling François, she appeared so small and lost. Her dwarf, a dark-haired, heavy-jawed girl, sat at her feet and tugged at her mistress's gown as the acrobats began to perform to cheers and claps. I smiled at Claude across the great chamber.

'She will not see you,' said Eliza, taking a piece of chicken from the platter, 'she is too short-sighted, as is her dwarf, Marie Darcille.'

My eyes moved farther across.

'And that old crow is Anne de Beaujeau, the Duchess de Bourbon. As the eldest daughter of King Louis XI, you must always refer to her as *Madame la Grande,* for she is a very powerful woman and a princess of France. She must be fifty if she is a day and resides at Chantelle, near Moulins.'

'She looks fierce,' I observed.

'She is, Anne, but she is well respected for she is still strong enough, and brave enough, to hunt the wolf with her pack of wolfhounds and a crossbow. The other woman is Louise's half-sister, Philiberte, the Duchess of Nemours.'

I then spotted a beautiful young girl and Eliza did not even bother to look up when I asked her name. She was, apparently, Mademoiselle Diane de Poitiers, and the loveliest creature at court. A year older than myself, Diane was a great favourite with François, and a fearless horsewoman, for no horse proved too bold for her, and she frequently led the chase. I studied the young girl with her thick, strawberry blonde hair wound up with a simple ribbon, her heart-shaped face and tilted sea-green eyes. Unlike every other woman in the *salle,* she wore no jewels or adornments of any kind, but a simple gown of apple green and white silk.

'She is to be married soon,' said Eliza, 'to the *grand senéchal* of Normandy. I gather he is old and hunchbacked, but she has agreed to the union, for it brings great wealth and power. *Madame la Grande* arranged the match.' Mary wrinkled her nose in distaste. 'When she marries,' continued Eliza, sipping her wine, 'she will be given the position of *Dame d'Honneur* in Claude's household, which for one so young is a rare honour. Watch her, Anne, for I believe there is something very special about her. She is simplicity itself, never adorning herself with tawdry baubles like the other ladies.'

'I think she and Marguerite are the most elegant ladies at court,' said my sister, 'for Marguerite well knows how to adapt herself to every mode, adjusting each new device in a way not seen before.'

'Well, I cannot wait to marry my Edward next week,'

said Ann Jernygham. 'I am so glad he remained here in Paris so that we can be married here in France. As the eldest son of the Marquis of Dorset, it is a very good match.'

As I wondered about this, I noticed Louise of Savoy whisper to her companion, who then hurried over and asked that I follow her. Perplexed, I quickly put down my napkin and rose, the girls watching in silence. As I approached François' mother, I gave a deep reverence. She waved me up to my feet and, leaning forward, laid her smooth hand on my arm. I looked down at the great emeralds and rubies on her fingers and noticed her perfect oval nails.

'That was most observant of you in the abbey today, my dear,' she said in a pleasing voice. 'Our dearly beloved queen was about to faint and had it not been for your quick-wittedness, might have slipped away from her throne – poof – like a dandelion head.' She waved her elegant hand in the air, and the ladies around her politely laughed. 'You appear to be a very bright young lady – a pleasant change at court – and I gather your name is Anne Boleyn.'

I must have looked somewhat surprised.

'Oh, I know all about you. The Boleyn girl from Mechelen, granddaughter of the old Duke of Norfolk, although I am better acquainted with your Uncle Howard. The duke speaks highly of you, and as it was he and your father who placed you here in France, he has asked me to make good use of your talents. I gather Margaret of Savoy spoke of you with some regard as well and was not pleased to lose so lively and willing a maid.'

I replied that I was content to serve in all things, and she flashed a brilliant smile.

'Oh, I do hope so, my dear,' she said, taking a sip of wine from her goblet and searching about the *salle* with narrowed eyes. 'I really do.'

● ●

The following day, as the mist lifted, the new queen left the abbey, and we began our journey south. I had lain awake most of the previous night unable to sleep with excitement, for I could not wait to dress in my new gown. All the young *demoiselles* were dressed the same, but with my dark hair, I knew that white would become me the most.

King Louis already waited in Paris, having left at seven in the morning, to make sure that all was in order for his queen's triumphal entry. Nothing was to be left to chance. We had fussed over and dressed the queen to perfection in a gown of gold brocade with a crown of pearls on her hair, and she now sat in an open chariot draped with cloth of gold and gold tinsel. A great company of archers provided the escort, and each mounted lady had her page walking beside her. François rode his bay horse, leaning down at every opportunity to say something amusing to her.

About half a league from Paris, the queen – to her chamberlain's horror, for the schedule was timed to the last second – stopped, for she wished to receive the kind gifts that many of the local villagers had prepared. The whole cavalcade waited impatiently as housewives brought forth cakes, pies and warm loaves of bread. It turned into the most wonderful, impromptu feast, the queen laughing with the weather-beaten women and showing them her magnificent diamond bracelets.

When we finally continued on our way along the wide, freshly sanded roads I noticed a strange smell and was told by one of the French ladies in our party that the sulphur-rich earth mixed with the recent rain caused the odour.

'Thus, you know you are nearing Paris!' she laughed. 'I tell you, Paris is the filthiest city in Europe – it stinks of manure, for ten thousand horses are ridden daily about its narrow streets.'

At four in the afternoon, we entered through the great

Port Saint-Denis, the main gate to the city of Paris, and as we clattered over the drawbridge the swift current of the River Seine below lashed against the mossy walls of the city. The two massive medieval towers fluttered with banners and flags, and trumpets blasted out accompanied by a great roar from the crowds. King Louis sat his horse on the other side of the bridge, surrounded by his gentlemen-at-arms, nobles and no fewer than three thousand French clergymen. He took his place beside his young wife, smiling fondly at her. I could not help notice that his cheeks had been rouged with a dab of colour high on each hollow cheekbone. He sat hunched, but at least he had managed to stay mounted, rather than lying prostrate in a chariot.

When we trotted through the port, onto the Rue Saint-Denis, we were greeted on the other side by a great marble fountain spouting red wine. Next to it stood a scaffold, upon which rested a ship in full sail, and on it, Bacchus and Ceres held a vine branch with grapes and a sheaf of corn. A girl, depicting Honour, stood holding the arms of France, and mariners sang of their beautiful, new queen. However, although the main street had been strewn with sweet-smelling herbs and covered with fresh sand, the fetid smell could not be disguised, and neither could the sight I beheld behind the colourful streamers and banners. No amount of fluttering cloth could hide the narrow, dark alleys, or the water dripping down the walls of the dilapidated, gabled houses. On the cobbles, blood trickled down these alleyways, and something akin to entrails lay abandoned on the stones. Thin, filthy children stood barefoot and glassy-eyed on cold stone steps, as greasy dogs growled and cowered with offal in their jaws. Was this the Paris of which the Regent had spoken? Was this how nine thousand Parisian beggars lived out their squalid lives?

We continued to the next pageant at the Painters Gate, admiring the church of the Holy Sepulchre, and continued to the church of the Holy Innocents. I could see that the church had a small cemetery and a tomb with a tall tower, upon which sat a stone statue of the Blessed Virgin. As we moved into a line, Madame d'Aumont squeezed her mule next to mine.

'It is impressive is it not?' she asked as I stared up. 'It is a grave, built as a fine monument.'

Mary Fiennes waited until she had moved forward again. 'Apparently,' she giggled, 'it was built thus so that the dogs could not piss on the man's remains.'

I put my glove to my mouth to hide a smile.

'In the church,' she continued, 'there is the body of an actual Holy Innocent child, encased in gold and silver. But how are you faring?'

I shifted position and told her that I felt cold, but in awe of the wonderful tableaux.

'France has the most ingenious workmen,' she agreed, 'and the artists and sculptors have been working for months on this *entrée*. Just imagine being a queen.'

I sighed, feeling jealous. To have so much made of oneself and be the centre of attention must surely be desired. How I wished that all eyes were only on me. Well, I would pretend.

As François leant down from his horse to say something to the queen, she blushed. He threw his head back and laughed, but King Louis gazed sadly on, for he could see only too well what a beautiful couple François and Mary made, so young and full of life.

Moving on, we arrived at a high-walled, turreted place, and I was told that this was the Châtelet. Staring in amazement, I saw that grass had been fashioned into strips of green paper, so lush it appeared real. I truly believe that it was during this extraordinary day that my love for pageants, plays, and masques was born. I was only young, but my eyes took in every possible detail, invention, and tableau for I had never seen such wondrous novelties and delights! However, halting once again to hear a long oration, I could only wonder at how the queen had never once stopped smiling.

Perhaps it was grace given to her by God on her crowning. How else could such patience and fortitude be had?

We then made our way along the Rue St Antoine to the Place de Grève, where stood the Hôtel de Ville in a wide, open square, close to the river. Although decked gracefully with roses and lilies, it had not been possible to hide the fact that the building stood old and dilapidated. I told Mary I thought the square charming with its stone fountain, but one of the French ladies, riding up close to me, shook her head.

'You are quite wrong,' she said with a shudder, 'it is a place of infinite horror. Many executions and punishments have occurred here and still do, such as hanging, boiling in oil, flaying, scourging – only last week they skinned a man for stealing a horse. They have removed the pillory today, of course.'

I felt horrified.

By five o'clock, with clarions sounding in the fading, wintry light, the convoy clattered across the Pont Notre Dame. A great many torches were now lit, and I could see that this bridge was quite different from the others. I found out later that an Italian had designed it in an entirely new style since the old bridge had collapsed from the ice of harsh winters. It had only recently been finished, having taken thirteen years to build, and the beautiful houses that lined it were all built to look identical, in stone and red brick. I hoped it would now take the weight of our vast, winding company.

'How does anyone ever find their way around here? I asked my sister as we turned yet again. 'Every street looks the same and I will never remember the names of the bridges.'

'You will not have to,' said Mary. 'I have been told that you just have to be aware that Paris is divided into three parts – the Cité, the Ville and the Université. Or to make matters simple, remember Paris thinks on the left and prays on the right.'

I was not convinced.

The narrow streets now appeared to be a jumble of

bookshops and printers, for in this part of the city all the schools and gentlemen of the university resided. We halted outside the church of St Jacques, where the gentlemen waiting in their fine robes bowed low to the queen in her chariot. They were soon staring up in annoyance. From the open windows of the adjacent houses, noisy students leant out, frantically waving flags and anything they could get hold of – shirts, caps, bits of cloth, flaming torches – anything. Some had even climbed precariously onto the roofs and were throwing paper roses down. The queen, waving up, blew them a kiss, causing the boys to shout and challenge her to come and kiss them in person. Everyone smiled indulgently, except the great doctors whose faces were strained in discomfort. None of them could make their lofty speeches until the noise had subsided. But all was not over yet.

We progressed to the Hôtel Dieu, on the Rue Neuve, and onto the Place du Parvis Notre-Dame, to the great cathedral. It was indeed beautiful with its two towers adorned with magnificent figures and a huge central rose window. It nestled among a myriad of other, lesser churches and a great many bishops and clergymen waited here. In the newly paved square, sprinkled with rose petals, the queen rose from her chariot to the joyous sound of bells.

Mary, stretched her legs as she sat on her mule. 'My toes are quite numb with cold,' she said, wincing.

As we giggled, Madame d'Aumont dismounted, as straight-backed as ever. 'Ladies, you forget yourselves,' she chided. 'Do not think for one moment – one single moment – that you are only here to display fine gowns and proud looks. You are here to complement our queen, even if it does mean sitting rigidly on a mule for eight hours. Now, do as *she* does – smile and look lively, not jaded like wilting daisies.'

François himself appeared as fresh and eager as ever, but Claude, clinging to his arm, looked tired and cold, as did King Louis. He smiled weakly, wrapped in his heavy fur-lined gown, and patted the gloved hand of his new wife as we picked up her heavy train. When the queen returned from making her private devotions, we processed back down the aisle and back out into the cold air.

'Good to see all the whores have been removed,' commented one French nobleman to another, pulling his furs tightly about his shoulders. His companion sneered. 'They will be back, my friend. What is Notre Dame without its bawds for our bishops?'

A little while later, all turned to mayhem and confusion, for as we rode through the archway of the palace, we discovered an immense crowd of people blocking the doors. Fortunately, a disaster was avoided by some quick thinking on the part of the guards who, shielding the queen, steered her towards the porter's lodge and bustled her up a back staircase. The girls thought this highly amusing as we hurried her up the narrow stone steps, tripping over our gowns and laughing. On reaching her chamber, she immediately flung her gloves to the floor and flopped down into a great, padded chair.

Madame d'Aumont, eying the discarded gloves, raised an eyebrow in disapproval.

'Thanks be to God and his good angels!' cried the queen, closing her eyes and resting her head. 'My face felt fit to break in two from smiling.'

She took the goblet of hypocras presented to her. 'Oh, *demoiselles*!' she cried, sitting forward. 'Did you see the faces of the good doctors when the students hooted and cried? Such a picture of discomfort. I had to try so hard not to laugh, for they looked fit to burst!'

Madame d'Aumont fussed about with brisk efficiency, clicking her fingers as we hurried forward with a new gown, jewels, and a coronet. The queen meanwhile sat, eyes closed, as her hairdresser re-dressed her hair and Ann Jernygham and Florence Hastings washed her feet in a bowl of warm, lavender-scented water.

'What a day,' she said, splashing her cold toes like a

child, 'and it is not over yet.'

Finally, with the queen refreshed, we all changed into gowns of pale blue silk and descended the magnificent staircase to the *grande chambre du roi*. A huge marble table had been placed under the west window, beneath the stained glass, and a golden canopy erected. As we maids and ladies took our places farther down the chamber, I felt so relieved to feel at last the warmth from the roaring fire and sip the warm, sweet wine.

The banquet that followed was a triumph of exotic dishes and sculptured subtleties, including a magnificent phoenix that mechanically beat its wings amidst real flames. The queen, ever charming and amusing, spoke to all around her with interest. However, by nine o'clock, poor old King Louis had to be carried from the festivities, utterly worn out by the day's events. He was not the only one. Just after midnight, the queen finally gave in to weariness and fell fast asleep on her canopied chair of State as François cradled her lolling head. He would happily have stayed like that all night, but Madame d'Aumont instructed us to escort the tired girl back to the king's chambers. François, ever the gallant, carried her in his arms, her sleepy, golden head resting against his shoulder, while we maids trotted behind.

Claude's eyes followed her glittering husband until he disappeared from her sight. As I glanced back, I saw her yawn and pick aimlessly at the plate of sugared fruit set before her. Even the gift of several jars of brightly coloured bonbons from the good citizens of Paris had not cheered her, and she had kindly sent them to her little sister, Renée, who remained at the château, at Vincennes. She then rose to join her husband. To Madame Louise's disgust, it had all proved too much for King Louis, Madame Claude and the new Queen of France.

The following day, the king and queen rested, and on Tuesday afternoon, we all left the Palais Royal and made our leisurely way back across the Seine. As the queen rode her horse beside her husband, I heard much chattering and laughing concerning the coming tournament. The queen's eyes were bright with excitement, for one of the chevaliers bet that this time my Lord of Suffolk would be unhorsed. No man could beat the French champion, and he had a purse of gold on the wager. The queen laughed and promised the chevalier two hunting dogs if Suffolk hit the ground.

After a while, the street widened out, and we came to a huge complex of over a dozen dark towers and chaotic buildings. This was the Hôtel des Tournelles and the mass of spires, chimneys, weathercocks, and towers gave it its name – 'The Palace of the Turrets.' As we rode closer, I thought the palace looked very run down, with ivy crawling up its walls, thick moss covering the stone, and black corbies hopping along its ramparts. I could not imagine why King Louis preferred this palace to the Palais Royal. As we trotted through the gloomy entrance, decorated with the arms of King Louis, I stared up at the imposing, oppressive walls, and thought it not hard to believe that this place was also a prison.

Chapter Two

'In soft deluding lies let fools delight.'

Paris and
Saint-Germain-en-Laye

I stared at the girl sprawled out on the gilded bed, a heavy gown folded over my aching arms. She had woken late and missed Mass but did not seem in the slightest bit perturbed. As Ann Jernygham and Eliza Grey busily picked up the gowns left scattered on the floor, Mary Fiennes gathered up shoes and stockings. Jeanne replaced a golden collar in its velvet box. Everything to do with the young queen was chaotic, from her carelessly thrown belongings on the floor, to the silver platters of half-eaten food left by her bed. She did not have the slightest idea of tidiness or care for her possessions.

However, although all around her was bustle and frenzy, Mary Tudor only stretched out like a contented cat before throwing back the golden bed cover.

'God, he lay dribbling,' she said, putting her hand to her mouth to yawn. 'And farting. Oh, my brother will be amused!' She then curled up and placed her hand beneath her cheek as I stood by the blazing fire, my arms flagging. 'Oh, ladies, I have so many wonderful things – gifts, jewels, furs, constant gifts from the king. He never stops giving me presents.' Then it caught her eye. 'What is that?' She leant up on her elbow and beckoned me to come closer.

I curtsied. 'Madame, it is *another* gift.'

She smiled in expectation. 'You see what I mean? Let me see.' Jumping excitedly off the bed, she grabbed the gown and held the dark blue velvet against her night shift. Gazing at her reflection in the long mirror, at the priceless diamonds fashioned into stars sparkling like the midnight sky, she laughed. 'Ah, to be adored so by one's husband,' she said. 'And he does, he truly adores me.' She swirled around the chamber, her golden hair falling beneath her waist, holding the gown out at the side with one hand.

'Madame,' I said. 'Madame, if you please, it is not from your husband, but from the Duc d'Angoulême.'

She stopped still as the girls looked up, all chattering ceased.

'François? *Monsieur mon beau-fils?*' She lowered the gown in amazement. I nodded. 'Such expensive gifts are not proper, not proper at all,' she said, turning away with a blush and tossing the gown onto the floor as if it were a rag.

I took her saffron yellow night robe from the chair, and as she raised her arms in the air, I dropped it over her head. Her cheeks were flushed, and her eyes bright as I tied the ribbons at the neck.

'Such a foolish boy,' she said, pulling out her hair from inside the robe and trying not to smile. Then she giggled. 'Can you keep a secret, Anne?'

I said I could and she turned abruptly to the other girls.

'Leave me. I wish to be alone.'

The girls stopped their tasks and stared back at her in surprise.

'Out!' she repeated sharply.

I watched as they hurriedly curtsied and left the chamber. 'Anne, bolt the door.'

I did as she said, and when they had all gone, she sat back on the bed with a mischievous grin. 'I have a serious admirer,' she said quietly.

I thought this hardly a secret, for everyone admired this lovely girl. 'Indeed, Madame.'

'Well, go on – ask me, ask me who,' she urged, with a giggle. I stared blankly at her. 'It is François,' she said triumphantly. 'He tells me that he adores me, and says I am the most enchanting creature he has ever seen. He has quite lost his head. What do you think of that?'

'Madame, everyone adores you, so that is no surprise,' I said, avoiding her eyes and placing her silver slippers on her cold, bare feet.

'No, Anne, look at me – look me in the face and tell me what you think. Go on, your sister, Mary, tells me you speak plainly and I want to hear it.'

I stood up. 'Well,' I began, 'for – forgive me, Madame, but – should he not be giving such gifts to his wife, Claude?'

She threw back her golden head and laughed. 'Ha! I knew it! You disapprove, and you are the only one who will dare say so. And I agree. He should not be paying court to me as openly as he does. He is a licentious lecher.' She began playing with her hair, twisting it between her slender fingers.

'Yes, he is, Madame, but I do not think it is my place to give an opinion.'

She stared at me with her piercing blue eyes. 'It is if *I* say it is,' she said sulkily. 'Besides, I want a friend I can talk openly with, someone I can trust. Someone who will be honest.' She fell back onto the bed with a sigh, arms above her head, and stared up at the rafters. 'It is so difficult knowing that I am watched all the time.' She sat back up again. 'Can I trust you, Anne? Your sister Marie is amusing company, but she gossips at every turn and is not discreet.'

I smiled. 'You can, Madame.'

'I like Ann Jerringham,' she said, 'and Florence, although she is twice my age at least. But as to the other girls, although sweet, they follow each other's opinions like simpering sheep.' She moaned. 'Oh, I *wish* Jane Popincourt were here, for we became very close friends in England. Nothing I ever said shocked her and I could tell her all my dealings.'

At that moment she appeared so vulnerable I desperately wanted to cheer her.

'I do understand,' I said.

'Well, it has not been easy for me here,' she said, rising and walking over to her dressing table. She handed me the hairbrush. 'Everyone scrutinises me and that Madame d'Aumont never leaves me alone.'

I took the brush, encrusted with gems, and as she sat down, started to brush out her glorious hair. She murmured her pleasure and closed her eyes.

'I am so lonely, Anne. Oh, it looks like I have everything I want, but I do not. Yes, I have the love of the king, but not of the people close to him. Even Claude feels sad that I have taken the place of her mother – and who can blame her? But she is kind. If it were not for her kindness, I would go quite mad. Louise is afraid of me for the power I might wield should I get with child, and Marguerite keeps her own counsel. They are all petrified that I shall become pregnant and deliver a boy, thus snatching the crown of France away from François.'

I twisted the queen's long hair up into a chignon and secured it with an ivory comb from the table in front of her. As I took the second comb, she put her hand over mine. 'Be assured, it will not happen.' With her face sad, her previously sunny mood had quite evaporated. I had seen her brother's mood change just as quickly; all bonhomie vanished as rapidly as the early morning mist.

'Oh?' I asked.

'It is the king,' she said. There was silence.

'Madame, you *can* trust me,' I said, moving round to face her. Her cheeks were pale as I crouched down and knelt before her, searching her eyes. To my horror, she put her hands up to her face and burst into tears, making such a great wailing sound that it immediately caused a loud knock on the door.

'Your Grace, what is the matter?' asked a muffled voice.

'Leave me, Madame!' cried the queen, angrily. The door handle rattled. 'Make her go away!' screeched the queen, and running to the door, I opened it just enough to see the flushed face of Madame d'Aumont.

'What nonsense is this?' she hissed, peering in. 'What is going on? Why are these girls standing here shivering? Let me in this minute!' She pushed against the door.

'Please, Madame!' I protested, 'the queen wishes to be alone. There is no harm, all is well, I assure you.'

I slammed the door shut, slid the bolt across and returned to the crying queen. She sat sniffling and wiping her nose, while outside Madame d'Aumont continued to bang frantically on the door.

'Let me in!'

I waited a moment for the knocking to stop and the angry footsteps to recede.

'Thank you, Anne,' said the queen. 'She is such a confounded busybody, and I am sick to death of not having a moment to myself. They are all driving me to distraction.'

'May I speak plainly, Madame?' I asked.

She sighed. 'I wish somebody would, Anne.'

'Why will you not have a child with the king?'

She blew her nose again. 'Because he is not strong and has – has difficulty with the consummation. Oh, he tries and is the gentlest of husbands, but he is feeble and cannot – cannot get ... you know...' Her voice trailed off.

'But you would like a child?' I tried to put the hideous picture she had conjured up out of my mind.

'I would like a child very much, more than I can say. Oh, I have every material thing I could wish for here – jewels, gowns, treasures, horses.' She waved her hand carelessly in the air.

'Everything, except a child,' I added.

'And a man I might truly love.' She started to cry again.

'My lady, may I continue to speak plainly?' Her lips

trembled as she nodded, unable to speak. I hesitated for a moment.

'Is – is it true that you love another?'

To my horror, the queen burst into more frantic sobbing, and rising, threw herself onto her bed. As she wailed, her face hidden against the bolster, her fists pummelled, and her body shook with frantic sobs. I stood staring at her slim body and lovely hair falling loose from the combs, as she worked herself up into the most dreadful state.

'Oh, how can I hide it?' she sobbed, her words muffled. 'It is gossiped about throughout Europe. I have always loved the Duke of Suffolk, even as a little girl. Who could not love him? He is handsome, strong and makes every woman shiver with excitement when he jousts. You must agree, surely?' It sounded like a command.

'He is, Madame,' I said.

'He promised me, he promised me!' she cried, as I stood by the bed, alarmed. 'Oh, Jesu help me. Do not let him go back on his word!'

'Who promised, Madame, the duke?'

'My brother! My brother promised that if I married old Louis, the next husband I took I could choose for myself. He swore to me an oath, and he cannot go back on his word!' She cried until, finally, the sobs subsided. Then she swung her legs round to the edge of the bed, and sat up.

'Madame, everyone agrees that next to King Henry, the duke is the most handsome man at court,' I said, trying to cheer her.

Her face immediately brightened. 'Oh, *yes*! I knew you would think so, too!' she said. 'Louis cannot live for much longer. My true love is Charles and only Charles, and I am aching for love of him.'

'And he feels the same?' I asked innocently.

She stared blankly. 'Well, of course, he does, how could he not? Charles is afraid of nothing except my brother's terrible wrath if we act against his will. I am also afraid of

your uncle, Thomas Howard, and the council, for they
are all jealous of Charles and would resent his influence
through me.'

'But Madame, you said the king –'

'Oh, you do not know my brother,' she said. 'I am a
political marriage pawn, and when Louis dies who knows
where he will send me? He blows hot and cold. I suppose if
I did, by some miracle, have a male child with Louis, I would
at least remain Regent of France. Then, to my brother's joy,
he would have one sister ruling Scotland, the other France.
Two troublesome countries taken care of in one swoop, and
he the ruler of the seas between with all the trade and wealth
that would bring.' There was a moment's pause. 'But if I do
not get a child, then I might be forced into another betrothal
with Prince Charles of Spain. I was but thirteen years old
when they betrothed me to him before, and I can still recall
with horror the celebrations. They sang in the streets how
'Dame Mary shall join the Golden Fleece of Gold – Ave
Maria!' and they made me drool over his portrait and sigh
with love.'

'Madame,' I said, 'I have met the Prince at Mechelen,
and he is not that ill-favoured. He is quite – acceptable – in
his serious way. I also believe you would be very happy at his
aunt's court, for she is a wonderful woman.'

'Yes, but I would not be marrying his *aunt*! Besides,
she cannot be that wonderful encouraging my Charles
in an embarrassing flirtation with her! The old fool was a
laughing stock.'

I lowered my eyes, aggrieved that the kind Regent could
thus be spoken of.

'Oh, God! Prince Charles is an awful fate compared to
my love, and if my brother gainsays his word, I shall kill
myself, so help me God I will!' Her eyes flamed dramatically.

'That would be a sin, my lady.'

'Well, you cannot imagine, Anne, how awful it is day
after day here, watching as the lusty duke cavorts his horse

at the jousts, knowing my husband is weak and feeble. Oh, Charles was so heroic in the tilt against the French. I could not believe it when I heard that François had slyly introduced a German mercenary to beat him. It was despicable, most unsportsmanlike, and my love might have been killed.'

'Do you not love King Louis at all?'

'Of course, I do,' she snapped, 'and you do me no good service if you thunder it about otherwise. I show him all the tenderness and care that becomes a good wife.'

I had angered her, but then her voice softened.

'Louis is the sweetest of men – well, apart from the argument over my ladies. I hated him then.'

I smiled, remembering the upset.

'He is kind, generous, thoughtful and oh, so desperate to have a son. He is good to me, but I do not love him physically. How could I? It is frightful to feel his cold hands, bereft of feeling on my body, and see the blood that comes when he goes to make w –' She stopped herself continuing. 'Tis naught,' she said, lowering her eyes. 'I shall not have a son by the king, that is certain.'

I thought about Charles Brandon. I thought of Madame Regent and hoped that the princess would not be humiliated in the same way, for the Regent had lost her heart to the duke when she met him at Lille. Why was everything to do with that man so complicated?

The queen then took hold of my hand. 'Anne, you must not repeat what I have told you today. Do you understand? This is between us. Do you swear on your life?'

I swore.

'Good. I do mean to have the duke, whatever the cost and however long it takes – and I mean to have his child.'

*   *

Frozen with cold, I held a piece of linen soaked in lavender to my nose. The *grande salle* of the Hôtel des Tournelles stank, due to its proximity to one of the greatest sewers in Paris, and as I sat on the wooden bench, my fingers numb, I cursed a king too mean to light the fires. Rubbing my cold hands, I gazed around as people went about their business. Young pages, messengers, noblemen, and their ladies strolled past the magnificent tapestries, and I thought about the court at Mechelen and Margaret of Savoy. No doubt she and her ladies were returning from Mass now, for it was not long since dawn.

A young woman approached me and interrupted my daydreaming, her face unsmiling. 'Madame will see you now if you would follow me.'

I rose from the bench just as I spied the queen at the far end of the gallery, tittering and laughing with my sister, her ladies, and a large entourage of gaily clad young gentlemen. The queen's laughter rang out, and my sister gave me a playful wave before disappearing through the door. I walked on a little farther until the woman in front stopped at a large, oak door and knocked. The voice inside sounded muffled, but the woman opened the door, and as I entered, closed it behind me. Astrological charts and a myriad of documents lay scattered across the floor. On a table lay an unfurled scroll of handwritten dates, with drawings of the planets around the margins. In front of me stood Madame d'Aumont, dressed in her usual black damask, her face set cold and imperious, and not a look that boded well. I gave a deep reverence.

'What in the name of Heaven do you think you were doing?' she asked angrily, twisting the ring on her finger. I stared at the large, white opal – a magical stone that gives insight to the wearer – and my heart began to race. 'Well? Get up and speak,' she said, moving closer, 'and do not play games with me, young lady. You are a bright girl, not a dolt.'

'Madame, forgive me. Are you referring to the queen's distress?' I refused to be cowed.

'You know very well what I refer to,' she said. '*I am* the *dame d'honneur* here, and I will not have my authority undermined in this manner. What gave you the right – *the right* – to be alone with the queen thus? Anything might have occurred. She could have been in mortal danger.'

'By your leave, Madame, the queen herself requested that all leave her presence and so I only did as I was instructed.'

She narrowed her angry eyes. '*I* instruct, mistress, I do the instructing!' she screeched. 'You have been here but five minutes and appear to feel it is your place to know what is best for the queen. Well?'

I felt my cheeks burn with indignation as I stood berated.

'What you did was quite outside the order of how things are done at this court. Do you hear me?'

'I do, Madame.'

'Here, we have precedents. Was nothing taught you at the court of Savoy? Should the queen be distressed about anything, you must fetch me, *regardless*,' she said, raising her voice as I opened my mouth to speak, 'of the queen's wishes. Although I stood outside the door, you rudely refused to let me in. Refused! How dare you behave in such a manner? I should have you whipped, sent from the court as quite unsuitable, and packed off back to England. It has been done before to other such busybodies.'

'Oh, Madame!' I decided that a defiant stance might not be the best approach after all. 'Please, please forgive me. I did not mean to offend you. I beg you not to send me away, for I mean only to have you satisfied with my conduct.'

One of the dogs by the fire whined for the raised voices had unsettled him.

'Madame d'Aumont, if you please,' came a calm voice from behind the high-backed chair in the corner. 'You are frightening the girl.'

With a heavy sigh, a woman rose up and turned to face me. She held an astrological chart, and I dropped a curtsey, not daring to look upon the dark, looming figure of Louise of Savoy.

'Get up, dear, would you care for some cordial?' she asked kindly, clicking her fingers to a page to hand me a glass from the table. She put the chart down. 'Really, such a fine intellect should not be cowed with harsh words,' she chided, glancing towards the duchess. 'Now, drink and recover your composure.'

I did as she commanded, nervously eyeing Madame d'Aumont, who appeared fit to burst like an overblown bladder. Louise, meanwhile, watched me with unblinking eyes, the folds of her ruby red gown falling like rivulets of blood in the candlelight.

'Are you happy here?' she asked with mild concern, plucking a grape from a nearby bowl. 'You should be.'

'Oh, indeed, Madame, although I have been here but a short while, and – and some of your ways are new to me.'

'But you would like to stay – yes?'

'Indeed, my lady, very much so.'

Louise walked over to the window and gazed down towards the noise outside. I could hear the queen's laughing voice and recognised my sister's high-pitched squeals. Barking dogs added to the commotion, and obviously, some great amusement was taking place below.

'Such a pretty girl,' said Louise, as she gazed through the thick, green glass. To my dismay, I heard my sister shriek again. The unmistakable Boleyn laugh sounded most unbecoming. 'Tut, tut – English girls, what am I to do with them?' she continued.

My heart sank as I feared we were both about to be sent back home - Mary for laughing too loudly, and me for having offended the *dame d'honneur*. I thought of my father and how he would be outraged. We had been here in France but a few weeks and now we would return home in disgrace. How humiliating.

'Our queen,' said Louise, moving from the window, 'is young and needs guidance, for she is apt to be wilful and domineers others to get her way. I cannot quite decide if she is a foolish girl – or rather cunning. Oh, I cannot fault her behaviour to our beloved king and the people adore her, but she is – headstrong. You understand me?'

I nodded, but, in truth, I did not. The queen had behaved impeccably at all the ceremonies and celebrations, impressing the ambassadors with her dignity and grace.

'Yes, Madame,' was all I could say.

'My dear, when you get to my age you learn to read people, to understand their true motives, and I understand the new queen very well. I know that she adores the exalted position of Queen of France, with its gowns, gifts, jewels, and attention. But she is not wise and puts her own needs and desires before all else. A queen cannot do that, and it is to this last matter that I must express my concerns.' She paused and studied my face as if expecting some response.

'How much do you wish to remain here?' She took another sip of wine.

My expression immediately brightened. 'Oh, more than anything, Madame!'

She smiled graciously. 'So you will help me?'

I nodded again, not caring what she asked, for I could not possibly return home in disgrace.

'Then tell me, what did the queen say to you when you were alone together?'

Madame d'Aumont opened her mouth to interject, but Louise held up her hand to silence her. I stood dumb, for I had given my word to the queen that what she spoke of would stay secret.

'You know your uncle speaks very highly of you,' said Louise, changing tack. 'Did you know that? He says that you are far brighter than that – that creature down there with the queen, a credit to your family.'

My face lit up at the comparison with my sister and the thought that my uncle had spoken of me to this great lady.

'Well?'

I turned to Madame d'Aumont for assistance, but she only looked away.

'Anne, dearest girl, if you want to stay at this court

you must learn to trust me. I have only the queen's good at heart and wish to protect her. Even now, I am consulting her planetary chart. She is young, and I love her as if she were my daughter. Through her, the royal line of France will continue – after all, she may be carrying the future king of France as we speak. I need to be sure that all is well and I can only do that if I have your co-operation. So, I am relying on you to help me, to be my eyes and ears. I need to know what worries the queen, what upsets her peace of mind or if she feels ill and so forth. How can I guide her if I do not know these matters?' She gave me a charming, concerned smile. 'Come, I am offering you a most important role here at court, one that your family will be most proud of – one of complete trust. Now, I ask you again. What was spoken of?'

Her smooth, silky voice sounded caressing, her eyes shone clear and honest, and at that moment, I found it hard to believe the things my sister had said about her. Surely Louise did not hate the lovely queen? Yet Duchess Agnes had said Louise was spiteful and bore grudges. No, she was mistaken, for Louise wanted only the best for Mary Tudor. I did not need to heed my sister's warning and could make my own judgement. Besides, I felt flattered, for here stood the great Comtesse d'Angoulême asking for my help – a girl of small account to anyone. Of all the young ladies at court, she had asked for my assistance alone, and at that moment I felt proud. I also knew that as one of the queen's maids of honour, I must do all I could for the girl, and protect her from her foolishness. To watch out for her, and serve her well. That is what I had been taught, and that is what I was expected to do. I already knew that the woman standing before me held immense power and worth and that I must try and please her if I wished to succeed at the French court.

'Madame, if it is truly to protect the queen,' I said, casually casting aside my promise to the girl, 'then it is my duty to tell you anything that you ask of me.'

Louise smiled with satisfaction at Madame d'Aumont

and gave me an expectant look.

'And?'

'The – the queen is desperate for a child.' I said simply, looking from one to the other.

'But that is good, is it not? And she is happy with her husband and his – attempts?'

Madame d'Aumont turned away with a faint smile, for I detected the remark from Louise was not sincere.

I shook my head. 'No, Madame,' I said sadly, 'the queen will not have a child with King Louis. She said he is not capable'

Louise moved forward and placed her hand on my arm, crushing my sleeve. 'She said that? Those were her exact words?'

'Yes, Madame, she said he cannot do the act. He has not been able to con – con –' I could not think of the word in French, but then surely this was no surprise, considering Louis' health?

Louise remained silent for a moment or two and folded her hands in front of her gown. 'Well, it is as we all thought. Now, Anne, that was not so difficult, was it?'

I shook my head.

'Tell me. Is there anything else?'

'Yes, Madame, the queen is in love with the Duke of Suffolk.' There was a moment's pause.

'The duke?' I nodded.

'Well, Mistress Boleyn,' said Madame d'Aumont, with a sneer. 'I think we can all see her admiration – and that of every other woman at court – for she never takes her eyes off him. But they are the doe eyes of a headstrong girl, no more.'

'No, Madame,' I said. 'The queen says the duke feels the same, and she will have him as her lover by whatever means possible. She is desperate and fears that if she is left alone with him, she will not be able to keep herself from getting with child.' I could not resist embroidering the facts for good measure.

Louise gave a start. *'Adultery?* With Brandon?' She turned away so that I could not see her face. When she finally turned around to face me, she appeared more composed. 'This puts a very different complexion on matters and is precisely what I mean about protecting our queen, whom I love as my own.' She piously kissed the crucifix hanging at her girdle. 'Do you see my dilemma, my dear? What if King Louis does get her *enceinte*? And what if the Duke of Suffolk also...' Her silky voice trailed away. 'How would we know if the child she is carrying is Louis' – or a Suffolk bastard? You understand the great danger her soul, and the kingdom, is in?'

Still immensely flattered, I most certainly did, and wanted to help this powerful, charismatic woman who, in effect, ruled France.

'Where is the duke lodging at present?' She turned to Madame d'Aumont.

'With the family of François' mistress,' came the reply, 'for your son has been most amenable to the duke, most amenable indeed.'

Louise narrowed her eyes. 'I see,' she mused. She then turned to me, the tone of her voice now cold. 'If you repeat any of this conversation, I shall find out, have you whipped, and sent home. Do you understand? Keep your ears open and your mouth shut, for that way you will serve your dear queen wisely. From now on you come to me, or Madame d'Aumont only, with anything you might hear. If you do as I ask, you will be very well rewarded here in France – and the queen's honour will be protected. Your family will also hear of how much you have pleased me.'

I watched as she moved away, seemingly deep in thought. After some moments, she turned around. 'Oh, and your sister – send her to me. I might yet have a use for such a creature.'

My audience had ended, and as I curtsied and made to leave the chamber, the black figure of *Madame la Grande* appeared from the shadows. As I walked back to my lodgings,

I realised that I had forgotten to mention that François had also bought the queen a gift – a very expensive gift indeed.

*   *

Throughout late November, at the château of Saint-Germain-en-Laye, just two leagues outside Paris, we attended the young queen as she greeted the many dignitaries who flocked to see her. Overlooking the River Seine with its bridge across the dry moat, the château appeared somewhat dilapidated, but inside its draughty chambers there continued a heady round of official banquets, dancing, and entertainments. At one such dinner, Claude asked me to play an English song on my harp for the mayor, and sitting on a cushion before the illustrious company, I thoroughly enjoyed the attention.

Meanwhile, King Louis remained behind at the Hôtel des Tournelles, too ill with gout to accompany his lovely wife. He had changed his dining hours to suit his new queen, retiring to bed far too late, having eaten rich, fatty suppers. He had a great love of sauce *a là bretonne,* which included ham, veal and partridge juice mixed with butter and chicken jelly, but sadly it did not love him back. Frequently sick and fearful that the smell of vomit would not be conducive to love, he had lain on his bed alone during the day, in the dark palace. Behind his back, the court smirked and sniggered, saying he rode a spirited horse to Paradise. However, every night, the queen dutifully returned to her husband to play music for him, keep him company, and feed him herself from a golden spoon laden with greasy meat.

In December, the Duke of Suffolk, to Louise's visible relief, was recalled to England. The queen, now feeling vulnerable from the ever more pressing advances of François, threw herself into a fever of nervous activity. We maids were so tired from the late-nights that we could barely keep awake during the morning Mass, but still, the queen insisted on late-night supper parties, dancing, and singing. She also had a passion for riding out in the snow or skating on the ice on the River Seine, wrapped in sumptuous furs. Poor Louis lay watching in his canopied chariot, his feeble breath barely making a wisp in the frosty air, surrounded by exhausted courtiers and ambassadors.

'Well, well,' he wheezed, 'see what a pretty conceit she is and I, I tell you, will soon regain my vigour. I will have an army in Italy by Candlemas, so urge me no more and heat yourself not. I am warmer than you all, and I assure you, the expedition will take place. It is just this gout that troubles me so.'

The ambassadors, stamping their snow-covered feet to try and keep warm, were not fooled. Louis waved as his queen swept away on the arm of François, blowing a kiss from her red, velvet glove. As he coughed into a cloth and observed the specks of blood, he sighed. He was not fooled either. He had promised her a wonderful Christmas in Paris, but he knew that he grew weaker by the day. He gazed sadly at François' jewel-encrusted cloak, knowing what it had cost the treasury, and mumbled to the Vicomte de Lautrec: 'Ah, that rude boy will spoil everything.'

The nobles, standing close by, nodded in solemn agreement, but all knew the frugal old Louis, and it was obvious to all that they looked towards the next young king. They were done with this burnt-out old fossil of a creature in his shabby coat. A king should look a king, noble and majestic. Claude, meanwhile, gazed on indulgently from her fur-draped sledge, and although distressed at her father's condition, put on a brave smile. As she glanced down at the medallion of St Margaret held tightly in her thin fingers, I knew that while some might mock her, none could touch her. François had done his duty and as she smiled, she was, no doubt, content in the knowledge that it would not be long before she gave him his greatest wish.

Louis felt too ill to attend Mass, and on Christmas Day, at the Hôtel des Tournelles, the physician ordered the court to remain as quiet as possible. There were no noisy carollers, processions or late night masques, no feasting, dancing, or gaiety – just an oppressiveness hanging over the gloomy chambers. It resulted in a very subdued day, more like Christ's death than birth. In the *grande salle*, courtiers gathered in corners, or warmed themselves by the meagre fireplaces and muttered in low voices. Meanwhile, the queen sat anxiously alone with Claude, having been advised by Madame d'Aumont not to leave the duchess's side for a moment, but to read her prayer book.

In our chamber, where my sister and the other girls sat playing chess, I strummed quietly on my lute and thought back to the previous Christmas at Mechelen. It could not have been more different. I wondered what the Regent and the other girls were doing, and if they were preparing for a masque. I thought of my dear tutor, Madame Symonnet, and pictured her laughing eyes and lilting voice. In England, my parents were attending the court at Placentia, and Mother had just written to Mary and me enclosing two sets of coral earrings as New Year gifts for us both. I put my instrument down and slipped the letter out from under my sleeve to read again. Mother wrote that the ladies were now much occupied with Queen Katherine and her terrible grief, for she had brought to almost full-term a longed-for prince. But it proved too soon, and he was stillborn. No one knew what had happened, but some said it might have been due to the queen's distress over the king's dalliance with a girl called Elizabeth Blount. It was foolish, for everyone had told the queen it meant naught, but she would not be calmed. For months the king had rejoiced in a fever of excitement and anticipation at the coming birth. This son, he had said, would be the finest Christmas gift the queen could offer him, a new saviour of the world, but one born in the most sumptuous surroundings rather than a meagre stable. The magnificent cradle and baptismal font had already been sent from Canterbury for the christening. Now, however, nothing but wailing and weeping drifted from the queen's chambers. The king, disappointed beyond all reason, behaved cold and distant and none dared approach him. In expectation of a prince, he had already received a congratulatory gift of twelve beautiful broodmares from Mantua, in Italy, each worth their weight in silver. He now spent his time down at the stable yard perusing them, far away from hysterical women. The Italian envoy, along with the Duke of Suffolk, had put them through their paces before His Grace, and the king was so impressed with the envoy's riding skill that he tried to persuade him to remain in England in his service. Mother wrote that as my father stood watching the talented display with my brother, George, the king had beckoned the boy over. Showing him special favour, George had, to his joy, been allowed to trot about the courtyard on one of the mares. The king seemed especially fond of my talkative, merry little brother and perhaps saw in him the boy for whom he yearned. There would be a wedding, too. Young Bessie Bryan – she whom the king had once been so enamoured of – was to wed Nicholas Carew before the Feast of the Purification of Our Lady.

• •

Matters took a turn for the worse. As I stood at the top of the great oak staircase watching the growing crowd of murmuring ambassadors and courtiers gathering below, I gave a little gasp.

'Oh, there is someone I know,' I said.

The girls followed my gaze.

'It is Signor Mercurin Gattinara,' I said, 'the Flemish ambassador from the Regent's court at Mechelen, and with him is Signor de Nassau and Signor de Saint-Py.'

I slipped down the staircase into the heat and press of the crowd and approached the ambassadors resplendent in their fur cloaks.

'Signor,' I said, with a respectful curtsey, 'forgive me, sir, for being so bold, but I served at the court of the Regent, Madame Margaret, last year and I wonder if you could tell me how does my lady?'

The gentleman turned around with a quizzical look. 'And you are, mistress?'

'Anne Boleyn, signor.'

He nodded slowly in recognition, his manners impeccable, and smiled indulgently. 'But of course, now I remember you. I remember you very well for it is my business to remember faces. And I remember how prettily you played for my lady'. His companions smiled too. 'Madame grew very fond of you and – if I recall correctly – felt somewhat put out when your father recalled you from her service. Well, now I assume you are here at the French court, serving our new French Queen.'

I nodded, eagerly, as he continued.

'I am content to report that the Regent is very well indeed and busy with plans to celebrate the prince's fifteenth birthday and coming of age.'

'With a grand boar hunt in Mechelen?' I asked.

Signor Gattinara laughed. 'Oh, something far more spectacular this time, I think. Ah, now, if you will excuse me, I think we are finally moving.' He bowed and turned away.

'Please, signor, give Madame my felicitations,' I added, 'and tell her she is often in my prayers.'

As the gentleman inclined his head and walked away, my sister beckoned to me from the balcony. I made my way back.

'You should not approach people like that,' she chastised when I reached her. 'You are too bold.'

As we stood observing the crowd, five grandly dressed gentlemen appeared in a cloud of scented silk. They were speaking so quickly and excitedly that I could not understand a word they were saying, and the cloying scent of violets hung in the air as they descended the staircase.

'Who are they?' I asked, picking up Bonny and nestling her in my arms.

'Men who can smell a corpse,' said Eliza.

I must have appeared alarmed for she smiled.

'Well, they smell like women,' I added, referring to the sickly aroma.

'Who is *that?*' asked my sister, leaning over the balustrade, revealing her ample bosom.

'The handsome gentleman in the blue cap,' continued Eliza, 'is Guillaume Gouffier, Seigneur de Bonnivet. They say he is the most profligate man at court, which is saying something for France. I hear from gossip that poor Marguerite felt quite passionate about him once. Truth be told, I think she still does.' She pointed again. 'The other gentleman there is Seigneur de Bayard, reputed to be the best horseman in France. I think that is Philippe Chabot and that is Anne de Montmorency – you pronounce his name '*Annay*'. Finally, there is Robert de la Marck. They were all brought up with François at Amboise, as *pages d'honneur* and they accompany him everywhere. See how they are hastening to the royal apartments.'

I watched as they disappeared, fascinated by the richness of their attire.

'Not that they have been kneeling with their rosary beads, mumbling prayers,' said Mary Fiennes under her breath. 'There have been complaints from the king's doctor that the laughter coming from François' apartments has been most disrespectful.'

'And I know why,' said Ann Jernyngham, 'for I hear François and his companions have been holding their own Christmas, celebrating the fact that he is about to receive the finest New Year's gift possible.'

'Is the king so very ill then?' I asked.

•   •

The year 1515 began with a terrible snowstorm, the like
of which I had never seen before, and I rubbed the dusty
window to watch the mayhem. Outside, horses whinnied in
the stables and boys frantically ran to bolt the barn doors.
Buckets flew, dogs howled, and geese and chicken scattered
as the tremendous wind raged. The snow appeared blinding,
and I watched as one of the young stable boys slipped to
the ground, harness in hand. I turned away, shivering, for
the windows in the draughty palace banged and rattled, and
no matter how much we stoked up the logs on the fire, the
snow-flakes gusted down the chimney into the chamber.

I returned to my place with the maids and recited prayers
for the dying king. Bonny and the other lapdogs lay wrapped
around each other, tail to head in front of the howling hearth
to keep warm, and made me smile. Even with coney furs
draped over our shoulders to block out the draught, we were
still frozen, and as I knelt on the rush mats, I smelt stale dog
piss. At home at Hever, Mother would have insisted that the
boards were clean and covered with fragrant rue and thyme.
I sneaked a look across to Madame d'Aumont as she led our
mumbling prayers. Her eyes were closed, but she seemed
distracted, for she would open them and glance towards the
door. Still, the storm continued to rage outside and the wind
whistled. As we prayed, we knew that François – along with
the king's confessor, Guillaume Petit, his captain, and his
men-at-arms – was with the dying king in his chamber. His
life, along with the wax tapers, was fading fast.

By nightfall, we were just about to proceed to the
grande salle to take some supper, when we were disturbed
by a commotion outside in the passageway. As we stood,
motionless, the door burst open, and Françoise de Foix,
Comtesse de Châteaubriant, flew in, flushed and breathless.
Dark haired, I immediately noticed how attractive she was.

'Quick, ladies, quick! Attend to the queen – she is with

Claude and has fainted. We cannot revive her for *le Roi* – *le Roi est mort!* She made the sign of the cross, and we all followed suit. My eyes then glanced towards the window, for outside in the courtyard we heard shouting, a dull thudding of horse hooves in the snow, and the cry of *'Romorantin! Vite!'*

As if stung by a bee, Madame d'Aumont scrambled to her feet and peered through the windowpane.

'Now – now is the moment she has waited so patiently for,' she said, her warm breath making a little patch on the diamond-shaped glass.

'And now *we* go home,' whispered my sister.

• •

The *grande salle* heaved with ambassadors, courtiers, nobles, and ladies. Pages scurried to and fro with dishes and platters, and the barking and whining of numerous dogs added to the noise. I glanced about to see where we could sit. Not over to the right – a woman sat there with a hideous monkey on her arm.

'Well?' I asked my sister as we squeezed onto a long bench at one of the tables by the window. 'What do we do now?'

Mary glanced up and smiled as a young servant placed two goblets before us. He flushed, much to my sister's amusement.

'I told you, Nan. For the present we are instructed by Madame d'Aumont to attend on Claude, so that is what we must do.'

'All of us? But she has her ladies.'

'I am not certain. I do not think I could stand all that weeping and wailing. I have nothing against Claude, but she is so *dull.*'

I began picking at our shared platter of goose, chicken and duck meat. It did not smell very appetising, and the chicken had a greasy sheen. I dipped my fingers into the finger bowl, my appetite vanished.

'The only good thing about being in her presence,' said

Mary, her eyes shining, 'is that we shall be in daily contact with François and therefore his gentlemen. Is not Monsieur Gouffier handsome with his golden beard? There is talk that one day he will be made Admiral of France.'

'Mary! Do not dare make eyes at him. Besides, you know he still only has eyes for Marguerite.' She cut a piece of manchet bread and dropped it to Bonny, sitting at my feet. The little dog snapped her jaws loudly, glad of any morsel, stale or otherwise.

'Oh, I have just thought of something, Mary. If we have to attend Claude, we might not be able to attend the coronation of François, for I hear Claude is ill. We cannot miss such an occasion!'

Mary laughed. 'You just want to be seen at every opportunity wearing an extravagant gown, Nan. You are becoming quite the little courtier!'

'Well, I mean to do well here,' I said, defensively, 'and that means being noticed by the right people.'

Mary pulled a face. 'Oh, do not think that you have not attracted attention, running errands for Madame d'Aumont, and then off to see Louise of Savoy. What was that about?'

I gave Bonny a piece of meat. 'Nothing,' I said.

'And we all know you are the favourite with the queen – I mean the Dowager French Queen – now old Louis is dead. If you carry on, you will make yourself unpopular with the other girls, since everyone sees how she favours you.'

'I care not a fig,' I said. 'Besides, the people I am unpopular with do not matter. Maids come and go. What matters is to please those people who have influence, who can be advantageous to you and your family.'

'Christ above, you sound like Mother.' She plucked a grape from the dish.

'I cannot help it if certain people see me as intelligent and bright,' I continued hotly. 'Anyone can simper and look attractive.'

'Oh, listen to yourself prattling on,' said Mary. 'What

would you prefer to be – attractive or intelligent?'

'Both.'

'Not in your case Nan!'

I stood up from the bench. 'Why are you being so hateful, Mary?'

'Because you are making a fool of yourself, tripping here, tripping there, that secret, smug look upon your face.'

'And you are not, I suppose, making doe eyes at every gentleman who enters the chamber? You told me that you had changed.'

'Oh, you are such a prig, Nan! What is wrong with a flirtation? Would you rather hole me up in a nutshell? This is France.'

'Nothing is wrong, Mary – absolutely nothing.' I picked up Bonny and with a petulant flounce left the table.

●   ●

'Madame d'Aumont, I understand exactly what is expected of me but you are going too far! I *will* have my attendants!'

A hairbrush flew across the chamber, narrowly missing the newly painted portrait of Claude, and hit the door with a thud.

'And can someone stop that infernal bell ringing outside? It is shredding my nerves!'

'It is the French custom, Madame,' came the haughty reply. 'You must remain alone for forty days until it is known if you are with child or not. Also, so that none might give you a child that you could later claim as your dead husband's. *I* do not make the rules.'

'What an insult! I am the French queen,' said Mary, imperiously, 'and that is how I will continue to be addressed. I understand full well what is expected of me. God's death, is it not bad enough that I am to be locked up, but that I cannot have an English attendant about me?' She sat down heavily on the bed with a pout. 'I can assure you I –'

'Assure me of what, Madame?' asked Madame d'Aumont, picking up the brush. As she handed it to me, I saw that the priceless jewelled top had been badly cracked.

'Tis naught,' replied the queen, sulkily. 'When do I repair to the Hôtel de Cluny? I trust it is not cold for I cannot endure the cold.'

'Madame, it has recently been rebuilt and refurbished and you will not have far to travel in this cold weather. Now, at Cluny your clothes must all be in the white of mourning. You know how lovely you look in white.'

'Ha! And who will see?' retorted the queen. She glanced at me and my sister as we cleared her little table of its scattered pots of rouge and perfume. Always in disarray, half the tops were missing, or on the floor. 'Can I take my dogs?' She picked up her little spaniel, and although Madame d'Aumont nodded, she buried her head into the dog's silky fur and began to cry. 'Oh, what will become of me, I am so afraid!'

My sister and I glanced at each other beneath lowered eyes, as the other girls carried on folding her gowns and placed them in the large chests.

'Come now – what is it that ails you so?' asked Madame d'Aumont, her voice now concerned.

The queen lowered her eyes.

'I – I am sad at the king's death. He was a good man to me and I mourn him for his chivalry and honour.' As she looked up, her soft eyes full of tears, her voice betrayed her insincerity.

'Would you like to rest a while?' asked Madame d'Aumont, playing the game and plumping up the bolsters on the bed. 'You are tired, quite overcome and need quiet. The king's death is, indeed, most distressing.'

As the queen nodded forlornly, the door burst open. All the girls and ladies, including Madame d'Aumont, swept to the floor, but the queen remained seated on the bed. The woman standing in the doorway appeared serene and behind her stood several gentlemen, bowing low. One I recognised as the queen's physician.

'My condolences to you, Madame,' came the calm voice of Louise of Savoy. From the state of her mud-spattered gown, she appeared to have been travelling for several days. She removed her green gloves, threw them onto a chair, and waved everyone to their feet. Then she took off her black velvet bonnet and fingered the magnificent brooch attached. It depicted the golden salamander of Angoulême, with eyes of flashing rubies – the device of her son. I wondered what it meant, and she followed the path of my eyes with her own as if reading my mind.

'I feed on fire – and I extinguish it,' she said, moving forward.

How could she read my mind?

The queen stood up and proffered her white hand and Louise kissed it as if it were a poison chalice.

'Madame Louise,' said the queen.

'My Lady Marie, forgive my rude condition,' she said, waving for the door to be shut on the gentlemen, 'but I have ridden hard from Romorantin with my beloved daughter here, through the most dreadful storm. The roads lay deep with snow and mud and I rode as quickly as I could to –'

'Put your mind at rest?' interjected the queen.

'To offer my sympathy,' continued Louise, coldly. She unclasped her fur cloak and handed it to one of the ladies. 'Yesterday my son began his reign, receiving ambassadors and members of *parlement,* appointing those he wishes to keep in office. Those *I* wish to keep. Now, consider how embarrassing it would be, to say the least, if –'

'There is no child, Madame, as far as I am aware,' interrupted the queen, quietly.

Louise furrowed her brow but her flashing eyes were as hard and bright as diamonds.

'And you are certain of this?'

'Madame, your son has already hastened to me and

asked the same question. I said I know of no other king in France, but he.'

Louise could not hide her triumph. 'Well, my dear child, you understand we must be sure? We must follow procedure and so I have asked your physician to attend you on this matter.'

The queen's face flushed.

'Now, I must change from this gown and go to my son. The palace has turned into a madhouse – I have never seen such a crowd of foreigners and young men seeking new positions.' She walked over to the window and, lifting the drape aside, peered down. 'See how they huddle like vultures, ready to rip at the flesh of favour – and yet still more people are trying to get through. If we are not careful, the guards will be quite overcome.'

A moment or two of silence followed as she stood, lost in thought. She then turned around as if surprised at our presence. 'Did you know my husband died on the first day of January? And now, on the same date, my beloved son became king.'

'As God wills,' said the queen.

'Indeed. Well, all the stars foretold this, that this year would be one of great marvels. Now, my dear, you must rest after your shock. Mary Boleyn here will read to you, while Madame d'Aumont and the other ladies will be right outside the door should you require anything, anything at all. I will tell the guards to admit no-one.'

The queen climbed back onto the great bed.

Louise paused. 'No, wait – let her sister stay instead. She can sing some French *chansons* for you. Most soothing.' Without a glance, she handed me the beribboned lute leaning against the table.

'I should like that, Madame,' said the queen.

Louise of Savoy then swept out of the chamber, and I noticed she had forgotten her gloves.

Madame d'Aumont clapped her hands and removed

everyone else, including my sister.

'I do not see why I have to go,' Mary hissed in my ear, before dipping low to the figure now on the bed. 'I can sing better than you.'

As the chamber emptied, Madame d'Aumont turned to me, her back to the queen, and leaned close.

'You know what is expected of you.'

●　●

The body of King Louis lay robed and sceptred in state at the Hôtel des Tournelles. His court painter, Jean Perreal, made a life-like cast of his face and placed it over the corpse. It appeared eerie in the blaze of torches that were continuously kept alight. The corpse was then transported with great ceremony through Paris, a city heavily draped with black from every corner and house window to the Cathedral of Notre Dame, for the service. François attended the Mass dressed in purple velvet and, with his dark looks and long nose, apparently looked like the very devil himself.

The following day, in the cold, drizzling rain, old Louis began his journey to Saint-Denis. However, what was supposed to have been a solemn day turned into a pitiful farce, for to everyone's embarrassment, the monks argued over the ownership of the golden pall covering the coffin. There ensued a tug of war with the French nobles on one side and the monks on the other. Then, in the pouring rain, the chariots got stuck in the muddy road, and a wheel broke. The velvet-clad horses, turning their heads away from the biting wind, could go no further and everything had to stop for the night. Finally, on the morning of the fourth of January, they hastily laid King Louis next to his wife, Anne of Brittany. His long reign over, his household was immediately dissolved. The king was dead. *Vive le Roi!*

No-one thought to offer Claude their condolences – not even her husband François – and she remained forgotten. Predictably, she fell into paroxysms of grief, for now she and her six-year-old sister, Renée, were orphans, both having dearly loved their kind father. He had spent many hours with Claude teaching her the art of governance, regardless of her being a woman, and she would miss his wise words. He alone had loved her for herself, not for how she appeared, with her twisted body and short sight. He knew that with her sound judgement and true instincts, she could be of great use to her husband if only he would let her. However, François did respect her position and loved her for her goodness, and although Louise might privately seethe, Claude's name always took precedence over hers on every official document. It was a small consolation for a girl who loved her husband so deeply.

• •

I stopped, curious. The muffled crying appeared to be coming from the entrance to Claude's royal suite. As I stood listening, the door opened and several anxious ladies of the chamber bustled out, led by Madame d'Assigne.

'Yes? What is your business?' she inquired, abruptly. 'Madame has not long risen.'

'My lady, if it pleases you, I have a message from the Dowager French Queen for the Duchess Claude which I have been told to deliver in person.'

Madame d'Assigne paused a moment and then nodded. As she led me into the gloomy chamber the lovely Françoise de Foix announced my name, and I saw Claude, dressed in black velvet, sobbing. Marie Darcille sat on the floor dabbing her eyes as I curtsied low and, on seeing me, Claude beckoned me to her.

'Please,' she sniffed, 'let us have no ceremony. Come, sit here Mistress Boleyn.' She pointed to a large, velvet floor cushion and her dwarf scuttled away. 'Now, I hear you have come from the widowed queen?'

'My lady, she sends her deepest condolences and felicitations.' Claude proffered a thin smile.

'Do you know,' she said, 'that kind-hearted girl is the first one to do so? Not a single courtier, ambassador or minister has comforted me thus. It is as if my poor little sister and I no longer exist.' She resumed her tears.

'Please, my lady, do not cry so.' The voice was that of Diane de Poitiers, dressed elegantly in black, compared to her feeble mistress who appeared dowdy. 'You are not without friends. Does not the king's sister speak gently to you?'

'Madame, there is more,' I said, as Diane smiled at me. She had the most beautiful smile I think I had ever seen.

Claude looked up and noticing my hesitancy, waved the other ladies away. When they were on the other side of the chamber, out of hearing, I whispered. 'Madame, the Dowager French Queen says you are not to be grieved on her account, for I am to tell you she will do you no harm.'

Claude's watery eyes met mine. Close to, her pale face had a gentleness and mildness about it. Of course, a little rouge would have brought colour to her cheeks, but I knew that she would not countenance such sinful artifice.

'And do you know, Mistress Anne, what she means by that remark?'

I shook my head.

'Come now, you are one of her ladies so surely you have seen how my husband admires her? Everyone at court has noticed, for he cannot take his eyes from her. He has practically forsaken his mistress, Marie Gaudin, for now he sees a greater prize in Mary Tudor. Do not talk to me of harm. Oh, how I long for him to look at *me* that way.'

'Madame,' I replied, 'he is the king, and you are his queen – soon Mary Tudor will return to England or marry another great prince. What harm *can* she do you?'

Claude put her face in her hands and her ladies looked up from their sewing. 'Oh, she can do very great harm to me by marrying my husband and taking him from me!'

'*Marrying,* Madame?' I asked. 'But you are carrying King François' child – and besides, he adores you. Why all know you for your goodness and grace and you are very much loved.'

'Anne, François loves the fact that through marriage to me, he gained the Duchy of Brittany. However, it is Mary Tudor that he truly adores and I am fearful he will not have me crowned if I do not have a son. I will be put away, but if I am, I tell you, I will take Brittany back with me!'

Diane hurried over and placed a warm cloak over her mistress's thin shoulders. 'Sweet Madame, crown or not, you are Queen of France,' she said, frowning at me. 'Come now, take care of the child you are carrying for these early weeks are fraught with danger. Do not vex yourself, or you will end up like poor Queen Katherine in England. Shall I ask Anne to leave?'

Claude shook her head and took hold of my hand. 'No, let her stay,' she continued, forlornly. 'It is true I am François' Queen. Mary Tudor will be forced to marry where she must, but I am well aware that marriage to France would keep the treaty with England safe.'

I knew that the widowed queen would never, of her own volition, marry François – but would she have a choice? Out of comfort, I could not help but put my other hand over Claude's and felt her ice-cold fingers. 'Hush, Madame.'

'I am also in much fear of my mother-in-law,' she continued, 'for she hates me. It is she who will have me put away.'

I looked across at one of the ladies, but she only shook her head sadly and carried on threading her needle.

'It is all so confusing,' continued Claude, 'for in the last few months she has tried to show me kindness, but I know it is only because she is as afraid of me, as I am of her. She is desperate to put her cold behaviour to rights in case I do her some ill. Is it any wonder I cannot trust her?'

I thought of Louise of Savoy and knew that this small girl was no match for her. Bold as I was, even I had found her intimidating.

'It is not,' I said.

'I am not feeble-minded,' said Claude. 'I want to be involved with the work of my husband, but *she* will not let me. She sees herself as the queen, with François as king, and her daughter at her side. And there is something else. My husband is determined to ride into Italy, at the head of a great army and take Milan. He is obsessed, like my father before, with its conquest, and will place himself in mortal danger. If he is killed or captured, I shall be left quite alone with his mother, unprotected, carrying our child.'

'Madame, that will not happen.'

'But now that my father has died, she intends bringing great changes, and will get rid of all those people who were once friends of my poor mother.'

This was true, for Louise had hated Anne of Brittany.

'What, my lady, can I do to make you smile again? I do not like sadness and from what I have observed, I can tell King Louis was a tender father to you and Princess Renée. You will always have that to cherish. My father is often cold and indifferent, and when he sent me away to the court at Mechelen, I felt so homesick in a strange country. I then lost the dearest person in all the whole world to me, for Mrs Orcharde, my old nurse, died while I was away from home.' I lowered my head.

'You understand grief then, Anne?'

'I do, my lady.'

'But you do not carry any sadness on your face,' said Claude, 'it is always merry, with laughing eyes.'

'Indeed, Madame, people say I am by nature lively. But I also like solitude and take great joy in reading the lives of the saints. Often I can spend hours lost in the beauty of their writings, so much so that I wonder if I should repair to a convent and take the veil. Such a life might, I feel, quite suit me.'

As my tongue ran away, I avoided Claude's gaze, knowing my words were insincere, and that to be hidden away in a convent would be a ghastly prospect. I loved beautiful gowns, gossip, dancing, and masques, and my fascination with the great personages at court grew every day. I relished the excitement and, it must be said, the feeling I was of some importance. I felt flattered and nursed great pride in myself. However, having heard that Claude felt such earthly sentiments were worthless and frivolous, I tried to ingratiate myself with her, to win her approval.

'But I, too!' she said, brightening a little. 'Such holy lives are my inspiration and comfort. Sometimes, I think the word of God is my only treasure. Have you read the life of St Ursula?'

'Oh, indeed, Madame,' I replied, hoping she would not ask me more about a book I had never even seen, let alone read, 'and it furnished me with great solace.'

Just as her eyes began filling with tears again, the door opened and Madame de Soubise entered the chamber with Renée. The girl stood holding a white rabbit in her arms, and I quickly rose to my feet.

'Why, my darling, come here, come to your sister!' cried Claude, as Renée's adored governess gently pushed the girl forward. She stumbled crying into her sister's arms, releasing her rabbit, and buried her face into Claude's velvet sleeve. 'Do you know,' said Claude, quietly stroking the child's hair, 'there is talk, as we speak, of marrying this girl to Prince Charles of Castile, for Burgundy now wishes to be on good terms with France.'

'Who?' asked Renée, raising her head.

I thought this interesting for I had heard how her father, old King Louis, had teased Renée for her plainness, jesting he would never marry her off.

'His councillor, Monsieur Chiévres, understands that by marrying Renée, the prince would reap the reward of the Duchy of Berry. My God, I could not bear to lose her!' She laid her head close to her sister's, and I thought this could not be true, for Margaret of Savoy hated the French with pure venom.

'I do not want to go away – they cannot make me!' cried Renée, her voice querulous.

'Madame Claude,' I said, 'I have something that would give your sister much cheer at this sad time. Can you guess what it might be?'

Claude shook her head.

'My little dog – I shall bring her to you, and your sister will not be able to stop smiling, for Bonny is the most amusing creature.'

Marie Darcille gave a clap of delight.

'Oh, but Renée is afraid of dogs,' said Claude, 'for she was bitten two years ago by my father's hound – see the scar on her hand. He had the dog hanged, which made me very sad for the creature did not mean to cause harm. That is why she now has her rabbit, Florie.'

'But Bonny does not bite at all, Madame. She will only lick you! While I am still here, I am happy to share her with Your Grace and your sister if you would allow it.'

'You are leaving?' asked Claude, alarmed.

'I expect I shall now be recalled to England with my sister,' I replied. 'My parents are hoping that we will attend Queen Katherine – unless the Dowager French Queen is sent to the Low Countries as a bride for Prince Charles. If that is the case, I may be sent back to Mechelen.'

'But to lose you would be a great shame!' cried Claude, standing up. 'Tell your mistress that you are a credit to her and that my sister and I would like to see you again, perhaps when walking in the gardens? You are so pleasant, and it is nice to have a girl of my age to talk to. Diane, of course, is very sweet and kind, but I think you understand the cruelty of being teased. Even for little things.'

I quickly hid my strange fingernail in the folds of my gown. Although a small disfigurement, it still made me feel self-conscious.

'What is more important, Mistress Anne is that you are

a good listener. That is a rare talent at court.'

I gave a low reverence and kissed her hand. Then, just as I started to leave the chamber, she called to me.

'Madame?'

'Anne, have you heard the news from Brussels concerning Margaret of Savoy?'

I had not. 'Concerning what, my lady?'

'That she is no longer Regent – the poor woman has just been deposed.'

• •

Madame d'Aumont stood with her back to me, staring down into the courtyard. She turned with a smile.

'Ah, Mistress Anne, please come in. I see that the crowds outside are lessening somewhat.'

Although only early afternoon the flaming torches flickered on the wood panelling, and a lap dog lay asleep on a cushion, twitching as it dreamed. In the fireplace, the logs crackled and burned.

'Madame?'

'You are proceeding very well here in France,' said Madame d'Aumont, 'after a rather unfortunate start.'

'Yes, Madame, I am very happy here, and my French improves daily.'

'Indeed. But tell me, what of our petite *reine blanche?* She moves to the Hôtel de Cluny tomorrow to begin her seclusion.'

I said nothing and she pressed on.

'How does she seem to you, Mistress Anne?' She walked over to the little dog and picked it up. 'Her courses are not due yet, are they? How is her health?'

'She is due next week according to the calendar, but she is much troubled with a severe toothache and her surgeon, Master John, hopes to assist her. Oil of clove is proving unhelpful, and the tooth may have to be pulled.'

'Anything else – generally?' She stood, smiling brightly,

stroking the dog in her arms.

'My lady has received secret correspondence from the Archbishop of York.'

'Wolsey?' she asked.

'Yes, Madame, she showed it to me, and I saw his seal. He assures her that he is her truest friend and that she is to do nothing without his advice. She is not to consider any offers of marriage, and in doing so, she will have her heart's desire and return to England.'

'And?'

'He assures her that he and her brother will never forsake her. However, the dowager French queen secretly fears that she will not be allowed to leave France, but be kidnapped on the way home to Dover and taken to the Low Countries to marry Prince Charles. It is adding to her distress.'

'French Queen, indeed,' tutted Madame d'Aumont, 'she should not be using that title. Well, tell me, how did you find Madame Claude?'

'Sad, Madame, as is Princess Renée.'

'The child is too much under the influence of that Breton woman, Madame de Soubise,' replied Madame d'Aumont. 'Well, the woman is soon to be dispensed with, for she is an enemy of my beloved mistress, Louise. Of course, old Louis and his wife insisted on keeping her as a governess, but her time with Princess Renée is done. Remember – anyone once a friend of Anne of Brittany is considered an enemy of Louise. Now, at last, we are to have only Louise's creatures in court posts – those we can trust.'

My smile faded for I knew Claude to be very fond of Madame de Soubise, for her religious thoughts were pure, and she laboured with pious care to impart wisdom to her royal pupil. This was yet another unkind act.

'You do not look very happy, mistress,' said Madame d'Aumont, staring at my face. 'If you want to get on at this court, you must know your enemies and be ruthless with those who might do you harm. Louise might not be loved, but she is wise in the ways of the court, as is *Madame la Grande*. It is a wisdom that can only be admired. Do you understand?'

I nodded.

'In future, you would do well to hide your personal feelings. Now, because you are close to the Dowager, we would like you to attend her in her seclusion at Cluny.'

Cluny! This time my expression remained impassive, but a myriad of thoughts rushed into my mind. Why, I would miss the coronation! The entire French nobility, anyone of importance, would be present as well as all the great ladies of the court.

'As far as anyone is concerned,' continued Madame d'Aumont, 'Claude made the suggestion herself, for she mentioned that you find a life of contemplation and solitude most pleasing. However, the truth is that your grandfather, Old Surrey, has personally asked Louise that you attend the queen. He wants to hear anything, anything at all that might relate to her and the Duke of Suffolk. As a family, bound by family loyalties, you will do this?'

I readily agreed for I would do anything to find favour with my family and the powerful Louise.

'Good. Since she is more likely to confide in a familiar face, you are a perfect choice. However, you are to say nothing to the other girls, is that clear?' Madame d'Aumont narrowed her eyes and I nodded.

'Yes, well I hope you remember why I want you there and do not let me down in this decision. That foolish girl *must* continue to take you into her confidence.'

●　●

The icy wind whipped against my cheeks as I pulled my woollen cloak and hood about me and mounted my mule. The frozen cobbles in the courtyard lay hard as iron as the dowager French queen climbed up into her chariot, and settled back against the velvet cushions. A large escort, clad in black, stood behind and in front, the warm breath from the horse's nostrils curling like wood smoke.

François tripped down the steps and leant into the chariot to kiss the queen's hand. Her face remained hidden beneath a white veil attached to a white velvet hood edged with ermine. François' lips lingered on her gloved fingers as he devoured her with his long, slanting eyes and smiled. Then, as the trumpets blasted their fanfare, he kissed his mother and sister sitting opposite her and bade them farewell.

We made our way on our caparisoned mules down the Rue St Antoine, observing the Hôtel de Ville, and down the Pont Notre Dame towards the Rue des Mathurins St Jacques. Pilgrims would gather here for their long journey to the Cathedral of Santiago de Compostela in Spain, but on this day there were none – just the proprietors of the bookshops and printing press houses, busily sweeping their steps.

All the streets had been swept clean of horse dung, and carpenters now noisily erected stands ready for the coronation of the new king. They stopped their banging and sawing as our procession lumbered into view, and knelt with caps in hand on the cold cobbles. On one side, I noticed several thin, ragged boys with fine metal nooses, pitchforks, and nets. They jumped up barefoot from their doorsteps, grinning toothless smiles.

'What are they doing?' I asked Mary Fiennes as she trotted up beside me.

'They are the dog catchers,' she said, with disdain. 'Hundreds of stray dogs are to be rounded up off the streets and destroyed and their carcases sent to the glove makers for skinning. For every dog removed, the boys will earn a sou. Events like a coronation demand a purge.'

As we trotted on through the gloomy, narrow streets, banners already fluttered from the houses ready for the celebrations, all-black cloth now discarded. I gazed up at the crooked windows and crumbling gables, and it seemed that mourning for old Louis had been abandoned with indecent haste. I later heard this was because François wanted to begin the celebrations, banquets, and revels before Lent began.

The Hôtel de Cluny appeared to be a large complex of buildings, overlooking the River Seine, and far more intimate than the Tournelles. Madame d'Aumont explained that it once belonged to the abbots of Cluny, but now the powerful Jacques d'Amboise, Abbot of Cluny, lived there. Some of it had recently been rebuilt in the modern style, with a beautiful gallery to the left of the courtyard, and a magnificent hexagonal stair tower.

As our large entourage came to a halt in the spacious courtyard, I was struck by the odd fact that the chimneys were not smoking. Usually, the air hung thick with wood smoke on such a cold day, but not a wisp rose up. The French queen stepped down from her chariot and allowed herself to be led inside to the great staircase by Madame Louise and Marguerite. On the first floor, we continued to the exquisite reception chamber, but instead of halting, the queen continued along the passageway, past the chapel, to a set of private apartments – *les chambres de la reine blanche.* When the door opened, and the queen stepped in, I could see, to my utter dismay, that the chambers were dark and the tall windows draped with heavy, black fustian cloth. Next to the canopied bed, the shadowy figure of the Comtesse de Nevers already waited, crouching low on the rush strewn floor. Candles flickered, casting great shadows on the walls, and as I looked at the queen, I thought she might burst into tears.

'My God, it is a very tomb,' she whispered in horror, waving the comtesse to her feet. 'And it is so *cold!*'

'Madame, I am sorry,' said the comtesse, 'but there has been very little time to clean the chimneys, hence not all the fires have been lit. We have had such a bitter, cold winter, too, but I will see what I can do.'

My sister and I stood staring about in utter disbelief. How could anyone stay in this dark, airless place for six weeks?

'Now, Madame,' said Louise, 'your ladies will dress you in your mourning clothes, and then, when you have said your farewells, they will depart. I have appointed four French ladies to attend your every need, under the charge of the comtesse here.'

Marguerite stood fingering the heavy cloth at the windows and threw the queen an apologetic smile.

'Come, daughter, we will return shortly.'

After they had left, we started to undress the shivering young girl. She stood, arms across her white body, her lovely hair falling about her shoulders like a mantle. On the bed, lay her mourning clothes, and Eliza Grey took the delicate white robe and lifted it over her arms and head. We pinned up her hair, and Ann Jernyngham placed the fine lawn cap and wimple on her head. The pleated barb fell to her shoulders, and she reminded me of Margaret of Savoy, who had dressed in the same way, being a widow. She wore no jewels, and as she stood, she might have been a girl about to enter a religious house. The whole ensemble could not have been more inappropriate to the gay, laughing girl encased inside.

'I shall *die* in this chamber!' she whispered to me, as I laced up her long sleeve.

I said nothing.

'So would anyone,' said my sister as she threaded the lace through the eyelet on the opposite sleeve. 'And as for that comtesse woman, she is so pompous. What will you do here all day, my lady?'

The queen sighed.

'Read, play my music – think. Oh, and I am supposed to pray, pray for the soul of my dear departed husband. In reality, I shall pray to go home.'

At that moment, Louise walked back into the chamber with four French matrons, each dressed in grey, and each carrying a lap dog.

'Madame,' she said, 'these ladies will attend you, and

your physician and the Duchess Claude's almoner, Monsieur Laisgre will, of course, be on hand should you require them. Now, we must bid you farewell. Be assured that I shall visit often, as will my daughter. Come, you must rest, contemplate your state and pray for the soul of your dead spouse.'

To all our surprise, the queen threw herself into Louise's arms and held her tight. Louise appeared aghast as she made to put her arms about the girl, but decided against such a show of affection and let them fall limp to her side.

'Come now, Madame, say your farewells.'

We curtsied to the queen, but she impetuously put her arms around each of us and became so choked with emotion, she could barely speak.

'Ah, my dear child,' sighed Louise, her voice forlorn. 'It is no use – this will not do at all. My tender-hearted Claude tells me we cannot be so cruel as to leave you here, friendless, and I agree with her.'

The queen looked up confused, her eyes brimming with tears. This was a turnabout.

'What would your dear brother think if he knew his beloved sister felt so unhappy?' She carefully perused all the girls and appeared to ponder some thought. Without any warning, she then took my arm firmly, almost in a pinch. 'Why, you must keep the little Boleyn girl here with you for company, for I hear she has the perfect voice for the reading of scripture, plays the lute and sings well.'

'But *Madame Mère*, with the deepest respect,' interrupted Marguerite, quietly taking her mother aside, 'we have arranged for our ladies, under the comtesse, to see to the queen dowager's needs. I do not s –'

Louise put her hand up in her usual way of tolerating no opposition. 'No, no, I have decided, my mind is quite made up.'

I stood there trying to avoid my sister's incredulous gaze, while the grateful young queen smothered Louise's be-ringed hand in kisses.

Madame d'Aumont then clapped her hands and the girls filed out through the metal-studded door, closing it behind them. Little did I know that when next I saw my sister, I was to feel naught but horror and shame.

Chapter Three

'Thus fortune turns.'

Paris

The monotonous days merged one into another, punctuated only by the unwelcome visits from François. On one particular Tuesday, late in the evening, he arrived with a small torch-lit escort and insisted on being immediately shown into the library by the Comtesse de Nevers. Demanding to be left alone, he would not allow the comtesse or the other matrons to follow him, for he feared they were his mother's servants and I knew he did not want the content of this meeting known.

As the comtesse opened the door and reluctantly withdrew, François flew in like a great gust of wind, grabbing the large, plumed bonnet from his head and sweeping it to the floor with a flourish. Dressed magnificently from head to toe in argentino and white, the diamonds on his coat glittered in the candlelight, and the smell of musk lingered in the air. Beneath his arm, he held a long, walnut box, and I noticed that one of his hands was lightly wrapped with linen strips as if from some injury.

'*Madame Mère*!' he cried in awe as if witnessing an apparition of the Virgin Mary herself. He eagerly took the dowager French queen's outstretched hand and smothered it with kisses.

As she sat there on a high backed chair, draped in white, she did indeed appear as if she had stepped down from Heaven. She inclined her head and François opened his eyes. As he did so he caught sight of me, standing in the dark by the tapestry.

'My most trusted chaperone, a mere child,' said the queen.

François shrugged and then continued,

'Ah, Marie, Marie, see how I, too, am in mourning, for I am dead to all joy without your presence at court.' He fell to his knees, eyes closed again as if deeply troubled.

The queen smiled and François, his eyes now flashing, opened the catch on the walnut box with deft fingers.

'Oh, your hand!' exclaimed the queen.

'It is nothing, dearest lady, a burn from a torch. Now, allow me to present you with a small token.' He opened the lid of the box and against the black silk lay the most exquisite collar of white enamelled roses and blue forget-me-nots, all linked with gold. In the middle of each blue flower nestled a diamond. As the collar twinkled and winked in the candlelight, the queen gasped. François carefully lifted out the piece and laid it in on her knees.

'Why it is *beautiful*,' she breathed, eyes alight with desire, 'and so heavy. My little neck will not be able to sustain it.'

François smiled, his dark, liquid eyes narrowing to mere slits. 'I am willing to hold it about your slender neck for eternity, just to be close to you, *ma chère.*'

The queen fingered the piece, replaced it on the silk and then closed the lid with a snap. Smiling, she put it down on the table close beside her.

'Thank you, *Monseigneur,*' she said, 'it is most gracious of you. But now I beg you to tell me what is going on. What is my position here, and when am I to return home?'

François appeared uncomfortable. 'Sweet Madame, on the faith of a gentleman, I will speak plain. Your position is perilous. The courts of Europe are full of rumours that you will not be allowed to leave France, and several names have been suggested for prospective bridegrooms such as the Duc de Bavaria, the Prince of Naples, and Prince Charles of Spain. There is even talk – God forbid – that the old Emperor Maximilian would have you. He has written to your brother to get you out of France as soon as possible – for his own ends of course.'

The queen's face turned as white as her veil.

'Calm yourself, Madame! He changes his mind like a weathercock doth change his turn. But all is not lost for I can save you from this terror. Consent to be my wife and you will remain Queen of France.'

'Sire, that is preposterous, you have a wife!'

'But Claude can be put aside – it is not a problem,' he ventured, leaning closer to her.

'On what grounds?'

'There are fears that she will not bring the child to full term, else it will be deformed like she. Of course, she might die in childbirth. My mother sees the signs in her astrological charts and is convinced she is too weak to bear a prince. But you – ah, if you and I were to marry we would have the most perfect, beautiful prince that ever sat on the throne of France! Give yourself to Caesar and the world would be ours together!' He took her hand again, and his lizard eyes perused her shocked face.

'Sire, I beg you for the love of God, do not speak of such things! I am forbidden to listen to you without my brother's leave! Besides I – I think I might be carrying my dead husband's child after all.'

François stood up, his expression now cold. 'Madame, you assured me that you were not,' he said, in alarm.

'I – I may have been mistaken – I – I cannot be sure as yet and have not told my physician. But if it is true and I am carrying Louis' child, even if I married you, you would not be king, for the crown of France would go to Louis' son.' Panic sounded in her voice as she continued. 'Would you deny your right to the throne and Brittany?'

François fell to her knees in a passion. 'Ah, seeing you now like this,' he said vehemently, 'I would deny the very Blood of Christ!'

The queen rose from her chair and began pacing about the chamber. Twisting her hands, she became agitated, and I watched as François followed her.

'Then give yourself to me as a lover, nothing more. I swear there would never be any other woman in my life.'

'Sire,' she said, turning, 'Have you gone quite mad? You do not know what you are asking! If you gave me a child it would only be assumed to be Louis', and you would never be king.'

'Then, Madame, if you do not want me as your lover or husband, why do you accept my gifts?' His lascivious eyes followed her slender form. 'Surely you accept them as tokens of love?'

'I most certainly do not!' The queen turned in indignation. 'Your wife knows that you give me presents as a dutiful son might to a mother, but I have assured her that I would never do her harm by betraying her with her husband.'

François, in a fit of pique, swiftly moved to grab the walnut box, but the queen moved quicker and put her hand over his to stop him. He grabbed it and put her fingers to his lips.

'I accept your gifts in friendship, nothing more,' she said quietly, removing her hand. I tried not to smile for I knew the queen loved jewels more than anything else, and this gift was particularly beautiful, displaying François' impeccable taste.

'Nothing more, Madame? Why, that is a great shame for I tell you, your brother will not leave you unmarried for long. You are too valuable, and all of Europe is vying for you.'

'Yes, like a fine mare to be trotted out and sold to the highest bidder!' retorted the queen. 'That is what I am so afraid of. Oh, I am going out of my mind with fear! What will become of me?' She appeared so utterly helpless that François, unable to resist a woman in distress, softened. He gazed at her with such tenderness that she broke down, and flung herself into his arms. He could not believe his good fortune. 'Oh, sire, I beg you to help me! I am so afraid. My brother promised that if I married old Louis, I could choose my next husband for myself. He *promised!*'

'Then choose me!'

She sobbed on his shoulder and François clicked his fingers. 'Your lady needs wine to fortify her,' he ordered, holding the quivering girl close.

I bobbed to him and filled one of the beautiful Venetian glasses to the brim. The red liquid flashed like rubies in the green vessel.

As he took it and gave it to the queen, I returned silently to my place, clean amazed by the scene unfolding before me.

'My God, I am on fire for you,' he said, 'and have been from the moment I saw you. My heart was breaking when I had to watch you, day after day, wife of that dying husk of man, knowing that I, *I* alone could satisfy you.'

'Fie! The king was good to me!' shrieked the queen, red-eyed.

'Madame, calm yourself,' he soothed. 'We have to face the reality of your position. Your brother will not stand by his promise.' His words produced yet more tears, and François took her face in his hands. 'Hush! If you will not have me, I can at least prevent you from being sent to Flanders. Let me suggest that you take Antoine, Duc de Lorraine as your husband.'

'Lorraine? That great beast who almost killed the Duke of Suffolk in a joust? Never!'

'But you would remain in France with the revenues from Blois at twenty thousand francs a year, and live a life of wealth and position. I would give you any château you wanted as a wedding gift. In time, if your husband proved not to your liking, we could become lovers. I swear on my mother's life, I would forsake all others. What say you?'

The torrent of tears that fell became so alarming that I moved forward, but François brushed me impatiently away with his hand. As I scurried back to my place, I felt the draught from the window, sharp as a knife, and shivered.

'Do not speak thus!' she wailed, 'how could I possibly be any man's when my heart belongs to another?'

François expression turned slightly bewildered. 'But all the world knows that the flirtation you speak of is but a flight of fancy. You are the queen dowager and he –'

'Is the man I *will* marry – must now marry!' She sat down with her head in her hands.

'Marry? Suffolk?' He was incredulous.

'Oh, François!' The queen appeared to be in utter despair. 'He is the only man I have ever truly loved. I beg of you, press your suit no further, and I will open up my heart to you. I will tell you, with true honesty, my whole mind, and how far this matter has gone with me. I am imploring you to help me by reminding my brother of his promise.'

Understanding women as he did, François now knew when to give up. He traced his be-ringed finger around the dark curve beneath the queen's eye and wiped away her tears with his thumb. She stood utterly helpless.

'Then, if that is truly the case,' François' face was soft with chivalric concern, 'and you will disclose your heart openly to me, I will pledge myself, as a knight, to assist you.'

Taking his hand in hers, the queen began. 'Two days ago, Queen Katherine herself, on the advice of the old Duke of Norfolk, sent a Father Langley to visit me here and urge me not to marry the duke. You must know that Norfolk detests him. I am horrified that the queen should do this since I thought we were very close and loving friends.'

My grandfather? I stood listening, all ears, as she continued.

'It was dreadful – he asked me to make my confession – which I refused – but he persisted saying he knew secret things that he could only tell me in the privacy of the confessional. Of course, I could not resist hearing what he had to say.'

'What things?' asked François, raising an inquisitive brow.

'Oh, terrible things! That the Duke of Suffolk is in league with the devil, along with Wolsey, and that together they have put a curse on Will Compton's leg making it ulcerous! But I care for none of this. My heart is with my Charles and his with mine. If you do not believe me, watch his face when you tell him this: 'I hold last May morning and what transpired at Eltham between us in my heart forever.' Promise me you will tell him that?'

'Calm yourself, Madame. I now believe you. But is Queen Katherine not your friend? She would not profit from such counsel – unless there might be some spiritual difficulty with such a marriage. Something which she fears might put your very soul in danger.'

The queen sighed. 'You mean the rumour that he cannot re-marry before he is legally divorced.'

François shrugged. 'His enemies,' he continued, 'say it is thus, for his amours have always been complicated, even by French standards. Of course, there is also the fact that Queen Katherine would like to see you married to her nephew, Prince Charles, and be the queen of an Imperial throne. Such an alliance would not suit France, but it might suit your brother and –'

'Then what do I do?' cried the queen.

'*Ma chère*,' he said, soothingly, 'it is plain where your heart truly lies. You married old Louis for peace – now you must follow your heart and marry for love. I have assured you of my help, and I will give it gladly. But as yet you are to say nothing to anyone.'

When François finally left, the queen ran to the window and gently pulled aside the dark drape. Peering down onto the courtyard, she laughed, all distress quite miraculously evaporated.

'See, Nan? See how I have him wrapped around my little finger?'

⁕   ⁕

In the small chamber, the queen ostentatiously picked at her food.

'The carp is not to your liking, my lady?' I asked.

The Comtesse de Nevers glanced up suspiciously from her platter. 'But Madame,' she said, 'I had it sent fresh this morning.' She leant over and sniffed the dish. 'I will see the boy about it when he next delivers.'

The queen then rose from her seat and walked over to the window.

'The smell is disturbing me,' she said, mournfully, 'take it away. I am not hungry.' She languidly moved the heavy curtain aside, hoping to gaze outside on to the courtyard, but the window had been completely boarded up. She sighed and placed her hand on the front of her gown.

'Are you ailing?' asked one of the matrons.

The queen did appear very pale and there were dark shadows beneath her eyes.

'Possibly. I feel quite out of sorts,' she said over her shoulder. She moved back and took my cold hand, then led me to the window seat on the far side of the chamber, out of earshot of the other ladies. 'Oh, Nan, how amusing this is. Keep asking me about the food. Louise thinks she knows everything, but she does not. This will throw her and her astrologers into a fit of panic. Old Louis up to the task after all, who would have thought it?'

'But Madame, what happens when they find out, which of course, they will?'

'And who is going to tell them? I shall just say it is a mistake – any woman can be mistaken.'

'But you are not *any* woman,' I countered, 'you are the queen dowager of France.'

I had annoyed her.

'What?' she hissed, close to my ear. 'It is only a game, and I am so *bored* here, I need some amusement or I shall go out of my mind. Day after day locked up, not knowing what is planned for me. It is making me ill, and my nerves are shattered. Migraine, toothache, and this gnawing pain in my side – I am going insane. What do you expect?' She arose, her face sulky, arms crossed. Then, in a fit of pique, she rushed out of the chamber, pulling the door behind her with such force the wooden crucifix fell from the wall with a thud, onto the floor.

'What on earth ails Her Grace?' The comtesse rose to her feet, her eyes following the angry queen. 'Is she truly ill?'

'My lady,' I said, 'the queen's head is aching, and the lack of exercise and fresh air are making her ill at ease. It is no matter, I shall go to her and read to soothe her mind.'

The comtesse nodded and fastidiously dabbed her mouth with her napkin.

'Since the carp is not acceptable, tell her I shall have a fish broth prepared. She must eat to keep up her strength.'

●　●

'With *child*? It cannot be! I cannot allow it!'

The shrieking voice sounded unmistakable, as were the brisk steps and dull thud of a walking stick echoing along the stone gallery at Cluny. My ears listened to the steps as they approached closer and closer until the door of the chamber flew open. Dropping hold of the linen I was folding with the other matrons, we curtsied and scurried to one side. There before us stood Louise, her lovely daughter, and Antoinette de Polignac, their cloaks wet from the rain. The Comtesse de Nevers stepped forward and swept dramatically to the floor.

'Well?' asked Louise, 'I arrived as quickly as I could.' As she lowered her hood, I saw her face, grey as ash, as she stared about the darkened chamber. 'Is it true?'

'We believe so, my lady,' came the reply. 'The queen dowager has fainted twice and we wanted to inform you before we called the physician. All the signs are there.'

'How long?'

'She will not say,' replied the comtesse, 'but she must have conceived immediately.'

'Let me sit, my gout is causing me great pain today.' Louise limped over to a chair. One of the matrons put a stool in front of her, the other offered her wine, and she drained the glass in one go. The glass was refilled, and she began to drink again. 'My astrologer will hang before the day ends,' she muttered, drawing her hand across her lips. 'This was *not* foretold.'

'Madame,' said the comtesse, 'the stars do not lie, but the astrologers lie about the stars.'

Louise grunted,

'Does my son know?'

The comtesse shook her head, and Louise gripped her daughter's hand, squeezing it so hard the blood drained from her fingers. 'Blessed God, preserve us. He is determined to undo himself and all I have laboured for.'

Unable to stand the tension, and knowing what I must do, I stepped forward. 'My lady, I must speak privately with you – it is most urgent.'

Louise stared at me. 'It was *you* who assured me that the French queen had said the king had not been capable. Well? Was that not true?'

I remained silent.

'I see,' said Louise, narrowing her eyes, accusingly.

I bit my lip as Louise pushed away the stool and, holding her daughter's arm to steady herself, rose up. Her stick fell with a clatter and I quickly picked it up and handed it to her.

'Come with me – alone,' she said, grabbing the proffered stick and turning to the door.

Comtesse de Nevers, obviously put out, bowed her head as we left the chamber.

I hurried along, ignoring the guards, trying not to step on the train of the limping woman in front until we arrived at a small anteroom. Inside, Marguerite pulled out a chair for her mother, closed the door, and then sat down herself. She smiled encouragingly at me.

'Well?' asked Louise. I froze under her icy gaze. 'Speak up!'

'Madame, it is not true. She pretended to faint, but it was a trick. She told me quite plainly that it is all a merry jest.'

'A jest?' Louise stood up, her pain forgotten, outraged. 'How *dare* she, the minx! Days before my son's coronation and she plays games with the throne of France! How long did she think that little ruse would work for – and to what end? God's blood, I will be glad to see the back of her!'

'Mother, calm yourself. All will be well,' said her daughter, soothingly.

Louise turned to me.

'You are certain of this?'

I nodded and repeated what the queen had told me herself.

Louise stood up, twisting the opal ring on her finger. 'And what of my son?' she asked. 'I gather he has been here visiting. To what purpose?'

'Madame, he continues to shower the lady with gifts, the latest being a gold collar of roses, enamelled with blue forget-me-nots.'

'She refused it, of course.'

'She accepted it, Madame.'

'God's blood! What else?'

'Madame, your son is so besotted with her that he says he would gladly risk losing his kingdom for her. He even talks of putting away Claude to marry her.'

'Marry that meddlesome, deceitful woman? The poor boy is addled. I knew it! This is my fault,' she said, wringing her hands. 'I encouraged him to be in that woman's company, but this – *this!* I must have someone speak to him and bring him to his senses. Someone he will listen to. Not I, though. No, I cannot chastise my beautiful boy, for it would break my heart to do so.'

'Madame, he said that if he cannot marry the queen dowager,' I continued, 'he will marry her off to the Duc de Lorraine and become her lover.'

Louise gave a derisive snort.

'However,' I added, 'the queen has no intention of marrying your son or the Duc de Lorraine. She assured him that she is only going to marry the Duke of Suffolk who is travelling with Doctor Nicholas West to Paris, as we speak. I stood present in the chamber when this was spoken of between your son and the queen dowager, and I speak the truth plainly.'

There was a moment's silence.

'You have done well to speak up, Anne,' said Louise, sitting down heavily in the chair. 'As for me, I must follow my own advice – '*je tiendrai*' – and hold firm to my destiny. His destiny.'

I stood feeling very proud of myself.

Her daughter nodded in agreement as Louise took her hand and patted it fondly.

'Well, I shall go to her now and tell her the game is up. My son will go to Rheims to be crowned – and that *she-wolf* can go to the devil!'

●   ●

The queen dowager sat at a small desk, reading by the light of a beeswax candle. Her long hair curled over her shoulders as she pulled her fur-lined night robe tightly about her. We were alone, since the other matrons had retired to their beds early to keep warm, and only the dogs lay dozing by the meagre fire.

She suddenly raised her head. 'Oh, Anne, he is coming! The duke is coming! It says here he will be meeting François with Sir Richard Wingfield and Doctor West this week, to discuss the situation between France and England. I shall see him and he shall – he *must* – take me home. Perhaps my endless letters to my brother have proved fruitful after all. Every day I have written telling him of my fears and reminding him of his promise. He cannot fail me.'

Knowing the queen's clever turn of phrase, I could imagine how persuasive her letters might have been. As to going home, matters were still by no means settled.

'Why, Madame, that is wonderful, but what does it say of the coronation?' I asked eagerly.

She found her place again on the letter and began reading out loud. 'On the day of the Conversion of St Paul, François, Duc d'Angoulême, became King of France in the cathedral at Rheims.' She stopped and thought for a moment. 'Do you know, Anne, that is the same day that the young François nearly died when a horse ran away with him. His mother thinks there is now good fortune on that date. How superstitious she is. Anyway, all the princes of the blood, the twelve deputies of France, the nobles, ladies and every representative from the courts of Europe were present at the magnificent ceremony. All noticed how triumphantly his mother had appeared, dressed in ermine, while little Claude stayed behind having felt unwell. Doctor West goes on to say that all of Louise's years of hardship, waiting and longing had finally come to fruition in the glorious *Sacré* of her beloved son.' She put the letter down on her knees.

'King Francis I of France,' I said.

'Yes – it is accomplished,' she mused. 'I am eternally grateful for his help for he did what he promised he would do, even though it suited him best.'

'But how did he help you, Madame?' I asked, glancing up from unpicking the golden stitches from one of her stockings. Her marriage device *The Will of God Suffices* now lay in bits of thread.

She frowned at me in the dim light and moved the candle on the table closer to my work. 'After Corbény,' she continued, 'where he went with his mother and sister to receive his power to cure the king's Evil, he travelled to

Compiègne, to meet Prince Charles' ambassadors, and they finalised the prince's betrothal to Renée. I am sad for her, but now my brother cannot force me to marry him, and I thank God and François for it.' She arose and walked over to the sprig of winter jasmine lying on the table.

'And he did that for you, Madame?' I asked. 'Then he is a great king indeed.'

She turned and smiled, the sprig in her hand. 'No, Anne, he did not do that for me. François does what is best for François for he knew that in doing this he would be thwarting my brother. Also, with France allied to Flanders, the country is safe from any Imperial attack. No, he knows that if I marry the Duke of Suffolk, my brother is robbed of using me to his advantage elsewhere in Europe. Better that I should marry a useless English duke than some foreign power against France. François is well pleased.'

I thought of the frail, young prince and Margaret of Savoy who, before long, would accompany her nephew, as the new King of Spain, in his triumphal journey through his provinces. Sadly, it was Monsieur Chièvres who now ruled in all but name – not something that Margaret would find easy to stomach.

'Poor Renée,' I said, 'why, I truly pity her betrothed to that solemn boy.'

'I am still puzzled as to how Louise found out so quickly,' mused the dowager.

I avoided her eyes.

'About my 'condition,' she explained, twisting the sprig about. 'I have never seen anyone, not even my blustering brother, so angry. I told Louise I was mistaken, so why did she accuse me of trying to trick them all? She was not to know I was play-acting. Well, no doubt she found out from the comtesse – that infernal busybody misses nothing.'

I folded the silk stocking, satisfied. 'Madame, would you like a jug for that?' I asked.

The dowager turned and smiled. 'Later, Anne, although

I fear the flowers will wither in this poor light.' She then picked up a small mirror and scrutinised her face, fingering the pale skin. 'Much like myself,' she observed, sadly. 'No, I am still afraid my brother will renege on his promise.'

'Is there nothing that would assure his support?' I asked.

She sat down on the bed with a sigh. 'The only thing that matters to my brother is not to be outdone by François. He must never be bettered and will want to trick him any way he can. After all, François is not above using underhand means himself. If I could just join my brother in tricking François in some way, I might get Henry onto my side – sister and brother together.' She rose up, her face thoughtful. 'Anne, fetch my jewel box. I have just remembered something Wolsey, my Lord of York, mentioned. Quickly, girl!'

I went over to the cabinet that held the queen's treasures and took out a large, black enamelled box inlaid with mother of pearl. She then sat down on the floor, produced a key with which to open the box, and began to empty the contents onto the turkey rug – brooches, earrings, pendants, and rings. Her hair tumbled down as she scrabbled about in all the secret drawers and compartments until, hidden beneath its false bottom, her fingers found a black velvet pouch. Carefully, she opened the pouch and held up the content. I gasped as it glinted in the candlelight. What I beheld before me was not mere paste, but the most enormous diamond with a pearl hanging beneath, the size of an egg.

'Oh!' I cried.

'The Mirror of Naples,' said the queen, 'a gift from my late husband.' I stared in awe. So this was the piece that Margaret of Savoy and Signore Gattinara had once spoken off. It was magnificent!

'May I hold it?' I asked.

She handed it to me and I turned it over. 'It is so –'

'Vulgar?' asked the queen, with a laugh.

'Heavy.' I held it up by its dark-blue, velvet ribbon and marvelled at the clarity of the diamond.

The queen took it and placed it against my throat.

'Diamonds suit you,' she smiled as I looked in the small mirror. 'This piece, Anne, is part of the French crown jewels and therefore French property,' she said, taking it back and replacing it in the pouch. 'It is as French as François, and I am going to have it sent to my brother as a bribe. He will not be able to resist it, and Louise will go out of her mind with fury, for she assumed it was returned to Claude on Louis' death.'

'But – then it belongs to her,' I said, thinking of how the kind girl had, herself, written to King Henry, begging him to let the queen marry the duke.

The girl before me shrugged. 'I care not a fig. Anyway, there is more still.' She opened another drawer and took out a string of lustrous, creamy pearls. 'Henry adores pearls,' she said, letting them slip like water through her slender fingers. 'Just eighteen of these are worth ten thousand crowns and he can have them all to adorn his queen. If this does not work, then I will have to think again.'

'But how do you intend getting them to him?' I asked, in excitement. She stared at me.

'That I have yet to decide, but it must be done quickly.'

'Madame, as these jewels belong to France, is it not theft to smuggle them out of the country?'

She smiled mischievously. 'I shall send them to my brother and he can return them – or not,' she said simply. 'The main thing is that they are not missed in any way. I just need time to get them out of Paris, but who with? I can trust Mr. Wingfield, of course.'

As I looked at her sitting there so innocently, I could only admire her nerve and audacity.

• •

When the ambassadors from England arrived, including the Duke of Suffolk, I took them straight to the queen dowager. They appeared agitated and told her that she must not marry anyone against the King of England's wishes. She was to beware of François and avoid his company. They were too late. After they had discussed other matters with her, she sat and chatted awhile but appeared pre-occupied with her thoughts, and was hardly listening to their earnest talk. When supper was announced, everyone finally left the chamber, except for Suffolk. The queen took him to the window embrasure and spoke in low whispers, so I was unable to hear what they said.

Later that night, the Duke of Suffolk unexpectedly returned with his servant, Monsieur du Pyne. The duke stood in the main gallery, waiting for his presence to be announced, bonnet in hand, pacing up and down. Then, aware I was standing there, he turned and stared at me, and I wondered if he knew, or cared, who my grandfather was or the damage he plotted to do him. I curtsied and led him down the passageway to the library, where he stepped inside and closed the door. Outside the chamber, I stood on guard in case anyone should venture forth. Then, with my ear to the door, I heard a great cry burst forth from the queen, followed by dreadful pleading. Much of what she cried sounded incoherent and there seemed to be a great deal of pacing about on floorboards. I did hear her say there was no way out, reminding him of his love tokens and presents. If he did not do as she asked, she threatened she would die of sorrow. He would never see her again, and she would make sure he was forever disdained by the nobles on the council. Danger threatened him from every side. I heard the duke then plead with her, but instead of calming her down, it only made her scream the more. Then something very heavy smashed against the door, causing me to jump back in fright. The library fell quiet, and I held my breath in expectation. What on earth had happened in there? Finally, I heard murmuring sobs and sighs.

After about ten minutes, the door opened, and a red-eyed girl peeped through the crack. With her hair tangled and free from its hood, her lovely face blotchy, she appeared utterly exhausted and resigned. Pressing her forehead against the cool doorframe, she closed her eyes. Behind her, the duke sat with his head in his hands.

'It is over,' she said. 'Go to your chamber, Anne.'

• •

As dawn broke and bird song filled the air I felt exhausted, for I had barely slept. I stared in the mirror at my red-rimmed eyes and pale face and pinched my cheeks to add a little blush. It did not work. I sat in despair. Why did she have to do such a thing? To go so far? Now my name would be forever linked with hers. The door burst open and caused me to start.

'Mary, Eliza,' I whispered, my eyes cast down, 'quickly – come in.'

'Dearest Nan.' Mary Fiennes flung her arms about me. 'It is ages since we last saw you!' She held me away at arm's length and perused my face. 'Why, you have been crying, whatever ails you?'

I shook my head.

Eliza Grey kissed my cheek.

'We have missed you *so* much, Anne, and it has not been the same without you. But why are you so downcast?'

Before I could reply she prattled on. 'Anyway, what on earth is going on? We were escorted here today at first light, by a gentleman in the Duke of Suffolk's livery, and told to say nothing to a single soul.' She pulled off her gloves and looked about the chamber. 'Dear God above, no wonder you look so pale,' she said, turning, 'shuttered up in this gloomy place.'

'Yes, but what is happening?' asked Mary, 'and why are we here under such secrecy?

'You will find out shortly,' I replied. 'All is done. The French Dowager Queen's official title of *La Reine Blanche* is no more, and Louise along with Sir Richard Wingfield, has ordered all the drapes removed, and the windows unlocked.

She has dismissed the matrons and had the comtesse sent back to the Tournelles. In a –' Before I could finish, the queen flew into the chamber in a haze of scent.

'Ah, my English ladies at last!' she cried with joy. 'Up, up quickly, we must hurry.'

I straightened the queen's golden veil, flowing from the back of her hood, and handed her an exquisite book of hours. It had been given to her by her sister, Margaret, and was inscribed with the words: *Madame, I pray your grace, remember on me when you look upon this book.* I thought it a charming sentiment from sister to sister.

The queen smiled and appeared lovely again now that she had recovered her spirits. 'Ladies,' she said, 'follow on if you will.' She then turned to me and whispered. 'Anne, I understand what I divulged to you last night must be difficult to comprehend, but *please*, try and be cheerful today – for me?'

As we bustled out of the chamber and through the open gallery, the girls chattered with excitement. It was good to smell the fresh air after the fetid chambers, but when we finally paused outside an arched, wooden door the queen hesitated.

'He *promised*,' she said firmly to herself as if trying to summon up her courage. She then took a deep breath as the guard opened the door, and we entered. There, with his back to us, stood the Duke of Suffolk himself. Dressed in a sober suit of dark green velvet, he turned, and I saw his face bore the colour of soured milk – to match my own. The queen moved quickly to his side, and he kissed her hand. '*Courage,*' she whispered, smiling.

I looked at the central pillar supporting the elaborate vaults, and then at the upper tier of carved, canopied niches containing statues of, I presumed, the Amboise family. The altar lay bare of candlesticks, plate, and ornaments, and cloth of purple lay folded ready to cover the Lenten statues.

Eliza moved closer to me. 'What is going on?' she

whispered.

An old priest, standing before our party, appeared most agitated. He gave a weak cough and fumbled about with his missal, his nervous eyes avoiding those of the woman before him. He began to speak, but the queen, gazing enraptured at the duke's face, stood barely listening to his words. It was not until the rings and coins were exchanged that she became emotional, and as the duke placed the gold band upon her finger, she started to cry.

'With this ring, I thee wed, this gold and silver I thee give,' he said, quietly reassuring her with a nervous smile.

A few moments later, the priest pronounced them man and wife, and prayed that God would keep them in his love and grace. It was done. What would Louise of Savoy say now? What would my grandfather say? He had done everything in his power to prevent this marriage occurring and yet here was I, his granddaughter, standing as a witness. I felt anxious – and not only on this count – for there was worse to come.

The queen flung herself into the arms of the duke and he held her close. The priest, ashen-faced, scuttled through a side door and we were left alone, somewhat dazed. The queen burst out laughing.

'Oh, Caro! When I think of this compared to my last wedding, it is hardly the grandest of ceremonies! And yet, my dearest love, I could not be happier – have never been happier. I am truly your wife – the new Duchess of Suffolk, although I do still wish to be known as the Dowager French Queen. We shall live together at Suffolk Place, and I shall supervise the renovations. You must also recall little Anne back from Mechelen for it will be good to have your daughter with us. Oh, Charles, we shall all be so happy!'

'Will we?' replied the duke, kissing her hand, 'I would feel more at ease if we could disappear to some far off land and never be seen again, for I fear you will not have a husband with a head on his shoulders for long.'

'Fie! It is too late,' she replied. 'We are married, and the thing cannot be undone. Do not fear my love, all will be well. Now, ladies, we are to have a private dinner in my chamber and so I will not require your services again until tomorrow.'

Mary Fiennes gave a mischievous smile and the new duchess laughed, clapping her hands loudly.

'Go to, ladies! You must enjoy the gardens and fresh air while you can. Then, please make sure that my gown is ready, along with my jewels, for the grand entrance into Paris.'

With her arm in the duke's, she then skipped through the same door as the priest, her eyes shining with happiness. Inside, I felt desolate.

Chapter Four

'Time discloses all things'

Paris

The gardens at Cluny lay deserted as we made our way down a pathway lined with almond trees. Above, the rose-coloured sky began to lighten and a new day dawned. I pulled my cloak about me, for it was chilly, as Bonny ran ahead, sniffing at every leaf and stone.

'Well, what did you make of that?' Eliza took my arm. 'A secret wedding!'

I shrugged.

'You do not seem very excited,' she said petulantly.

'Should I be?'

Mary took my other arm and led me over to a stone bench. 'What *is* the matter, Anne? You are not your usual talkative self at all.'

I stared blankly at her. 'Surely you have heard?' I asked.

Both girls shook their heads and my eyes filled with tears.

'What on earth ails you?' asked Eliza, anxiously.

'It – it is Mary.' My voice was barely above a whisper.

'The dowager queen?' they asked, in unison.

'My sister,' I replied. 'She has been staying at the king's château at Senlis, on the outskirts of Paris. He was en route returning from his coronation when he decided to hunt in the forest of Chantilly.'

'Yes, we know,' said Mary. 'The king's mother asked your sister to join her son and a small company of ladies there. None of us were invited.'

'You mean ordered her,' I replied. 'Anyway, why would you be invited? Those 'ladies,' according to the dowager French queen, are the king's *petite bande*. Those he shows great favour to – and they to him.'

'How do you mean?' asked Mary innocently.

Eliza sniggered. 'She means as whores.'

'But the king invited your sister as a guest,' protested Mary, casting a frown at Elizabeth.

'No,' I sighed, 'she was sent as a pretty diversion for François. A diversion that worked, for now, he is enamoured of her. The Dowager Queen told me last night as she wanted me to know before I heard it from anyone else.'

Both girls gasped in disbelief.

'It is true. The queen said that since Claude is with child, she understands that the king is entitled to his affairs, but she is insulted and angry that he has picked one of her ladies to dally with.'

The girls sat in shocked silence, and as Mary squeezed my hand, my eyes burned with indignation.

'Dear saints above, Anne, no wonder you are so upset, but maybe all is not lost. You know, there is great advancement to be had if one pleases the king – which she obviously does – and is clever.'

'Which she obviously is not,' I retorted. 'He will tire of her very quickly, and my whole family will be disgraced!'

'Not necessarily,' said Eliza, 'your sister is very entertaining and amusing. She is also kind and warm-hearted – everyone loves her. Besides, if that is the case, the king will marry her off to some splendid nobleman, and she can remain here in France in a grand château. Just think – a count or a duke for her, and you, as her sister...why, who knows? You, too, might marry well from this.'

'And which of them would marry an English girl with

no title?' I asked. 'Is it likely when there are girls from the highest French nobility to choose from? We all know full well that marriage is a transaction, a union of rank, responsibilities and family interests. No, I tell you my family will be enraged at my sister's behaviour and there will be no gain for the Boleyns.'

Mary smiled brightly. 'I disagree, for there are many men who would be honoured to –'

'What? Have the king's cast-offs?' I cut her off. 'Because that is what she will be!'

'No! Anne, that is not what I mean, please do not be angry. Besides, until you speak to your sister, you cannot be sure of her position.'

Eliza nodded in agreement.

'I do not want to see her!' I rose from the bench.

Mary took my arm and drew me back.

'Then let us talk of the new duchess,' said Eliza, smiling as Bonny dropped the twig, begging for it to be thrown. 'How did this wedding come about?'

'Do not call her duchess,' I said, 'it is supposed to be a secret!'

'There is no need to snap,' came the reply.

'The dowager French queen,' I continued, 'told me that it was at Senlis when François summoned Charles Brandon to his chamber and berated him for his intentions of spiriting away the queen without his, or King Henry's, permission. François said he knew of the queen's love for Charles, but the duke utterly denied it. François then repeated to him a secret that was only known to the two lovers. Horrified, the duke then knew for certain that the stupid girl had confided everything to François, and the game was up.'

'What secret?' asked Eliza.

I said I knew not, but something that occurred at Eltham. Both girls groaned in disappointment.

'However,' I said, 'it seems that François only pretended to be angry and assured the duke he was still his friend.

He promised he would write to King Henry in England, reminding him of his promise to allow his sister to choose Brandon for her next husband. The duke was not convinced and departed in fear.'

'Ha!' said Mary, 'it seems the duke, yet again, has found himself tangled in a hopeless romantic affair.'

It was true. How could one man have such complicated dealings with women?

'He just cannot resist a pretty face,' she continued.

'No, he cannot resist a woman who might bring him wealth and position,' said Eliza.

'The queen,' I said, 'told me how the duke was frantic with fear over what the king of England would do if he married his royal sister. He could be executed for such presumption – in fact, I would go so far as to say my grandfather on the council would demand it.'

'Would he dare?'

'Mother says so. She also added that the king's word can never truly be relied upon.'

'So what happened next?' asked Mary.

'The duke came straight to the queen, here at Cluny, with no other intent but to comfort her, but she gave him an ultimatum – it was now or never – and – well, he gave in. He has married her, and we three have just borne witness. So there you are – now you know everything.'

Both girls stared at me.

'I suppose the least the council might do is have the marriage annulled – it being Lent,' said Mary.

'Well, you know what the wise women say, marry in Lent and live to repent.'

'Yes, Eliza, but according to Madame d'Aumont things are done differently here in France.'

'Well,' I said, leaning down to stroke Bonny, 'I care nothing for the stupid queen, or duchess or whatever she wishes to call herself, and I think the liturgical calendar is the last thing on her mind.' Even my little dog's eager face could not cheer me.

'I wonder how long it will be before his new wife rails at him, saying she married beneath her,' said Mary, yawning. 'It is always the case.'

'Yes, a man relying on his wife's income is shameful,' added Eliza. 'It is one thing to have romantic trysts, ballads, and gifts but quite another to *marry* someone with such a disgraceful reputation and at least three illegitimate children. Who in their right mind would want sullied goods?' Who indeed? I thought.

* *

If I leant forward slightly, I could just about see the Duke of Suffolk watching the procession, picking at his nails.

The dowager queen and the other ladies, including the ever-watchful Madame d'Aumont, were seated nearby, beneath a cloth-draped canopy. The window of the house we occupied had been removed to provide space, and once or twice, the duke glanced our way. The dowager queen sat draped in sable, a matching hat tilted beguilingly on her head, and smiled back at him. I shivered thinking of the dread secret they shared. On the other side, in the royal box, sat Claude, Louise, Marguerite, and *Madame la Grande*. Behind them stood a host of titled ladies in sumptuous gowns, amongst whom were Madame de Châtillon, Marguerite's *Dame d'Honneur*, and Antoinette de Polignac, Louise's *Dame d'Honneur*. Claude's ladies, Françoise de Foix – a cousin of Anne of Brittany – Diane de Poitiers, and Madame d'Assigny, stood nearest to her. Fashions seemed to have changed overnight, for apart from Diane and Madame d'Assigny, their gowns appeared far more provocative than I had seen before. Now, the looms of Flanders and Genoa yielded exquisite fabrics of silk, velvet, and damasks in the colours King François preferred.

As I glanced at Louise, I saw tears of joy in her eyes as she savoured the triumph of her son's official entry into his city of Paris on that cold, February day. My sister sat opposite and tried to catch my eye, but I sat, stony-faced, refusing to look at her. When I did steal a look, she appeared rather pale and subdued.

Below, the noisy crowds lining the route were exuberant, for they knew that as the new king rode past on his journey from the Chapelle Saint-Denis to Paris, he would throw them fistfuls of gold coins. A month's wages could not be missed, and apprentices, fishwives and labourers pushed hard against the barricades, breaking them down in parts. The soldiers, their gold-embroidered salamander devices glinting on their coats, linked arms and pushed them back, cursing under their breath as the royal cavalcade lumbered on. As the king came into view under a silver canopy, the mayor, aldermen, and representatives of the companies and *Parlement* escorted him on either side. He sat astride his favourite warhorse, its white plumes matching his suit and hat of silver and white. Flashing with diamonds, and throwing up coins, he waved to the crowd who, with outstretched arms, cried '*Vive le Roi!*'

As trumpets blasted from the roofs of the buildings, great baskets suspended from ropes tipped over, and a thousand white rose petals fluttered down like snowflakes onto the procession below. As they fell, Claude's ladies clapped excitedly, and we turned to see Diane flush. Below, her intended husband – Louis de Brèzè, the *grand senechal* of Normandy – rode behind the Princes of the Blood, followed by a hundred gentlemen carrying lances fluttering with white, yellow and red streamers. All the ladies gasped in admiration, but all I saw was a hunched old man with a large nose. Mary Fiennes whispered to me that this was only the second time that Diane had seen her betrothed, but that she was more than content for she would soon, as the Comtesse de Brézé, rank as one of the first ladies of France. She was surely the envy of them all – all, but not quite. As I studied the lovely dowager French queen I wondered if she pitied Diane, betrothed to a man forty years older than herself.

The king halted beneath the royal box and bowed deeply to his mother, hand on his heart. She rose from her seat, and a great roar ensued as she stretched out her arms to him. She then held out her hand to her daughter and she, too, stood up and blew a kiss to her brother. He saluted her, but his eyes rested on Françoise de Foix, exquisite in her colours of tawny, black and white. She must have been about twenty-one years old, but she appeared to have the bearing and confidence of a much older woman. I watched her avert her eyes as the king, one hand tightly controlling his impatient, foam-flecked horse, then trotted on towards the Cathedral of Notre Dame to give thanks to God and the Virgin. He had not looked once at my sister.

That evening at seven o'clock, we enjoyed a magnificent banquet at the Palais Royal. François sat on a great dais with the Duc d'Alençon and Duc de Lorraine on his left. On his right, sat the ambassadors of the pope, Venice and the King of England. His constable, Anne, Duc de Montmorency, his *grand-maître*, Artus Gouffier, his Admiral of France, Guillaume Gouffier seigneur de Bonnivet, his Treasurer, Florimond Robertet, and his Marshal of France, Robert Fleuranges, all sat close by. They were mostly young men, but some were older like Robertet and the new chancellor, Antoine Duprat. Duprat was unpopular, ruthless and violent, and I had heard that he was very close to Madame Louise. He was her creature, and I knew that Claude feared him.

High up on a balcony, close to the Chamber of Requests, sat Claude, Louise, Marguerite, and *Madame la Grande,* and below them, in order of precedence, all the nobles and ladies. I sat with the other maids, next to Eliza, and stared at my sister at the far end of the long table. She waved at me, but I turned my head away with shame.

'You will have to speak to her at some point,' whispered Eliza.

'I will not – I shall *never* speak with her again,' I said, unfolding my napkin with an angry flick. Mary Fiennes and

Ann Jernyngham took their places on my left. 'Everyone is staring.' I felt mortified.

'No, they are not.' Mary leaned towards me. 'I doubt it is even common knowledge.' As I looked across the *salle* to Claude, I saw François kiss her cheek. She flushed a little.

'I bet *she* knows,' I whispered, my voice petulant.

'Stop it, Anne, you are being foolish.' Mary held her goblet up to be filled. 'And anyway, you are wrong. I hear François is not cruel and does not flaunt his conquests in front of his wife, particularly in her present condition. The rule here at court is that nothing must be known, and so everyone's honour is respected and order reigns. Now, try and enjoy the food – the quail eggs are delicious.'

I took a sip of wine and over the rim of the glass gazed across the great sea of people towards Louise. The man standing behind her chair appeared splendidly dressed, almost outshining the king, and as he leant forward, his head brushed against hers. They were whispering, and as he kissed her hand, she flushed and laughed like a girl.

'Who is that gentleman?' I asked, of Eliza. 'I have not seen him before, and he is being very familiar with the king's mother.'

'That is Charles Montpensier, the Duc de Bourbon, the most important prince in France under François, who is jealous of his good looks and wealth. He is married to *Madame la Grande's* daughter, Suzanne de Bourbon, and although he is much younger than Louise, at twenty-seven, he is –' and here she whispered in my ear, 'her lover.'

I felt my mouth drop open.

Attired in cloth of silver, embroidered with tongues of fire, a rich border of gold decorated his robe, upon which blazoned the motto, '*A toujours jamais.*' Forever and ever.

'Apparently, he resides in the most beautiful château in France,' said Eliza, 'and owes his advancement to Louise. I hear she is besotted with him and has him trapped like a spider with a fly. It is strange how she exercises such an extraordinary fascination over men's affections.'

'Is there no-one here at this court, apart from Claude and Marguerite, who does not have a lover?' I asked, glancing under my lashes at my sister. I noticed a beautiful gold necklace about her neck and felt instantly jealous.

Eliza followed my eyes towards the piece. 'Oh, Marguerite is not as pious as you might think,' she said. 'She designs the jewellery and devices for her brother's lovers herself and takes great pains to find out their tastes so that he pleases them – and vice versa. Such a strange devotion to her brother is remarkable – do you not think?'

I shrugged. My sister always had a yearning for expensive jewellery and cared not a toss who designed it. 'Perhaps.'

'Come now, Anne, everyone here has a lover in one form or another,' she said, smiling. 'Does not the king himself say that a man without a mistress is a nincompoop?'

Better a nincompoop than an adulterer, I thought.

●　●

'How appropriate amidst the shit and filth.' I glanced around for somewhere remotely clean to sit down.

'Nan, please do not be angry, it is the only place I could think of where I could talk to you alone. I had to speak to you, for you cannot keep avoiding me, it is cruel. Please, sit.'

My sister appeared pale as she sat down on the bale of straw. Across the cobbled yard several horses, heads over their stalls, gazed in curiosity, and at the far end of the stables, a boy splashed a metal bit in the water trough, whistling a tune.

'I cannot stay long,' I muttered, sitting down on the opposite bale. 'I have to attend Madame Louise, and she is in a foul mood.'

We stared at each other before I spoke.

'Oh, how *could* you, Mary! You told me that you had changed, that everything was different, that you would keep yourself chaste. Now we are shamed, and Father will be furious! Besides, you said you did not even like François.'

'Nan, softly,' pleaded Mary, her eyes filling with tears. They did not soften my heart, and as I stared at her, I felt nothing but contempt.

'You did not waste any time, did you?' I asked, accusingly. 'The minute I turned my back you were up to your old tricks. Six weeks – just six short weeks whilst I am locked away in Cluny, you run straight into the arms of the new king. You – *you* – are the eldest who is supposed to know better!'

Mary jumped up and fell at my knees, her expression pleading. 'It is not what you think, Nan,' she said, clutching the fabric of my gown.

'Neither was it last time,' I said, tugging it back.

'Nan, please, I had no choice! I was put in his path by his mother.'

'Really?' I asked angrily. 'And you could not have said no?'

'She is a difficult woman to refuse, and like François, always gets her way. Besides, she threatened to send me home as entirely unsuitable. Can you imagine what our parents would have thought?'

'And what will they think now, Mary? Father will be furious at the position you have put him in, and how do you expect to ever attend Queen Katherine? Any hint of a bad reputation and she will not countenance you at court.'

We remained in silence before I asked her what had happened.

'He said he first noticed me, Nan, at the dowager French queen's coronation. Yes, of course, I was flattered by his smiles and winks, but I thought no more of it, for everyone here at court teases. Then, just before his coronation, he started to seek me out and to talk to me. I saw no harm in him.'

'Oh, for the love of Heaven, Mary, a practised roué?' I sighed, gazing up at the stable beams. Water from a leak in the rafters plopped into a nearby bucket. She sat back on her heels, frowning.

'You do not understand. It was while we were talking

that I said I loved to ride and I made a wager that I could beat any of his ladies in a race. He roared with laughter and said that I must prove it. His mother then suggested I accompany him and his other ladies to Senlis and if I won the bet, he must bring me oysters on a silver platter. So, I went.'

'And you believed him?'

'Why should I not?' asked Mary, surprised.

'And you had no idea who these 'ladies' were?'

'Of course I knew who they were!' she cried, indignantly.

'But still you rode out with the man who devours women merely by looking at them? Did you not think that odd?'

She stood up, exasperated. 'I told you – I was ordered by his mother. She said it would please her if I joined her son, and she did not like to be disappointed.'

Without warning, I pushed her hard.

'Why did you do that?' she shrieked, brushing off the straw as she scrabbled to her feet, hair tumbling about her shocked face.

'You gave yourself to him, didn't you?' I asked, glaring at her.

She straightened herself up, her eyes blazing. 'Nan, I have done naught to be ashamed of. I – I tried to stop him, but could not.'

My face fell as her words sank in. 'My God, did he force himself upon you?'

'No! François would never hurt a woman in that way. He was gentle, and although at first I did not want to give in to him, I could not help myself. You know my nature.'

I stared at her, appalled. 'But what about your restraint, your self-respect?'

'Nan, you have never been in such a perilous position, how could you know how difficult it is to reason at such a moment? Oh, do you not see? This was not some coupling with a simple boy of no standing as at home, but with the King of France. François promised me so many beautiful things if I gave myself to him, so of course, I weakened.

Besides,' she added, 'there are such secret things I could tell you, things that no-one else knows about.'

I sat down again on the bale and sulkily chewed at a straw. We said nothing until I broke the silence, unable to stem my curiosity.

'What things?' I asked, annoyed with myself for asking.

'Well,' she confided, in a whisper, 'he is not as versed in the pleasures of the flesh as all the court imagines.'

I stopped chewing.

'Oh, he is very sensuous, but – well, he does not have the patience to please a woman. Everything is over very quickly as if he cannot wait to be about some other business. He also asked me to do things that I – I did not like.'

'But surely you were there just to please him,' I said, sarcastically. 'What you like is of no matter.'

Mary shrugged and in the silence that followed my curiosity got the better of me again. 'What things?'

Mary's cheeks flushed. ''Tis naught, but there is something very odd about him.'

'Go on,' I said, not even trying now to contain myself.

'Well,' she said, slowly, 'a coldness. There was coldness about him, for he would not talk about himself. He hated answering questions and seemed quite awkward with intimacy as if one should not get too close to him. People think he is very playful, but he is quite heartless in private because of his impossibility to show affection. His nature is cautious and reserved, and I believe he thinks too much, which gives him that distant manner.'

'I had not noticed,' I replied.

'Why, yes, when you see him laughing with his women, he seems so at ease, but when it comes down to it, in private, he is tightly shut like an oyster shell. What do you make of that, Nan?'

'What should I make of it?' I asked. 'If you disliked him so much, why did you give yourself to him?'

'Because I had no choice! Matters went too far,

too quickly.'

'He is married, and I think he is disgusting,' I said. 'Naught will come of this sordid affair, you see.'

'But why, why should nothing come of it?' she countered. 'Was it not you, Nan, who once said that you wanted to please only those people of influence who can give you things, such as Louise? Well, who has more influence than the King of France? You love expensive gowns and everything good that life can bring. Do not pretend you do not. This way, you can have them through me – I can help you obtain anything you ask for.'

'Do not place this at my door!' I glared at her.

'Anyway, Nan, François now says I can stay here in France as part of his *petite bande*. He promised.'

'Oh, I *see*, Mary, would that be with those clever, wealthy, highborn noblewomen who amuse him and are his closest confidants? How marvellous – so where will you fit in?'

'Why, you evil, little bitch!' she squealed, flinging herself onto me. A fight ensued, with hair pulling, grabbing and pummelling, causing the horses to snicker nervously and weave about in their stalls. A pail of water tipped over and splashed across the hay as dust and straw flew into the air making us both cough. The stable boy ran over and was immediately followed by two of his friends, jeering and hooting. They clattered their empty buckets against the iron railing to add to the noise and called to yet more friends to come and watch the catfight. A couple of barking dogs ran in to add more mayhem.

Finally, an older man ran forward and pulled Mary and me apart. My nose was bloodied and Mary had a scratch across her cheek. We stood glaring at each other, trying to catch our breath, and I glanced down at my torn sleeve. The man dusted me down, but I pulled away, mortified by the laughing boys. As I picked up my hood and ran out of the stable, I heard Mary's breathless voice cry out:

'Sister, dear, you did not ask me if I enjoyed the oysters!'

* *

Although she had her back turned to me, I sensed that something must be wrong. I gave a small cough, and she flinched.

'Leave us,' she commanded. The maids dropped their embroidery, scrambled to their feet, and hurriedly left the chamber.

When the door had closed, the woman turned and placed a piece of paper down on the table. Even though it lay upside down, I recognised the writing.

'Read it,' she said.

I stepped forward and picked up the paper, perusing the words.

'Out loud!' she cried. 'I want to hear every single word.' She then sat down on the high backed chair, imperiously watching me. I began:

> *'Watch for your servants,*
> *Find out about them beforehand, my demoiselles,*
> *And you will discover which ones are the deceivers.*
> *When they speak, their language*
> *Is sweeter than the talk of young girls,*
> *Watch out for it.*
> *In their hearts, they are aiming to deceive,*
> *And -'*

'Enough!' The dowager French queen, no longer in her white weeds, held up her hand. 'Who wrote that?' she asked.

I put the paper down to my side. 'Why, my lady, it was written by Margaret of Savoy and given to me.'

'And given to you. Wise words from a wise lady, would you agree?'

I nodded, solemn-faced, as her narrowed eyes pierced through me. Then, without warning, she sprung forward, forcing me to take a step back.

'How *dare* you!' she cried. 'How dare you spy on me

and run to Madame Louise with my secrets! I took you into my confidence and my care. I trusted you as I trusted no other. The court is full of malicious gossips, and I thought you were different. But you are not. What did she give you? Trinkets, gowns?'

I remained motionless.

'Nothing, Madame,' I replied, in a firm voice.

'Then,' she said, folding her hands, 'you are even more of a fool than I thought.'

'Madame, forgive me, but she said it was necessary to protect your honour. She wished to help you and –'

'Mistress *Bullen*, hear this once and for all. She was – is – my enemy. A ruthless and controlling woman who hated me from the moment I married Louis, in case *my* child robbed her son of the crown. You are an ambitious minx – a trait she quickly recognised in you – and one that served her purpose well. I hear she is now aware that the duke and I have married? Is that true?'

'Yes.'

'Well,' she said, nervously pacing about, 'he and I have lain together as man and wife, and it cannot be undone.'

It was obvious that she still felt afraid that her brother would not recognise her marriage.

'What else have you told her?'

I informed her of all I had said since first joining her in Paris – her visits by François, her false pregnancy – everything. When I told her how Louise had raged when she found out that she, via a trusted courtier, had smuggled the 'Mirror of Naples' out of the country, she appeared panic struck. She continued pacing up and down, muttering to herself. Finally, after several minutes, she turned to me.

'You will remain here with me at Cluny, for the time being, where I can see you. But beware – I now know your tricks – and after that, you are dismissed from my service. I will not tolerate a girl I cannot trust in my household. You will never serve me again – *ever* – and I will do nothing for you, should you ever enter the English court and the service of Queen Katherine. I shall, in fact, ignore you if our paths ever cross in the future. Do you understand?'

'Madame,' I replied calmly, refusing to be cowed, 'I did not mean you harm. My grandfather –'

'Your *grandfather!* Do you think I do not know the calumnies he has rained down on the duke and the trouble he has made insulting him as a mere horse master to the council? No, you have done much harm, for you are muddled about whom you serve and therein lies the greatest danger. You are not of the French court, but the English, and as such you are *my* creature.'

I stared defiantly at her.

'Why,' she said angrily, 'I see that you are proud, proud enough to think yourself of some use and importance to Madame Louise. No doubt she flattered you?'

I continued to stare ahead.

'Well, you Bullen girls have not made a good start. One has proved disloyal to me, and the other has behaved shamefully. If I were your mother, I would have you both whipped in front of the Place Maubert and left there to rot.'

I wondered what Mother would, indeed, say.

'Now leave me.'

I was just about to go when Madame d'Aumont flew unannounced into the chamber, her arms flapping. Ashen faced, she swept to the floor.

'My lady, forgive my intrusion, but there is news from Blois,' she said, breathlessly. 'Madame Louise is near to death! It began as she set out on the road from here. She suffers a great flux with dark outpourings and continually lays siege in the privy. She lies sweating and is very weak. François, Marguerite, and *Madame la Grande* are with her as we speak, and her closest council have made their way to the château. They fear she will not see the light of dawn. They say she has been poisoned!'

The great kitchens at the Palais were turned upside down in the uproar that ensued. The cooks and young boys were questioned throughout the night until they wept with exhaustion and fear for their lives. Someone was responsible, but no culprit could be found. To be safe, carts loaded with meat, fish, custards, and tarts were thrown out and taken to the palace gates for the waiting beggars. They scrambled, arms outstretched, to grab what food they could, devouring it with famished eyes, and caring not if it was tainted. But poison had not made Madame Louise ill. It appeared to be some type of contagion that had remained behind after she had left for Blois, and it swept through a great many people at court.

We were not even safe at Cluny and unable to leave the stool closet, spent a miserable few days in our chambers, gripped by stomach pains and enduring foul odours. The chamber smelt of vomit as I lay shivering, then burning on my bed, my knees drawn up. I even wanted my sister, but she remained in Blois with François. The dowager French queen had reluctantly agreed to allow me to stay with the other ladies until she departed for England, but I would not be returning with them to Calais. What was to become of me? I tossed and turned knowing that my father would have to decide what to do. Would he send someone to come and fetch me home? How humiliating!

Nobles came and went, and messengers brought forth the news that King Henry of England stormed through the palace, incandescent with rage at his sister's marriage to his best friend. She, a Princess of the Blood! Finally, after great personal effort, Wolsey wrote to the dowager saying that due to his sole intervention and support, he had succeeded in calming the king and saved her and Suffolk from danger. However, the leniency of his master would depend on a favourable financial settlement of his sister's dowry and possessions. Wolsey would do his best but hinted that when the duke returned to court, he trusted he would not forget his help. We also heard that the Mirror of Naples had arrived safely in England and that the king wore it openly in his bonnet for all the court and its ambassadors to see. He insisted that the taking of it had been no more than a merry jest and promised to return it when negotiations were settled. Unconvinced, the French ambassador became decidedly alarmed and protested loudly for all to hear. Meanwhile, the king's anger began cooling, temporarily placated by Wolsey and the value of the diamond, and secure in the knowledge that he had tricked François. Now, it was François' turn to be furious at the underhand dealings of the dowager queen. Rumour had it that in a fit of pique, he had scribbled the words *'Pleus sale que royne'* – *'more foolish than queenly'* across a drawing of her, and threatened to consign it to the fire. However, on second thoughts, he threw it into a large drawer to lie there forgotten forever.

As to Louise, she did not die. Thanks to the large number of rhubarb pills prescribed to her by her physician, she was soon out of danger and sitting up dictating letters to her secretary.

Chapter Five

*'From vanished night the sun now
reappears.'*

Paris

Two days after the spectacular wedding celebrations of Diane de Poitiers at the Hôtel de Bourbon, in Paris, another wedding took place at Cluny. Afraid that the King of England would not accept the marriage of his sister and the duke as legal – and outmanoeuvre him – François insisted on a public ceremony with himself and Claude as guests. The only snub came from Madame Louise, who did not see fit to attend the wedding since she deemed Suffolk a man of low estate. She remained behind in Blois to regain her strength and fume over the stolen diamond. Now, with the ceremony sanctioned by the bishop and with enough guests and ambassadors to make it formal, the dowager French queen enjoyed a public marriage. It was done, and her brother could do nothing against the law of God and the sanctity of the sacrament.

After the ceremony, we left the chapel and made our way to the *grande salle* for the celebrations. I stood alone, holding my posy of pink roses to match my gown, and noticed that François, although charming, appeared to behave in a very cool manner towards the newly wedded couple. He mingled among the guests and placed his hand conspicuously over

Claude's. My sister, standing to one side in a new cream gown, looked lovely with her hair tumbling down to her shoulders beneath a gold, netted cap. However, François did not look at her once, and I moved reluctantly to her side.

'That's done then,' I said. It was the first time I had spoken to her since our fight in the stable.

She hesitated, then broke into a smile.

'Oh, Nan, my darling Nan, am I forgiven? I cannot tell you how much I have missed you! Are we sweet sisters again?' She eagerly took both my hands and I gave a nonchalant shrug.

'You have heard?' I watched François laughing with Claude.

'About you?'

I nodded.

'Of course, Nan, all the girls have been gossiping. At least it takes the attention away from me. But you must not worry so, it is just a storm,' she added, soothingly. 'Besides, you do not need the dowager French queen any more for I will insist that you stay here in France with me if that is what you wish. It is in my gift. Trust me. I can obtain anything I want from François for he is quite besotted with me.'

'Does Father know yet?' I watched Claude as she sat down. She seemed so insignificant next to her magnificent husband.

'I doubt it,' said Mary.

I asked if Claude knew.

'Her ladies do not tell her anything that might upset her, and she does not ask. She accepts that her husband has 'appetites' and she is charitable towards his amours, but when he is with her, he is with her alone. Besides, he does not want to distress her in her condition, which is why he does not acknowledge me in front of her.'

'What will Father say when he finds out that the French queen is to dismiss me?' I asked, not convinced.

'Why, Nan, none of our family cares a fiddle for her

or the duke, and she knows it. It will just be seen as spite, so what is all the fuss about? There is nothing new about passing such information on, as well the queen knows. Most of the ladies-in-waiting here are in the pay of somebody at court, for how else can they afford those extra luxuries that are otherwise unobtainable?'

'But I did not receive any pay,' I said.

She smiled as Françoise de Foix swept by, her seven-year-old daughter, Anne, close behind. Mary's smile was not returned and it was obvious that she did not like my sister.

'Mary, what gifts has François given you?' I asked. She put her posy to her face to hide her excited smile.

'Well, I have a new neck chain,' she giggled, putting her fingers to the gold Italian links about her neck, 'and a new gown of gooseberry-coloured satin – one of his favourite colours. He always chooses his ladies gowns himself, as he has exquisite taste, and even matches them to the colour of the chambers they are in, so that they look – *we* look – our loveliest. Did you know it takes ten ells of fabric just to make up one luxurious gown?'

'Why should I?' I gazed about. 'I am not some common seamstress. Anyway, I suppose as the deed is done you might as well accept his gifts. What is there to lose now?'

'Oh, stop it, Anne. You are only jealous. No, best of all, François has promised to give me a horse, stabled at his expense, at Blois. I am to choose it next week when the new Arab mares arrive from North Africa.'

A horse? I began to feel sick with envy, for she was right. I always felt jealous when it came to the good fortune of others.

'What is the château at Blois like?' I tried to change the subject.

She frowned. 'Old fashioned. François plans to update it, and at present, it is covered with scaffolding because of the restoration work due to start in June. He intends building it in the Italian style, and Claude has asked him for a new façade in front of the old court. Inside the walls are gilded and the floors are covered with colourful glazed tiles to keep the chambers cool – unlike in our own English houses. François wishes to do away with the old colours of crimson and gold and introduce lighter colours such as silver, white and mulberry. But the gardens are exquisite with arbours and pathways, and bushes curiously cut into the shape of birds.'

'Like Hever Manor then?' I asked, not entirely serious.

She laughed. 'It makes Hever look like some squalid old gatehouse in comparison, and as for Rochford – well!'

'You once said that you wanted to live at Rochford forever,' I said, as we moved out of the way of the gathering musicians. 'Now it is not good enough for you.'

'Yes, but that is before I saw the delights France has to offer.'

'You mean François,' I said.

'François *is* France,' she sighed.

'Well – I feel the same, Mary. I have grown to love everything French and do not want to be sent back. I miss home, of course, and George, but I love the banquets and entertainments here. It is so different from the court at Mechelen – everything is so lavish, free and without restraint, even the gowns. I have never seen such richness.'

'But, Nan, just a moment ago you said how –'

'I know, but I do not want to return to the quiet of the country at Hever – not just yet. Mary, let us not argue again, but what will happen to you if François tires of you?'

'He will not – I am no Marie Gaudin to be cast off for the entire court to mock. You wait and see.'

The musicians made their way up to the gallery and began tuning up their instruments. The king, seated with Claude, signalled to my sister to approach him. With a swish of gown, she moved to his side, and he whispered something in her ear. She smiled, blushed and then walked to the centre of the *salle*. With a clap from the king, silence fell, and my sister began to sing before the company to the accompaniment of a viol. I noticed that the dowager French queen lowered her eyes throughout the *chanson* as if distracted. I was not surprised. Although now married to the man she loved, she had had to surrender her official seal and was now as good as penniless. With all her money spent, she was unable to pay her servants, victualler or seamstress. Even her gambling debts were left unpaid, a galling situation for a spoilt woman used to obtaining anything she desired. Wolsey, she knew, continued to work tirelessly for her, for he alone could get her home, but at what financial cost? He had informed her that her brother still planned to inflict a ruinous fine on her and the duke since the 'Mirror of Naples' had not fully appeased his greed. It was a grim situation. Her brother, still haggling over her dowry and her expenses, remained in a difficult position, for the French refused to agree to terms unless Tournai and the diamond were returned to them.

As the dowager sat pensively next to her new husband, François appeared lost in his thoughts. His fool, Triboulet – a dark, swarthy little man, more imp than human – sat hunched at his feet. Garbed in black, he dabbed his large eyes and blew his great, bulbous nose as if a mourner at a funeral, rather than a wedding guest. They said he was the only man in France with a nose larger than the king's, and I could see why. He glanced at the dowager, placing his hand to his heart and sighed. When François kicked him playfully with his soft shoe, Triboulet whimpered liked a craven hound, causing Marie Darcille to bark like a dog.

Meanwhile, Claude, sitting next to her husband, fanned herself in the heat of the *salle* and smiled at everyone in her gracious way. She placed her hand on the front of her gown, her thoughts, no doubt, on her coming child. As for me, as I sat on my stool listening to Mary's lilting voice I could only muse at what the future might bring.

• •

'We are going home! We are going back to England!' laughed the queen dowager, spinning Ann Jernyngham around the chamber at Cluny. In her excitement, she immediately tripped over the scattered gowns discarded on the turkey carpet. 'Thanks be to my Lord Wolsey, for he has finally assured a treaty with France – oh, and thanks be to God,' she added, making the sign of the cross.

I opened up the lid of a large basket as my sister handed me a pile of folded linen, both of us silent as we went about our task. At that moment, the duke strode into the chamber, picking his way across the gown-strewn floor, and took his wife into his arms.

'I will not be sorry to leave this accursed place, my love,' he muttered, 'and yet I am fearful of what awaits.'

She gazed up, smiling sweetly. 'Yes, but at least a settlement has been reached, and I can leave with my dowry. I must return my jewels and revenues from my French properties, but I care not a whit so long as we are together.'

'And what do we live on, sweeting, fresh air?' he asked, holding her close. 'Your brother is demanding a ruinous fine of four thousand pounds a year from me until your death.'

'Well, I could die tomorrow if that would be more convenient,' the dowager pouted.

He laughed and steered her over to the window seat.

'Thank God, indeed, for Wolsey,' he said, as she sat beside him. 'I have managed to keep and obtain for him the bishopric of Tournai, which will please your brother, but it is a small thing I do for so great a favour.' He frowned. 'It is difficult for me to do anything for anyone at present.'

'Well,' said the dowager, 'we must now face the fact that, diplomatically, we are judged to be persons of no import.'

The duke raised a worried brow.

'Oh, believe me, Charles, the Venetian ambassadors were very quick to 'accidentally' forget to bring a gift for me when they visited a few days ago.'

'Why did you not say?' The duke was concerned. 'They brought you nothing?'

'Not a pin,' came the flat reply. 'I am dynastically of no further use, and I am glad of it.'

'I fear it is just the start of things to come,' said her husband. 'Our reception in England will be difficult, to say the least.'

'From my brother and the council?'

'No, Wolsey has beaten down the council. I was thinking more from the people. You know how the Londoners love you, and here I am married to their princess. You must be prepared for their hostility – as must I.'

She smiled and rose up. 'Why should I worry when I have you by my side? Come now, let us talk of more amusing matters. I have something to tell you.' She took his arm and walked out of the chamber, then turned around at the door. 'Ladies, please have everything packed by tonight, and do not squash my bonnets – they each have a satin box ready for the pallets.' She glanced vaguely around. 'Somewhere. Oh, praise be to God we are going home!'

When she had left the chamber, Mary and I stopped and looked at each other.

'*She* might be going home, but what of us?' I watched as two of the French maids folded up her fur cloak.

Meanwhile, Ann Jernyngham scrabbled about on her knees, frantically searching for something beneath the gilded bed. 'This is hopeless,' she grumbled, 'half of her shoes are missing. Where is the other blue velvet one?' She finally arose, red in the face, the dusty shoe in her hand. 'Really, I have never known such a careless woman, for she just flings off her shoes without a care. See how the buckle is broken – how am I to fix that?'

My sister took the shoe from her and studied it.

'We will never be packed in time if you worry about that right now,' said Mary Fiennes, grabbing it. 'All the gowns still need laying in their linen covers – Honore, Lucille, get to it!'

The two chamberers immediately stopped clearing the table of brushes and combs.

As Mary and I turned back to our basket, Madame d'Aumont swept into the chamber and silently surveyed the array of boxes, chests, gowns, and shoes. 'Mistresses Mary and Anne Boleyn, I wish to see you both in the *grande salle*. Tidy yourselves up and come down within the next five minutes.'

When she had left the chamber, Mary and I ran to the mirror.

'Perhaps Father has sent for us,' I whispered, rapidly undoing my apron.

'But I do not want to go home!' cried Mary, alarmed, 'and besides, Louise will insist I stay here.'

'That remains to be seen,' I said, as we hurried out of the door.

Down in the *salle*, Madame d'Aumont sat in a high backed chair, two ladies standing on either side of her. She stared at Mary and me as we waited for her to speak.

'I have had a letter from your father,' she finally said, unfolding the paper on her knee. As I recognised the wax seal impressed with the bull's head, my heart began to race.

Madame d'Aumont raised her head. 'Mistress Marie,' she sighed, studying my sister carefully. 'What are we to do with you?'

Mary stood, hands behind her back, her ample bosom rising as she tried to calm her breathing. Two pink spots highlighted her cheeks, giving her an irresistible flush.

'Your father has been informed – as we knew he would – that you have been favoured by the King of France. However, he said that as the king has a wife already with whom, at present, your father is in correspondence, this puts him in a rather delicate situation. He does not wish to anger the king, or, indeed, interfere with his pleasures, particularly as matters here are already tense between our two countries. He does not wish to upset Claude, or for that matter, Madame

Louise. So what is the remedy?' She paused a moment.

'I know not, Madame,' said Mary, now reddening.

'Well, you will be pleased to know that your Howard relatives have seemingly overruled your father and his qualms. In fact, your uncle himself wrote to Madame Louise and Marguerite to ask their advice on this delicate matter. Madame replied that it was her dearest wish for you to remain in France and attend her, as one of her maids.'

My sister's face brightened while mine fell. *Louise's* household? But that would surely keep Mary firmly in François path? He would have access to her any time he wanted. What was my uncle thinking? All he seemed concerned about was upsetting Claude or Louise.

'Oh, Madame.' Mary could hardly believe her good fortune.

Madame d'Aumont did not smile – it was clear she found the conversation distasteful – but turned, instead, to face to me.

'Mistress Anne, you, on the contrary, have proved yourself a most pious young lady, obedient to your family and Madame Louise. She is most satisfied and regrets that the dowager French queen no longer wishes to have you in her service back in England. Your father and mother are also pleased with your conduct and bearing here, serving your family well.'

I smiled with pride.

'Madame,' I said, in a honey-sweet voice, 'I ever owe my good fortune to my family's kind offices and understand I am here only to do their will.'

Madame d'Aumont grunted. 'Good, I am glad you are so amenable, because your father, after careful consideration, has decided you would be better away from the court for a time. He will be placing you in a convent in Brière, five leagues from Honfleur, in Normandy. Since it is a house renowned for its learning, he feels you will do well there – for a while least. Madame Louise, of course, is happy to release you from court as soon as it is convenient for you to go.'

The smile on my face froze. I knew of the place, for my Uncle Howard owned a house nearby, and would sail from Portsmouth when on business there.

She continued. 'We will, of course, arrange for you to be safely escorted to the village, where you will be met, but after that, you are your family's responsibility and care.'

'Yes, Madame,' was all I felt able to say.

'So – everything is settled. When the dowager queen has departed, and your duties to her are done, you will both await further instructions. Now, you are dismissed. Please return to dismantling the queen's chambers. Incidentally, Mary Fiennes and Eliza Grey are to serve Queen Claude, and will not be returning to England either – for the present. However, Ann Jernyngham will be returning with her husband to serve the queen in her new household.'

One of the ladies standing behind her gave a curt nod to indicate that our audience had ended, and we left the *salle* without saying a word. Outside was another matter.

'A *convent*!' I shrieked, when we reached the staircase, not caring that other people nearby had turned to listen. 'Mary, this is so unfair! I have done nothing wrong, and yet it is me that Father wants to send away from court! You should be the one locked up, not I!'

My sister stood smirking like a cat with a bowl of cream. 'Only here to do his will,' she purred, mimicking my words. Then she saw how truly miserable I felt. 'Oh, Anne, I am so sorry, but –'

'You are not one bit sorry,' I said, as a group of ladies quickly walked away. 'Why am I to be punished for your behaviour?'

'It is not a punishment, how can it be?' asked Mary, putting her hand on mine.

I swiftly pulled it away in disgust. 'Yes, it is – stuck in a convent while you hunt, dance and trip prettily around every château in the Loire valley – with *him*. Fêtes, entreés, and banquets for you – sitting alone at a refectory table with a bowl of broth and a Latin book for me. What can Father be thinking of?'

'Well, he must want you out of my company for a while,' she said. 'Or maybe he has been swayed by Uncle Howard. How do I know? Either way, I am glad that I am staying, but I am sorry we will not be together – truly I am.'

'No, it is her,' I said, tears of frustration pricking my eyes. 'She wants you, Mary, in her household because of her son. He desires you, and she is more than happy to put you in his way where you are easily available to please his every whim. She cannot deny him a thing.'

'Well, I told you she was a ruthless woman,' said Mary, smugly, 'for since you are no longer of use to her, she is happy to let you go.'

I clenched my fingers, seething with anger. 'And Father has meekly agreed with the plan,' I said.

'Well, if truth be told, he is afraid of Uncle Howard,' continued Mary, 'afraid of all of the Howards in fact. Have you not seen how they gainsay him on every matter? Perhaps our uncle sees my pleasing François as an advantage. Maybe François will give him, or Father, a grand château with a fine hunting park?'

'And what if France and England decide to go to war against each other again – then what? We will both be sent straight home. Besides, Mother will not see it as an honour.'

'I care not, Nan. Besides, she will have no say in this matter – as well you know.'

'Well, I refuse to go,' I said, sitting down on the cold, marble steps of the staircase. 'I am *not* going off to a convent. Mary, you have to do something. Ask François – you said he would grant you anything – promise him anything – do what he asks of you – but do *something!*'

• •

At Cluny, my sister and I watched the crowd below in the courtyard. Many officials had come to pay their last respects, and several foreign ambassadors stood in the warm morning sunshine exchanging pleasantries. François sat astride his great bay horse, raising a glass of wine to the woman he had once tried to seduce, and wishing her a safe crossing. The dowager French queen nodded and smiled graciously to him, but it was all a sham. She knew that he and his mother were glad to see the back of her, and the feeling was mutual. In fact, to the people's great happiness, François had even announced that the following day would be a public holiday. Was this a slight or a compliment to the queen?

Now the horses were saddled, the carts loaded with exquisite belongings, and the queen and her new husband were ready to depart. Dressed prettily in Tudor green with a velvet cap set jauntily upon her head, she looked a picture of relief. Ann Jernyngham sat on her horse, her husband beside her, for she would soon be joining the queen's household in England.

Some weeks later we heard from one of the ladies-in-waiting that François had escorted the new Duke and Duchess of Suffolk out of Paris as far as Saint-Denis. He then kissed the duchess's hand and embraced the duke several times before turning his horse towards Paris, throwing his cap into the air, and galloping away with his friends along the stony road.

From there on, a large party of nobles rode with the couple to Beauvais in Picardy, then Abbeville, and finally on to Montreuil, where the duchess rode up to the fortress to admire the valley. I imagined her laughing in the evening sunshine and ambling down the steep, cobbled streets to rest at the monastery for the night. There, amidst the blossoming hawthorn, she might have walked with the duke in the gardens until evening, planning their future together and allaying his fears with sweet kisses.

The following day, we heard that they rode with their escort across the River Canache to Calais, where they stayed awaiting permission from King Henry to set sail. Sadly, at their lodgings, the duke had to bolt the door against the English garrison for fear they would murder him for his audacity in marrying their beloved princess. Even the citizens of the town mocked the couple over their garden walls, throwing filth, and shouting that the princess should have married the Prince of Spain, instead of a commoner. In fact, matters were so grave that the couple did not dare venture out into the street for fear they might be stoned to death by the rabble. For a while, it looked as if they might not reach home at all...

● ●

I stood outside Queen Claude's apartments, at the Palais de Louvre, and watched as her women filed past. Since each of them carried several gowns piled high over their arms, they could barely see where they were going. In the dark passageway, young pages struggled as they dragged the heavy trunks along the stone floor, one of them cursing as he tripped. My sister, bumping into one of them, came to my side.

'Nan, I have been searching for you,' she said brightly, biting into an apple.

'I have been asked to see the queen.' I moved back against the wall as a boy, struggling to hold four unruly wolfhounds, slid past. 'Mary, what is happening, why all the commotion?'

'Have you not heard?' she pulled me into the alcove. 'It is thrilling! François is crossing the Alps and invading Italy! The whole court is to accompany him to Amboise to make ready before he continues to Lyon to join his army. He is going to fight with twenty-five thousand knights and forty thousand soldiers. There is to be war!'

'War?' I asked, alarmed.

'Well,' she said, 'Uncle Howard says François will never actually go over the Alps, as France has been reduced to too much misery already due to previous wars. But *if* he does, there is a rumour that François will have to sell the queen's possessions to fund the campaign.'

'Did François tell you this?' I asked.

'Of course not, he tells me nothing of importance. I overheard him discussing matters with Signeur de Bonnivet and the Duc de Montmorency, as he was rising from his *lever.* He was still wearing his night robe as I was hurried out by his *valet de chambre,* and told to wait outside. Naturally, I listened at the door and heard that the duc, who finances the army, advised François to melt down all the gold plate that belonged to the queen's parents. What he could not melt, such as her china and valuables, he was to sell, and so fill the treasury with a million *écu.* He knows her mother's gold plate is still in old Louis *cabinet* at Blois, along with other treasures there.' She stared at my amazed expression.

'But sur –'

'He has no choice, Nan. The dowager French queen has pilfered so much money that he does not have the wherewithal to undertake the Italian campaign without selling them. The queen, of course, dared not express her horror at this action, but is deeply upset.'

I was just about to speak when a boisterous group of young men ambled down the narrow passageway, laughing aloud. One of them draped himself languidly around the smaller man's shoulder, talking close to his ear. They appeared very slightly drunk.

'So my friend, it is settled. The king will make war on Milan, and we will make love to the girls. I hear Italian girls are dark, fiery, full of passion – and available!'

'Not if the Switzers ravage them first!' said the shorter man.

His companion shrugged. 'I hear the king is already dreaming of meeting the beautiful Clarissa of Milan. They say he is only going to war to win her heart!'

'Well, while he is busy on an errand of love, we will hunt the stag, for the season has come upon us, and the hounds are eager for the chase after their winter confinement. I have a new white pack to show the king, bred by the Comte de Chalons, for he says they are faster than the grey and cleverer than the black.'

'Talking of dogs, I hear the Swiss are ready to give France a good reckoning, and Ferdinand of Spain is to join them with a large force of canon and artillery.'

'They are curs indeed,' said his friend, 'such perfidy!'

Mary and I stood aside to let them pass, but one of the gentlemen stopped.

'Ah, Mademoiselle Boleyn,' he said, taking my sister's hand and kissing it, 'why are you loitering here when the king pines for his sweet, English rose?'

My sister's face lit up eagerly as she curtsied. 'The king asks for me, Monsieur? Where is he? I must go immediately!'

'Not so fast,' countered his friend, staying her arm, 'such haste is unbecoming. Besides, you have not introduced me to your companion here.' The others laughed as Mary turned to me.

'Monsieur de Foix, may I present my sister, Anne.'

'As dark, Marie, as you are fair,' said the man, gazing at my long, lustrous hair. 'And may I present my brothers, Thomas and André.'

The two men bowed politely and the shorter one spoke. 'We are on our way to see our sister, Françoise. Is that not so, Odet? You have perhaps seen her, Marie?'

'Sirs,' I interrupted, 'I think your sister is with Queen Claude – I am about to go to her. Is there a message you would have me give her?'

'You are one of her *demoiselles*?' asked Thomas.

'Yes, sir – I mean no, sir – that is what I am to discuss with her. I served the dowager French queen, but since she has returned to England I am awaiting her instructions.'

My eyes then wandered to the figure standing behind the man's shoulder.

'Ah, we have not introduced you,' said Odet, following my eyes and moving to one side.

The gentleman behind bowed, took off his bonnet, and stared at me intently. For once, Mary stood forgotten.

'Clément Marot, *demoiselle*,' he said.

At that moment, I observed gentle, dark eyes that expressed an amused curiosity. Although swarthy of complexion and not strictly handsome, the way he held my gaze with those eyes felt compelling and caused my heart to stir.

'Hopefully, I shall see more of you,' he said, taking my hand and brushing it lightly with his lips.

Smiling, I gazed down on his dark hair, glossy as a raven's wing.

Mary then stepped forward. 'Oh no, sir, that will not be possible,' she said, twirling her hair seductively around her finger. As she slid smoothly like a snake, brushing her breasts close to one of the gentlemen, she smirked. 'My sister here is about to leave for a convent, although I, of course, shall be staying. Now, sirs, will you walk with me to the king's apartments?'

With that, she tossed Thomas de Foix the remains of her apple as they followed her down the passageway. Only Monsieur Marot looked back.

●   ◉

'*Entrez!*' It was the voice of Diane. 'My lady will speak with you now,' she said, her green gown swishing as she turned.

I noticed a maid walk away carrying a large box.

'No, not that, that can go separately,' said Diane, impatiently, taking the box from the girl. 'Really, must I do everything myself?'

She handed the box to a page and asked me to follow

her until we reached the quiet of a small *cabinet* or chamber. Diane knocked and opened the door, announcing my presence. I entered a pretty chamber with pale blue walls painted with silver *fleurs-de-lis*, and a beautiful pastoral tapestry that filled an entire wall. Queen Claude stood in front of a great pile of unframed canvasses, carefully sifting through them.

'Anne, my dear,' she waved, 'please come in. Thank you, Diane. Please close the door behind you.' She turned to me with a bright smile. 'Now – we are alone. What do you think? Should I take this picture of St Jerome or this one of the Annunciation? I do so admire Signore Angelico.'

I rose from my curtsy and moved closer to the canvasses.

'Madame, I think the Annunciation would be the most inspiring in your present condition, whereas that depicting St Jerome, surrounded by his books, is of a more sombre theme. Besides, his expression is somewhat weary as if burdened or bored by a dull lesson. Hardly a cheerful prospect.'

The queen turned and laughed. 'Oh, indeed so, Anne, how right you are! Now, please sit here on this cushion.' She sat down herself on a gilded chair and gave a wriggle, her silk slippers not quite reaching the floor. 'Now, I hear that you are leaving us to go to the good sisters at Honfleur,' she said, resting back against the cushion. 'Is that what you wish?' she asked, kindly.

I shook my head, dejectedly.

'But it is as your family wishes, is it not?'

'Yes, Madame, but not as I would wish. I would miss my life here very much.'

'Of course, you would. That is understandable for a young girl with such talents as you possess. I have seen how you love dancing and playing the lute – all agree you perform exceptionally well. And you sing like an angel. What a loss to the court such a bright star would be.'

'Thank you, Madame.'

'So, you would stay if you were able?'

I said I would.

'Indeed. Well, what I have to say is not entirely selfless. I am lonely here. I long for a girl I can talk to, and although I have Diane, I must say, she intimidates me with her beauty.'

Poor Claude, I thought, just about everyone frightened her.

'Besides, Anne, I like your company. Renée likes you too. She says you are amusing and always gay. Would you like to remain at my court?'

My eyes widened. 'Why, yes, oh, yes indeed, Madame! I do not want to go to Brière. Oh, I have nothing against the holy nuns, truly,' I blustered.

'But, Anne, did you not tell me once that you thought you might like the convent life, spending your days in quiet contemplation and reading?'

I recalled the conversation we had had, and how I had hoped to ingratiate myself with her by agreeing with her views. Sadly, I had overdone my enthusiasm.

'Oh, yes, Madame – I mean, no, Madame! I do not want to be away from the court or my sis –' I stopped abruptly, but it was too late.

'Ah, yes, your sister, Marie,' she said quietly. 'Do not worry. I am not completely blind, just a little crook-eyed. I do know the situation, although my ladies think otherwise. Well, I am sorry for her.'

'Sorry for Mary?' I asked, somewhat surprised.

'Indeed. None of this is her fault, for she has been used by Louise to please her son. Oh, I envy her looks, and I understand why, for a fleeting moment, she captivates my husband. But that is all. I am his wife, descended from a true and noble line of kings, soon to bring forth the future *dauphin* and one day to be crowned queen. I am untouchable – even by his mother.' She sat there, hunched and fat, yet with her little chin raised, she appeared more dignified and noble than a hundred pretty Mary Boleyns.

'And you do not rail at him?' I asked.

She laughed. 'My husband? No! These fancies come and go and the king must take his ease where he can since at present, I cannot oblige him. That I understand. No, I am more disturbed by those ladies who stimulate him intellectually, for they are the ones who truly hold his affection, such as his sister, Marguerite. As it is, all here think me stupid, but I can debate as well as any man or woman on any subject. I was brought up by my parents to have a sharp mind if only given the chance. But what can I do? Rage and become a shrew? Would that make him love me more? No, it would not.'

'But, Madame, how can you ignore these slights?' I asked.

She smiled. 'I place myself above them, for the eagle does not capture flies, Anne.'

'Do you think he loves my sister?'

'Anne, I have seen many such pretty women come and go, but Marie is not one he will ever love. But what is love? It is not some lowly, superficial thing, or vile sensual matter. It is lofty, spiritual and intellectual, and your sister, forgive me, does not possess the mind to hold him. Besides, there is none he truly loves – only his mother and sister – they have his very heart and soul, even before God.'

'But he loves *you*,' I replied.

'No, he loves me as much as François can ever love the mother of his future heir. But he is not a cruel man and often comes to my bed in tenderness to get me with child. I thank him for that.'

I felt disgusted and perplexed at the same time. How could she possibly put up with such humiliating behaviour, and yet be so forgiving?

As if reading my mind, she spoke. 'I am his queen, and although I pray every night for forbearance, patience, and understanding, my life is good.'

As I listened to her words I wanted to shake her. I would never allow my husband to humiliate me in such a way!

'Besides,' she continued, 'I have my gardens at Amboise

and Blois, my paintings, and my charitable work – all these give me great comfort, as do you. That is why I should like you to stay. I shall write to your father informing him that I need an interpreter. Would you be happy with that arrangement? You would reside at my court, under my careful protection, in case he has any, well, shall we say qualms?'

Rising from my cushion, I knelt at her knees. 'Oh, Madame, I should desire that above all things!'

She took my hands in hers. 'Then you must promise me one thing. If you are to serve me, you must do just that. Madame Louise is unkind to me, and if I reveal my heart to you, I do not want my words repeated to her.'

I opened my mouth in protest, but she stopped me.

'Hush, hush, I understand what happened before, and how manipulative Louise can be. It is very hard to stand against her and, like me, you are young. But can you be loyal to me? Can I trust you?'

'I promise, Madame, on my soul, to be always discreet and wise.' This time I truly meant it, for I could never betray this devout, innocent girl.

'That is good for I have very few friends here. There is also Renée to consider and I would like you for her companion. I shall say as much in my letter to your father. I think you will be very happy in my care, for I have few rules. However, one thing I will not countenance is dalliances amongst my maids. Marriages are arranged by parents who only have your good at heart, and I will not tolerate any light behaviour that might jeopardise your reputation.'

She waved me to my feet and I begged leave to speak. She nodded.

'My lady, why are you so solicitous to me when my sister is causing you much hurt?'

'Because I do not blame her,' she replied, 'and besides, you are not responsible for her behaviour. However, although I try to be forgiving – for dignity and courage never offend God – to have her in my household would try the soul of a saint, which I am not!'

I laughed. Mary would, indeed, try anyone's patience.

'Now – I shall write immediately to your father. Then, if he is in agreement, which I am sure he will be, you must help the other ladies pack.'

I thanked her profusely.

'I am afraid we will have several 'Annes' so I hope it does not become too confusing!'

'I am happy to be called Nan if that would help,' I said.

She gave a pretty laugh. 'Now, let me tell you about my ladies. Madame d'Assigny, Vicomtesse de Coëtmen, is my *Dame d'Honneur*. Madame Anne de Graville, Madame de Tournan, Madame Françoise de Foix and Diane de Brèzè are my close attendants. Then we have the French ladies, Madame de Brissac, Madame de Bouyan, Mademoiselle de Chaigny, Mademoiselle de Guiny, Mademoiselle de Fonguyon, and Mademoiselle de Guilleton. The youngest maids are Anne de Pisseleu and Anne de Foix. Old Madame de Tournon likes to fuss over them so you must indulge her. Oh, and as I mentioned, Mistress Fiennes and Mistress Grey will also be staying behind to serve me, so you will have some English company.'

My face lit up.

'I think you will be most taken, Anne, with the charming Anne de Graville, for she is the only female poet here at court. She loves to sing and is highly gifted, so you will find her most entertaining. Marguerite loves her dearly for she was the first girl with whom her brother fell in love. At barely fifteen, he was full of boyish romance.' She looked pensive as if remembering something private.

'I do not think I have met her yet, Madame,' I replied.

'No, but you will. Now, my court is quiet and God-fearing for I continue in the way of my mother. She helped so many young girls starting out in life, even paying their dowries. Like her, I expect my young maids to be modest.'

I lowered my eyes and hoped I looked suitably demure.

'And you must always pay heed to Madame d'Assigny. A woman, such as she, at the head of a *hôtel* is responsible for the good behaviour of the ladies and *demoiselles*. She must closely supervise her staff and above all, ensure respect for hierarchy and rank. It is she who ensures that women are decent in clothing and speech and occupied in honest pastimes since leisure leads to vice and perdition.'

Her serious face broke into a smile. 'But let us move on to happier matters. On the twenty-six day of this month, the whole court moves to Amboise to celebrate the wedding of Renée de Bourbon, sister of the constable, to the Duc de Lorraine and there is much to do. The *fourriers* will have the usual, unenviable task of finding accommodation for everyone, and there will be sour faces on those who feel slighted by their lodgings. Some will, no doubt, end up sleeping in the open air, but that is the price they pay for their ambition for they follow court in their lust for advancement.'

She arose awkwardly from her chair, as if in some discomfort.

'Now, back to my pictures. Thank you for your candid advice, Anne – I shall take the Annunciation. The other I will give to Diane as a belated wedding gift. I do hope the marriage does not bring her disappointment.'

As I left the *cabinet*, I looked back to where she stood, and it was then I saw her press her hands to her eyes, look up and quickly wipe a tear away from her pale cheek. She straightened her bent back a little and turned away.

'Anne, do not put too much faith in the court,' she called. 'It is corrupt, with every incentive to evil and none to do good. For all its allure, you will find it an empty vessel.'

'Then may God preserve me, Madame,' I replied, sweeping low to the floor.

●   ●

I nervously fingered the sealed parchment in my hands and turned it over. For the second time, I put it down by my side, afraid to read the contents. Outside in the courtyard, I heard a great deal of noise, for the exodus to Amboise had begun and, distracted, I watched as the *fauconniers* tethered their birds of prey to their wooden travelling frames. Horses pranced skittishly upon the cobbles as the young grooms tried to settle them down, and the buckhounds howled in their travelling cage, eager to be set free.

I sighed. It was no use – I would have to read the letter. Opening it, my eyes quickly scanned the script:

> *'Turning to you, Nan, Queen Claude has written to your father and has asked that you remain with her court as her interpreter. As a result of the queen's request, you will not be going to Brière…'*

'Oh, thanks be to God!' I crossed myself. I sat like that for some minutes as immense relief swept over me. Finally, I continued to read:

> *'My heart breaks at the folly of your sister, but I cannot be surprised that, in her weakness, she succumbed to the king. It is why I sent you, not her, to the Regent at Mechelen. Still, I only delayed the inevitable for beauty without wisdom is like a ship without a pilot – bound to run aground. But what is done cannot be undone, and I implore you to be a gentle sister to her. Do not compound her folly by carrying vengeance or anger in your young heart, and refrain from discord. It is unchristian, and she is your sister. I know you can be full of spleen, like your father, but I have written to Mary, and she knows my mind.'*

Mother wrote that she had begged my father, in tears, to bring my sister home immediately, and he had agreed he would. Having recently been appointed to the Privy Council he wanted no lewd gossip. Then he executed a complete volte-face when my uncle Howard stepped in, convincing him that Mary would be better off staying in France since there might be some gain to be had. Grandfather Howard then quarrelled with Mother, advising her to keep out of the fray, saying Marguerite – whom he knew well – was the wisest woman he had ever met and that since she had pleaded so prettily to let Mary stay, it was the least he could do. God forbid he upset the king's sister, and so, as far as he was concerned, there was nothing more to be said. Besides, he cared naught for domestic matters and was far more preoccupied with the prospect of France invading Italy.

I raised my head and thought of Marguerite, feeling a pang of disappointment in her. Whomsoever her brother loved, she loved too, and like her mother could only ever indulge him in all things – sinful or not.

'Finally, Nan, as you can see, I am writing from Eltham. I have not been well and think I may soon return to Hever to recover my health. My prayers are with you both...'

Although concerned for my mother, I could not imagine her tucked away in the quiet of the countryside. And now Queen Katherine was to have another child. Surely, this time, all would go well? My thoughts then turned back to Mary. Let her find her way. I cared not a fig. I was about to travel to the warm south of the Loire valley – and I would see *him* again!

Chapter Six

*'Love stands constant whilst the
world turns.'*

The road to the Loire

The blustery April wind whipped against my face as my hackney tucked her head close to her chest. As she sidestepped and pranced, I did my best to hold her steady, and turning in my saddle, I saw the other girls on their mounts splashing through the stream. The court – some ten thousand people and three thousand horses in all – were not travelling together, but had split up into smaller columns so they could move across the countryside at their own pace. The old and infirm had taken litters, most of the men were on horseback, but many other, less noble folk trudged on foot. The slowest were those transporting supplies such as food, birds, dogs and even exotic animals like lions and a lynx, for Amboise. There had been much for the *grand-maître* to prepare.

'How much farther?' I called out to one of the squires, pushing my hood from my face. The wind carried my words away, and he did not hear. I narrowed my eyes, gazing into the distance at the great train following behind, and saw a cartwheel stuck in the mud. As the men pushed and pulled at the axle, the mules brayed angrily as the grooms tugged at their bridles. Sighing, I gazed up at the grey, leaden sky and felt the drops of rain against my face. One of the French ladies rode up beside me, her hair loose and in disarray from the high wind.

'*Ma foi*!' she cried, 'this weather is bitter! Why could we not continue by barge?'

We turned our skittish horses against the gust of leaves.

'Because I hear the river is too low!' I was almost shouting. 'When we reach Gien the royal barges should be waiting.' The woman wrinkled her nose.

'I do not envy the *prevote de l'hôtel* his task of finding accommodation for this huge amount of people,' she said, gazing around at the great convoy.

Somewhere in the long line, a dogfight had broken out and the sound of vicious snarling snapped in the air.

'Come,' she said, 'we must catch up with the queen.'

Our horses scrambled up the muddy slope and cantered on towards the queen's litter. Its blue and white plumes blew in the gusty wind, and one of its many ribbon streamers slipped loose and fluttered away. The queen put her gloved hand out over the leather door and tried to catch it, but it had flown away. Next to her sat her almoner, Monsieur Laisgre, and the lovely Diane. Madame Louise, a sable draped across her knees, sat opposite with Renée. The little girl appeared bored and rested her head on the side of the litter.

'Why is it so unseasonably cold?' grumbled Louise. 'We should be enjoying the warm sunshine. It is intolerable.'

'My husband cares nothing for the weather and has ridden ahead to hunt,' replied the queen as I rode close to the litter. 'He has even taken his bed so that he can stop where he wills.'

I immediately thought of my sister, for I knew that even now they were probably tumbling together on those silken sheets. I also knew he liked to keep his staff and those who amused him close by, and that meant Clément might be with him, too.

'How far have we travelled, Madame?' I moved my

hackney aside as two gentlemen, in an obvious rush, cantered away in front.

The queen leant out a little and I could see she looked pale and in some discomfort. The faint odour of vomit clung to her, for she had been sick again. On her knees lay the book of romances that she took everywhere, for it had once belonged to her beloved mother.

'About ten leagues, I believe, Anne,' she said, 'for we are approaching Melun – look, you can see the water mills there built high on stilts along the river.'

I peered ahead to the arched bridges topped by strange wooden constructions.

'And do you see the lamprey nets? There will be a fine catch today.'

'Madame, is the valley of the River Loire very beautiful?' I followed her finger as it pointed.

'Ah, Anne, you will soon see!' smiled the queen, giving a slight belch and settling back against the cushion. 'The valley is low lying, full of ancient forests, and châteaux of creamy-coloured stone. It has a great abundance of wildfowl and game. Is that not so, Monsieur?'

Her almoner looked up. 'Indeed, Madame, the Loire itself is wide and unhurried and brings life to the land, making it green and fruitful for the vines. The sandy soil is perfect for growing vegetables, and the orchards have the best cherries in all of France.'

'And mushrooms!' Renée raised her head.

'To Marguerite's great joy,' he agreed, closing his prayer book, 'for they are grown in the caves along the banks of the River Samur. However, tonight we shall enjoy fine eel for supper, for they eat the flour that falls into the water from the mills and it makes them taste very good indeed. They will satisfy your craving, Madame. We might even finish our meal with succulent melon.'

It all sounded quite wonderful.

'We shall stay,' he said, 'at Melun for a while and then

progress farther south, where you shall see for yourself the pleasures that await you.' He smiled at the queen and her face lit up.

'Anne,' she said, 'the month of May is quite the most perfect time to visit Blois, for it is a riot of cherry blossom. It has a terrace, which my mother named the 'Breton Perch,' for it is there that her trusty Breton guard would wait to accompany her wherever she went – perched on their terrace, like pigeons. The bridge from the terrace crosses the city ramparts, and there are ten hectares of gardens on three levels. I cannot wait to show you my beautiful orangery, pears, and plums trees. The greengage plum has been imported from the Orient and nurtured in Touraine. I hope t –'

'I detest the place,' interrupted Louise, pulling the sable over her knees, 'for it is there that I was once spied upon and kept practically prisoner when Louis married *that* woman. Worse still, it is there that I nearly lost my life.'

'What happened, my lady?' I noticed the queen's face cloud at the reference to her beloved mother.

'The ceiling to my chamber collapsed one sultry, July day as I lay resting from the heat. It was terrifying! My dwarf ran in, raised the alarm, and Monsieur Desbrules carried me to safety. To them and the Virgin, I owe my life. As for my little dog, he was crushed to death.'

'But with God's protection, you are here with us today,' added the queen quietly.

Madame Louise glanced at her with disdain. 'Was I not destined to see my son crowned king?' she asked coldly. 'But I still do not like Blois, even though Louis made his court there. I never will. I prefer my own home at Romorantin where I do not suffer the ague, although the disturbance from the workmen re-building the old palace tries me. I also have my beloved tapestries from Paris. Such beauty gives me solace.'

'Speaking of ague, Madame,' said the queen, 'they say there is a pestilence in Italy, and I fear so for my husband.

Should anything befall him I –'

Louise snorted: 'I forbid harm to befall him. It is his destiny to be master of Italy, and he is hungry for glory, although the English council is convinced that my son will not cross the Alps.

'War is a glorious thing,' I said, half to myself, remembering the fêtes and banquets at Lille, where I had accompanied Margaret of Savoy in her train of young *demoiselles*.

'Is it?' Louise peered out at me. 'Did you hear, Monsieur, how that Wolsey fellow has the effrontery to say that should my son mistreat with him, sixty thousand men will invade France within eight days?'

The almoner sighed. 'I heard some such rumour, Madame, but he does all with the love and connivance of his king. That said, Wolsey is telling the pope that no man is fit to deal with the king, only himself, and he has persuaded the pope to send gold to the Switzers. He rules England in truth – *Ipse Rex* – for no one in that realm dare attempt aught in opposition to his interests – or ours.'

'Possibly,' said Louise, 'for I hear that his heart is bent towards a French alliance, but I am disappointed to find that Archduchess Margaret has also promised victuals to the Switzers should they need assistance.'

I thought of Margaret.

'And what of Albany?' she continued.

'As you are aware, Madame, Wolsey was not best pleased to hear that the Duke of Albany is sailing from France for Scotland to take over the regency there. It is obvious that since the death of King James at Flodden, Queen Margaret Tudor's infant son, James, cannot rule, and as Albany is Admiral of France and the next heir, it is fitting he should go. It is fortunate for us that of all the Tudors, Margaret is the most foolish, since by marrying the Earl of Angus – against her council's express orders – and naming him co-regent, she has stirred up jealousy and faction among her nobles.'

'Both of King Henry's sisters are foolish, but still, they have played right into French hands,' said Louise.

'The Venetian ambassador writes to King Henry that François has only sent Albany to Scotland to butcher the queen and her young babe so that he can be master there.'

'So I hear, Monsieur, and I gather the Duke of Suffolk is furious, since a regent with French interests so close to home, is not what he desired'.

'Talking of the duke,' said the queen, 'I hear that he wishes to bring his daughter, Anne Brandon, back from the court at Mechelen. There is the suggestion of placing her here in France if Queen Katherine will not take her. Anne, you were maids together, would you recommend her?'

I pushed aside a low branch and thought of the little girl. I would have loved to see her again and said she would make a charming companion.

'Then we shall wait and see if the duke writes,' the queen continued, 'and I will welcome yet another Anne.'

'Christ's nails, I'll have none of his brood on French soil!' exclaimed Louise, making Renée start.

Queen Claude lowered her eyes and the smile vanished from her pale face. 'Then *Madame ma mère,* I see I must wait until I am actually crowned queen, and then order my household as I see fit.'

∙   ∘

Although May was upon us, the weather did not improve greatly, and we spent much of our time inside the château at Melun, busying ourselves with sewing, and mending the torn gowns that had been damaged on the journey. The queen's keeper of the wardrobe, Monsieur Normain, despaired at the ruined silk.

We heard that in England, the king had finally relented and allowed his sister, the dowager French queen, and the Duke of Suffolk to set sail from Calais to Dover. To their great comfort my Lord Wolsey and other courtiers – the

Howards not among them – met them there, but on the journey to Lord Bergavenny's house at Birling, the good people of England pelted the duke with mud. It was hardly a good start, but at least the king appeared pleased to see his favourite sister and closest friend, Charles, arrive safely home.

Meanwhile, we saw little of François or his party and watched as Doctor West waited patiently for an audience to discuss the payment of the dowager French queen's money, into the English coffers. Every morning he paced the château terrace, becoming more and more irritated, but François preferred to hunt and only returned occasionally late at night to talk with his wife. She, of course, was ecstatic, but I knew that in the early hours as she slept, he slipped from her chamber and went to my sister's bed. I longed to talk to Mary, but our paths did not cross, and I would have to wait until we reached Blois. There, I hoped, I would see Clément again.

When we continued our journey to Égreville, a great hail storm destroyed some of the baggage train, including the gowns we had only just repaired. Such rain had not been seen for years, and we were forced to stop for shelter for two days in the woods under hurriedly erected canopies. Although the rain lashed down, the River Yonne still lay too low for the barges, and yet again we took to our horses and litters, making our way to the imposing château at Montargis for shelter and rest.

On the twelfth day of May, with the early morning mist cleared, we clattered over the great bridge at Gien. The lovely château belonging to *Madame la Grande*, Comtesse de Gien, sat proudly on its promontory on the edge of the *Forêt d'Orléans*, the May sunshine sparkling on its golden weathervanes and pointed turrets. I marvelled at the many glass panes as they glinted, for I had heard that the comtesse had wanted a residence, not a castle, and the red and black brick – laid in so many different patterns – gave it great charm and warmth. I watched as Louise, now on horseback, trotted before me and I wondered what she might be thinking as we crossed the twelve arches that spanned the wide river. Having an affair with the husband of the daughter of *Madame la Grande* seemed a strange way to repay the woman who had done so much to teach her the ways of the French court, and how to be humble in all things.

We stayed twelve days at Gien and while we were there we heard that a third wedding for the dowager French queen and the Duke of Suffolk had taken place at the Palace of Placentia, in the presence of King Henry, Queen Katherine and all the nobles. The new duchess, we were told, felt grateful to Queen Katherine, for she had played no small part in encouraging her husband to be lenient to the newly-wedded couple, and a great masque and tournament were held in their honour. At the tournament, the duke in green velvet and cloth of gold, had valiantly seen off all comers, and my uncle, furious at the way matters had turned out, only glowered and vented his spleen at my father. Arms folded, he had leant on a post by the lists, growling under his breath like a whipped dog.

The news made Queen Claude laugh, which was good to see, for thus far she had felt the strain of her pregnancy, and her back ached day and night giving her no rest. Her sickness should have passed, but it continued and she could only pick at her food and offer titbits to her dwarf. We also heard that the Duke of Albany had landed at Dunbarton, in Scotland, and that Queen Margaret rode out from Edinburgh castle in full state to meet him. He refused to throw off his French ways, and it was not the best of starts.

As the weather improved, we were able to sit out on the terrace but as I read to the queen, she appeared listless, a distant look in her eyes. I paused and laid down *The Ship of Virtuous Women* – one of her favourite books – but she took no heed. Even Renée could not cheer her as she played with her doll and dressed its hair, or poked at the bright, green lizards basking in the sunshine. *Madame la Grande* tried to discuss the gardens but had little response. Diane and I discovered that the queen's low spirits were due to Madame Louise. She had maliciously warned her that since her body was ill-formed, there might be difficulties with the birth and she must take great care. God knows, Louise had said, carrying a child was hard enough with a strong body such as her own – but with Claude's feeble frame? The child might be deformed like herself. The queen feared the effect that this would have on François, since the Prince must be perfect in every way like his father. What Louise did not say, thank God, was that most of the court assumed she would die in childbirth. So suspiciously adamant were they, that ambassadors mentioned in their despatches to King Henry that they thought poison had been prepared to murder her, should all not go well. Thus, François would be free to marry again.

Needless to say, the queen sank into a black dolour. She sat with the bottom lace loosened on the front of her gown, sipping at her ginger-infused cordial, for her digestion was troublesome, and gazed across the river into the distance. We all knew what she searched for, as did the frustrated Doctor West. It was the royal banner and it did not appear. She tried to accept that François had ridden away with his gentlemen and favourite ladies hunting the boar, but sometimes he disappeared for days on end, and she longed for his company. However, the more I watched her, the more I felt afraid that something else might be amiss, for she gazed at me with something akin to pity. Although loving as ever, something in her demeanour made me feel very uneasy. It would not be long before I was to discover the reason.

•   ◦

The royal barge, pennants fluttering in the breeze, sailed lazily along the wide River Loire, past the town of Orléans, and towards Blois. In the distance, I would catch the shimmering glimpse of a château turret, or strange cave-dwelling hewn into the rocks by the riverbank. The weather had mellowed, and now everyone enjoyed the warmth of the sun. It could not have been more idyllic with the sky above as blue as Our Lady's mantle. The king had insisted on his musicians playing, and the noise attracted the town officials who came to greet him in their flat-bottomed boats, all bobbing on the glinting water.

François sat with his wife, mother, sister, and Renée in the first barge, a great silver salamander standing proud on the bow, its feet raised and tail curled. As the liveried oarsmen rowed on in perfect unison, each pull of the oars took them smoothly down the river towards the château. The queen smiled beneath the embroidered silk canopy, waving at the people on the riverbank who had come to cheer their new king and his queen and throw their caps in the air. Cries of '*Vive le Roi!*' resounded from the banks as the king tossed baskets of coins towards them and many waded into the water to grab them. I sat with Anne de Pisseleu, a beautiful child with vibrant blue eyes and golden hair, and Diane, looking as pretty as ever. As a contrast, I had hoped to show off my dark hair, but the queen did not think it fitting for young girls to be seen as such, and it was plaited and coiled beneath a cap. Louise's *demoiselles* wore their hair loose, crimped and bejewelled, and I felt dull in comparison. As I took a cherry from the silver bowl on Anne's knee, she suddenly grabbed my sleeve.

'Look – Anne, look! See, the gentleman in the blue striped barge?'

I twisted around and then quickly turned back.

Diane lent forward.

'It is *him!*' I hissed, almost choking on the cherry stone. 'Oh, what do I do?'

The barge drifted up beside our own, and I wanted to flee but had nowhere to go.

'Ladies, please, stop turning about,' said Madame d'Assigny. Her hideous pet monkey clung to her neck and let out a squeal. 'All eyes are upon you, and it is most improper. For shame!'

The oarsmen stopped rowing and the barge bobbed and lilted in the swell of the lapping water.

'Good day, sweet ladies!' came a cry, as the gentlemen doffed their caps. 'Sister, dear! How divine you look today – the hue of the lily becomes you.'

A gentleman blew a kiss to Françoise, and we all sniggered as her cheeks turned pink. One of the men then placed his foot upon the bow of the barge and tossed a posy to me. It landed on my lap, and I held it up to my nose.

'Oh!' I spied something tucked into the blooms. Madame d'Assigny eyed me suspiciously, but I placed the posy by my side.

The gentlemen in the barge clasped their hands to their hearts and pretended to swoon, but my eyes were fixed on Clément. He lay back languidly against a cushion, finger to his lip as if deep in thought, perusing me with interest. For a brief second, I held his gaze, and he smiled, giving a slight nod of his head, making my heart race a little. His barge then pulled away.

'Anne,' I whispered, excitedly, as Madame d'Assigny spoke to one of the other women. 'There is a note in the posy.'

She turned her bright face towards me.

'Look, the paper is folded, but I dare not open it here.'

'But you must!' she said.

I turned away from the prying eyes of Madame d'Assigny and opened the note with trembling hands. I read the elegant script:

> *'My dearest Anne, I have not been able to put such a winsome creature from my mind since we first met. Your dark eyes have captured my heart, and it lies bound in chains. Tonight there will be a feast to celebrate the king's preparations for war. Will you do me the honour*

of dancing with me if I dare to ask such a favour? I hear
you are the most accomplished dancer of all the young
maids at court. Until then, my heart commends itself to
you, your servant ever, Clément.'

I hid the note down the front of my gown and steadied my rapid breathing. He had said my eyes had captured his heart! No-one had ever said that to me before; it was only ever said to my sister. She was the lovely one who stole all the compliments, with her soft brown eyes and seductive looks. At that moment, as trumpets sounded and crowds of courtiers ran to the water's edge to greet the royal family, I felt beside myself with excitement and just had to find my sister to share my news.

● ●

The horses carried our litter across the *port-cote*, around the *basse-cour* with its double line of guards, through the arch of the *salles des guards,* and round towards the Château of Blois. At the magnificent archway, I shielded my eyes from the brilliant sunlight and stared up at the stone statue of King Louis XII. The sun glinted off the bejewelled trappings of his destrier and beneath, the device of the porcupine lay set between the initials '*L*' and '*A*' in lapis lazuli.

'That is how I remember my dear father,' said the queen, gazing up, 'a noble warrior full of vigour, astride his favourite warhorse, Gringolet. Did you know, Renée, on this very spot the Maid of Orléans raised her army?'

Our litter lurched forward through the archway and into the large, cool courtyard of the château. Although wooden scaffolding obscured much of the building, I could still see that it had a homely charm and the queen told me that here her father had been at his most relaxed. In the middle of the courtyard stood a very large column that appeared to be made of jasper, decorated with idols of antiquity. On top stood a statue of a child bearing a torch, and the queen explained that this statue represented the union of Louis and Anne, bringing light and peace to all of France. The château itself, built from red brick and stone, appeared a mix of flamboyant golden archways, square pillars and balconies, with stair towers at either end to service the galleries. Every inch of carved stone made a dizzy array of colour, and every arch and column bore the initials '*L*' and '*A*' alongside the devices of the *fleurs-de-lis*, porcupine, looped *cordelière* and ermine.

Having alighted from our litter, we entered the *grande salle* with its barrel-vaulted ceiling and arcade of columns adorned again with *fleurs-de-lis* and ermine tails. I followed Diane and Françoise de Foix as they held up Claude's train with the help of Madame de Tournan. Madame Louise held Marguerite's arm, and in her other, she carried a small, brown yapping dog. *Madame la Grande* pushed in front with her daughter, Suzanne, and I noticed Louise lower her eyes.

As we fell into place behind her, I saw that the Duc de Bourbon, Constable of France, and his entourage, were waiting to greet the queen. I could not help but stare about at the vastness of the chamber, and the dazzling array of crimson and gold decoration. I had been told that here, audiences, balls and great masques were held for up to seven hundred guests, and its arched windows let in a beautiful, soft light. There were tapestries depicting Alexander the Great, scenes from Troy and golden pillars; old Louis' love of Italy could be seen in the decoration of putti, angels and magical beasts. Even the great candelabra appeared to be of Italianate design.

As we gathered, I heard a loud commotion from behind our party and the king himself burst in with a crowd of gentlemen. My eyes searched in vain for Clément.

'Ah! Greetings my good Duc, gentlemen.' François turned to his companion and handed him his hazel switch. 'Tis *true*, I tell you, on the faith of a gentleman, that hound there – the white one – but yesterday caught a heron, and dragged it to the ground in front of me. I saw it with my own eyes.'

'We believe you, sire,' said one of the gentleman.

'Such a shame the meat is so unpalatable,' continued François. 'Well, the Comte de Chalon assures me that the *chiens blancs* cannot be faulted for bravery, and work better in packs than the grey.' He then turned to the aged Florimond Robertet. 'As to the reds, why my brave Myrault here is not old, and there is not a horse that will not break his neck trying to follow him.' He slapped the excited dog on the back. 'I shall take him with me to Italy – 'tis you, my friend, who is decrepit!'

A loud chorus of laughter rose up, led by Florimond himself.

The king then draped his arm around the shoulders of the Duc de Bourbon, and called for wine as his beloved hounds barked and dashed about, pissing against the stone pillars.

'And talking of hunting, where is the leopard you promised me, Charles?' He punched him playfully. 'I want to see for myself how quickly the beast can bring a quarry down, for they say they are faster than lightning.'

I noticed Renée move nervously behind her sister's gown, unsettled by the big, boisterous dogs with their furiously wagging tails.

Bourbon bowed as François then asked what progress had been made in finding a suitable location to build a new hunting château.

'Sire, the area around the old lodge at Chambord is thick with forests and wildlife, and I think it would suit you very well,' said his friend. 'Perhaps we could survey the area with your architect, Signore di Cortone, when we return from Italy?'

'Nothing too grand, eh?' François whispered, with a wink. 'Suitable for intimate parties? Ha! I am only teasing, my friend, it must be magnificent.'

The queen proffered a faint smile as François then engaged Bourbon and Bayard in conversation, and the pages scurried forth with refreshments.

Leaving the king with his companions, the royal ladies walked up the winding stone staircase of the *logis neuf* towards the royal apartments. I stared up at the beautiful painted ceiling and the tapestries displaying pastoral scenes. The sun, pouring in from every window, lit up the glazed tiled floor and gilded fireplaces, highlighting their carved royal devices. Not a single surface remained uncovered. Every few steps, a liveried gentleman bowed, and the queen stopped to exchange a few kind words. As one old man kissed her hand, tears in his eyes, I could see how her people loved her. She patted the man's hand and put something into it, closing his bony fingers.

'We must never forget,' she said, smiling at Renée, 'that much work is done to prepare for our stay. If we have not visited for a while, everything has to come out of storage, including pictures, tapestries and furnishings, and I do not like to be a burden to these good people. Many were servants of my mother, and I shall always remember their care for her. That is why I keep the town of Blois free from taxes, and my husband agrees that although *Madame Taille* is most lucrative, I will not have it here.'

The ladies about her clapped in approval at her generosity, and the queen gave a shy smile. I then remembered hearing how her wet nurse, Charlotte Pele, had received a generous pension, and her governess, Perrette de Las, given the right to the revenues from Blois for ten years in thanks for her loyal service. Baron Semblançay, the Minister of Finance, had been somewhat alarmed at the generosity of these gifts, but the queen had stood firm. She then turned to me.

'Did you know, Anne, that Renée was born here, and that I gave my husband this château as a gift? Blois instead of Brittany is a poor exchange, I know. Perhaps that is why Madame Louise does not like this place.'

We continued to the queen's apartments, which, I was told, had belonged to her mother and it was here that she had died. Finally, we reached a smaller, more intimate bedchamber. Queen Claude took a seat in a high backed chair, beneath a golden canopy, while Madame de Tournan placed a cushion embroidered with the arms of Brittany, beneath her swollen feet. We maids then began to unpack the great trunks and baskets of gowns that had arrived, and hung them high on the curtained rails to air and allow the creases to fall out. Claude watched as she unfastened her gloves.

'My dear husband has written to the Marchioness of Mantua to ask her what fashions they are wearing in Italy at present, and she replied that everyone is mad for devices. Flaming torches, animals, mythical beasts are all to be seen embroidered on the ladies' gowns. She says it is fashionable to display these secret meanings. What say you, Renée, what device would you wear?'

The girl ran to the queen and put her arms around her.

'A beast with prickly spikes like papa,' she said, shyly.

The queen laughed and kissed her hair as her dwarf, Marie, entered the chamber. Today she had decided to dress as a Turk in a strange, billowing coat.

'Ah, sweet sister, the porcupine of Orléans. But why not a pearl in honour of dear Marguerite?'

'Or a marigold?' offered Renée, looking up.

'No, no, a Piddlybed,' said Marie, hands on her hips as she surveyed the scene. 'Your device should be a Piddlybed.'

'Oh, really!' cried the queen, 'a dandelion, indeed. But what of Madame Louise's device of four wings tied by a cord – a symbol of destiny?'

Renée wrinkled her nose and shook her head.

'Then what of my coming babe, what device should he have, for I do believe I carry a *dauphin*.' As she spoke, she pointed to a golden cradle, draped in green damask, standing on one side of the chamber.

'A bird!' cried Renée.

The queen laughed.

'Birds, indeed, are in fashion, as the marchioness is

aware. She is such a captivating woman, and everywhere she goes, women rush to see what she is wearing. Her beauty advice is sought all over Europe, and I have asked her to send some scented hand cream to me. She promises she will, but she is very guarded about her beauty secrets.'

She gave a wince as she shifted in her chair. 'Now, ladies, Signor Francesco Grossi, the Mantuan envoy, has said he will bring me some fabric samples and we shall have the finest gowns made up in Lyon. The city has already paid six thousand livres in taxes for the coming war, so we will buy their silks to compensate. My husband wishes to know everything that is worn by the Italian ladies from chemises, to sleeves and headdresses.'

I caught the eye of one of the ladies and knew her thoughts exactly. Of course, he did – François would demand that his favourite women dressed in a style to complement his coming campaign. Surely the queen knew this? I had heard that the purchase of the château of Blois had cost old Louis two hundred thousand livres – the exact amount that François had spent on one bolt of fabric for his women. I instantly felt disgruntled at my sister. Here was I, hanging up gowns, running hither and thither, while she, no doubt, sat perfumed and pampered awaiting a visit from the king. As I moved away, the queen caught my hand.

'Anne, please fetch the holy water from my oratory – it is just through that door. You cannot miss it, for the bowl has seven large diamonds and seven rubies and was a gift to my mother from my father. It is of great value, so please have a care.'

I curtsied and walked through to the private chapel. Candles flickered, and gules of light from the beautiful stained glass windows fell across the floor like pools of blood. However, before the statue of Our Lord on the small altar, there stood – nothing. I looked around but saw no bowl and nothing of any value, just a wooden statue of Our Lord and a crucifix. Then, in horror, I remembered my sister's words.

Could François have sold it?

•   •

Our tasks completed, Queen Claude made ready to receive her husband for their afternoon audience, and we maids were allowed to explore the château. I immediately took Anne de Pisseleu by the hand.

'You must view the gardens,' said Madame d'Assigne, over her shoulder, as she carried a tray of food to the queen, 'for they are famous all over France and are quite captivating. You will have to cross the ravine to enter the passageway, so be sure to be back in time for tonight's preparations – and do not scuff your slippers on the gravel!'

As we walked, I gazed in wonder at the stuffed stag heads, wooden dogs and falcons – all once favourites of old Louis – lining the length of the gloomy passageway. We were glad to reach the warm sunshine, where there before us lay the most beautiful sight I had ever seen. An enchanted garden, enclosed by trellis-covered galleries – so long a horse might have galloped their length – with row upon row of pink blossoming cherry trees. There were wonderful vegetable gardens and flower borders with peacocks strutting about, their tails shimmering in the sunlight. In the middle distance stood a magnificent marble fountain inside a wooden pavilion, topped with a great statue of St Michael.

'Quick, quick, let us pick some flowers,' said Anne, as we wandered down towards the fountain.

When we had approached a little nearer, Anne plucked an iris and offered it to me. 'Anne?'

I ignored her and stared ahead, rooted to the spot.

'Mary?' I asked quietly.

'Mary who?' the girl replied, her back to the pavilion.

'My sister,' I said.

The young girl spun around to look.

'Mary!' I called, running down the gravel path.

As I reached her, my sister disappeared behind a tree.

'No, Nan! Go away, I do not want anyone to see me like this, I look frightful.'

'But where have you been, what is the matter?

'What is it?' asked Anne, as she hurried towards me.

My sister moved around the tree again.

'Anne, leave us, I said.'

The girl stood still, curious.

'Go and pick some blossom for the queen's chamber, but do not forget you are helping to dress me later.'

She gave a little shrug and I watched as she walked away, reaching up to pluck more blossom. She disappeared far down the path and out of hearing.

'Sister,' I began, 'tell me what is wrong. We are alone now, please look at me.'

Mary stood hunched and sullen.

'Mary?'

Nothing.

'Look at me!' I cried.

She turned slowly. She wore no jewels but a simple pale, sea-green gown, and her hair had fallen loose from its coiled plaits and ribbon. She pushed a thick strand from out of her blood-shot eyes and glanced at me.

'Hateful, hateful bastard.'

'Who?' I asked, fearing the answer.

'Who do you think?'

'Well, I assume we are talking about François here?'

She nodded and gave a great blow into the piece of cloth clenched in her damp hand.

'Tired of me,' came the muffled response.

'Well, how predictable,' I said wearily. 'You said he would never tire, *he* said he would never tire – and guess what? He has tired of you. What did I tell you? What made you think you could ever compete with the brilliant women around him?'

'Not all are brilliant, Nan,' she said.

'Well, obviously!' I snapped. We stared at each other in

silence. 'So, what will you do? Will you stay here or ask to return home?'

She shrugged. 'I do not know, Nan. Louise promised that any woman who once pleased her son could expect a good marriage, so I was hoping to stay and...' Her voice trailed off.

'Well, has she someone in mind?'

She shook her head.

'Oh, *Mary*, of course she hasn't!' I wanted to put my arms about her, but I was afraid that I might shake the foolish girl instead. 'Did he give you anything? A château, money? What about the Arab horse he promised you?'

'It never appeared,' she said.

'But he gave you jewels? I saw you wearing them. What about the gold neck chain?'

'Madame Louise took it back – you know how avaricious she is. I only have the gown I am wearing.'

I stared at her in disbelief. 'So he has abandoned you. When was it?'

Mary sighed 'At the hunting lodge at Melun. All was well at first. We rode out, we hunted the boar, his favourite saker on his arm, but then he preferred to ride ahead with just one or two other ladies. In the evening, when I sat with him, he barely spoke or acknowledged my presence until at midnight when, having drunk heartily, he would rise unsteadily, take my hand and pull me towards his chamber.' She turned to me in despair. 'He is ruining my looks! See the lines about my eyes from crying.'

In truth, she appeared no different to me, just dishevelled.

'And?'

'Oh, Nan, I believed everything he said, and when he said he adored me, I wanted to please him. I did whatever he asked and refused him nothing, but as the days wore on, he came to me less and less. He was either too busy talking about the coming war, or disappeared hunting before I had even awoken – sometimes he did not return to our lodge at all. I do not know where he went.'

I knew. He had returned to his wife for some intelligent conversation.

'God, I wish with all my heart I had conceived a child with him, for perhaps then things might have been different.'

'Mary, his wife is pregnant. Why would he want *your* bastard?'

'Yes, but with the king's child, I would have some position at the court.' She stared sulkily into the distance. 'I knew he was tiring of me when *she* came along, all sloe eyes and ambition. I am sure they are having an affair but none believe it. Well, *I* know. I have seen him wearing her colours. So you were right. How can I compete with a woman who speaks Latin fluently and writes poetry?'

She began to tidy up her hair and I watched her, shocked.

'Not Anne de Graville?' I handed her a dropped hairpin.

'No, that Châteaubriant bitch,' she mumbled, the pin in her mouth.

'Françoise de Foix?'

She nodded.

'My God, the poor queen, how does she suffer it?' I said.

'How do *I* suffer it!' cried Mary. 'He did not mind his wife knowing about *me*, but with that woman, it is different. He worships her from afar as if she were the Madonna. Why is that?'

'Mary, you were not his mistress, just a brief diversion. He was never going to admit you to his circle of women.'

I wanted to add that Françoise de Foix had breeding and intelligence, having been raised at the court of Anne of Brittany. Happily married, she had a child, and – more importantly – the backing of a powerful family. Her brothers could serve the king, in more ways than one, for by bribing them with favours and positions, he no doubt hoped to seduce their sister.

'Is he serious about her?' I asked.

'One of his friends says he is becoming more smitten by the day. He has ordered her a gown worth one hundred and fifty thousand livres, and even his beloved sister designs jewels for him to tempt her with. They say she loves her husband, but she will still succumb, you wait and see.'

I asked if the queen knew.

'She knows that her husband has already tired of *me*.'

I then understood why the queen had appeared so ill at ease in my presence. She must have felt sorry for me – or embarrassed. Which was worse?

'I shall win him back,' said Mary, her voice defiant. 'I shall not hide away in shame but make him desire me again. I pushed that simpering Gaudin girl out of the way, and I will do the same with Françoise.' Her eyes blazed. 'If I cannot push her out of the way I shall tell François that he has competition for her affection, and he won't like that.'

'You will do no such thing! Besides, do you think he really cares?' I asked angrily.

She pouted. 'He will care when he finds out that his close friend, Seigneur de Bonnivet, is the one sniffing after Françoise. Anyway, *I* care not, Nan. Now let us return. I need to cool my face to get rid of the blotches before tonight.'

As we walked back in silence down the path, I wanted to feel sorry for my sister, but I could not.

'It doesn't suit you,' said Mary, glancing at me.

'The queen insists,' I replied, knowing that she referred to the Breton hood which did not become my oval face.

'Have you heard from home?' she changed the subject. 'No-one ever writes to me.'

'Of course, letters arrive via the despatches – Mother tells me that everyone is well and George is still talking about the court and how much he loved the pageants last Christmas. I cannot believe our little brother is twelve years old. Uncle Edward married – did you hear? He finally settled on that Tempest girl whom nobody likes, except Dame Margot. Talking of our grandmother, I hear she keeps forgetting things, and Mother says she is losing her mind.'

Mary pulled a face. 'Does Tom Wyatt write?'

'Not much, for he is too busy studying at St John's College, Cambridge. As to the court, there are rumours that Queen Katherine is with child again. No-one is allowed to speak of it and the queen herself remains silent.'

'What a bore,' sighed Mary.

'Anne Brandon is now at the English court, although I had hoped she would come here to France. Queen Katherine said she was most desirous of seeing her and sent Sir Edward Guildford over to Mechelen to fetch her back to Placentia. She is such a sweet-natured girl. Oh, and Mother writes that the May Day celebrations at Greenwich were the finest she had ever attended. Twenty-five damsels on white palfreys attended the queen, and twenty-five thousand people watched the procession.'

'What a sight it must have been!'

'Mother mentions other matters, but she is more concerned about you.'

Mary cast her eyes down.

'But what of your news, Nan? What have you been up to?'

I reached up, snapped a sprig of cherry blossom from one of the trees and placed it in the front of my gown. I spun around and smiled at Mary's blotched face, feeling immense satisfaction.

'Oh, I have been up to lots of things,' I said, teasingly, 'and tonight I wish to look my best for someone *very* special.'

Mary's face brightened. 'You? Oh, do tell!' she cried.

I started to run ahead and called back to her over my shoulder. 'Wait and see! Your sweet, clever little sister has an admirer of her own.'

•   •

'Oh, make it stay up!' I cried in despair.

'I am trying to, my lady,' replied my maid, 'but please keep still. Your hair is so thick and heavy it tumbles back down.'

As the rest of the excited girls preened and fussed, the chamberers brought forth sleeves and caps, everyone jostling each other for the burnished mirror. With my hair coiled up for the fifth time and secured into place, my maid carefully wound in a grey ribbon. Finally, Anne de Pisseleu handed my maid a silver-netted cap, and she placed it over my hair.

'Anne – do you think I am comely?' I asked, anxiously, of Anne de Graville. 'I mean, like this? Would my hair not be better loose? Do men not prefer a maid's hair to fall free? After all, I am not promised or married.'

'Of course they do, and it is a shame to hide it so, but you know the queen prefers our hair covered in the Breton style. She still wishes her maids to follow the modest fashion of her mother's day, saying that if a gentleman were to gaze upon the hair, it could lead to him harbour lustful thoughts.'

I sighed, for that is exactly what I had been hoping for.

'Come, Nan, you know what she is like, forever saying matters were so much better in her mother's day when maids were thus attired. It was not so of course. On the good side, it makes you appear sophisticated and with your heart-shaped face and these –' here she took the amethyst earrings from my hot hands and fastened them into my ear lobes – 'you look enticing. All melting dark eyes and long, white neck.' She kindly did not mention my flat, underdeveloped breasts.

'But my nail,' I whispered, 'I must keep it hidden.' I took off the ring to make it appear less noticeable and tugged down my puffed and banded sleeves. 'If these sleeves were wider I could tuck my hand away,' I said, studying the reflection in the mirror to see the effect. 'Look, if I pull them lower, thus – what do you think?'

'It is hardly noticeable, and there is no time to fuss about it now.' She fastened the clasp of a fine chain around my slender neck and placed her cool hands on either side of my shoulders. She smiled. 'There – you are done. A triumph.' She then moved away to get ready herself and I sat staring into the mirrored glass.

Was I comely? I had certainly noticed young men glancing my way and smiling when I followed behind Claude. And I was never short of partners in any dance, yet it was said that without fair hair there is no charm. Anne de Graville had blonde hair with brown eyes that sparkled full of fire, arched eyebrows, a high forehead and a smile both inviting and spiritual. The fair Diane had the most translucent, pale complexion I had ever seen. How could I compete? Staring at my reflection, I observed my sallow, oval face, pointed chin, large dark eyes with thick lashes, and well-formed brows. On the good side, my expressive, mobile features were considered charming. Plus, I was the perfect age to attract men, and I decided that I must learn how to use what I had to good effect. I eyed the pots of rouge and lip stain on the table in front of me and opened one. I dabbed it on my lips – just the faintest touch – and my lips came alive. Full and red, they were ready for kissing. Perfect.

At that moment, my sister Mary leant towards the mirror to fasten her earrings. They were the pair that mother had sent her. She looked at me in the mirror.

'You cannot wear that,' she said, nodding towards the pot. 'You look foolish, and the queen will not allow it. You know she forbids such artifice.'

'You are wearing rouge *and* lip stain,' I countered.

'Yes, but I am older, and Louise insists her ladies look alluring for her son – anything to set us apart from the queen's dull entourage.'

'So you are to stay at her court then?'

'For the moment.' She winced as she jabbed at her earlobe with the awkward earring.

As I stared at her, I thought she did not look like the Mary I knew. With her pink colouring, rouge on her cheeks was hardly necessary, and her primrose yellow gown appeared far too low at the front, showing her highly trussed bosom. The shoulders, edged with gold, were pulled down and her chemisette of white lawn lay open not tied. She, too, had coiled up her hair, but left a tantalising strand loose at the back, so that it tumbled down to her waist. She smelt of amber and, frankly, looked like a courtesan.

'Ladies!' It was Madame d'Assigny, clapping her hands and strutting about like a ruffled pigeon. 'Quickly, quickly, we are summoned.' She then pulled me to one side and ordered me to wipe my face clean.

In the *grande salle,* the king sat with his wife on one side, and his sister on the other. Madame Louise appeared deep in conversation with the ambassador from the Low Countries, Monsieur Jean Jouglet, and laughed heartily. *Madame la Grande* sat perusing the large crowd of guests, drumming her fingers on the chair arm. To the right, sat the king's gentlemen and friends. Although the pillars were obscuring my view, if I moved slightly, I could just see Clément, deep in conversation with his companion, dressed in dark-blue velvet, his hair glossy beneath a bonnet devoid of feathers. When he saw me, he raised his glass, in acknowledgement. My stomach tumbled as I lowered my eyes and tried to hide my smile.

'You must eat something, or you will faint in this heat,' advised Anne de Graville, leaning towards me. 'You will need your strength for the dancing and leaping about.'

I picked at a piece of fine, manchet bread, but I could barely chew it. When, oh, when would the dancing begin? I started to feel uneasy, aware that my sister was becoming more raucous in her laughter by the minute. She did not take her eyes off the king but watched him constantly over the rim of her glass. I glared at her, and she pulled a face in defiance as she held up the glass to be refilled. Eventually, the king called for the tables to be moved back and the great chequered tiled floor to be cleared, ready for the entertainment. I barely watched the jugglers, fire-eaters and fools tumbling about the *salle* in their gaudy coloured costumes – my eyes were only on Clément. When I did turn away, I saw my sister clapping wildly to the pipes and tabors, people staring at her exuberance. Flushed and excited, she began weaving her way in and out of the nobles, occasionally whispering something to them and laughing. Their wives glared at her, but she seemed oblivious to their sullen faces and mutterings. Gillette tugged my sleeve.

'For God's sake, your sister is drunk,' she said. 'Do something.'

'Do *what*?' I asked, aware of the embarrassment that Mary appeared to be causing.

Louise of Savoy watched like a hawk from the dais and glanced at her son. He also sat watching Mary as she approached one of the gentlemen and took his arm, her hair now completely tumbled loose, just as she intended. The nobleman, aware of the stares from his angry wife, tried to step away, but Mary seemed determined to entangle him. François smiled at his mother, but she only whispered something to the woman standing behind her. I then watched as the lady pushed through the crowd to where my sister began annoying yet another young gallant. Mary turned and stared at the woman, and then swayed slightly as she was manhandled to the side of the *salle*. She became agitated, and I heard her raised voice, but due to the crowd, I could not see what was happening. I glanced across to Clément and noticed the amused expression on his face. How humiliating!

At that moment, the sackbuts, shawms, and hautboys sounded, and the chamberlain announced the dancing. The king led his sister from the dais to the floor, and the two of them danced the stately *basse danse* together. Such a dance demanded excellent bearing, and to dance it well showed true breeding. Few could dance it like Marguerite, and as she held her brother's hand in affection and tenderness, I noticed that Clément could not take his eyes off her. After they had progressed around the *salle*, the rest of the nobility were invited to join in, and the king returned his sister to her place of honour. Clément made as if to rise, but sat down when he noticed my sister had pulled free from her captor. I felt excruciatingly embarrassed, for there was nothing graceful about the way she wobbled and tried to keep her balance. She even slipped twice and clung to the nearest person's arm in an attempt to recover her poise. What a disgusting display. After what seemed like an age, the dance ended and everyone moved away – all except Mary. As she staggered close to the dais, she sank in front of the king, her breasts heaving seductively over her gown. There was a gasp at her effrontery. How dare she approach the king thus?

'Monseignor,' she panted, unsteadily, raising her glazed eyes to his, 'will – will you do me the honour of dancing the Bourée with me?' François appeared bemused and taking his wife's hand, kissed it tenderly and slowly for all the court to see. The queen's face brightened at the gesture.

'Mademoiselle Boleyn, you must excuse me, but the Bourée is fast and furious. I think you would do well to sit for a moment.'

Mary remained on the cold floor tiles, alone, like a fish stranded on the beach. Madame d'Assigny stepped down to the floor and a tussle ensued as Mary, confused, tried to push her away.

'Oh, my dear Lord,' gasped Anne de Graville, turning to the shocked Diane.

By now people started tittering, and two of the gentlemen ushers quickly removed Mary from the *salle*, calling to the musicians to strike up a tune. They stood bows in hand, looking towards the king, bewildered. I felt I wanted to die. Within moments, Madame de Châtillon hurried over to me.

'Anne, go to your sister. She has been escorted to the maids' chambers.'

I stood up, pushing back the bench. 'Now, Madame? This minute?'

'Immediately, and remain with her for the rest of the night, for we do not want her returning to repeat that dreadful performance. Do you understand?' I watched as she returned to the dais.

'Oh, God, Mary,' I wailed, in despair, 'why, *why* have you done this to me?'

I left the *salle*, head down, and then made my way up the winding stone staircase, incandescent with rage. I stormed through the chambers, brushing aside any who blocked my way, ignoring the stares from the tittering pages. When I reached the maids' chambers, I felt too angry to enter and sat down on the draughty steps, trying not to cry. How *could* she do this, tonight of all nights! I had looked forward to this moment so much, had taken such care with my gown and now – now what would he think? I wished I were back at Mechelen with no Mary to spoil things – and I missed Symonnet. I missed Beatrice. I missed everyone sane. Eventually, I flung open the door and saw Mary sitting in front of the mirror brushing out her hair. The candles flickered in the draught, and their light illuminated her pale face.

'What do *you* want?' she asked, glassy-eyed, glancing at my reflection in the burnished steel.

'Me? Oh, do not trouble yourself about me, Mary!' I said. 'My needs are irrelevant. I am only here to clean up shit after you.'

She put the brush down on her knee, plucking at the bristles, and sat in silence.

'Nan, did I appear foolish just then? It was –'

'Mary,' I interrupted, 'did you see Louise's face? If you were aiming to make an exhibition of yourself in front of the entire court, and in particular the king, then yes – you appeared foolish.'

She twisted round to me, turned the colour of ash, and vomited onto the turkey carpet. The red wine splashed out and it was apparent that she, too, had not eaten. It had not even been watered down.

I called out to the chamberer and she scuttled in.

'Bring water and cloths,' I snapped, covering my nose in

distaste. The child appeared terrified, but I cared not.

Mary stood up, wiping her mouth, and then flopped onto the bed with a groan and a belch.

'God, that's better.' She raised her dishevelled head, then flopped back again and closed her eyes. 'Ugh, the chamber is spinning.'

In frustration and anger, I pulled down my coiled hair, tugging at the pins and breaking the ribbon. Then I took out my earrings and threw them angrily onto the table with a clatter.

Mary sat up on one elbow and stared at me as the chamberer returned with a bowl of lavender water.

'Well, who is to see me now?' I asked, eyes wide in anger.

'Oh, please, Nan, his father is a mere *valet de la garde-robe*,' she replied, sitting up and struggling to undo the bracelet at her wrist. 'He is not a *gentilshomme de la chambre*. You can do better than that.' She tugged at it and watched as the stones scattered onto the floor.

'Damn!'

'No, Clément's father was the poet laureate to Claude's mother and her writer of history. His son wishes to be the court poet, too. I will never know now, though, thanks to you. We shall be sent home. Again.'

'A poet? A poor choice from what I have seen of them – forever out of useful employment. I feel better now,' she said, brightly, 'better for being sick.'

'How lovely. I feel worse, and I am starving,' I complained.

'Did you hear what François said to me?' she asked. 'The Bourée is our – was – our favourite dance.'

'What did you expect?' I said. 'Claude is his Queen. Matters could not be plainer.'

'*She* is plain.' She yawned.

I moved over to the window and stared out onto the torchlit courtyard. A boy ambled along leading a horse to the stables, a messenger had just arrived, and a group of black-robed monks walked silently towards the Saint Calais chapel. In the distance, the sound of music and laughter drifted from the *salle*, and I felt tears of frustration slide down my cheeks. I had taken so much care with my appearance and all for nothing. Now, I felt afraid that Mary's behaviour might have us both packed off back to England since she was obviously of no further use here and had angered Louise. It was bad enough that she had dallied with the king, but to have no reward whatsoever would incense my acquisitive father and the Howards.

I stood gazing through the window, lost in my thoughts. When I turned round to tell Mary I had been ordered to stay with her all night, she was asleep, her long hair spilling down the side of the bed like a waterfall, and her mouth open. With her red lip stain smeared across her cheek, she looked like a harlot ravished by ten men. I stared at her. Her nut-brown hair might glint with gold, but she was not truly beautiful. Not in the sense that the French women were beautiful. So what had François seen in her? Perhaps it was her inviting eyes and voluptuous breasts. Perhaps it was her eagerness to love and be loved. She had no ambition, no thought beyond the moment. Was it the fact that she asked nothing in return and was sweet and willing? Did she not know that he liked a woman with spirit?

I sighed, picked up the lute lying by the bed, and began to gently pluck the strings, thinking of home. I had been unable to play the instrument competently when I left Hever, and yet now I played for the queen and her sister. My parents could not fail to be pleased with me, for I could also speak French fluently, converse intelligently and dance. What had Mary done but embarrass herself?

I must have finally drifted to sleep, for I awoke to a dog barking and the dawn chorus. I opened my eyes and saw the young chamberer standing on tiptoe as she reached up to replace the burnt-out torches. I leant up on one elbow, yawned, and looked across to the still sleeping Mary. She had moaned and snored all night but had not been sick again.

Rising sleepily up, I put on my slippers and smoothed down my crumpled gown. I did not bother to brush out my long hair and left the chamber, yawning. The château had begun to stir, and pages stood silently lighting the candle sconces down the passageways. I felt tired and hoped that Bonny had been fed. Lost in my thoughts I rounded the corner towards the staircase.

'Oh!'

'Mademoiselle Boleyn, forgive me, I startled you, but thank God I have found you.' It was *him* and my heart began thumping so hard I feared it might choke the life from me.

'Monsieur – I – I have just this moment left my sister. Forgive my appearance.'

As I stood there, I was aware that I could not have appeared more unbecoming if I had tried, for my hair lay loose and tousled, and my face stared up as pale as a church candle. What little jewellery I had been wearing now lay in the maids' chamber, so I stood completely unadorned.

'Is she all right? Oh, Anne! I could not believe you had to leave before I had the chance to dance with you.'

I stood mute and gave a shiver.

'Why, you are cold,' said Clément, taking my hand.

'I am cold *and* hungry,' I said, glancing up at the concern in his eyes.

He smiled, and as he placed his woollen cloak around my shoulders, I felt the heat from his body and smelt the aroma of wood smoke.

'Then come, we shall eat.'

'But, sir, I cannot – not unchaperoned and certainly not like this,' I said, dismayed, 'I am not fittingly dressed or presentable. The queen would be most displeased.'

He laughed, 'Anne, believe me, you have never looked more lovely or more natural. You do not need jewels or artifice to gild such a perfect frame.'

His words pleased me.

'Come, we will sneak down the back stairs and steal some newly baked bread, fresh cheese and milk. As we eat, I want you to tell me everything about yourself. Just the two of us away from the prying eyes and gossip of the court.'

He placed my hand on his arm as we made our way down the stone spiral staircase leading to the kitchens. As I stole a glimpse of his face in the dawn light, I thought I might expire with desire.

• •

We stayed five days at Blois, and I could not have been happier. Clément sought me out every day in Claude's garden as I walked her dogs, and together we meandered down the covered bridge with all its great hunting trophies, and over the moat to the artificial ponds. There, we trailed our fingers in the water, amidst the darting fish. He told me how he and his father had fished together when he was a boy, and I told him about Hever and my brother George. I discovered that Clément had grown up in Cahors and that his father, Jean Marot, had served at the court of old Louis and was introduced to Anne of Brittany by Madame de Soubise, Renée's governess. He owed everything to her, for he soon started writing poetry for Duchess Anne. When she died, his father continued as *valet de chambre* to François, and Clément was placed as a page in the rich household of Seigneur de Villeroi – just as I had been placed with Margaret of Savoy – remaining there until he became eighteen. Too old to be a page, he then studied at the university and qualified as a law clerk at the Palais de Justice. Returning to his father at the Valois court, he was now nineteen years old.

'There is no city quite like Paris,' he sighed, as we strolled towards the tennis courts, 'for it is there that I am inspired to think and write as I wish. Ah, Paris! There I often drink with my dear old friend, Jean Lemaire and –'

'Why, sir, I knew him as the librarian to the Regent Margaret,' I said, recalling the name.

'Indeed, and when he comes to France, we visit the bookshops together on the Rue St Jean de Beauvais, or amble down the Rue de Fouarre where students sit idle, a book in one hand and a pretty maid in the other. Often I dallied with such maids at the Porte Babette, inspired by their beauty, and read verses to them.'

I looked up at him.

'Was inspired,' he corrected, squeezing my arm. 'I no longer dally thus. But it is my father I am most indebted to, for he taught me to understand the sweetness of poetry and the art of verse. Ah, *demoiselle*, there is nothing finer than words. And words are powerful, too – look at your own John Skelton at the English court, harassing that Wolsey fellow! He risks his life denouncing him. Words can bring a man down, raise him, force him to hide or proclaim him a genius. Well, I choose to be a genius.'

'But what do you write about?' I asked, as we sat on the bench by the marble fountain and watched the sparrows dip in and out of its cool water.

'I write of love, loss, people who have touched me in some way,' he added, earnestly.

I gazed at his sweet face, taking in his dark hair and liquid brown eyes.

'I composed *Le Temple de Cupido* on the marriage of Claude and François, and last year presented the king with a book, *The Judgement of Minos*, as a gift, hoping he would grant me an appointment. I asked Monsieur de Pothon to put in a good word for me, but it has not happened yet. Still, the king will not be deaf to the requests of a talented poet for long! Besides, I do not wish to be dependent on my father. My ambition is to be the court poet and to serve Marguerite. She is an angel with the mildest face I ever beheld.'

The sparrows twittered noisily as they splashed and bathed.

'But it is the word of God that fascinate me,' continued Clément, turning. 'Not doctrinal controversy, but what is written in the Bible. I worry at how men discard such words, for you must have heard of the great lamentations at this time? Everywhere is talk concerning concubines and profane priests.'

'But who has seen such things?' I asked.

'Only those who want to see, for the Church, once such a blessed thing, has turned into a nest of murderous vipers, with sins worse than the Turk. How can it burn parents for teaching their children the *Credo* in English? As to Rome, once it professed to be the door to Heaven, but now it is the gaping mouth to hell.'

'And do you dare write of these things?' I asked, enthralled.

He nodded. 'I do, but only in private – for the present. Not even the beautiful sister of the king would pen such thoughts, although she is for reform.'

'Does Louise know of her daughter's beliefs?' I asked.

'Louise agrees with her opinions, but she is too clever to acknowledge them openly. Her Franciscan advisor, Francis du Moulin, has contact with men such as Guillaume Budé and Jacques Léfevre – Claude's tutor – and Louise uses them to keep her informed, without appearing to support them. I admire Léfevre and agree with his bold words.'

'I have heard, sir, that Anne of Brittany felt that the church could, one day, place genuine power in the hands of women.'

'Perhaps, in time, for the roots of the old Catholicism as we know it are already loosened, and a storm is coming that will tear off its degenerate branches.'

I stared transfixed at his excited face.

'Change is coming, *demoiselle*, it *is* coming – and I want to be part of it.'

'What do you think of King François?' I asked, changing the subject. 'Do you think him a better king than King Henry?'

'I know that François is too lax,' he said, 'and he is

already bringing harm to his court. For a start, the court is too big, and anyone can access it. He also has far too many churchmen about him, and – although none will complain – too many women.'

'And do you agree?' I asked, intrigued.

'Not at all. Ladies are the main attraction of the court, since discussions between men about matters of state, hunting and games are so dull. One is never bored when conversing with honest ladies.'

'I have heard it said, sir, that because of their influence, the behaviour of the noblemen has become more polished and it has introduced into court society a new civility.'

'That I cannot argue with!' laughed Clément.

'But what of King Henry?' I asked.

'I hear he is nothing but a bigot ruled by priests and women,' he replied.

'Well, I do not like him,' I said. 'He is rude and boorish and once insulted the name of my mother. I never forgive a slight.'

'Then I do not like him, either,' said Clément. 'More importantly, he still has no son.'

'But they are still both young,' I said.

'Maybe, but without an heir to follow him he is vulnerable. The Yorkist '*Rose Blanche*' is highly favoured by François, and he promises him money and assistance to restore him to the English throne. He has a great house in the northeast of France, and is popular with princes and soldiers alike.'

'Can this Richard de la Pole do much harm?' I asked.

'With twelve thousand troops? Yes, I imagine he could. Old Louis gave him a pension, and now François continues the favour. Anything to discomfit your king who has tried to have the imposter assassinated many times, but has not yet succeeded.'

We laughed together, and as he took my hand, I gazed at his slender fingers.

'Anne – may I call you Anne? Why are we wasting time talking of the court? Let me teach you to write verses, rondeaux, ballades, and chansons.'

'In truth?' I asked, eagerly, taking back my hand from his grasp.

'Of course! Marguerite writes with extraordinary intelligence and spirit, as does Madame de Graville, so why not you? From what I hear, you have the wit and intelligence. Were you not chosen for Renée's companion?'

'Well, I have written some verses for myself,' I said, 'and Tom Wyatt thinks they are amusing.'

'Oh?' he said, his bright expression clouding a little.

'The Wyatts are good neighbours at my home in Hever.'

He relaxed again. 'Well, amusing is good, but there has to be passion – there must be a passion, a longing in the soul. I see a passion for something in your expressive eyes.'

'I, a passion?' I exclaimed, rising to my feet. 'Why, I have a passion for music, dancing, fine gowns, and hunting.' I danced a few steps, swirling around in my green gown as he watched in admiration.

'So, you enjoy the fine life that the court offers with all its intrigues and gossip?' he asked, clapping.

'Indeed I do, Monsieur – or may I call you Clément?'

He laughed and nodded.

'It is the most exciting place I could ever imagine and France is the loveliest of countries.'

'But you cannot stay here forever. Have your parents not arranged a match for you, back in England?'

'Not that I am aware of, but besides, they will try and find a husband for my elder sister first – if they can.'

'Come now, talk of your sister does not fascinate me. You do.'

'Well – nothing has been spoken of, but I expect when the time comes my father will find me a husband of good standing.'

Clément smiled.

'Anyway, Father is progressing well at court and – well, I am sure he will find me a match, if not in England, then mayhap in Ireland.'

'Ireland?' Clément appeared surprised. 'They say it is a land of saints and scholars yet I know it is a troubled land with centuries of feuding and quarrels. Surely there is nothing for you in that bog of a place.'

'Not so!' I cried, feeling affronted. 'My grandmother has estates in Kilkenny, and I could easily live there as the lady of a grand property. The Irish also have the best horses in all the world, and so I would have the finest of stables.'

Clément laughed at my indignant face. 'I disagree, Anne! The best horses are bred in Ferrara and Naples or come from the stables of the Marquis of Mantua himself. There they train their horses to leap and cavort with just a word or a light touch. No, the English and the Irish train their horses too young, and with a harshness that quickly renders them lame.'

'And you have been to Italy?' I asked, quite fascinated.

Clément turned away to hide the seriousness in his face. 'No – but I have a restless spirit and wish to go. Oh, there is something in me that will not be still, and I yearn for I know not what!'

'Then you must pray to God for peace and guidance,' I offered.

There was a moment's pause before he turned to me.

'Tell me, Anne, if I might make so bold – have you ever loved another, even from afar? Has any man ever stolen your heart?'

I lowered my head, taken off guard by the question. How should I reply at only fifteen years old? I liked Tom Wyatt, I had found Jamie Butler attractive in Tournai, and I had noticed the attractive young courtiers around Prince Charles in Brussels. Foolishly, I had even found the Emperor Maximilian an attractive, charismatic man. But that was all I could think of.

'I have not sought such things,' I said, 'and do not know

of them. Besides, such thoughts are a sin un –'

Without warning, he lent down and kissed me full on the lips.

'Was *that* a sin?' he whispered.

I quickly moved away, my hand over my mouth.

'Monsieur!' I cried.

He reached out for my arm. 'No, Anne, wait!'

We stood staring at each other as he held my sleeve fast.

'Has no man ever kissed you before?'

I wanted to lie but instead gave an embarrassed shrug. 'I am not like my sister,' I mumbled.

He smiled and took both my hands in his.

'Then I am honoured,' he said, kneeling, 'and crave your forgiveness. But Anne, it was an honest kiss, pure and discreet. Still, I vow I will not kiss you again save by your consent.'

I felt my breathing quicken as I stared down at him.

'I – I do forgive you,' I said, not at all certain of my feelings. 'I mean – I mean I do gi –'

Seeing the eagerness in my eyes, he jumped up, and holding me close, kissed me again. This time I did not pull away.

•   •

To my utter astonishment, Mary remained in Louise's household. There must still have been some use for her, but I knew not what. François, too pre-occupied with war to give her a second thought, spent his days in conference with his advisors, and the balmy evenings in the queen's gardens. With the queen's hand on his arm, they admired the newly planted flowerbeds and tender saplings and strolled together beneath the arbours. The queen loved to talk to him about her plants, and he would nod kindly at her animated face. I suspected he knew his time with her was short, and so he could feign polite interest in her garden for just a little while longer. His mind, no doubt, was on war and not weeds.

Always in the queen's sight, Clément and I could only exchange secret, loving glances, but we did manage to converse one evening in the orangery as we watched a game of archery. He stood, the evening sun setting golden behind his head as we spoke quietly and earnestly about the state of the church, and how no man should suffer persecution for telling the truth. I felt utterly captivated by our bold conversation, so different from the foolish babble of the girls about me. Did such evils exist? Could they be stopped?

He moved me to one side, away from the others, and whispered close. 'Anne, a tide is sweeping across Europe as we speak. Intelligent men are no longer prepared to be led by evil men, or have their faith soiled. They believe that every man should be able to read the word of God himself without interference.'

'But Clément, how would that be possible?'

'How indeed,' he replied, 'for no man can translate the Bible without the Catholic church's approval.'

I felt a thrill inside as he spoke.

'Wycliffe did, of course, but he acted boldly.'

'And he was punished,' I whispered back, inclining my head to a passing couple.

'Yes, Anne, but to reform the church, we need to read Christ's words clearly, not from the Latin translation but the original Greek and Hebrew. Is not Erasmus working on this very thing as we speak?'

Marguerite drew her bow and let the arrow loose. François clapped, and Clément shouted 'Bravo!' She threw him a dazzling smile, which for some reason, I did not like.

'Now there, Anne, is a lady who can do much good, for she, too, believes the church must be reformed and freed from persecution. She far outstrips her brother in learning with her grasp of Latin, Greek, and Hebrew, and ideas flow from her brilliant mind.'

Sadly, our conversation was interrupted by my sister's laugh – that shrill Boleyn laugh – surrounded as she was by her admirers. She glanced towards François, but he did not return her gaze. She laughed again excitedly, clapping as an arrow hit its mark, and insisted on pulling a bow herself. I felt embarrassed as I watched one of the gentlemen lean in close to her from behind, peering over her shoulder at her swelling bosom, too close for decency.

'Watch the mark, my lady, not the arrow's end,' he said, as she steadied the grey goose feather.

However, Mary's gaiety could not fool me, for I knew that look of desperation in her over bright eyes. I should have felt concern, but I did not. Tomorrow we would celebrate the Feast of Pentecost. It would be a beautiful ceremony to celebrate the birth of the Church and the promise of summer. No, I only felt an immense excitement at Clément's bold words and nothing Mary could do would spoil things. Or so I thought.

Chapter Seven

*'That thou shalt die is plain: when thou
shalt die is hidden.'*

The Loire

e left Blois on St Boniface's day, a week before
the building work on the northwest wing began,
since François did not want Claude disturbed by
the noise of the workmen. Standing in the courtyard holding
the plans and pointing towards the windows, he gave final
orders to Raymond Phillipo, who was in charge of the works'
progress, and Jacques Sordot, his Master Mason. Marguerite
then appeared wearing a black damask hunting gown faced
with gold, and a plumed bonnet over her gold-netted hair.
Later that day, François planned to hunt in the forest of
Amboise with her and their closest companions, and arrive
at the château in the evening. I watched as she squeezed her
brother's arm, and he kissed her fondly on the cheek.

'Ah, *mignon*,' he said, excitedly, 'see – I shall have two
new façades in the Italian style – such as in St Peter's, in
Rome – with modifications to the roof, and a high balcony
with commanding views of the gardens. It shall be a sweet
marriage of all that is best in France and Italy, and for you
– the finest library in France. Eight thousand livres will see
it complete.'

His sister smiled indulgently and fondled the silky ears

of his hound as she saw their mother walking with her ladies towards the waiting litter. My own sister sauntered behind, smiling brightly at François, but he did not notice her – or chose not to – for he strolled off towards the Saint Calais chapel, his hound at his heel, and his dark head close to his sister's.

• •

The morning sun felt warm as we sailed alongside fruit orchards, golden sandbanks, and green islands studded with weeping willow trees. On the busy river, small boats bobbed as the light breeze tugged at their sails, their occupants cheering and waving their caps at the royal progress.

Queen Claude lay back on her cushions, hand on her growing belly, and savoured the fresh peas held in a bowl by her dwarf, Marie. Knowing they were beneficial to pregnant women, she took another handful and spoke of Amboise. She told me that the château – heavily garrisoned, unlike Blois – had once been an old fortress, built high overlooking the Loire so that any flooding from the river could be seen. There were two great towers on the north and south side, with inclined planes of cobbles which wound upwards in the midst, instead of stone steps. One was called the *Minimes* and the other the *Hurtault*. Thus, she explained, chariots and litters could proceed from the lower ground to the courtyard above, and when François rode his horse up, he was accompanied by such a blaze of *flambeaux* that a man might think it day.

The queen explained how her mother had occupied the second floor of the château, and from her window, she could see the pretty white houses of the town below, as well as the lovely River Loire. As a little girl, the queen had lived in these chambers, and they were still covered in the yellow silk as a reminder of those happy days. Her mother had also enjoyed a wonderful collection of priceless ornaments, for a great deal of beautiful pottery had been brought back from Italy by

King Louis XII as presents for her.

'You will soon see such delights for yourself, Anne,' she said, brushing away a fly, 'unless –'

'Oh, Madame, tell me of your gardens,' I interrupted, afraid to think where those treasures might be now. I did not put it past François to have the gardeners dig up her flowerbeds and sell the rare bulbs for gold.

'My gardens, like Blois, are beautiful,' she continued, 'designed, by order of my dear father some fifteen years ago, by the Italian gardener, Signor Pacello de Mercogliano. He created beautiful arbours, flowerbeds, and alleyways, and there is a very pretty pavilion named after my mother.'

'And orange trees!' cried Renée, 'do not forget the oranges!' She was an amusing girl, and I could see why her sister felt so protective of her.

The queen smiled.

'Indeed, sweetheart, for the orange and lemon trees yield fine fruit in this climate. Do you remember last winter, how you helped me plant them in boxes with little wheels so they could be brought in to protect them from the frost? This year you shall have as many as you like, my darling.'

Renée smiled and began stroking her rabbit.

'What is that lovely place?' I gazed into the distance.

'That is the château of Chaumont,' said Anne de Graville. 'The king will stay there while he hunts, before moving on to Amboise, and we shall rest there, too, for the night.' I stared at the beautiful, white château on its mound, shimmering in the hot sunlight against the deep azure sky.

'Do you not have such châteaux in England?' asked the queen.

I said they were called palaces, but I had not seen any – except at Thornbury, when I had attended a wedding – but I had heard that the one at Hampton, built by Thomas Wolsey, Archbishop of York, was a wondrous sight to behold.

'Indeed,' she said, 'we hear a great deal about your Thomas Wolsey and his magnificent red brick palace. It is his good fortune that you do not have a jealous king.'

She yawned and trailed her hand languidly in the cool water. 'Monsieur Bohier is investing his fortune in a fine new château at Chenonceaux, but having seen the plans, my husband already has his eye on it for himself.'

She turned away with a sigh. Her face, a moment ago so happy, appeared pensive as she laid her other hand upon her stomach. Finally, Dr du Puy leaned forward, concern in his face.

'Are you unwell, Madame?'

The queen shook her head and shifted her position a little. 'No, not at all, but I have such a foreboding about this coming war. I want to confide my fears in my husband but dare not for fear of upsetting him before he leaves for Italy. He does not want to hear his wife chiding him. I told the Venetian ambassador that I understand it is his duty to go, for he must maintain control of Milan and Genoa. Is Milan not the gateway to all communications with Spain, the Netherlands, and Austria? But for all my brave words, I am afraid.'

'Indeed so, Madame, but you must not worry about the king. He is young, but he is also strong and beloved by his people.'

'But the people, dear doctor, are fickle, and he gives them little enough reason to love him. Did my father not once say that only two things are vital for the contentment of the French people – to love their king and to live in peace? Yet no sooner is François crowned than he rushes them into the toils and charges of war. Such a cost, such a terrible cost.'

'Madame, your husband has written again to the Duke of Suffolk reminding him he still owes him fifty thousand francs, which would go a long way towards the expenses of the campaign.'

'Surely King Henry would not haggle over the amount?' asked the queen.

'Well, Madame,' continued Dr du Puy, 'the French forces

have now crossed the Alps with their artillery and cannot go back. Maximilian is ready to march into Burgundy, and the Spaniards are about to join the Swiss with a large force. Your husband needs money to stop them both. As England is France's ally, he expects King Henry's assistance. All he asks is financial help to annex Milan to France.'

'And he must give it, for I will not have my people so oppressed.' The queen's face was full of concern. 'Such thoughts fill me with horror.'

Dr du Puy placed his hand on her lap. 'Then, Madame, we will talk no more of it. You must distract yourself with thoughts of the coming wedding of Mademoiselle de Bourbon. I hear Marguerite helped to design the bridal gown herself.'

'How can that distract me, when I know full well her new husband will forsake her immediately to accompany my husband to Italy. Should any ill befall him before a chil –'

'Come now, Madame, your condition causes you to have these womanly fears. Let your young lady here play you something cheerful.' He turned in his seat. 'My dear, play *Printemps* for it tells of the coming of spring, the season of love'.

This was a song I knew from Mechelen, and I started plucking my beribboned lute. As I did, I thought of Clément and wished he were beside me, but instead there was only the queen, fat and ungainly, her eyes closed as she fingered the ivory rosary beads she always carried. Then, as I began to sing, we heard a dreadful shrieking from the direction of Louise's barge – in fact, it came from Louise herself. The queen sat up, pulled back the silk of the awning, and stared short-sightedly, towards the disturbance. Foolish Marie began to squeal to add to the noise.

'What is it,' asked the queen, 'what has happened?'

In Louise's barge, Madame de Châtillon stood over her mistress in bewilderment as *Madame la Grande* handed her a phial of smelling salts.

'My leg! It is my leg!' Louise writhed in pain, her eyes tightly closed.

'Dr du Puy, get to her – quickly!' cried the queen, knocking over the bowl of pea pods.

All was commotion as our barge drifted up beside Louise's and the doctor scrambled over the frightened women, rocking the barge in his haste.

Louise, lying down, clutched her lower thigh.

'Ladies, please, if you will, stand back and give me room!' The doctor pushed his way forward. 'Madame, are you cut? Has your dog bitten you? Is it a bee sting?'

Louise, white as a lily, let the doctor rip down her stocking and slip off her shoe. He looked up at her, puzzled. There was nothing to see – no puncture wound, no rash, and no swelling.

'Such pain! Such pain!' gasped Louise, her eyes now aflame. By now all the other barges had gathered about, and courtiers stood craning their necks to watch the commotion.

'Madame, I am at a loss to say what this pain might be,' announced the doctor in despair.

Louise attempted to sit up, clinging to his sleeve and pulled him to her. 'It is my son,' she breathed, hoarsely. 'My *son* – some dreadful ill has befallen my son!'

As she gasped, she fell backwards in a dead faint, straight into my sister's arms.

•   •

At Amboise, the courtyard lay in confusion. Hunting hounds barked as horses clattered across the cobbles and courtiers leapt from their saddles, the skirts of their grey tunics splattered with mud. Grooms ran out to grab reins as Monsieur de Ruthie, the *lieutenant de la venerie,* cracked his switch at the brace of mastiffs crowded about him, bringing them to heel. Their thick, protective felt jackets were covered with dirt and river water from the chase, and they whined in excitement.

'Make room!' bellowed the Duc de Montmorency, grabbing the reins of the foam-flecked horse.

'Fetch the physician!' Marguerite dismounted, her hair loose and her sleeve tattered.

At that moment, Louise threw herself onto her son as he slid down from his saddle. Grimacing with pain, he fell into the arms of the Comte d'Estampes, his hose bloody and the grey felt skirts of his hunting garb badly torn. I watched in horror with the other ladies.

'*Ma mère*, please, it is nothing, a mere scratch,' he said, breathlessly, slumping as he trying to stand.

'My God, what happened?' she asked the comte, with Marguerite close behind.

The comte, assisted by the Duc de Lorraine, helped François into the chamber of the *salles des gardes* where the king's guard were housed.

'Fetch water, cloths and some wine!' called the duc to the startled men, who abandoned their game of dice.

Louise hurried after them, and Marguerite turned to take the hand of Madame de Châtillon.

'It all happened so quickly,' she said, amazed, as the queen appeared through the wooden archway with *Madame la Grande* trotting behind.

'What is all the noise about?' she asked, sleepily. 'I lay resting and then heard the hunting party return. What has happened?' She stared at the silent faces. 'Is it the king? Tell me!'

'François is hurt but there is no need for concern,' soothed Marguerite, walking towards her.

The queen squealed.

'But I must go to him!' Her eyes were wide with fright.

Marguerite stopped her. 'No! Let the physician do his work first,' she counselled. 'Trust me, he is not in any danger. We will move him to the *logis du roi* shortly when the bleeding has stopped.'

She steered the queen to a stone seat, and the two of

them sat down together as we crowded around. The queen began crying as Madame de Tournon put an arm about her shoulders to comfort her.

'My husband!'

'As you know,' said Marguerite, 'we were out hunting the boar in the forest. François, Diane and I were alone, apart from a couple of courtiers, and about to turn for home. There seemed little point in trying to continue, for the trees were dense and difficult to ride through, and our nets rendered useless. But then we saw it – a great white beast rooting in the undergrowth. It must have been the largest boar I have ever seen, with gnarled tusks and a scarred face. Startled, it looked up, caught our scent and scrambled away. In the excitement, we chased it deeper into the wood, François with his spear raised, and Diane close behind. At that very moment, a wood pigeon flew up and startled François' horse, causing it to rear and plunge straight into a thorn bush. The king slipped sideways and impaled himself on the branches. His horse became agitated and, panicking, swung about, entangling itself and François further, so that even more thorns cut through the cloth of his hose, slashing him like knives.'

The queen put her hands to her face in horror and wailed louder.

'Hush, hush, he managed to disentangle himself but one of the larger thorns has embedded itself deep into his leg. It must be removed.'

'Dear God!' The queen crossed herself.

Marguerite took her arm. 'Come now, the surgeon is with him as we speak, be calm. All will be well once the thorn is cut out. Accompany me to my chamber, and we will wait together.'

With the commotion over, I wandered towards the *logis de la reine* where a group of nobles stood talking amongst themselves. Seeing a blue velvet bonnet lying on the cobbles, its white plumes now broken and splattered with horse dung, I picked it up. It must have been Marguerite's. Then, as I continued down the steps, my sister appeared from the portico. She threw her arms out to the side in despair. 'I tell you, Nan, that woman is mad. Weeping and wailing over a thorn, beating her breast over omens and signs. Whose is that?'

I ignored her question. 'Hush,' I glanced back at the gentlemen, 'the king might have been killed. Anyway, why are you not with her?'

'She dismissed us all and is now with François in his chamber, fussing over him like an old hen with a chick.'

'Have you spoken to him?' I asked.

She shook her head. 'He barely acknowledges me,' she said, her face downcast. 'It is as if nothing ever happened between us. Nothing of any importance to him.'

We walked over to a tethered mare and watched the steam rising off its flanks. A groom rubbed it vigorously with wisps of hay and then threw a cloth over its back. I stroked its pink nose, and it flinched as another groom bathed its wounds with strong, warm vinegar.

'Be still, sweetheart,' he said, in a soothing voice, 'we must get these thorns out.' The mare gave a quiver at his touch and turned her eye towards him.

'François' favourite,' said Mary, as she too, stroked the velvet nose. 'She is called Artemis, and he will be very angry if she is scarred. See the device of the salamander branded into her flanks? They say the creature has magical powers, for it can live in fire and not be destroyed.'

I turned and rested my back against the mossy wall, thoughtful. 'How did she know?' I asked.

Mary did not look at me, but carried on with her stroking. 'Because she is a witch.'

'Mary,' I whispered, 'do not say such a dangerous thing.'

She shrugged. 'It is true. She has supernatural powers that bind her to her son. What he feels, she feels. You saw it for yourself.'

'It might have been just chance,' I offered, trying to convince myself.

'Hardly,' she said. 'I tell you she is a witch and a mad one at that. Madder than usual at present, since she is furious that her lover is going to Italy – you should have heard the argument they had at Blois.'

'But the Duc de Bourbon is a distinguished soldier – the king would never allow him to remain here, even for his mother's sake.'

'Well, she will not accept it and has been in a blazing mood. Nothing we ladies do can please her. She also insists that Francis du Moulin remains with her, although he, too, is desperate to get away rather than discuss pious thoughts with her. What a shrew.'

'So you are staying here?' I asked.

'It would seem so for the moment.' She ran her hand along the mare's mane. 'We are only here at Amboise until the wedding is over and then we return to Louise's château at Romorantin. She is planning a new residence there.'

'Well, it is better that you should be out of the way so that any gossip dies down.'

She stopped her stroking. 'I think, Nan, you will find that you are the one causing the gossip.'

'I? But how so?' I was alarmed.

She linked her arm in mine as we walked back towards the chapel of Saint Blaise. 'You know very well – that dark Marot fellow. Some of the girls are gossiping about how he stares at you. The queen will say something if you are not more discreet. What do you see in him? He is just like his father – a rhymer of words; there is nothing noble in that. What happened to your pride and ambition in aiming high and, besides, what on earth would Father say?'

My mouth dropped open as I stared at her in complete amazement. How *dare* she!

'You are wrong,' I said. 'I told you before, he is held in great esteem by François and one day hopes to be appointed as either the court poet or as a *secrétaire*. He has even translated Virgil.'

'A poet,' she repeated.

I felt crestfallen at her remark. 'No, Mary, poetry is a supreme art, for a poet paints with one stroke the body and soul, and so paints in the heavens.'

'Oh, really. Have you given him any favours yet?' she asked.

'Do you mean trinkets and such?'

My sister stared at me in disbelief.

'Mary, of course not! How could you ask that?' I cried, catching her lewd meaning.

'Because I am your sister, and I love you, and we have no secrets.' She squeezed my arm.

'No, Mary, we have not done anything improper, but I love him more than any man I have ever met. He knows so much about the court and fascinates me with his love of books, poetry, and religion. Words come tumbling out when he speaks, and his enthusiasm is infectious. He has written a poem for me and –'

She rolled her eyes. 'Nan, how exactly do you propose to keep him? To draw a man out, you must throw him the bait.'

I looked at her confused.

'You will not hold him if you are not kind to him, and I am trying to help you if you will let me.'

'You did not hold the king's affection,' I replied.

'Do not change the subject. Now, do you want to keep your foolish poet or not?'

I nodded.

'Then listen to what I have to tell you.'

I was about to speak, but she turned, her eyes wide. 'Oh, Nan, I had forgotten my errand! The blue wedding banners have just arrived from the town seamstress, and Louise is furious because they are the wrong shade. Damn! I was instructed to bring them to her immediately, so I must hurry back.'

I watched as she turned to go. 'Mary – stop – what do I need to know?'

'I will explain later!'

As I stood watching her hurry away, I began thinking of Clément. This was not what I had planned at all. Mary was right, he *was* just a poet and hardly a grand match, so whatever could come of it? Where, indeed, had my ambition gone? My family would be doubly appalled for while Mary had, albeit briefly, cavorted with the King of France, I was aching to do the same with a man of much less standing. He was not rich, he had no title, and he was not what I had dreamt of. And yet just thinking about him put me in such a state of nerves and excitement I could hardly sleep, eat or breathe.

François recovered. The curved thorn in his leg turned out to be five inches in length and embedded like a meat hook, but once removed, the healing quickly began. In fact, within three days, I saw François, wearing a soft slipper, back in council with his advisors, either deep in discussion or scribbling orders and instructions for the coming war. When not inside, he rode out in the tiltyard, practising skill-at-arms with his favourites, smiling up at his mother as she stood on her balcony. Her face appeared anxious as she watched his dangerous demonstrations of physical prowess. She was pale as she watched him brandishing his sword, padded coat open to his opponent's blade, fearful as he parried and thrust, and parried again with his headstrong friends. How could I know that those very skills she feared were about to save my life?

●   ●

The echoing and rumbling of iron wheels on stone drifted upwards, as litters, chariots, and horses wound their way up the wide, spiral ramp of the great *Minimes* tower. Today, it was decorated with tapestries and hangings, and sweet-smelling herbs lay scattered on its cobbles. When the rattling procession of chariots finally arrived at the large, open terrace, ambassadors and guests alighted from the cool of the tower to the sizzling heat. Fanning themselves, they smiled and admired the fresh flowers bound into great swags and draped around every column. The king and queen, dressed in argent and white tissue, flanked by all the great nobles of France, greeted their arrival. Louise, Marguerite, and the Duchess of Nemours, standing beneath the shade of a canopy, nodded graciously as the guests entered the château, each appearing far more magnificent than the poor, hunched queen. She only seemed to be wilting.

As I watched, I noticed that Marguerite did not appear her usual, cheerful self but was somewhat quiet. I suspected she already dreaded her return to her château at Argentan with her dull husband, away from the sparkling company of her brother. There, she had her household to run and domestic matters to attend to, but she would much rather have debated with François than listen to the grumblings of her cook. She gazed across to the magnificent view of the River Loire, sunlight glinting on its water, and sighed. Normandy could never match her beloved Loire, and I knew she would miss the hunting. However, today was a propitious day, being a full moon, and a good day to celebrate her brother's accession to the throne. A happy day with no talk of war, no talk of her brother leaving – and no grumbling from her mother as she accused her lover of abandoning her for the coming campaign.

As we made our way to the *grande salle,* I glanced across to where Clément stood with a group of courtiers. He tipped his head towards me and I repaid him with a coquettish smile. I was, by now, totally besotted and only lived to see him, no matter how briefly. Helpless to stop my feelings, I knew my family would not approve, but still, I yearned for his attention.

Then, quite without warning, François leapt onto a table and announced that all his guests must proceed to the arched gallery, overlooking the *basse-court.* There he had a surprise waiting for them.

I moved to my sister's side as the excited crowd jostled around me.

'What is happening?' I said, as we reached the top of the spiral staircase. When I looked down over the balcony, men-at-arms appeared to be blocking the entrance to the courtyard with great chests, tables, and chairs. 'What are they doing?'

Mary leant over the balustrade, her gown cut low, and her smile enticing. As she wafted her silk fan back and forth, she seemed to be her ever-cheerful self again.

'Wait and see, Nan. The king has a great feat to entertain his guests. It is supposed to be a secret, but I overheard him talking to the Duc de Bourbon.'

I looked across to see the queen, Louise, Marguerite, and *Madame la Grande* take their places on four sumptuous chairs. Finally, all were seated, and with a great flourish of trumpets, François appeared in the courtyard below. The queen smiled as Françoise de Foix held the excited Renée's hand. Another woman whom I had not seen before, small and dark, with a pretty heart-shaped face and large almond-shaped eyes, stood next to her.

'Who is that?' I nodded to the young girl.

Mary screwed up her nose. '*That* is Jeanne le Coq, wife of the Parisian lawyer, Jacques Disomme. Françoise de Foix does not like her, and neither do I.'

'Why not?' I asked.

'Because she is pretty and unhappily married and that makes her irresistible to the gallant François. She is also very provocative – look at that extravagant gown. It must have cost a fortune.'

Below, the king, now wearing gauntlets, breastplate, and light tassets over his thighs, strutted around, hands on his hips. The noise fell to a murmur of expectation as he strode over to the large pile of leaves and branches in the middle of the cobbles, and gazed up at his audience.

Without warning, he kicked the branches, and an immense snorting and squealing erupted from inside. A loud gasp filled the air, as people moved closer to the balcony's edge to see what had made the noise. The king then placed his foot on what seemed to be a large crate beneath the leaves and drew his sword from its scabbard. It made a sharp, rasping sound, and his mother jumped to her feet in alarm, her eyes transfixed on him.

'This is the beast that would have my crown and lame me when I tried to hunt him down!' shouted the king, 'but see – he is now my captive!'

With that, he swept aside the leaves and branches, and from behind the iron bars, we all saw the terrifying, scarred face of a white boar. Snarling and pushing its great weight against the crate, desperate to escape, its eyes flashed red with rage.

'Release the traitor!' The king stepped back. Two grooms ran forward as I grabbed Mary's arm in anticipation.

'No!'

The grooms stopped in their tracks as the shrill voice filled the air. It came from none other than Louise. The crowd looked towards her as she stood, arms on the balustrade. Then the queen rose unsteadily to her feet.

'Husband – I beseech you, do not do this thing!' she cried.

'But Madame,' exclaimed the king, grinning, 'on the faith of a gentleman, I intend killing this beast in single combat and placing its head on a spike as a trophy for you.'

He glanced up to his friends, who were drunkenly cheering him on, clapping and stamping their feet, and raising their goblets of wine in salute.

Louise glanced over to them, and the queen appeared agitated as the boar became more and more aggressive in its confined space. Ramming its great weight against the crate, it almost tipped it over. It was then that Marguerite spoke, beads of sweat visible on her brow. How could he do something so reckless with the queen in her delicate condition?

'Loving brother,' she said loudly, as she leaned forward with her hands outstretched, her words faint amidst the noise.

The crowd fell silent.

'Loving brother, such an animal is not the equal of a king, and cannot thus be pitted against such nobility. You are a Valois, he but dust beneath your shoe. Let him play the fool, by all means, but devise some other game so that we might laugh and jeer at the unworthy creature he is!'

A murmur of approval rose and the king, hearing the mood of the crowd and smiling at his beloved sister, bowed low. He could refuse her nothing and beckoned to the grooms and men-at-arms, who rushed forward to talk with him. As the frustrated boar continued to grunt, the men ran off and returned with great sacks filled with straw that they then tied to ropes stretched across the courtyard. The king deftly leapt to the safety of a barricade just as the rope on the crate door was tugged open, and the boar dashed out in a frenzy of frustration. It ran straight for the nearest sack, spearing it through with its great tusks, and then spun around with such speed that it caught another sack within seconds, throwing it into the air. Straw rained down about it. Standing with legs apart, it then sniffed the air as the crowd roared, booed and stamped their feet. Maddened by the noise, it charged again, tossing the sacks and ripping them to pieces. The flying straw covered the beast, and the young nobles in the lower stalls began placing bets on who could hit it first. I watched as small knives, silver goblets and other missiles were hurled at the boar, and it screeched at a dagger protruding from its shoulder. No-one knew who had thrown it, but it came from somewhere up in the gallery. Too much for the frightened animal to bear, it ran towards the staircase, tossing aside the old chests and chairs that were blocking its way as if they were hay. The roar of laughter became quite deafening.

'Mary!' I grabbed her arm.

As the boar began to scramble its way up the stairs towards the guests, the laughter faded as people scattered and vanished through doorways. Ladies screamed as they ran towards the staterooms, knocking over chairs in their panic, their lapdogs barking with excitement. The younger gentlemen leapt up onto the balustrade and continued to pelt the beast with whatever they could get their hands on, including bread, fruit, cups, and plates. Debris rained down like rose petals, taking no effect as the boar advanced.

'Mary, get to the door,' I said, as the men-at-arms surrounded the royal ladies, including Renée, and rushed them out of the way.

'Quickly, Nan!' Mary reached out for my hand. 'The animal is almost at the top of the staircase!'

I ran towards the door but slipped over on the marble stone. The door slammed shut. As I looked behind, I could see that although someone had thrown a piece of furniture in its way, the boar was almost upon me. I stared in horror through the wooden legs of the table at the boar's slavering jaws and foam-flecked mouth and grasped blindly at the tapestry behind. From its shoulder, ruby-red blood dripped onto the stone and I stared as it trickled slowly down the steps forming a pool. Very slowly, I rose to my feet; all jeering stopped and I huddled behind the pillar.

'Sweet Jesu,' I said, as I stood rooted to the spot, my hair tumbling free from its hood. The animal raised its head over the obstruction; its nostrils flared as it smelt my scent, and I stood there, trapped, with my back to the wall.

'Stand very, very still, *demoiselle*,' came a calm voice from the crowd.

I glanced over to see the handsome Seigneur de Bonnivet step out from behind one of the walls. He moved silently towards me, and the boar momentarily spun round to face him, grunting.

'Do not move,' he whispered.

I stood fixed to the spot, all eyes upon me. Somewhere,

from behind a door, I heard little Renée crying.

There was then a great commotion, as with a cry François leapt forward from nowhere, sword in hand, in front of the boar. Everyone seemed to hold his or her breath and then it happened – faster than a bolt of lightning. The enraged beast lunged at François, tossing the table away as if it were a stick. The king deftly stepped to one side, forcing the boar to stumble and slip in its dripping blood. As I ran out of the way, he drove his great sword deep into the animal's neck, and it tumbled, with a squeal, down the staircase, mortally wounded. François then leapt down after the beast and plunged his sword into its body three more times. He then cut off its front foot in triumph. A tumultuous roar filled the air as François' friends ran to his side, lifted him onto their shoulders, and carried him back up the staircase.

'*Vive le Roi!*' they shouted, as he grinned, his eyes shining with excitement.

Mary ran towards me, followed by Clément.

'Oh, my Nan,' she said, 'my darling Nan, thank God you are not hurt!'

She held me so tightly in her arms I could hardly breathe. When she released me, I saw my hands were shaking. What if the boar had reached me and tossed me to my death? My life would have been snuffed out like a candle before it had begun.

'My God, are you hurt, Anne?' Clément pulled Mary away as the other girls gathered around.

'I was so afraid!' continued my sister, tears in her eyes.

Louise ran out from behind the door, the queen, pale and trembling, close behind, clutching Renée's hand.

'My Caesar!' cried Louise, triumphantly, as she reached up to kiss her son's hand and hold it to her cheek. François leapt down from his friend's shoulders, his eyes glancing about as if searching for someone.

'Come now, *Madame Mère*, see how my practice with the arming sword and falchion have made me stronger than a lion. You must not fear for me – I have provided a fine beast for the roast!'

A great laugh rose into the air but then, seeing the queen's tears, he took her trembling hand and held it to his lips.

'Be calm, Madame, I trust no harm is done. Is the *demoiselle* hurt?' He looked towards me.

'Why, sire, you saved her from certain death,' said Clément, over the queen's shoulder.

Louise then turned to me, her face calm, and her eyes unblinking. She held me in a cold, blank gaze as if she could see into my very soul, but I refused to avoid her stare. She raised her hand, almost as if in benediction, and then finally spoke, her voice a mere whisper.

'This child will not die in France – but she will die by the hand of a Frenchman.'

I stared at her in astonishment and wanted to laugh at her absurd words, but dared not. Mary was right – she was a witch. Then, as if snapping out of a trance, she turned from me and smiled at her son.

My sister sprang forward, dropped to the floor and kissed the hem of the king's coat. 'Sire, I must thank you for saving my sister's life. Never have we seen such a great feat and we – I – am forever in your debt. Tell me how I may please you.'

She looked utterly desirable on her knees. François gently raised her and kissed her fondly on each cheek. Horrified, I stared as he slowly and sensually brushed the hair away from her half-closed eyes, and she blushed in triumph. He was hers again and all the court had witnessed his desire. He then leant close to her ear. 'Then run along, Marie, and tell Madame Desomme to come immediately to my private chamber.'

From the desolate expression on Mary's face, I thought she might burst into tears.

●　●

'But *why?*'

The sun beat down as I moved to the shade of the Porte de Lions gate and turned my back to the wall. The burning heat felt oppressive as a green lizard lifted first one foot then the other, and darted into a cool, shady crevice. Across the terrace, a young page sat on a stone water trough, doublet open, languidly tossing stones into the shimmering heat. Some distance away, two young men practised their swordplay, their doublets on the ground and their shirts open to the waist. The metal of their blunted practice blades clinked with little conviction as they slowly circled each other.

'Anne,' said Clément.

I saw the despair in his face and turned away.

'Anne, it is not for long, and I am not accompanying the main army – I might not even see a battle. The king is using German mercenaries since the Swiss are not available. They will be fighting, not I.'

'But you are a poet!' I cried, 'what care can you possibly have for war?'

'For experience,' he said, taking hold of my shoulders.

I felt the hot sweat prick beneath my arms.

'I must feel all things, savour all things if I wish to write truthfully, just as my father did in the battle between the French and the Venetians. I was but fourteen years old when he left. He wrote about the things he saw, from dying soldiers crying out to God, to the flag of St Mark trampled underfoot. He even described how the roaring cannon at Peschiera terrified the king's jester who crept under a bed. Poor Triboulet! Such tales, I, too, would tell in heroic verse. It will not be for long, I promise you.'

His eyes, one moment alive with excitement, now dulled. 'Anne, I cannot stay here forever, restless and yearning. Idleness and melancholy are my two great foes, and I am struck with the ardour of the adventurer. I will be the storyteller of all circumstances, imitating the Italians but constantly reinventing. Independence, excitement, and discovery push me on, for I *must* see something of life!'

'You mean of death,' I said. 'Anyway, what is this stupid fashion for adventuring? It is all you men talk of.'

'Please understand.'

'I do not – I *will* not.' I folded my arms and turned my head away.

'Marguerite understands,' he said. 'She knows her brother must go to Italy and fulfil his destiny.'

'To hell with Marguerite!' I cried. 'You are leaving *me*, not her!'

He appeared surprised at my outburst of temper, as in the distance the pageboy glanced my way.

'I have a gift for you,' he said, fumbling in his coat. 'It is a translation of the epistles of St Paul, the work of Lefèvre. Keep it safe.'

I grabbed the small book and made to throw it back at him.

'No, Anne, please,' he said, holding my hand fast. 'Our time is short, and I desire you so much. Let us not waste what chance we have. Walk with me to the church where it will be cool and – private.'

I narrowed my eyes and he nodded. 'It is true. You have stolen my heart away beyond all imagining. You are my dark-eyed lady, my muse, my darling Anne.'

I felt my heart beat a little faster. 'Am I truly?'

He gazed at me. 'I want you to be mine, my only love.'

Seeing the earnest look in his eyes, I threw myself into his arms. Eventually, he pushed me gently away. 'Be kind to me, Anne, before I leave. Let me hold the memory of you before I go away, for my nights will be long and lonely.' I gazed up at him and entwined my fingers about his neck, but he took my hands and kissed them. I laughed. 'Will they?'

'Please, I am in earnest, I am *begging* you,' he said, his eyes closed as his lips brushed my fingers.

I took his arm and we walked out into the white glare of the sun, across the shimmering terrace and towards the cool of Notre-Dame de la Grève. The old bell struck three.

●   ●

Tossing and turning, I found it impossible to sleep. Closing my eyes, I relived the urgent kisses that had made me moan with no thought of shame, and the kisses he had asked of me in return as we lay on his cloak in the cool, dark crypt. I closed my eyes and felt again the touch of his hands. God, I loved him so much. He had begged me to give myself completely, but I had felt afraid. I turned his words over and over again in my mind.

'Why, Anne? Why do you hold back thus and behave so cruelly to me?'

'*No*,' I had whispered, before pushing him gently onto his back and kissing him passionately again. His response had seemed lukewarm as he stared up, eyes open. I had paused and gazed into them.

'What is the matter?'

'Nothing,' he had said, sitting up, as I peered provocatively through the strands of my hair.

'My God, Anne, do not torment and tease me thus.'

Smiling to myself, I now closed my eyes and thought how strange it felt to be desired so, to see a look of longing and lust in a man's eyes, to feel a thrill of power. Perhaps I was not so different from my sister after all. How I longed to talk to her, but she was at Romorantin with Louise.

The hot, humid night caused me to throw the coverlet off the bed, and just at that moment, several horses neighed outside. Bonny growled. I sat up and leant on one elbow, peering across to the sleeping girls as they lay lit by the full moon pouring through the open casement. Rising from the bed, I moved to the window and leant out into the still air. The clear sky twinkled with a million stars, and an owl hooted in the trees. Where in the palace was my love now?

I thought of the words he had said to me before parting: *'Put me as a seal upon your heart because love is strong like Death.'*

The clattering of hooves on cobbles cut across my thoughts. However, although I stretched and peered, I could only see the dark shape of a large hound springing away beneath the gateway. Then another commotion broke the hot night, and I heard the sound of loud sobbing. Alarmed, I tip-toed over to the door, waking one or two of the other girls.

'What is it?' asked Collette sleepily.

One by one the other girls turned over, grumbling at the disturbance.

'Shush, I am listening,' I hissed, over my shoulder. 'It is the queen. Something is wrong with the queen.'

Mary Fiennes climbed out of bed, pulling her chemise about her. 'Is it the baby?' she asked.

We stood in silence, and as I carefully opened the door a little, I spied old Madame de Tournan shooing away the dwarf, Marie, who darted away in her night robe.

'Calm yourself, Madame, you must be still,' she called, 'I will fetch Dr du Puy.' She roughly pulled the arm of a chamberer. 'Go to, girl! Where is Monsieur Edevin and his potions? Can you not see my lady needs calming?'

'I have lost him!' cried the queen. 'He is gone, he is gone!'

I stared at Mary in alarm as the other girls, now quite awake, huddled behind me.

'My God,' said Gillette, as Bonny began frantically scratching at the door. 'I *knew* she could not carry the baby to full term, she is too feeble.'

We stood peering through the crack and watched the arrival of the doctor. He swept into the queen's chamber, followed by Françoise de Foix, Diane and a host of gaggling ladies in their nightcaps and robes, spinning round like weathercocks. *Madame la Grande* finally slammed the door shut.

'The poor queen,' I whispered. 'But where is the king – where is François?'

I moved back to my bed and picked up Bonny. As I sat there stroking her ears none of us spoke a word. Then, without warning, our chamber door burst open and Anne de Graville, her hair falling in two long, thick braids beneath her night bonnet, walked in, making us start.

'So – you are awake,' she observed, looking around at our faces. 'Anne, come with me please.'

I put Bonny down and grabbed my night robe, the other girls watching in silence. When I entered the queen's chamber, she was sitting in a chair, her fair hair falling about her shoulders, dabbing her eyes. The simple Brittany cross about her neck glinted in the candlelight, as Diane removed her book. The queen asked everyone to leave and I remained alone with her.

'Madame, is it the child?' I asked, tentatively.

She immediately burst into tears. 'Oh, Anne, come and console me.'

I hurried towards her, and she took my hand.

'François has gone. He slipped secretly out of our chamber as I slept, and I now hear he has ridden to join his mother at Romorantin. Only yesterday I publicly gave over to him the Duchy of Milan, received from my dear father, and assumed that we would travel together to Lyon. Ah, sweet François. Last night he held me in his arms and stroked my hair until I slept, so gentle and loving. Such tenderness means I cannot help but forgive him his women.'

Horrified, I thought of my sister, and she began crying again.

'Did you know they have been meeting regularly in secret again since the wedding?' she sobbed, 'and yet I dared not chastise him before he went to war. How could I reproach him? I could not.'

I began to feel anxious.

'Indeed, Madame,' I murmured.

'For her to meet my husband in the gardens of a monastery is – is bordering on sacrilege and he is becoming a laughing stock. I cannot bear it. Oh, I care nothing for myself, but I hate the way the people mock François in the streets with their lewd mummings, particularly the players of the *Bazoche*. My father thought them amusing, but I do not. I know that Madame Disommes is bitterly unhappy with her husband, but –'

I felt relief wash over me. Thank God. This time it was not Mary. And then I had the most awful thought.

'Madame, has the king taken all his gentlemen with him?'

'Not all, just his closest friends. Why do you ask?'

I shook my head, knowing it unlikely that Clément had ridden with him.

'François has agreed, on his mother's advice, that I could join him after the birth of the child, but not before, as I intended. I so wanted to be with him, but he would not hear of it, even though I pleaded. That is why he slipped away in the dark to avoid my tears. Well, at least he is not with *her*. Now, I am left alone with my imaginings, and I so fear for François' safety, for he is reckless and has no thought of danger, as his mother well knows.'

'Madame, perhaps this shared fear for his welfare will bring you and Madame Louise closer,' I said.

The queen put her hand to her cross.

'I pray constantly for it and trust a new *dauphin* will soften her heart towards me. There is also my concern for the good people of Lyon, for thousands of soldiers have swarmed into the city around the Place Fort, and the citizens will be much burdened. They have already paid sixty thousand livres towards the campaign and the joyous entry. Even the Venetian ambassador is alarmed.'

'Well, you must not be.' I took her damp hand in mine.

'I – I suppose not,' she added, raising her head. 'And I must be cheerful for it is at Lyon that François is to proclaim me regent while he is in Italy. He knows France will be in safe hands.'

'And that is how it should be,' I said.

'Indeed, I welcome it gladly, and I shall prove my worth and not disappoint my husband. My father taught me sound judgement and compassion – Orléan traits – and I have a thorough knowledge of state affairs.'

We were silent for a moment.

'Tell me of your news, Anne, distract my sad mind.'

'My mother has written to me and tells me that the court has departed to the West Country, on its summer progress. She says the land lies fresh and lush from the summer rain, and they are enjoying outdoor feasts in the woods, by candlelight, before repairing to great canvas marquees. All the court is there, except the king's sister, Mary, Duchess of Suffolk, who has returned to her estates in East Anglia to await the birth of her child. She still insists on being called the French Queen.'

'Well, I wish her a safe delivery, for she was ever kind to me,' said the queen.

'Oh, and Margaret of Savoy has written to me, too,' I said. 'She tells me she is quite well, as is Prince Charles. King Henry sent her a fine pair of hunting birds from England and she has enjoyed hawking frequently with the prince. She felt sad, privately, not to have attended the coronation of your husband, but is determined to push for peace with France as well as England.'

'Indeed, poor lady,' said the queen, with a sigh, 'yet her minister, Chièvres wants her completely out of the way, as does my mother-in-law with me.'

'And there is to be a wedding, Madame. In a few weeks, Mary of Austria will marry Louis of Hungary and Bohemia, at St Stephens Cathedral in Vienna. After the ceremony, fourteen-year-old Frederick, brother of Prince Charles, is returning to her court, from Spain. Oh, and Margaret has found several grey hairs, which have greatly dismayed her.'

The queen broke into a wide smile. 'Ah, see, you have cheered me in the way only you can.' She gave me a thoughtful look. 'You were happy with the Regent, were you not?'

'Indeed, Madame, but I am far happier here with you.'

And in that moment, thinking of my desire for Clément, I truly meant it.

* *

War fever engulfed the court, and many an old man wished he was accompanying the king, for war – they said – was a noble art. We heard that the king's great entourage, including his mother and sister, reached Lyon on the twelfth day of July, amidst the spectacle of arriving and departing troops. Over thirty thousand warhorses stood caparisoned in their finest harness, and their riders, their long, single feather gracing their helmets, vied with each other for richness of apparel.

King François wore a new suit of German armour covered with blue devices and enjoyed the many pageants and orations. He had also been presented with a great mechanical lion that spewed forth lilies, designed by a Signor Leonardo da Vinci. As a present, the king immediately sent the queen a magnificent silk coat covered with priceless emeralds and pearls. We stood in her chamber admiring it as she twirled about like a child, marvelling at its great cost. If sold, the money would have fed the poor folk of Amboise for a year, but the queen treasured such precious gifts from her husband and refused to take it off all day. However, it was nothing but a salve for the dreadful hurt that was about to come.

Chapter Eight

'Naught remains sure.'

The Loire and
Central France

The privy councillor held the arm of his companion, 'It cannot be,' he hissed, 'we are destroyed.'

They scurried along the gallery, papers in hand, throwing on their gowns as they walked, muttering to each other in low voices. The English ambassador, Lord Worcester, watched them pass. My thoughts flew to the war and Clément. Had there been some disaster? Every day the pages pinned fresh bulletins to the wall of the *grande salle*, but as yet, no such news had been posted. I felt myself shiver as dogs barked, servants ran behind their masters and messengers leapt up the staircase, two at a time, despatches in hand. Something was afoot, for as I stared out of the window at the litters, chariots, and horses clattering into the courtyard, it seemed like the whole world had descended upon us. Even *Madame la Grande*, usually at her château in Chantilly, arrived and alighted the steps, her ugly, yapping little dog in her arm. It had to be serious to drag her from her vineyards. I turned to see my sister.

'Mary, I thought you were at Romorantin. Oh, Mary, Clément has gone to war. I searched everywhere for him but could not find him, and finally received the news from his

servant. He left no note, no words of comfort – nothing –
I feel desolate! Do you know anything? Have the French been
defeated?'

She took me aside, her long hair frizzed in the latest style
and her silver-grey gown shimmering in the cool, dawn light.
'Nan, forget Clément – have you not heard the news?'

I felt angry at her unconcern at my plight. What could
be more important than my heart breaking?

'But – Mary, I must talk to you,' I protested.

She stopped and faced me, her eyes ablaze with
excitement. However, before she could speak, we heard
a great chattering noise, and both turned to see Louise,
accompanied by a trail of fawning courtiers, march towards
the *Logis of the Seven Virtues,* where the queen lay resting in
her apartments. Louise carried no walking stick and appeared
more vital and energetic than usual, eyes flashing as she
strode ahead.

'Make way for the king's most illustrious and clement
mother, the Duchess of Angoulême and Anjou, Madame
Louise!' cried the man-at-arms, as she flounced past Mary
and me, now bent low in obeisance. My sister fell behind
the other ladies and signalled me to follow on. When the
doors to the apartments were flung open, the queen turned,
startled, her book of hours in her hand. The crowd behind
Louise tumbled to an untidy halt.

'Dear God, what has happened? Is François hurt?' The
queen was pale.

'Madame, I am here to announce that you are to vacate
these apartments and repair to your confinement chambers
immediately. From this moment, I am endowed with power
over all men and princes alike. As regent, I now rule as Queen
of France here at Amboise, while you rest and await the birth
of the Dauphin.'

An expression of utter astonishment appeared on the
queen's face. 'But – my lady mother, my husband informed
me that I am to be regent before he left. It was agreed, for h –'

'Daughter, this is not a request. It is an instruction. You are about to give birth, and you will not be in any position to carry the great burden of state. We cannot have you endanger the child or exhaust yourself, can we?'

'But it was my husband's wish,' countered the queen, 'announced at Lyon.'

'No – since I was there, I shall tell you *exactly* what my son, himself, announced at Lyon. These are his own words:

> *'We have decided to leave the government of our realm to our well-beloved and dear lady and mother, the Duchess of Angoulême and Anjou, in whom we have entire and perfect confidence.'*

I stared at Louise as she folded her heavily ringed hands, the gold salamander on her forefinger appearing to flash its ruby eyes in triumph.

'Do not look so downcast. You and Renée were glorified in your absence, but my son instructed me to return to Amboise with Baron Semblançay, who is to direct my council. All that matters now is the success of the campaign, that the alliance with the Venetians stands sure and that old Marechal Trivulce stays close to my son.'

The queen appeared dumbstruck as her ladies stood in silence. Then Louise spoke, her voice high and imperious. 'Come now, did you not like the present François sent you? Such a valuable coat fit for a –

'Regent,' the queen interrupted coldly.

'A duchess,' came the reply. Louise could not resist the cruel taunt and so made the gift sound like some consolation prize.

Queen Claude crumpled into a chair and took the hand of Madame de Tournan, the old lady's eyes burning with venom. Dazed, the queen stared ahead at Louise's triumphant figure towering above her. She did not have the strength to fight her mother-in-law, and besides, it would have been useless. She raised herself unsteadily, but with dignity, placed a wrap around her shoulders and limped out of the chamber. Louise stood stiffly as the queen brushed past, chin held high.

'Madame, it is only as your husband wished,' said Louise, stepping aside. 'I am but his humble vessel, I must do as he bids.'

The queen made no reply as she continued with her ladies out of the door.

As I followed, Mary took me aside, and I watched as the queen retreated down the gallery.

'Dear God,' I said, in disbelief. 'Did you see that?'

'Yes,' whispered Mary, 'but there is worse. Louise is about to expel from their posts all those ministers she feels gave bad advice to her son, particularly those not considered *her* creatures. The *Parlement* in Paris is in an uproar, and all the court is outraged. And there's more, she wants immediate control of the treasury.'

'But the queen was expecting to rule, she said as much.'

'That may be, but her husband – no doubt pushed by his mother – decided otherwise, even though he is concerned Louise is not loved. He knows the people are afraid of her. I hear one of her first acts is to commission a family portrait to celebrate the war, omitting the queen. Is that not mean? Anyway, I must leave you here and wait on Louise, but it is very exciting. As one of her ladies, I shall be at the very centre of events. She is queen in all but name and will rule over all. What Louise wants, Louise gets. Now, I must hurry,' she said kissing my cheek, 'I will see you later.'

●　●

Inside her new apartments in the west wing, a fat, unsightly Queen Claude sat peering mournfully out at the Church of Notre-Dame de la Grève. Her ladies moved silently back and forth, carrying holy statues to place by her bed, and gradually the chamber began to take on the appearance of a tomb. The queen's dwarf, Marie, rubbed her mistress's feet and applied a dandelion poultice as she kneaded the swollen skin. Although many candles were lit, due to the poor light, the chamber appeared dreary, and I unfolded the blue silk gown, resting on my knees. It needed letting out, and I hoped I could sit quietly with my thoughts concerning Clément. It was not to be.

'I do not understand,' sniffed the queen. 'François knows that I am capable of ruling, whereas Louise is feared by the people. Did I not deal fairly with the recent jewellery theft in Amboise? Did I not hang the sow that attacked the child in Tours? No, I fear Louise will rule unwisely for she insists her lover, the Duc de Bourbon, returns to her side. As a great soldier and Constable of France, he must remain with François.'

'Indeed,' agreed Madame d'Assigny, 'but you know how François is in awe of his mother. We can only hope that Marguerite will restrain her.'

The queen gave a great, juddering sigh.

'Madame, do not forget,' Madame d'Assigny continued, 'Louise's authority will be somewhat limited since Duprat, as chancellor, has taken the Great Seal with him to Italy.'

'But since they work so closely together,' said the queen, 'that is of little comfort. Even the *parlement* has protested at her being given such wide powers.'

'Indeed, Madame, but perhaps it is best to leave you in peace, considering your condition, away from the affairs of state. Did not the Queen of England lose her child from acting as regent when her husband rode to war? You carry the most precious jewel.'

'Yes, but I do not intend galloping about the country,' said the queen. 'Besides, I hear there is a rumour that the queen is with child again. She recently launched a great galleass, *Princess Mary,* appearing plump and happy, but my ambassadors said it was impossible to tell her real condition beneath her full robes. If she is pregnant, she is still close laced.' She turned sadly away. 'As for me, I am perceived as worthless by this family, only suited to provide an heir, study building plans and tend to my gardens.'

'That is not true!' cried Anne de Graville. 'Your husband holds you in high esteem and relies on your sound judgement.'

A murmur of agreement filled the air.

'Oh, how I long to see him again,' said the queen. 'I hear from despatches that all goes in our favour, for his troops have captured Prospero Colonna, the commander of the pope's forces, near Villafranc. The Swiss had barred the high Alpine valleys, but my husband would not be stopped. He found even higher trails, blowing the narrow roads wide with black powder through the ice and craggy passes, towards Italy. He wrote that no-one would believe it possible to bring horses and artillery through raging torrents and precipitously steep mountains, yet now he is marching his army across like Hannibal. I pray every moment that God will protect him.'

She kissed the crucifix at her neck and then turned to me. 'You are very quiet, Anne.'

I started, for I had been lost in my thoughts.

'Perhaps you are sad that the court has lost all of its young gentlemen as they follow my husband to Italy?'

'No, no, not at all, my lady,' I stammered, my thoughts on only one of them. 'I have received a letter via Lord Worcester, informing me that my great-grandfather, Thomas Butler, the seventh Earl of Ormonde, has recently died at almost ninety years old. He was once chamberlain to Queen Katherine, and has left my father a very ancient gold and ivory hunting horn in his will.'

'Then you have my deepest sympathy, Anne,' said the queen. 'Were you fond of him?'

I said I did not know him well, but I had liked the blustering 'wool earl', with his Irish temper, afraid of no man. As a child, I recalled him hobbling along trying to chase me as I squealed in delight. However, although sad that he had died, I could not help but think of the great fortune he had

left behind, for he had been one of the richest men at the
English court and our family could only benefit.

'Well, we must have a Mass said for his soul,' said the
queen, her voice soft with kind concern.

•   •

Birds rose up in startled flight from the rooftops of
Amboise as a great cacophony of church bells announced
the arrival of the royal babe. The queen had laboured for
over ten hours and eventually at ten o'clock on the morning
of Sunday, the nineteenth day of August, the babe – a red,
mewling scrap – arrived. Sadly, it had all been in vain for the
long-awaited child was a *dauphine*.

As the archbishop, ambassadors and ministers filed
out in silence, I entered the crowded chamber with Renée.
I watched as the matrons fussed around the exhausted
girl and Marguerite handed the babe to the midwife to be
swaddled. The queen held her hand out to Renée as Anne de
Graville dabbed her brow with cooling water, for it had been
a difficult birth. As she smiled at her little sister, a shadowy
figure moved forward from the corner of the dark chamber,
and I drew back from the bed.

'Well, what will you call it?' asked Louise, as Dr du Puy
bowed and crept silently past.

The queen tried to sit up as the Duchess of Nemours,
standing behind Louise, stood pale-faced.

'We will call her Louise, in your honour,' she said weakly.

The duchess gave a nod as Diane curtsied, fresh towels
in her arms.

'You understand he will be disappointed – in private,
at least,' said Louise, staring down at her defeated
daughter-in-law.

The queen turned her face away.

'Your only task was to give him a son, nothing more.
Well, the despatches have gone forth, and he will know
within the fortnight. Now, you must try and sleep and regain

your strength. The baby is healthy, and there is no reason why you cannot have another. Marguerite and I, of course, will direct the care of the child, wet nurse, and nursery, having already appointed Madame Jeanne Brechenie. I am leaving now for Romorantin.'

With that, she turned and left the chamber, my sister following behind.

The queen sank back against the bolster, desolate. 'I had hoped to appease her by calling the baby Louise,' she said, as old Madame de Tournan pulled up the fresh coverlet. 'François will be so angry.'

'Madame,' said the old lady, 'the king is never angry with you. He will thank God that you have both survived. You have a beautiful little daughter. Next time, a fine little boy.'

'But if he does not come back to me – what then?'

'Nonsense, Madame, he will return in triumph,' soothed Madame de Brissac, 'they all will.' She threw me a sideways glance.

'We must, indeed, thank God you are both safe,' added Marguerite, as Renée sat on the bed beside her sister. 'The babe is beautiful, and my brother will love her tenderly. Is that not so, sweetheart? I hear that the council are to appoint a master of each guild for every town in celebration.'

'But I have failed him!' cried the queen.

'No, do not listen to my mother,' Marguerite chided gently. 'She is just disappointed. A daughter is not a failure as you well know. Do not be downcast, for to be born on the Lord's day is a blessing in itself. How could the king not love her as he loves you? Now – we must look forward to the celebrations for my dear brother's birthday. I cannot believe he is twenty-one.'

●　●

Desperate to hear from Clément, I cared naught for the new babe as everyone fussed around her, particularly Marguerite. She was besotted, while I thought only of him.

As crowds gathered inside the *grande salle* to hear of the latest developments, messengers waving their despatches clattered their exhausted horses up the *Minimes* tower ramp, and onto the dusty terrace. One despatch reported that the king had remained twenty-eight hours in the saddle, in full armour, with no food or drink. There appeared to be great terror and disorder. However, when the next messenger reached Amboise, great cheers rose into the air for we heard that French canon had reigned supreme and the Swiss had been routed back to Milan. After a fearsome battle at Marignano, three-quarters of the Swiss army had been destroyed, and Milan had capitulated on the fifteenth day of September. As Duke of Milan by right and conquest, the king made his triumphant entry and his new citizens showered three hundred thousand ducats upon him. Surely Clément would be returning soon?

King François had, apparently, happily celebrated the birth of his child, too good-natured to be disappointed for long. At Pavia, he was further amused when the artist Leonardo da Vinci designed another golden lion, this time spewing forth roses as he approached. François was so enchanted he made the artist promise to return with him to Amboise. He also sent the queen a set of wax dolls dressed in the latest Italian fashion, and his mother a medal, set in diamonds on a gold chain, engraved with the words: '*I overcame those whom only Caesar could conquer.*' She wore it constantly around her neck and ordered all the castles and towns along the Loire to be illuminated with torches and bonfires. Even the boats bobbing on the water were lit up like so many fireflies. Louise continued to arrange extravagant celebrations and for holy relics to process throughout the land, ordering that no expense was to be spared. Once recovered, the queen and her intimate ladies set out for the Abbey Notre Dame de Fontaine to give thanks for her husband's safety and the birth of her child.

Meanwhile, we heard from the English ambassador that

King Henry, hunting in Wiltshire, was furious at the king's actions, for daring to attack the pope, and refused to believe his exaggerated exploits. Thomas Wolsey had already warned the pope of King François' intent and reaped the reward of a cardinal's hat on the proviso that England supported the Holy See. Henry, for his part, promised to appoint Wolsey Lord Chancellor of England. Then, in London, a dreadful flux broke out, causing great fear and distress; and in Spain, we heard that King Ferdinand, that wily old fox, had fallen in a fit. Apparently, his wife had given him an aphrodisiac to eat. There also ran a rumour that he intended to make peace with England. I cared not a fig for any of this, for I yearned only to hear of Clément.

Late one afternoon, as I helped Eliza Grey and Mary Fiennes carry new shirts of linen to Madame de Tournan's apartments, a messenger stopped me. He bowed and handed me a folded letter, the script I recognised. My heart began racing, and I placed my shirts on top of Mary's pile and waved the girls away. Settling myself on a nearby step, I began to read:

> *'My dearest Anne, how I hope this finds you well and of good cheer and not still aggrieved at my departure. Please forgive me, but I could not bear your tears or reproaches. And please forgive my lack of writing, too – as an aspiring poet, I have no excuse! But I am safe and well and have such tales to tell of our campaign. How high were the strong hearts of our knights, how skilful the art of our captains! How bright the ardour of the Adventurers! The king was magnificent in his courage and has proved himself the most valiant prince, leading a charge against the Swiss. Yet all he wanted to hear before he rode into battle was that he had a male heir. I, amongst others, stood close to him at Vercelli – between Milan and Turin – when he heard of the birth, and I have never seen a man so broken. To the world, he*

appears overjoyed. He wrote a long letter to his mother, but only a short note to Claude, enclosing a gold ring. I do not think he knew what to write to her. But, I tell you, Anne, war is not of God – it is a pitiless serpent obscuring the pure, clean air with saltpetre, artificial powder, and wood smoke. I am done and ready to return and will make my way to Paris first, before I return to the south. Ah! I have seen many brutal – and noble – things, and I write with a fire I knew not existed. Ceaselessly all night I write, not caring for food or wine. Everything I see, touch or smell I put to paper. It burns me now with even more of a desire to make my way at court, consumes me with an ambition I cannot quench – If I can but find a way…'

As I looked up and gazed across the courtyard to the distance, disappointment filled my heart. I was not interested in the feats of the king, or the war, and although Clément wrote he would return soon, I felt sad. This was not the love letter for which I had hoped.

• •

'Stop fidgeting,' urged my sister, as she moved my long hair aside to fasten the necklace.

I stared in the mirror at the slight figure nervously picking at her nails. 'Mary, how can I be still when I am about to see him again? I am trembling.'

The chapel bell sounded a mid-day clang. Earlier, we had celebrated the feast day of the Nativity of Our Lady, and I had had quite enough of incense and Masses. 'Holy Mother, I am late.'

'Well, stop moving, this clasp is very awkward. Which earrings have you decided upon? The amethysts or the garnets?'

'The garnets. Oh, hurry, Mary!'

'There – anyway, I cannot be long as Louise has asked

for me. She is at this very moment with her astrologers, determining the best day to start the great journey to Marseilles. A Friday, of course, would bode ill. Marguerite said the queen is unhappy to be leaving her baby but is desperate t –'

'What did you just say?' I spun around to face her as she picked up the brush.

'Some promise Louise made last year to St Mary Magdalene. If the king proved victorious, she, along with the queen, Marguerite and the whole court would make a pilgrimage to the south to her shrine, and then meet the king in Italy. They – we – are leaving in a few weeks.'

'But what of Clément, will he go?' I sat down on the stool and looked anxiously up at her.

'How should I know? Perhaps your lover will stay here.'

'He is *not* my lover, I told you, Mary. I shall not lie with him until he marries me. I am not like you.'

'Marries you? Are you quite mad? Nan, you cannot marry him any more than I can marry François. Father and Uncle Howard really would send you away. Why can you not just enjoy the moment without foolish complications?'

I grabbed the brush from her and started frantically brushing my long, glossy hair. 'No, Mary, I mean to marry him – I mean it, so go away!'

I watched as she pulled a face in the mirror, and flounced out of the chamber. Why did we always have to argue with each other? But she was right – I *was* mad and until that moment had not seriously thought of marrying Clément. However, as usual, my defiant nature took over whenever she crossed me and yet…I had never met a man who engaged my mind with such a passion before. Other young men I spoke to bored me, but not Clément. Now, all thoughts to obey my parents in whatever advantageous match they might propose seemed to have disappeared in a puff of smoke.

When Mary had gone, I dabbed a little red paste on my lips and pulled my burgundy red gown down at the shoulders. My dull Breton bonnet lay forgotten. The queen would not approve of my loose, long hair on show, but I cared not. I felt bored under her watchful eye and, besides, she would not see me. Anyway, why should Mary be the one to wear her long hair crimped and enjoy all the amusements, gambling and flirting? All I seemed to do was sit sewing shirts while the queen read her bible, fussed over her baby and repeated over and over the king's tedious exploits. I glanced one last time in the mirror, pinched my pale cheeks, and nervously stepped into the late September sunshine towards the Church of Notre-Dame de la Grève.

In the cool deserted church, I crossed myself with holy water, my heart racing.

'Anne?' I spun around.

'Clément!' I threw myself into his arms, and he swung me around, my feet lifting off the floor. It was hardly the decorum I had been taught. 'Why did you leave Amboise so suddenly?' I chided, as he put me gently down. 'Why did you not write? I only received the one letter a –' I did not finish my sentence for he kissed me into silence for what seemed like an age.

'Come, sit with me,' he finally said, leading me to a bench. 'Dearest Anne, I have such things to tell you, but right now seeing your sweet face, I cannot. I only want to feel you close to me.'

I nestled into his shoulder.

'Has all been well with you? Are you still with Queen Claude?'

'Yes, but the days have been *so* tedious, and the nights even worse. The queen's court is stifling. Oh, I have missed you so much, why did you not write more often?'

'Anne, I thought of you each day I was away, truly I did. You are as charming as I remember.'

I smiled up at him as he stroked the hair tumbling over my shoulders.

'Here, I brought you this from Italy.' He delved into

his doublet and pulled out a small, silver brooch depicting a red enameled rose. 'I had it made in Italy, to remind you of home.'

I carefully pinned it to my gown, joy in my heart.

'Clément, have you heard of the progress planned in October? Do you know anything about it? It will take months and months and if you are left behind I will be parted from you again. I could not bear it!'

Clément smiled. 'Hush, what is this talk so soon of parting? I heard about the progress in Italy, for Louise is desperate to see her son again, and he has agreed to a reunion at Lyon in the spring. I assure you, I have no intention of remaining behind, and to that effect, I want you to give something to the queen. It is a poem I composed on the birth of baby Louise. I am hoping it pleases her so that I will be allowed to take part in the progress and, more importantly, be in the presence of Marguerite.'

'And mine,' I ventured, raising my head. 'But why can you not present the poem yourself?'

'I would. I would give it to the king, but now everything written, no matter how inconsequential, has to go through Louise first. She does not approve of me and Father says she deplores my religious ideas, which is strange since she is all for reform, albeit secretly. She only tolerates me for my father's service to her son. Did you hear that she is calling for an agreement between the pope and King François that, in effect, will place him at the head of the church in France? Only he will be able to approve appeals to Rome, tax the clergy and appoint new bishops. Through religion, he will thus entirely control the state. With such power, he will not have to accept any of our reforming ideas concerning the faith.'

'My sister calls her a witch behind her back,' I said.

'And so say I,' said Clément. 'Oh, Anne, I have returned with such hopes to succeed at court, but with King François away, my progress can only be through Marguerite. We think the same, hold the same religious views, read the same books. She holds the key to my success and I mean one day to do her service.'

'But when can *we* be together again?' I didn't want to talk about Marguerite.

He took my fingers and kissed them. 'Tonight, sweetheart, I will come and find you. And then...' As he put his arms around me and held me close, I noticed the shadowy figure of Françoise de Foix genuflect and leave through the chapel door.

＊　＊

On the fifteenth day of October, the king gave his mother permission to leave Amboise and give thanks for his victory at the shrine of Mary Magdalene, at Saint-Maximin-la-Sainte-Baum, in the south-west of France. The pilgrimage was to be called the 'Journey of the three Queens'. Of course, neither Claude, Louise nor Marguerite were crowned, but as the idea came from the king, they had to be accepted as such.

Once the letter arrived, Louise consulted her astrologers, and five days later, on a clear morning, thirty litters and chariots stood on the terrace at Amboise, laden with linen, tapestries, plate, and religious relics. Half of them belonged to Louise alone, since accompanying her would be her apothecary, her surgeon, her tailor, her seamstress, and a hundred other servants, either in carts or on foot. The advance party had already left to find suitable accommodation for the court, with mules laden with tents should it not be forthcoming. It had been a vast undertaking to organise, with everything packed from horse fodder to the royal wardrobe; but finally, all stood ready to depart.

I descended the steps holding Renée's hand, my other on the arm of the elderly Baron Semblançay, Minister of Finance, for the younger children and myself had been placed in his care during the progress. Before me, a great assembly sprawled across the courtyard, as horses jangled their harness with impatience. *Fauconniers* checked and re-checked the jesses and leashes of the hunting birds perched on their frames. As usual, *Madame la Grande* sat fussing over the cushions in her chariot and demanded they were changed. I stepped up into the queen's litter as Renée settled down with Bonny on her knee, and Marie, chattering excitedly, moved aside. Behind, I noticed the two young sons of the King of Navarre, Henri, and Charles, along with Anne de Pisseleu and Anne de Foix in their chariot. Anne sat fondling the ears of Renée's rabbit, aware of Bonny's amusing interest.

Meanwhile, the children's tutor, and their governess, Madame de Brissac, mounted their horses, their leather panniers bulging with books and papers, for nothing must interfere with their education.

My sister turned her horse in behind Louise, and my dearest Clément, hands resting on the pommel of his saddle, sat mounted beside her. The wet nurse held baby Louise up to the queen for a blessing, and she kissed her tiny hand saying that leaving her was the hardest thing she had ever done, except for parting from the king. Now, at last, she was on her way to greet him, and with trumpets blasting, the litter lurched forward, and we began to wind our way down the great ramp of the Minimes tower. Immediately behind our litter, Marguerite, dressed in plum-coloured velvet, walked her grey horse beside the Venetian ambassador, Signor Pasqualigo.

'I tell you, Signor, my brother is determined to make Venice greater than she has ever been before. As for the impoverished Emperor...'

The ambassador smiled and inclined his head. 'Madame, if all the leaves on the trees in Italy were converted to ducats, they would not be enough for Maximilian. Do they not call him *Massimiliano poco danari*? But we might yet see peace between him and your brother, even though Spain has been warring with France these hundred years, insisting she has claims in Italy.'

I smiled to myself for it seemed that Margaret of Savoy's father still lacked money.

'And now,' continued the ambassador, shifting in his saddle, 'we are on the road again, for if not chasing your brother through the forests we poor ambassadors must follow his mother halfway across France.'

'Is François so elusive?' Marguerite smiled.

'You know as well as I, Madame, that the court remains only in one place as long as the game lasts. Anyone who wants to speak with the king must find himself a horse and hie to the green woods.'

I turned to the queen, who told me autumn was the perfect time to visit the south, and that there would be fine hawking. But she felt concerned that the townsfolk would be burdened with the expense of entertaining her.

'I hate to put them to any trouble, but it is good to let the people see me,' she added, waving up at the open windows in the street as housewives cheered.

They loved the queen for her generosity to the town, and several ran out from the half-timbered houses with little gifts of bread and pastries, which she accepted with graciousness. We then proceeded through the main city gate with its great belfry and past the mill of armaments, towards the river.

Louise, seated in her ornate chariot, head down, peered at papers through an eye-glass. She handed them to her first councillor, Monsieur Charles du Plessis, who sat opposite her, clutching a leather bag. The work of government could never stop. As the horses carrying the litter continued to lurch and slide down the steep cobbled hill, the papers, to the councillor's utter dismay, fell from the bag and blew away. It was not a good start.

● ●

That warm, balmy autumn we continued south by barge to Bléré, and on towards the town of Mézières en Brenne. The countryside blazed with the red, gold and amber colours of the season, and the days, although shortening, stayed dry.

Our great convoy, with its golden, triple *fleurs-de-lis* embroidered on blue banners, rested a few days at the Château de Chemeray, overlooking the River Creuse. There we attended a splendid banquet hosted by the local mayor and dignitaries. The animated mayor talked of nothing but the hawking to be had. The wetlands, rich in fowl, such as heron, grebe, and tern, left Louise and Marguerite in raptures. Not so the queen. I noticed her drooping in the heat of the *grande salle*, for a great many people were present, and I knew, thank God, that she could not stay awake much longer.

I felt desperate to join Clément, and when everyone had gone to their beds, I hurried down the gallery of the château, down the stone spiral steps and entered one of the unused chambers. Seeing Clément standing there, I rushed into his arms. With the door locked, we were safe and kissed passionately without restraint. When his ardour became too much to bear, he deftly began to unlace my gown. As it dropped to the floor, I clutched at my silk shift, my heart beating so hard I thought I might die. I quickly moved onto the pallet and pulled Clément's cloak over my body to hide my embarrassment. I turned away as he removed his doublet and hose, and when he lay down beside me in his long shirt, I clung to his warm body as we kissed again.

A little while later, as I lay with my head on Clément's shoulder, he stroked my cheek.

'Why?' he asked, softly.

I turned onto my back and drew his cloak over my cold shoulders.

He sat up, moved it down a little and tenderly kissed the white skin. 'All summer I have waited and soon it will be the feast of All Souls. Do you not love me?'

I put my finger to his lips. 'Hush, you know I do. I love you more than I have ever loved anyone before. My love consumes me like fire, and yet I will only give my maidenhead to my husband.'

He fell back with a sigh and placed his arm beneath his tousled hair.

'God, when will you end my torment?' he asked.

'When you end mine,' I replied.

He opened his eyes and stared at me. 'What?'

'Marry me. Marry me here in France.' I leant up on my elbow. 'It would not be difficult to find a priest in any of the towns we pass through.'

'Your parents would never allow it,' he said. 'Besides, where would we live?'

'England, of course.'

'*England?* Why would we live there? My place is here at court.'

It was not the answer I was expecting.

'Well, then we could stay here,' I said, brightly. 'I could continue in the queen's service – Renée is very fond of me – and I am sure the queen would help us.'

'The queen would dismiss you today if she could see you – like this.' He pulled the cloak clean away, pulled up my shift and uncovered my naked, slender frame. Rolling on top of me, I felt his prying, urgent fingers between my legs.

'No, Clément, please!' I gasped under the weight of his body. *'Please,* I cannot breathe!'

He fell reluctantly back. 'Heaven forfend,' he murmured, 'I did not mean to do that.'

I lay there not knowing what to say, shaken by his passion. He closed his eyes and I could feel his heart racing.

'I – I can still please you,' I said, my hand sliding beneath his shirt. My sister had told me how to do that much at least. He abruptly clasped my probing fingers.

'No,' he said, with a sigh, rising off the bed. 'No, we must return. It is almost dawn and the queen may call for you. We must get dressed.'

I watched him as he hopped about with first one leg in his hose, then the other, and then fastened the points on his doublet.

'Let me,' I offered, sliding up behind him, my long hair falling like a mantle. He proffered a sleeve in silence, and I pushed the hair teasingly from his eyes. I kissed his neck and moved round to his lips, but he would not look at me. Instead, he gently took both my wrists and kissed me on the forehead. It was the kiss of a father, not a lover. He then helped me back into my gown.

'You go out first, Anne, I need to stay here a moment, alone.' As I kissed him on the lips and turned to leave, he suddenly caught my hand.

'Tell no-one of this, Anne. No-one.'

I smiled and stepped quietly down the torchlit gallery towards the queen's chamber. Smoothing down my hair, I hoped I did not appear too dishevelled. On the left, a beam of light from Louise's apartments streamed down the passageway, and I did not doubt that she had been working all night. She seemed to need very little sleep, and I knew that she had been closeted with Signor Dandolo, one of the Venetian ambassadors, and *Madame la Grande* for hours. As I approached the queen's chambers, Antoinette de Polignac, followed by Diane and several other ladies, swept in front of me, each carrying a framed oil painting. Perhaps these were some of the spoils of war from Italy that Louise had spoken of and was so keen to acquire. They knocked at Louise's door, and as it opened, I saw her head bent over her desk, writing.

'Leave them there, if you will. Now, Signor, you must not vex yourself, for we have heard this before. Embassies are coming and going from all the greatest princes in Christendom and all hammer at the same anvil.'

My sister then appeared, carrying a large pile of rolled documents. As they slipped and cascaded to the floor, I quickly helped pile them back into her arms.

'All night we have had this,' she whispered, 'I am exhausted. She cannot fart unless the position of the planets is favourable.' She giggled and glanced around as the ladies disappeared into the queen's chamber. 'Listen, Nan, if you were seeing *him*, you must be careful, for I heard a complaint that the queen asked for you twice last night after she went to bed. Poor Renée had a bad dream and cried and cried saying she wanted to see you. You will be caught, so have a care.'

'I will Mary, I promise, but wait, I must speak with you.'

'I cannot,' she said, 'I must take these to her astrologer and then return with him. There has been a great earthquake in Normandy and it bodes ill for the French, hence *she* is not in the best of moods.'

• •

Pulling on my green leather gauntlet, I took the hobby from the *fauconnier*. Her wings were outstretched and her feathers ruffled, but I soothed her with my voice, and she turned her head inside the red, tufted hood. She was a pretty creature, sure and swift in flight and I looked forward to the day's hunting. Marguerite and her mother, both with a merlin on their forearms, chatted as their ladies, my sister included, sat mounted behind them. Mary, laughing too loudly as ever, sat her horse wearing a charming blue hunting gown, her hair piled high beneath a silver bonnet. The queen, on the other hand, only appeared tired and worn out as she sat in her litter, for she did not feel well enough to ride today.

I turned my Spanish Jennet around and trotted away, the sleek, golden-haired dogs barking and tugging at their leashes. To my surprise, Clément did not acknowledge me, but kicked his bay horse ahead, his eyes lowered as if troubled. As I watched him go, I admired his horse – a present, he had told me, from the king, in exchange for presenting him with the *Judgement of Minos*. So, he had managed to attract the king's attention after all. Well, I would attract his, for he would now observe how well I rode and handled my bird, my feathered lure ready.

Our hunting party rode out through the mews and ambled towards the open ground of river inlets, reed beds, and woodland. A distinguished-looking old gentleman on a sleek black horse commented on my attractive plumed bonnet, and smiling, I trotted away lost in my thoughts. Beside me, falconers ran with leashes, lures and leather bags of raw meat strapped to their belts. Others carried gyrfalcons and peregrines, the Milan bells on the birds' legs jangling as they flexed their wings and ruffled their feathers. Diplomatic gifts, no doubt. My sister pulled her grey mare up beside me, and I watched as Clément spoke with Marguerite.

'I did not receive a falcon from François,' said Mary, glancing back towards Clément.

'Do you not think he looks handsome?' I said. 'Black is so very stylish – and expensive.'

'Yes, Nan, he does and how clever of him to match his coat to his mood.'

I sighed as she stared at me.

'What – have you two argued?" She looked over at Clément. 'He has not come near you, but only talks to Marguerite or the other ladies. I understand you both must be cautious, but he could at least have the manners to say good day.'

I gazed across to where Clément sat, his horse now surrounded by courtiers, stroking the tiercel on his wrist. It began to spit with rain.

'I know. Something is wrong, but I do not know what. No ill words have been exchanged between us.'

'Are you really in love with him?' Mary soothed her bird as it turned about on her gauntlet and stretched out one wing.

'I am and I do not know what to do, for I did not intend this to happen.'

She laughed and glanced back to Clément. 'I told you what to do, goose,' she said, gathering her horse's reins and trotting away. 'Do as he asks and make him happy!'

I gazed up at the sky and then, un-hooding my bird, watched as she roused herself and cast off from my left fist. Shielding my eyes from the low sun, I watched her spiral up to a great height and then hang in the air. Motionless, she hovered until the quarry was flushed out by the dogs and beaters, before diving to make a kill. One of the *fauconniers* ran to her, taking a small piece of meat from his bag.

'She is a beauty.' I turned to see Baron Semblançay cantering his horse up to my mine.

'Oh, yes, yes, indeed, sir, I hunted with my father at Hever. But not with such beautiful creatures.'

'And he taught you well, for you know how to handle a falcon,' came the reply. He took off his bonnet and glanced about, wiping his brow. 'It is good country for birds. Did you see how well Marguerite fared with her white gyrfalcon? It flew straight and fast, bringing down one bird after another with its powerful flight. Louise has also triumphed for her large, black-eyed merlin caught several skylarks with great ferocity. She is hoping to use the peregrine next to bring down a crane.'

We walked our horses together in silence and then I spoke: 'Monsieur, what is your impression of Madame Marguerite?'

The gentleman smiled. 'And why, *demoiselle*, do you ask?'

'I would like to know, the more to please her.'

He pulled his horse to a halt, rested his arms on the pommel of his saddle and turned to me.

'In truth, she is a joy, and I hear a very easy person to please; you have only to love her mother and brother. I can honestly tell you that I have never met such an extraordinary person, for although she appears to be a woman, she has a man's heart and wit.'

'But why do people think she is so attractive?' My voice was a little too high. 'I mean, she has a very long nose, small slanting eyes and is too tall for a woman. Do you not think so, sir?'

He laughed. 'You have missed the point, *demoiselle*, for beauty comes from the soul and is nothing to do with the physical. If the heart and soul are full of love, it shines through the eyes, and that is what makes Marguerite so beloved. She also captures men with her conversation, for she ever prefers her dinner to contain more wit than meat!'

I narrowed my eyes and stared into the distance. 'Indeed, Monsieur. Well, I see she wants you back.'

As I bent down to take my hobby from the returning *fauconnier,* Baron Semblançay turned his horse and cantered away. The old gentleman on the black horse followed him.

The afternoon wore on. Clément, often at Marguerite's side, helped her with her bird, her gauntlet, or with whatever else she needed. Marguerite, for her part, appeared happy with his attention and I began to seethe. When not with Marguerite, he accompanied another of the ladies, and it seemed impossible to speak to him alone.

I sat in a daydream as Diane trotted up to my side. She smiled in greeting as her horse shook out its long, white mane.

'What ails you, Anne?' she asked.

I was surprised, for I thought I was hiding my feelings rather well.

'You have been very quiet all afternoon,' she continued. 'It is not like you.'

I blustered some excuse, but she only frowned. 'I do know,' she said, her voice kind.

I sat feeling mortified as she reached out and rested her hand on my arm.

'Am I being foolish?' I asked. 'I cannot help my feelings, truly I cannot.'

'Only if you let the queen find out. You must be more careful.'

'Is it that obvious?' I grimaced.

She smiled and sat back. 'If it is just a dalliance, no harm will come of it. But you must not think that it could be anything more.'

'Why not?' I stared up at the clouds. 'Other women have married for love. It is – well, it's just that I am afraid that my parents will betroth me to someone I do not care for. I did not think much about it before, but now that I have lost my heart and understand how it feels, how could I live in a loveless marriage?'

'Anne, your parents cannot force you into a hateful match, for the church does not allow it. No, they will only want a suitable marriage that will increase your standing and prospects. That is to be expected from loving parents.'

Somehow I did not feel comforted since Mary Tudor had been forced to marry old King Louis before she married her true love, Charles Brandon. Where had the church stood in that frightful match?

'Anne, I am not much older than you and I had such hopes of a man nearer my age. When I first heard that I must marry the old Comte de Brézé, grandson of King Charles VII, I cried. However, *Madame la Grande* made me see sense with her kindness and wisdom.'

'Kind? She always appears so formal and frightening,' I said, none too convinced.

'Not at all. About ten years ago, she wrote a wonderful piece for Suzanne called *'Lessons for my Daughter.'* You should read it.'

'And what is your point?' I asked, stroking my horse's neck.

'Her wise words, Anne: 'Love who you will, but marry well.' Brought up under her kind guidance, I owe everything to her, and there is not a fine lady in France who has not come under her care. She has shaped my mind, developed my taste in art and instilled in me the highest principles of honour. To be worthy of my name, I must be a mirror, a pattern and an example for other women in all matters.'

'Do you love your husband?' I asked.

Her face fell a little.

'I did not at first,' she said, 'but he knew this and made me a promise. He would make me the finest lady in France, after Marguerite. Yes, he took away my youth, but he has given me great riches, and I have become fond of him. He may be old, but I will never betray him.'

'Do you mean with the king?' I asked. 'I have seen how he stares at you.'

'Oh, the king knows he is wasting his time with me!'

'But how does this affect me, Madame?' I asked.

'When the time comes, Anne, do the right thing for your family and its honour.'

'But I am only a knight's daughter, not some great noblewoman.'

'At present, yes, but who knows what may happen, for I hear your Howard family are ambitious. Be guided by them. Let them decide, not you, for that way lies ruin.'

I could not agree but felt too confused to argue.

At that moment my sister trotted up, her cheeks flushed.

'Nan, Diane, I have just heard that we are travelling on to Aigurande and Hérisson and then on to Montluçon.'

Diane smiled and turning her horse's head, cantered away.

I stared into the distance at Clément, his head now bent close to the king's sister – too close in fact.

'Are you listening?' asked Mary, following my eyes. 'You know you really must learn to hide your feelings.'

'Why is he doing this?' I asked, 'when he knows how I feel? Look at him.'

'Your jealous streak is getting worse by the day,' said Mary. 'Anyway, you know he only seeks Marguerite out for her patronage and what she can do for him.'

I sat, my face sullen, as my horse cropped the ground, and roughly pulled up her head. The long blades of grass looked comical as they dangled from her mouth.

'I just feel a fool,' I said, 'watching him thus and not knowing what I have done wrong.'

'Well, perhaps now you understand how I feel now,' replied Mary, 'and will try to be kinder…'

Chapter Nine

'Abandoned am I as all constant are.'

Central France and
Auvergne-Rhône-Alpes

We travelled over thirty-five leagues, taking barges down the River Indre when we could, or moving over land. However, the sinking tracks and floods now tried everyone's patience. Carts stuck fast in the mud, one of the horses bolted, and a litter overturned when the mules carrying it stumbled. The ladies inside had to recover at Chamblet, where the villagers stood dumbstruck at the sight of so rich an assembly. When the convoy finally lumbered away again, a drizzling mist had set in.

On arrival at the town of Montluçon, there began the usual bickering and squabbling over the fact that there was not enough accommodation at the château, despite tickets being allocated. An unseemly rush ensued as courtiers tried to find shelter in the town, bribing their way into family homes, hostels and even stables. Louise, comfortable in her chambers in the château, appeared far too busy to notice their plight as messengers and ambassadors hurried to her with news from her son. The queen, however, lay exhausted and, to Louise's immense irritation – for she was eager to see her son – she announced that we would have to stay put for the week while her daughter-in-law recovered.

Unpacking trunks and airing gowns with the other ladies, I hoped all the while to see Clément. But he was nowhere to be seen.

On the third night, we attended a reception and banquet held in the *grand salle,* and anyone of note from the surrounding towns swarmed to the château. Dish after dish of pheasant, red-legged partridges, heron powdered with sugars and spices, roast suckling-pig, Genoa artichokes, and Barbary cucumbers were placed on the long tables. Although a fire raged in the great fireplace, I felt chilled, for the heat only reached the place of honour where Louise, the queen, Renée, and Marguerite sat.

After the feast, as the rain pattered against the windows and the candles in the iron candelabra flickered in the draught, musicians took up their instruments, and we rose from our places to begin the dancing. Where *was* Clément? I had to know what I had done to displease him. Louise, Marguerite, and the queen stepped down and took their places with their hosts, waiting for the pavane to begin.

'Can you see him?' I asked.

My sister stood on tiptoe and craned her neck.

A gentleman asked if I would dance, but I declined, caring not if my refusal might be deemed rude.

'No, but another handsome gentleman is coming this way,' she replied excitedly.

Bowing low, Monsieur Jean Jouglet, the ambassador from Margaret of Savoy's court at Mechelen, took hold of my sister's hand and escorted her towards the dancers. Mary Fiennes and Eliza quickly followed, as Anne de Graville, Diane de Brézé and several other ladies-in-waiting took their places.

I stood amongst the younger girls, tapping my feet to the beat of the tabor as the dance progressed. Another dance began and finished. And then I saw him enter the *salle.* He appeared nervous as he removed the bonnet from his head and smoothed his ruffled hair. My face lit up, but on seeing me, he whispered to his companion and quickly made to leave. When my sister walked towards me, her face flushed from her exertions, my face burned with indignation.

'Nan?'

'How dare he continue to ignore me like this!'

Sweeping her aside, I moved forward, my eyes blazing in anger, pushing as best I could through the great crowd of revellers. I was just about to reach the other side when I felt someone grab my arm and force me behind one of the hanging tapestries.

'Oh!' I stared into the face of Françoise de Foix. 'Madame, what – what on earth are you doing?'

'Preventing you from making a fool of yourself, like your sister,' she whispered.

'But I – I do not understand.' I rubbed my pinched arm.

'I think you do. There is something of grave importance I must impart to you.'

I stared at the woman standing before me in the cream-coloured gown, sparkling with sapphires, and felt alarmed.

'Come, Anne,' she said, glancing about, 'let us go where we can be private, though God knows where in this crowd.'

'No, Madame, I cannot,' I said, glancing back towards Clément, but my words were lost as she steered me towards a wooden door. Once through, she closed it, dropped the latch and sat down on the bench.

'Please – sit.'

Reluctantly, I did as she said. On the other side of the door, I could hear the muffled sound of music playing and feet stamping. I hoped this would not take long, for I had to find Clément.

'Now – you must give him up. And do not insult me by asking who.'

My mouth dropped open a little. 'Madame, I do not know…'

'Yes, you do.'

I looked at her calm face and unblinking eyes. 'Then,

Madame, I can only assume you mean Monsieur Marot.'

I felt uneasy. First Diane and now Françoise.

'You saw us together in the church. How long have you known?'

'I have known for a long time, but the queen, thank God, does not. She has been too pre-occupied with the war, her pregnancy and now the child.'

'But I have done nothing wrong, Madame,' I said. 'I wish to marry Clément, and he wishes to marry me.'

'And you are sure of that? Anne, your family will have plans for you of their own, and besides, the queen will not countenance any of her girls having affairs while in her care. If she is told, well, that will be two Boleyn girls disgraced. Everything has a price, and impeccable behaviour is the price you pay for bed and board at her court.' Françoise's pale face softened, and she showed concern in her eyes. 'Please, Anne, I am not your enemy, but you must tell me. How far has this affair progressed?'

She took my cold hand but I pulled it away. Silence filled the air as I stared sullenly down.

'Are you with child?'

I stared at her in horror. 'No, Madame! I wish him to be my husband first. He – he urges me to – to do as he begs, but I have not yet done so.'

'Anne, you must forget this man.'

'But why, Madame, why should I forget him?'

'Because he has asked me to tell you that you must. Matters are over between you.' She turned around to avoid my eyes.

'But I do not understand. Why would he speak to *you* before me, about something so personal and private?'

She sighed, clearly finding this whole interview most disagreeable. She then told me that Clément had sought her out since he had not the courage to face me himself. She had begged him to do the honourable thing, but he said he could not trust himself to speak to me. Now she was to tell me that all affection between us was over and that his heart lay bound to another.

'*Another?*' I asked, in disbelief. 'How can there be another?'

Françoise began twisting the ring around her finger. My eyes widened in realisation.

'It is her, isn't it? It is Marguerite.'

Silence.

'Tell me!'

'Not – exactly.'

I burst out laughing.

'Ha, he thinks to have *her,* but she is the king's sister and married! Does she feel the same?'

Françoise sat down again. 'I doubt that she is even aware of his feelings. He is just a moon mad poet, but an overambitious one at that.'

'So what am I to him?' I asked, barely above a whisper.

'A fancy, a dalliance,' Françoise said gently. 'But you are young, and …'

'Exactly! And being young has proved my ruin. If I had acted like a woman and given him what he wanted, shown my love completely as he begged…'

'No, Anne.' Françoise voice was firm. 'If you think pleasing a man so will make you his wife, it will not, for what he gains too cheaply, he esteems too lightly.'

'But was declaring my love openly to him not enough? No, I am sorry, but I do not believe any of this. We are still to be married.'

'Anne, to declare your affection so openly was very foolish. Besides, he has no intention of ever marrying you, for he is besotted with Marguerite and has been for some time.' Her face softened. 'Come now, you know at fifteen it is easy to confuse sensations with sentiments; and that is why, if we are lucky, real love is not known until we are older. It is a gradual unfolding, and you have much time ahead of you, for you are still young.

'But this *is* real love!' I was not a child.

'Anne, let me plain with you. Clément Marot is an unstable young man. He is dangerous, outspoken, and headstrong, and one day he will be in trouble, taking you with him if you let him. He keeps bad company and is hungry for recognition. That makes a man rash. His head is full of ridiculous ideas on religion and while Marguerite has her brother's protection, he does not. Please, Anne, you will thank me one day for telling you this.'

Thank her? How could I possibly thank her for breaking my heart?

'He *does* love me,' I said, raising my head, 'for he says I am the most beautiful creature he has ever seen.'

'If that is what you wish to believe, then so be it, but to enslave a man completely, there must be spirit and intelligence, as well as beauty.'

'Do I not have spirit? Am I not intelligent?' I asked.

As I stood, utterly desolate, I asked if Clément knew her opinion of him.

'No, I keep my own counsel, as must you,' she replied. I felt stunned and utterly humiliated by her words.

'What am I to do, Madame? I have lost the dearest heart in all the world.'

'Forget the ideas you find so exciting, for they are dangerous. Heed my advice. Learn from this.'

I looked at her through my tears.

'I know what a debauched court we reside in. The men compare the ladies to fortified towns, which leads them to the conclusion that it is perfectly acceptable for any gentleman to enter there if he wishes. When this desire for conquest is put into practice, there is no risk for a nobleman but a real danger for the lady: a bad reputation, or even worse a pregnancy, could destroy the prospect of a suitable marriage and bring discredit on her family.'

I turned back to the window and placed my hot forehead against the cool pane of glass. I felt such terrible confusion.

'Anne, look at me. I know how the king himself leaps over the walls of other men's gardens and drinks from their wells. And I know what you are thinking, but you are wrong. I do not vie for his attention, or keep him from his wife, but when he orders me to court I must obey.'

'But *why*?' I turned to face her. 'Why must you do his bidding?'

She opened the door a little to see if anyone stood listening outside. Light, music, and heat poured through from the crowded *salle*. She clicked it shut and turned, lowering her voice.

'I am a pragmatist. If that is how it must be, then I accept the situation for what it is. But I am ambitious, and if I lose my good name, I will gain whatever advantage I can for myself and my family. That will be my price.'

'Well, I still do not believe that Clément does not want me,' I murmured.

'You will recover from this setback, believe me,' said Françoise. 'There will be other admirers, men who will be enraptured by your dark looks. You will survive.'

Survive? I wanted to die.

I turned away, my finger tracing the raindrops outside sliding down the windowpanes. No stars or moon could be seen, and it appeared black outside, like the desolation in my heart. What would I do now? How could I bear to face him again? I wanted to return home, to escape, but I was trapped on this accursed journey through France with him in my sight every single day. I felt foolish now, in my new gown and slippers, and fingered the rose-enamelled brooch that Clément had given me. As I pulled it off, breaking the pin, my heart broke too, and I wished that this dreadful night might prove just a bad dream.

I pressed the heels of my hands into my red eyes and said that I must return to the *grande salle*. Françoise nodded and said she would follow me, but on no account was I to betray my true feelings of misery. I must dry my tears, smile and show myself a courtier. Tonight, I must learn how to deceive.

* *

Over the following days, only my pride helped me save my tears for bed. When asked by the concerned girls what ailed me, I said my teeth were troubling me and turned my face to the wall. Even my little dog could not cheer me.

Lying there, unable to sleep, I became obsessed with Marguerite and hated her. How could I compete with her spirit and intelligence? Every man flocked to her, yet she wore no ostentatious gowns, or jewellery, and did nothing but smile and act graciously. Adored by her brother and protected by her exalted position, she was free to do whatever she wished. Nothing and no-one could touch her, whereas I was but a green girl of no account.

After all our arguments and competing, it was my sister who proved the greatest solace at this painful time. Watching me carefully, full of care and concern, she put colour on my cheeks, brushed out my hair and told no-one of my plight. She knew the pain of a broken heart and was the greatest comfort. When we were released from our duties, I would lie across her lap in some quiet corner, sobbing until my eyes were red and raw, and my kerchief wet with tears. What would become of me, who would love me now? How could I ever love again? I tortured myself thinking of Clément's gentle eyes, the smell of his hair, the touch of his skin. Our secret talks on religion had been exciting and forbidden but now…

Unfortunately, Mary's sympathy did not last. When I told her again that I had meant it when said I would never lie with a man until we were man and wife, she changed tack, and we were back to bickering. Could I not see, she argued, that Clément had wanted a woman, not a fond, frustrating girl? If all I could offer him were kisses and sweet murmurings, no wonder he had walked off in frustration and found solace in the arms of the painted whores who trailed after the court. And then we came back, always back, to my stinging barb that she had tossed her virginity away to the first boy who would catch it back at Hever. And now the king. Well, we had both been cozened and thrown aside, but unlike her, I was determined that no man would ever put me in this humiliating position again. I would learn from this; she would not. What she had given away, I still had – but more importantly, I was resolved to keep.

• •

The queen turned and smiled as I entered the chamber with Renée. Around her, ladies laid furs and gowns in trunks as Madame d'Assigny clapped her hands at the scurrying young girls. There was too much chattering and not enough packing.

'Renée!' The queen peeled back the linen cloth from the basket in front of her. 'Come, look.'

The girl walked towards her and stared down.

'Bonbons!'

'Me first!' Marie Darcille tripped over her exotic gown in her rush to reach the box. I wondered how her mistress tolerated her, but she only laughed.

'The council at Lyon has sent me twelve boxes of sugared almonds, and two boxes of raisins. They are too generous.' She slapped Marie's hand away and handed the boxes around to all present. 'No, Renée, you have already received yours,' she said, shielding the box from her sister's fingers. She then paused. 'Diane, I do not want to go to Lyon for I fear the town will spend far too much money on an *entrée joyeuse* and entertainments. They gave a great deal to my husband for the war, and I cannot ask them for more.'

Diane turned to speak but was interrupted.

'There is no need to be alarmed, all is arranged,' announced Louise, waving her hand in the air as she burst into the chamber with her ladies.

Marguerite followed behind, a book in her hand. She

wore a simple black gown, adorned with a white fur collar, and a matching hood studded with pearls. Tall and elegant, she smiled at all. I did not smile back as foolish Marie hid behind the table.

'The mayor,' continued Louise, 'has already sent a message to say they cannot house a great many men and horses, due to the lack of bread, wheat, and stabling. If we descend upon them, it would be ruinous, and since we shall be staying a month, I must agree.'

'Then, *Madame Mère*, so say I,' added the queen, turning around, 'and any money they might have spent shall go to the poor.'

'If you insist,' said Louise, 'but as a gesture, the council of Lyon wish to repair a rain-damaged bridge, at the Porte Saint-Georges, and decorate it with tapestries for our *entrée*. I have agreed that would be sufficient. We shall, of course, be warmly lodged, but the rest of the court must find accommodation outside the city walls. The *fourriers* have been briefed.' Glaring pointedly at Françoise de Foix, she turned with a swish of heavy gown towards the window and gazed out at the heavy rain. There would be no hunting today.

Françoise walked over to me, and taking a piece of silk from inside her sleeve, began wiping Renée's sticky face. She had managed to steal a treat after all.

'See how she hates me,' she said, as the girl screwed up her eyes. 'But as one of the queen's ladies, I must go where she goes.'

Renée wiped her hand across her mouth and escaped to the window seat to enjoy the sticky almonds in her hand.

'And I hate *her*,' I said as I glanced towards Marguerite.

I asked if Françoise had seen a certain gentleman, but she shook her head. He had not appeared at Mass, nor dinner. Perhaps he was hiding in shame for the way he had treated me.

'You are thriving, my dear,' observed Louise, turning to the queen, 'unlike the Scottish Queen, the Tudor, with her many troubles.'

The queen offered Louise an almond, but she refused, saying they did not agree with her digestion. She then began discussing the health of Margaret Tudor, describing how the birth of her daughter had made her so ill that she still needed to be carried about in a chair. Fleeing Scotland with her husband to England, to her brother's protection, she now left the Duke of Albany free to seize the reins of government.

'Had she not married again, as she solemnly promised,' said Louise, 'she would still be regent, but then that family has no self-control. No thought beyond their immediate gratification. As for France, we can only rejoice, for Margaret's folly strengthens the old alliance.'

'But a woman forced to give up her two little boys,' said the queen, 'is unimaginable.'

'To a natural mother, yes,' said Louise, watching as I helped Françoise place a collar of creamy pearls back in their velvet box. 'But all she cares about are her fine gowns. She even had them paraded in front of her while she lay in bed, unable to rise.' She walked over. 'A gift?' she moved to take a closer look at the collar of pearls.'

The queen nodded. 'From Cardinal Wolsey, on the birth of the baby.'

'Wolsey,' said Louise, tracing the pearls with her long, acquisitive fingers, 'sees fit to remind me of the friendship between King Henry and my son, and says that if we recall Albany to France and allow Margaret her rights, there will be no occasion for war; but if this is not done, Henry is determined to assist his sister to obtain what is due to her. He tells me the treaty with King Ferdinand has been renewed, and that Spain has promised to assist Henry in case of a Scotch war.' She paused. 'Is that old fox Ferdinand not dead yet?'

'I believe he is ill,' replied the queen, 'but still insists on hunting.'

Louise shrugged. 'Did he not once say: 'the King of

France complains that I have twice deceived him. He lies, the fool; I have deceived him ten times and more.' For that comment, alone, I wish him dead and in Hell.'

'*Madame Mère*,' said Marguerite, moving to her mother's side, 'I hear that the pope already regrets his hasty negotiation with France; after the retreat of the Swiss, French interests are supreme in Italy. I fear that when the pope can find his opportunity for expelling the French, he will use all his efforts to do so.'

I should have been interested in this turn of events, but I cared nothing for King Ferdinand, the pope or Margaret Tudor. What was she to me? Her sister Mary, the French Dowager Queen, had proved troublesome and Margaret appeared just as unruly. I moved aside to the next box and laid a set of brilliant red rubies on top of the white velvet. They lay like great drops of blood from a bleeding heart: my heart. I stood lost in my own sad thoughts, as ladies and maids moved back and forth with armfuls of robes.

When all the precious jewellery was packed safely away, the boxes were locked and the keys handed to Anne de Graville. She attached them to the chain around her waist.

'You are paler than usual, Anne,' she observed, as I placed the boxes in the trunk. 'Are you unwell?'

I shook my head, closing the heavy lid.

'Come, tell me,' she persisted, placing a hand against my forehead.

I tried to turn away, but she stopped me. Then, unable to hold back any longer, I bobbed quickly to the queen and Louise and, to the alarm of all, fled the chamber. I could not hide my breaking heart a moment longer.

'What on earth is the matter with that girl?' asked Louise as I closed the door and was promptly sick.

⁕   ⁕

Taking my bow, I narrowed my eyes and aimed carefully at the butts. I let loose my arrow and, with a dull thud, it just missed the bullseye. The queen clapped as I lowered my bow and then she took an arrow from her quiver. Stepping up to the mark, she drew back the silken string. The arrow flew wide of the bullseye, but she only grimaced and took another from Renée.

Today was our last day before we continued to Lyon, and around us, ladies and gentlemen enjoyed the pale, November sunshine, including Louise. I saw her out of the corner of my eye, pacing back and forth, her secretary hovering around her like a tiresome black fly.

My sister pulled on her red glove and allowed her new admirer to adjust her hold on the bow. A kitchen boy standing by a brazier turned small currant cakes over on a griddle and the smell of wood smoke drifted across the terrace.

'May I speak with you, Anne?'

Surprised, I turned to see Marguerite, standing in a violet gown, her smile benign. I gave a deep reverence and lowered my eyes, afraid they would show my seething dislike of her.

'In private, if you please.'

We walked in silence to the far end of the terrace, disturbing the sodden, red autumn leaves, until we reached the gate of the outdoor tennis court. There, Marguerite finally spoke.

'Anne, I fear you think I have done you some ill,' she said, searching my solemn face.

I felt alarmed.

'Françoise has spoken to me of what has occurred, but in thinking badly of me, you do me a great disservice.'

My heart began to race, and I felt terrified at the thought I had displeased her. Like her or not, she wielded great power.

'Speak, child, I cannot think what you have heard, for a woman is only gossiped about when there is something bad to say.'

I turned my face with its expression of puzzlement to her. 'Madame?'

'Come, Anne, there are no secrets at court, as you well

know,' she said kindly. 'Even I cannot command discretion.'

'Very well, Madame, if I may speak plainly, is it not true that you can do whatever you desire? Have whatever or whoever you wish?'

'Desire? And do you think that is what an exalted position brings – your desires? Such a position brings responsibility and an unblemished reputation. Now, I assume by 'whoever,' you are referring to Monsieur Marot?'

I felt alarmed.

'Please be assured that whatever I may feel, Anne, duty must always come before personal choice. You will, no doubt, have heard that when I was forced into marriage, I was so horrified at the prospect I collapsed. However, since my brother and mother decreed it for political gain, I had to obey, for that was my duty. And I will not desecrate those vows for any man.'

'But my lady, how can you exist in such a miserable marriage?'

'Ah, you think only of romantic love and the troubadours. In reality, an intelligent woman knows that marriage is not a perfect state and wisely accepts it for what it is – makeshift, but reputable.'

'Surely, Madame, in accepting such unhappiness, a woman will only wither away and die.' She smiled at me, her face gentle, and I could not believe she was standing there discussing such things with me.

'Yes, Anne, if she chooses to be a mirror of the ideas of others, destitute of a mind of her own, knowing nothing beyond the narrow confines of her bedchamber. But she can also choose to be an active, educated creature, with an individuality of her own, capable of reason.'

As I looked at her serene face, I felt desperate to ask her the one thing on my mind.

As if reading it, she spoke: 'But you are right. There is another, and I must still, to this day, watch him in my brother's company and force a smile as if no fondness existed between us – but he is not your poet.' I gazed across to the woodmen chopping their logs and plucked up my courage.

'Madame, are you referring to Seigneur de Bonnivet?' I asked, remembering my sister's words.

'I will speak nothing openly about this matter. That way, I do no-one harm.'

'Madame,' I said, my eyes pricking with tears, 'how can you bear to live so close to one you cannot have? You have the love of the court, but –'

'But what? I can only accept with graciousness its adulation and nothing more. It is the price I pay for privilege.'

'So how do you bear such a fate?'

'Fate, Anne, is for the heathen, providence is from God – you must bless providence. Everyone carries their burden, and although a child would be a great consolation to me in my unhappy marriage, it is not to be. Now, you too must discover patience and trust in God.' She gently touched my cheek. 'I know Clément has proved unkind, but as for his great admiration for me, I understand he only seeks my patronage. He admires Françoise de Foix; he admires my beautiful young cousin, Anne d'Alençon. But he intends to rise at this court – as much as a poet can – and he does not wish to have a wife to encumber him.'

'Only, Madame, if that wife is of no standing,' I replied, sharply. 'And yet if I had given myself to him as a wife, as he begged…'

'He still would not have married you,' finished Marguerite, 'and you would have lost that, which by the laws of holy church, must only be given to your future husband.'

I stared up at the scudding clouds, blinking away my tears of despair.

'Anne, look at me. If you learn nothing else from me, learn this.' I turned my face and raised my eyes to hers. 'Once a man has possessed your body, there is nothing left for him to desire.'

'No, Madame, that is *not* true!' I cared nothing for my

rudeness or impertinent outburst. 'Françoise de Foix lived unmarried in sin with the man who married her. She was not abandoned.'

'That I cannot argue with,' replied Marguerite, with a smile, 'but believe me, when she did so, there were exceptional circumstances which I will not discuss with you.'

I started to protest, but the expression on her face silenced me.

'Anne, to return to the matter in hand. I have taken the liberty – purely as a kindness to you – to ask Monsieur Marot to return to Cahours for a few weeks – to let matters settle.'

'Madame, he can jump into the River Lot for all I care,' I said. The fur at the neck of my cloak felt as if it might choke me.

'Anne, I am sorry for your plight, but I am warning you to act wisely. My brother likes Clément. He would not have him gone long from here just because of some indiscretion on the part of a careless maid. He, of course, knows nothing of this matter, but if he did and told the queen, I fear it is *you* who would be made to leave.'

'But Madame, it is so unfair!' I cried, in frustration. 'Why should I not expose Clément for what he is? A liar who led me to believe he loved me.' My eyes blazed as Marguerite took my hand.

'Because no-one would listen, and you would be held to blame. I know only too well how men attempt to destroy a young girl's will in the hope of making her pliable to their desires. Do they not boast that the bough must be bent while it is still green?' I replied that I longed to speak with my mother.

'Well, there I am lucky, for I have my mother close and could not wish for a better mentor.' She must have noticed my surprise for she gave a little laugh. 'Her care and encouragement have never failed, and it is to her that I owe my love of books and learning. I grant you that, yes, her zeal, energy, and passion cause her to be impatient with certain people.'

'You mean the queen?'

She nodded. 'My mother does not wish ill on her, but she will bully those whom she feels are weak. You must not be afraid of her, but rather emulate her strength of character and clarity of mind.'

As we walked, we moved aside to avoid the noisy geese crossing our path.

'I am concerned for Claude, though,' she said, her voice tender.' The girl is lonely and from what I have observed you of all the maids cheer her the most. How could you not, for you are so bright and lively with such a youthful curiosity.'

I began to feel guilty and seeing my downcast face, her own brightened.

'Come, we have a great deal of travelling ahead of us, and I hear that you are interested in books. Have you seen the library at Blois?'

I said I had not.

'It is a sizeable chamber, with shelves stuffed from floor to ceiling with handwritten books on every subject. All printers and booksellers must deliver one copy to the royal library, and many are waiting in chests to be dealt with. Perhaps you can help me weed out those not of interest?'

She then enquired about the library of Margaret of Savoy, in Mechelen. I told her of the two hundred velvet-bound manuscripts holding the works of Aristotle, Livy, the letters of Seneca, and the works of Froissart, and how I had loved spending my time there. Her face showed utter joy.

'Well,' she continued, 'I cannot wait to buy more in Lyon as there are a great many printers in Haberdasher Street. I would love to discuss my books with you and, if Claude agrees, would like you to travel with Madame de Châtillon and myself in one of the litters as we journey to meet my brother.'

Now I felt quite dreadful. Why was this illustrious woman even speaking to me, let alone showing such kindness? Perhaps I had been hasty in my venom towards her.

'I also have a mind to write to while away the time. And talk – yes, I know I talk too much and confess that when I open my mouth, it is long before I shut it again – but I want to have discussions and debates. Ah, I fear that dullness is an incurable malady, quite hellish, and one should guard against it. Tell me, what do you fear most, Anne? What would be your idea of Hell?'

I stopped to think and then turned.

'I think, my lady, it would be to exist in a state of perpetual inconsequence.'

She laughed as we approached the butts. A courtier clapped my sister for having scored a bullseye, and she now jumped about like a child. Nothing ever dampened her spirits.

'But what of Clément,' I asked, my face earnest again, 'when will he return?'

Marguerite smiled. 'He will return to the court soon enough,' she whispered, 'so you must not be concerned. In the meantime, I have a gift for you.'

◦   ◦

As we alighted from the mossy steps on the riverside landing of the Pont du Change, François de Rohan, Archbishop of Lyon, welcomed our party to his residential palace. Outside the old priory, curious pilgrims jostled to see our party and, overhead, the great bells of the Cathédrale Saint-Jean Baptiste rang in welcome. We had travelled down the River Saône by barge to Lyon, for it was gentler than the Rhône that flowed from the Alps, and it had proved a bitterly cold journey.

Now, as we entered the apartments, I felt glad to escape the northerly wind, and enjoy the warmth of the fire as it crackled in its magnificent fireplace. Dark and dismal, the palace needed re-furbishing, even though it had been expanded, but it appeared comfortable and now large enough to house many of our noble entourage. The queen immediately thanked the representatives of the council for their present of bonbons, and as I took the fur mantle from her shoulders we ladies followed Madame d'Assigny to the queen's chamber. Facing the river, its diamond-paned windows reflected the glinting sun, and as breathless servants carried the heavy baskets and trunks through the arched door, we started the usual task of unpacking the gowns. At that point, my sister flew into the chamber, gave a quick bob to Madame d'Assigny and excitedly beckoned. Putting down the black furs, I hurried to see what she wanted. She immediately grabbed my hand and took me to one side.

'He's here,' her eyes sparkled, 'in the courtyard. I have just seen him!'

I froze.

'Are you sure?' I asked.

She nodded. 'I bumped into him as he was carrying a bundle of books. It was him, I tell you.'

'What do I do?' I glanced back at the bustling girls.

'Smile sweetly, be nice to him. That way, he might want you back again.'

I stared at Mary as she nodded her head, her expression eager.

'*What?*' I asked, incredulously. 'When all I want to do is box him about the ears in front of the whole court?'

'I would be kind.'

'Yes, Mary, you would.' My face was grim as she left me standing there. 'But I am not you …'

●　●

Eliza Grey moaned as she inspected the hole in her gown. She glanced up.

'Anne?'

The chattering stopped as the girls turned around, and there was a moment of surprised silence.

'Well, what do you think?' I ask, holding out my arms.

'You look like an angel!' cried Eliza, as she moved towards me.

'And your hair is enchanting,' added Mary Fiennes, lifting the long curls in her fingers. The other girls gathered about.

'Why, the sleeves are beautiful! Was this your conceit?' asked Gillette, in admiration.

I swirled around, laughing, for my new gown was indeed beautiful, the most beautiful I had ever possessed. Marguerite had kept her word and sent me ten ells of fabric to be made up by her seamstress in any way I wished. Her kindness had proved extraordinary, and I regretted ever having hated her. Now, skipping over to the long, burnished mirror in my blue velvet slippers, I turned this way and that, admiring the vision before me. The bodice of my new gown, made of pale blue silk and edged with silver braid and pearls, was cut low to show two unusually full breasts. The matching kirtle spread out about my slender form, the underskirt starched to give a fuller shape. Over the close-fitting silver sleeves, puffed with white lawn, I had devised long, trailing over-sleeves of blue silk, scattered with silver stars that reached almost to my fingertips. On my head, I wore a matching round blue cap, edged with pearls, and beneath it, with my sister's help, I had curled my waist-length hair.

I smiled with satisfaction, for I knew that tonight Clément would see what he had lost. Having pondered carefully on Marguerite's words, I knew I now had two choices: to rant and rave and show him how much he had hurt me – or pretend that he had meant nothing to me and thus keep my pride. Well, I would not beg for his affection. From now on, I would flirt and tease and make every man desire me until they went quite mad, yet give nothing in return. From now on, I would hide my true desires and never give my heart away again. Not until it was worth my while.

'Will not the queen complain,' asked Diane, her soft voice betraying a note of concern.

'I care not,' I replied, boldly, causing a great deal of

mirth. 'I am sick and tired of the way we are forced to dress with such restraint.' The laughter stopped abruptly as Madame d'Assigny entered the chamber.

'Why, you have excelled yourself, Mademoiselle Boleyn,' she said, pacing behind me. 'One would think you were dressing for an admirer.'

The girls giggled as I threw a glance at Mary Fiennes, but when Madame d'Assigny moved round to my front, she frowned. 'But less is more modest,' she whispered, deftly plucking out two wool pads and tugging my bodice higher. 'Now, stand up straight.'

To everyone's amusement, my full 'breasts' fell instantly flat.

Down in the *grande salle,* all the nobles, clergy and officials of Lyon gathered to celebrate the magnificent meeting in Bologna of the king and the pope. Louise, standing on the dais, announced to all present how the king and the French nobles had received the sacrament from the pope's own hands, on St Lucian's day. This meeting of princes had been a triumph, with gifts exchanged, and alliances mended. Now, with a concordat reached, the king, as well as appointing clerical posts, would deduct ten per cent of all the church's revenues in France for himself. Louise did not mention that the *parlement,* the universities, and the religious houses were against such princely power. But such detail could wait.

A roar of polite approval filled the air as she sat down, and dishes of lamprey, sturgeon, carp, and pike were brought forth, followed by meat courses surpassing even the king's table. For entertainment, the archbishop produced a famous dancing bear from the Pyrenees, and it pawed the air as if dancing, accompanied by a merry tune played by a dwarf on the flageolet. Marie, the queen's dwarf, smiled at him with a besotted expression. On the dais, the queen, sitting next to her almoner, now Canon of Lyon, clapped with pleasure. She appeared comely when she smiled, and her fair hair, plaited high and decorated with pearls, along with her violet gown, perfectly suited her pale complexion.

Louise, on the other hand, sat seething, fastidiously holding a clove-studded orange to her nose every time the ragged muzzled bear ventured too close.

'Damn them,' she muttered, to Marguerite. 'How dare they say my son's guard looked like bargemen, dirty, greasy and shabby with not four chains between them. They say that he appeared more as a citizen than a king. Do they not recognise humility when they see it? No, they expected to see French vanity primped out with Burgundian gold. Do they not know that my son has put aside all princely interests? He is an example to all of Christendom, but now King Henry fears he will take the state of Naples.'

'Mother,' said Marguerite, 'it is Wolsey who directs the affairs of England. He has been, as you know, these past four months endeavouring to keep the pope firm with the emperor, King Ferdinand and the Swiss, and did all he could to delay the meeting at Bologna. Now he says unless France removes Albany from Scotland, England will make war on us and break the peace. But we cannot command Albany, a prince who is next in line to the Scottish succession, to do any such thing. No, Wolsey overstretches himself.'

Louise sighed and waved the bear away distractedly, for she could not abide by such shows. Besides, her gout troubled her, and the healing sulphur water rushed to her by a courier from her province of Aix-les-Bains had not eased it. She appeared only slightly more cheerful when acrobats vaulted across the hall. Tumbling and jumping, the troupe even leapt blindfolded through burning hoops held high in the air. Louise's new dwarf, Cosima, fell about trying to join in and even Renée had to be told to sit down. The finale was the appearance of a half-naked woman, her body painted with strange symbols, representing an ancient Pict. Her wild, red hair straggled below her waist, and she brandished a long spear as she danced and leapt, baring her teeth like a wolf. The strange woman's contortions were remarkable and resulted in tumultuous applause from the audience, except for Louise, who sat stony-faced. She languidly raised her orange again. The poor archbishop sat with a dejected face, painfully aware that the entertainment he had provided had not been the triumph he had hoped.

As the night wore on, I moved in and out of the vast company of courtiers, ignoring their murmurs and stares, my breathing rapid. I could hear them discussing me with admiration, but did not stop to listen. Somewhere *he* was here, but where? When one of the handsome Venetian ambassadors asked if I would dance with him, I readily agreed. If I could not see Clément, he was about to see me.

The musicians noisily tuned up their instruments: Poitevins their bagpipes, Provençales their viols and cymbals, Burgundians and Champagners their hautboys, bass viols, and tambourines. Moving towards the floor for the Burgundian dance, I noticed nods of appreciation as courtiers parted to allow me through. Was that the younger Boleyn girl?

I knew all eyes were upon me as I began to dance, my long curls bobbing at each hop and turn. My sister danced too, but this time she could not outshine me, even in her crimson red gown. I recalled the time she had danced in desperation before the king, and yet here was I doing much the same thing for Clément, using my dark eyes to play the coquette. As the music faded, my partner stood, mesmerised, and as I curtsied, I thanked God for all the long hours I had spent in my dance classes, perfecting my poise. None could match me, and even Marguerite nodded her head to me in secret appreciation, for she knew how much this brave show hurt.

A cry went up: 'The Moresco! Play the Moresco!'

Marguerite, on the arm of the Archbishop, quickly stepped down from the dais, for she loved this boisterous dance. As pages handed out silver wrist bells from a large basket, the musicians struck up their tune, and the circle parted to allow Marguerite to take her place. It was then that I saw him. Sitting alone, goblet held to his wine-stained mouth, unshaven, he was looking at me with glazed eyes. I defiantly stared back until he lowered his eyes, abashed.

When the dance finished, I was immediately asked for another and another, laughing my way through the Estampe and Salterello with a variety of noble young men. Even Françoise smiled at my exuberance. When the dancing finally ended, I watched as Clément wiped his hand across his mouth, rose unsteadily, and leaning on his young page staggered from the *salle*. Instead of feeling elated at my bold show, I only felt sad and empty, and returned, despondent, to wait upon Claude. He had gone, and the rest of the evening would be empty. I sat, deflated, trying hard not to weep in frustration.

Chapter Ten

'I stay for no man.'

The South of France

I sat beside Marguerite in her litter, both of us warmly wrapped in furs as we jolted down the Quai des Romains, towards the market and past the gabled and timbered shops. Marguerite had announced that she wished to buy a present for her brother and since Lyon was renowned for its gold and jewellery shops it was the best place outside of Paris to buy such goods.

As the snow fluttered down, all appeared noise and bustle as citizens cried out their wares. I peered from behind the leather curtain to glimpse a barber shaving a man in a shop doorway, a grocer standing beneath his striped awning and another cutting fruit tarts on a wooden block. He roughly brushed away the settling snow as housewives gathered about him trying to get the best price, and shouting him down as they haggled. They looked cold with their hands encased in grey, woollen mittens and their rabbit-skin hoods pulled about their faces. Above the noise on an upturned crate, a mountebank waved an array of coloured, silk scarves in the air, announcing they could cure any disease of the throat, having been blessed by the pope himself. Further on, I leant out and stopped a woman with a tray of ribbons and fancies, and bought a length of intricate black lace to use as a trimming.

When we left the narrow, confining streets, Marguerite pointed out the vineyards high up on the Fourvière hill and the ruins of the marble Roman Amphitheatre. She told me that Lyon was a city of wealth and elegance, the rival of Paris in fashion, and the 'Florence of France.' It was a thriving city, and being so close to the Italian border attracted merchants and bankers from Northern Europe to its four great trade fairs held each year. Drapers and haberdashers flocked to settle within its walls, and printing presses abounded. Marguerite told me that the fishwives, butchers, river people, and herb sellers spoke many different dialects in the city. She was right. When we stopped at one stall to buy the king's Christmas gift – an Italian gold brooch depicting a boar impaled on a lance – the talk seemed incomprehensible. As Marguerite handed the gift to me, I turned it over in my hand. Intricately modelled in solid gold, the boar's diamond eyes flashed. It was an exquisite piece and of great value.

We continued through the *Traboules*, or internal passages, that ran from one street to the other, past the church of Our Lady of Comfort, until we finally arrived at one of the printers' shops. Marguerite explained that since the first printing establishment had been set up in Lyon over forty years before, it had become one of the most important printing and publishing centres in Europe. Here we could purchase books in Hebrew, Greek, Latin, Italian, Spanish and French, as well as the works of Erasmus, Rabelais, Poliziano, and Fausto Andrelini – whom Erasmus called divine – from the German and Flemish booksellers. She and her brother had spent many an hour browsing through the stalls, often in disguise and thus unknown to the hawkers.

Now we sat, to my great interest, talking in one of the dark little shops, poring over the translations. Even the printer, wiping his inky fingers on his dirty apron, paused to listen as Marguerite read aloud from the barely dried sheets, and paced up and down the creaking, straw-strewn floor. When the lanterns were lit, the printer's wife insisted we ate, and set down goblets of fragrant red wine, freshly baked bread, and blood pudding cooked with apples. She apologised for not being able to offer her speciality of hot Lyonnais sausages, but they were fasting that day. When we rose to go, and I helped fasten the mink fur about her neck, Marguerite handed her new purchases to her servant to carry and pressed a gold *écu au soleil* into the printer's palm.

When we returned to the palace, I told Marguerite of my love of French books and how, through my discussions with Clément, I had found religious doctrine of great interest. She seemed pleased and explained to me that the mind was not a vessel that needed filling but wood that needed igniting. If Clément had ignited that interest, then I must rejoice and not be sad. She told me that she – and the Lyonnais themselves – longed to see the excesses of the church dealt with. Even the Archbishop of Lyon had spoken out against the abusive practices by Catholics, and as we strolled through the covered gallery, we discussed the merit of his words.

'Our churches and monasteries,' continued Marguerite, 'are full of valuable treasures, yet I cannot help but wonder if they are for repentance of the contrite, or the admiration of the beholder?'

'But you would not want to see the church stripped of its beauty,' I said, picking up Aurora, Marguerite's little spaniel. Bonny had nipped her yet again, and the poor, trembling creature stood pleading to be carried. As I fondled the dog's silky ears, Marguerite turned to me.

'Never! I love the statues, relics, and ceremonies, but I have to ask what has this imagery to do with the spiritual mind? The church is full of splendour and wealth, but alas for the poor. And yet is it more important to admire the stonework, or listen to the word of God and give of our charity?'

I admitted that the poor surely came first, but that such treasures were for the glory of God.

'But are they for God?' Marguerite's face was earnest. 'Statues are but a symbol, and yet they are worshipped as a god in themselves. It is not the statue or relic that has power, but our prayers to God, and to pay to see such relics I cannot condone. Yet I know some churchmen live comfortable and sinful lives on these churches' treasures. Did not Saint Bernard say that all riches lead to corruption, that man pollutes the office, rather than the office ennobles the man?'

'I believe so, Madame.'

'All I know is that chanting does not save one's soul; only faith, charity, and good works can do that. Sadly, I know not the remedy or how to bring about a new understanding of God's word.'

'I believe, Madame, that all men should be able to read and understand the words written in the Bible.' I echoed Clément's thoughts. 'We should not hear only those words we are allowed to hear. I believe preaching and printing are the way to teach God's word.'

'Exactly, Anne, yet five hundred years ago, Pierre Valdo, a rich merchant here in Lyon, stood excommunicated for translating the Bible into the vulgar tongue. One hundred years ago, John Huss was burned for daring to translate the Sacred Word. Yet how can one ever reach spiritual perfection without knowing the true word of God? How, unless by reading the words, does one gain true understanding?'

'Madame, Lefèvre states that Christ is the central subject of the scriptures, and if they are approached devoutly, God will give understanding. However, I do not think one can ever achieve perfection working in this world, for temptation is all around.'

She stopped, her face an expression of surprise. 'But – but surely we must strive?' she lowered her fur-lined hood. 'I could not bear to think that for all my spiritual struggling, I can never please God.'

'I have read, my lady, that a man who strives after goodness in all his acts is sure to come to ruin since there are so many men who are not good.'

'Why, then you have read the words of Niccolo Machiavelli.'

'Indeed, and I believe despair is a sin, for it clouds faith and hope.' I said, repeating Clément's words for the second time.

'I see that you have dwelt long on this, Anne.'

I smiled, pleased with myself.   'Well, *I* believe that trying pleases God, but those in an ordained position must try the hardest!'

Marguerite then opened the small door to the chapel and, after leaving the dogs outside with her lady, we entered to pray.

•   •

And so it was that during my time at Lyon, Marguerite and I became further acquainted with each other. We could never be friends due to her station, but the more she spoke with me, the more fascinated I became with this strange woman, nine years older than myself. Of course, I missed my wonderful conversations with Clément, but she proved just as illuminating. The queen, neither jealous nor possessive, seemed happy for me to learn as much as possible from her sister-in-law, and gave her blessing to serve her as well if she wished, when we returned to Amboise. Her only condition was that I must not abandon Renée, for the girl now felt inordinately attached to me.

Louise, plagued by a stiff knee, found the cold so disagreeable in Lyon that it was decided to move to the south quicker than planned, travelling through Valence and Montélemar. Besides, she wanted to be at the Basilica of Mary Magdalene for Epiphany, and we were already well into Advent.

Marguerite departed and agreed to be our host at her château until St Stephen's Day, overseeing the Christ-tide festivities. To her relief, her dull husband was presently occupied in Armagnac, near Toulouse, since the king had given them full rule in that region and there was much business to conduct. This was not just a gift of brotherly love; Armagnac needed stability and King François relied more and more on his sister's wise advice. She was a good assistant to her brother, for ambassadors always waited on her after their principal audience, and frequently, when the king had affairs of importance, he referred them entirely to her determination. He knew that she could be relied upon to engage and entertain them with her fine speeches, and being very artful and dexterous, could quickly weed out their secrets. These qualifications, the king would often say, made her of great use to him in facilitating his affairs, and he watched her almost with a lover's jealousy.

The pure sisterly love which Marguerite bore him, so unselfish in its devotion, was inexpressibly soothing to King François, oppressed as he often was by cares of state. No one could take her place, and although Louise dominated in the council, it was Marguerite who consoled the king in his hours of depression. Thus, he made her the keeper of his secrets, desires and future designs. He would use her wisely.

●   ◉

The weather turned pleasant as we travelled through Nîmes, although a great many of the court, including myself, had succumbed to a cold and troublesome cough. Wrapped in furs, we celebrated the Feast of the Immaculate Conception, and by the twenty-first day of December, having stopped briefly at Avignon, we reached Tarascon-sur-Rhône. As we sailed up the river, I spied the most imposing château with crenellations and round towers, sitting perched on an outcrop of limestone rocks, like some great Moorish prison. The queen, sniffling into her silk kerchief, explained that it had been built some sixteen years before by René d'Alençon, the father of Marguerite's husband. Legend had it that once a great beast terrorised the local people and that only St Martha could tame it. However, the queen was more concerned with the town than legends, for the council had promised to replenish our horses' oats, hay, and supplies while we stopped for the week, at no small cost. She fretted for the townspeople, and without the king, she had little cause to celebrate, although her family would later be joining the party. This would include the lovely Anne d'Alençon.

Inside the château, Marguerite had excelled herself, for swags of greenery and mistletoe decorated the *grande salle* in abundance. Gold, green and red ribbons wound around each stone pillar, laden with red berries, and with the great candelabra blazing, the *salle* appeared truly festive. Turkey carpets lay on the stone-flagged floors, and an enormous log fire blazed in the hearth.

While my sister and I tended to the queen and Marguerite, Louise, hobbling with her stick, set to work with her ministers. Carrying the queen's nightingale in its golden cage, I smiled to Louise's travel-weary ambassadors as they sat slumped on a bench in their mud-stained garb, waiting for an audience. Christmas or not, Louise would continue to govern the realm and would not be disturbed by anyone except her daughter. I had to admire her dedication, for I knew that if she was not at her desk, she was outside in the damp, handing out food and fuel to the many beggars and whores at the gate, oblivious to the mistral wind bending the trees. Requests, court appointments, and assigning new officers to posts in Bordeaux, all had to be dealt with. There were also gifts to accept, for the Mayor of Tarascon arrived carrying twelve golden images, each representing St Martha, with the offer of a visit to the saint's tomb the following day.

On Christmas Day itself, after Mass, we all enjoyed the entertainment that Marguerite herself presented. It was a merry affair – unlike last year with old Louis dying – with a choir from Avignon singing carols. It made me wonder about Margaret of Savoy and, of course, my tutor, and I hoped they had received my New Year's gifts. Margaret had sent me a gift but I was not to open it yet, and I thought of her letter telling me her news. Four marriages had been suggested for her dear Eleanora, and although the emperor was set on the king of Poland, Margaret thought the girl would be happier with the Duke of Savoy. No doubt she would be overruled. She had been suffering from back pain, but the saddest news concerned my dear friend, Beatrice. Margaret had heard from her family that she had died, not ten days after giving birth to a baby boy. She felt deeply shocked, as was I, and she lamented having to impart such sad news to me. Poor, poor Beatrice – she had proved a good friend to me when I had none, and I hoped she had found some happiness in her brief marriage.

My thoughts then turned naturally to home, and I realised again how much I missed my family. Mother wrote to tell me that, due to the sweating sickness, it was a cheerless season at court, with many noble knights and officers dead. The king would see no-one, not even the queen, so terrified was he of the contagion. All fairs were forbidden, markets closed, and herbs – such as rue, wormwood, sage, balm, and rosemary – were crushed and ground into prescriptions and sold on street corners. In churches, seven Paternosters, seven Ave Marias, and one Credo were advised to be recited every morning to ward off the contagion, followed by a pottage of almonds. For many, it proved in vain.

Glancing about the *salle*, I noticed that many of the court had straggled back home to their families, although a number remained, including Clément. I watched him as I sat with my sister and the other girls, partaking of the roast boar. He pulled the tender meat apart, laughing and talking to his friends, but when Marguerite arose to greet a beautiful girl I had not seen before, he rose to his feet and acknowledged her. She smiled graciously and from the look of admiration on his face – a look once given just to me – I knew this had to be Anne d'Alençon. She stood there like a tiny little bird, with sparkling brown eyes and nut-brown hair, dressed in a gown of the latest Italian fashion, its close-fitting sleeves puffed, banded and slashed with black and gold. Adorned with several gold chains, she wore her hair plaited and coiled with braid and, although the same age as Marguerite, who towered above her, she appeared much younger. I paused, my goblet to my mouth. The girl's husband, the Marquis de Montferrat, led her to their place at the top table, and all the while Clément could not keep his eyes from her. He appeared entranced, just as he had been with me, but although I felt uncomfortable watching him, the pain I felt had eased a little.

'I cannot see what you saw in him,' mumbled my sister, popping a piece of tender meat into her mouth. 'I mean, look at him.' She glanced at me, her cheeks flushed as she held up her glass goblet and beckoned impatiently to a page.

'Indeed,' I said, 'and I do not like his new beard. It makes him look like some greasy Spaniard.'

We both burst out laughing, causing the other girls to lean forward to share the joke.

Madame d'Assigny frowned from across the table, and Françoise de Foix shook her head in disapproval.

'You were right, Mary, I can do better than a poet and from now on I shall seek out only those who can be of use to me. One day he will know what he has lost.'

'And when would that be?' she teased. 'Once we are back in England he will never hear of you again.'

● ●

We reached Arles early on St Stephen's day to the sound of an artillery salute and cheering crowds. Although the town was poor, it had raised enough money to honour its royal visitors, and the gables of the houses fluttered with flags and pennants. I watched in fascination as we passed the ancient Roman theatre and arena, and continued to the house of Monsieur d'Arlatan, Lord of Beaumont, who had spent a fortune repaving the front of his house and installing new windows for his guests. Unfortunately, all had been freshly painted, and I noticed the poor queen blanch at the odour. When he presented a meal of onion tarts, crab and oysters, I thought she might void her breakfast, and realising his error, he swiftly showed her his aviary.

Later, Marguerite re-joined our party, for she had remained behind to give the annual arms to the poorer folk of Tarascon and deal with the business of her territories. She was wont to say that kings and princes were not masters and lords of the poor, but only their ministers, and gave of her time and money accordingly.

The following day, we trotted our horses out of the courtyard with our escort, for a brief visitation to the abbey of St Peter. As Marguerite rode her red-plumed horse beside Louise's litter, she gazed in concern at her mother, muffled in furs, sitting between the queen and Renée, and suffering from toothache. As Louise gazed stonily out of the leather half-curtain and narrowed her eyes, deep in thought, she fondled the medallion of King François nestling at her throat.

I rode close by with my sister and Monsieur de Beaune, and soon glimpsed the abbey, perched high on a rocky outcrop, standing like a fortress. This, I learnt, was a thriving community, with vineyards, a farm and an extensive library of manuscripts. Much good was done by the abbey for the local community, for the poorer people relied upon its herbal cures, food, and education. Here, Monsieur de Beaune said, his voice barely a hoarse whisper from his inflamed throat, we would see a piece of the True Cross from Calvary. Pilgrims travelled from miles around to gaze upon it and find God's forgiveness – or, he winked – a cure for toothache.

As our horses clopped noisily into the courtyard, the Archbishop of Arles, Monsignor Jean Ferrier, greeted our party with the abbot. The archbishop smiled warmly at Louise as she knelt to kiss the ring on his finger, and with grey clouds threatening snow, we made our way into the warm refectory while the monks tended to our horses.

Having rested and dined on fine lobster and wine, we walked to the Chapelle de Sainte-Croix, close to the Abbey Church of Notre Dame. Here was housed the very relic that Louise was most eager to see, and now the royal party, including the ladies, myself and my sister, would have that chance, too.

As the abbot swung his thurible from its chains around an elaborate, gem-encrusted case containing the piece of the True Cross, the incense-clouded air made me cough. Louise knelt with some difficulty as the golden case was brought to her, and kissed it over and over with great fervour. However, once outside, it was evident that she had not found relief from her toothache or her painful knee, and she was not pleased with God.

●   ●

Staring in the gloomy, early morning light at the crucifix in the Chapelle de Sainte-Croix, I pulled my new, white fur collar – my present from Margaret of Savoy – higher about my ears and shivered. Reneé's pet rabbit had disappeared, and I had offered to search everywhere I could, even the church, taking Bonny with me. When she gave a little bark, I swung around to see a dark silhouette before me. Flustered, I tried to step past, but the shadow caught hold of my hand.

'Anne, please, I need to speak with you.'

Bonny bared her teeth.

'No, sirrah!' I hissed, 'I – I do not wish to know your business.'

He followed me and blocked my way to the little wooden door, making my heart beat faster. Taking off his bonnet, he shook the snow from it.

'Anne, do not draw back from me,' said Clément. 'Please talk to me. I can tarry but awhile.'

'And why should I talk to you?' I asked, terrified that I might desire him all over again, just when my broken heart was healing.

'I miss you, Anne.'

'But you chose that path, not I,' I countered. 'You spurned and humiliated me. Why should I even deign to look upon you?'

'I am sorry for the pain I caused you.' Clément took my hand again but I pulled it away. 'I did – I do love you – but I am not ready to be married. A poet should be free to have mistresses and muses, not a wife. Besides, I think I would make a poor husband, forever restless and brooding.'

'So cries the popinjay,' I replied, coldly, 'and it is a great pity you did not think of that before you deceived me.'

We stood in silence before I finally spoke. 'Well, it is of no matter. My heart is now with another, and so the world wags on.' I stared sullenly at him, and he stared back, shocked by my sharp tongue. I also felt shocked by how lightly the lie tripped off my tongue – and in a holy place.

'Then I – I hope in time you will forgive me. Is it someone I am acquainted with?' He was taken aback.

I shrugged and sat down on the bench.

'Firstly, I will never forgive you, since I never forgive a wrong or a slight. And secondly, it matters not who. He is kind, generous and noble and asks nothing of me. Nothing.' As my tongue ran away, I saw with satisfaction that my barb had hit its mark.

Clément sat down beside me.

'It does not surprise me,' he said, 'for you are the talk of the court, after your last appearance. It broke my heart to watch as you danced with every man in the chamber. You were – are – a vision.'

'And you are not – you should shave.'

He fingered his beard and glanced at me in hurt surprise. Good, I thought, he deserved that.

'Anne, I do not want to be your enemy. Can we not speak civilly together on an important matter? I do miss speaking with you.'

I felt my resolve weaken, for I had missed our

conversations too, and although I would never let him back into my heart, I was curious as to what he had to say. Besides, it would be most gratifying to see him squirm further.

'Why not?' I regained my composure, for I did not feel quite the same any more. He had proved he was neither trustworthy nor honourable, *and* he was hot-headed.

'It has disturbed me, Anne, since we arrived at this wretched place, and it involves the relic of the true cross of Jesus Christ.'

'And what of it?' I felt disappointed. I wanted to talk of love, not relics.

'The pilgrims who come here are being charged exorbitant fees to kiss and touch it in exchange for God's forgiveness.'

'And?' I asked. 'Other places of pilgrimage charge to see their treasures. We do the same in England. That way, the monks can feed and clothe the poor. It has always been thus.'

'No, Anne, that way the monks can feather their pillows, get drunk on good wine, eat roasted boar and pay for their bawds. One of their outlandish privileges here is the right to fish sturgeon in the nearby Rhone. It would seem that not all of the men here are humble Benedictines who serve God.'

I felt myself shiver.

'Are you cold? No – you do not believe me.' He sat back and folded his arms. 'I think you are too afraid to face the truth and prefer theological theories instead.'

'Never!' I cried, turning to face him.

He smiled. 'Ah, that is the Anne I know, with those great, dark eyes on fire.'

'You should not meddle, Clément,' I warned.

'And that is the other Anne – the complacent, unworldly child – in all things.'

'How dare you,' I said, rising to my feet. 'I am not a child and I am not afraid to face the truth.'

'Then you should know that the abuses I speak of are very real.' His eyes flashed in earnest. 'Marguerite knows this.'

'She would,' I muttered.

He stared at his shoes.

'Anne, she dreams of reforming humanity, not dogmas.'

'Well, she can dream about what she likes. King François knows she will never go against his thoughts on the subject, and so she has his full protection. She loves him too well not to be of that religion which is most useful to him and the State. Did you know her gospel is: In Heaven: God, on earth: François?'

'No, but Marguerite has a taste for notoriety and seeks to bring together all the men who can voice various religious opinions in France. Of course, she is too clever to say what she thinks out loud.'

There was a moment's silence before I spoke again.

'Oh, Clément, I cannot believe *all* men and women of God are mired in sin.' I felt exasperated that he was here, just when I was trying to forget him.

He stood up and placed his bonnet back upon his head.

'No, but a great many are, and their behaviour is spreading like a canker. It cannot continue this way.' He paused.

'But you are devout,' I said, looking up at him.

'Anne, I love the church and all its rituals, and I bless the Virgin Mary daily. She is very forgiving. Can you find it in your heart to forgive me?'

I looked at him in surprise. 'I told you. I never forgive a slight, and I am not generous like the Mother of God.'

He gave a wan smile. 'Come, we cannot tarry, for we must reach Salon-de-Provence before the snow settles. The litters are waiting. Go to your lady.'

Genuflecting towards the altar, he made the sign of the cross and left. I felt sad, confused and angry in equal measure.

Just as he reached the door, I turned around.

'If you find a white rabbit, it belongs to Renée,' I called.

•   •

Standing by the arched doorway of the courtyard, I watched as a courier jumped down from his sweating, foam-flecked horse and hurried up the steps of the Château de l'Emperi. Mud-stained and out of breath, he had ridden hard from Milan and insisted to the guard he would only see Madame Louise. I followed him to the gallery to see him, hand on his despatch bag, stride across the stone-flagged floor. I stopped as he was admitted to Louise's chamber. Something must have happened to François.

The man remained in Louise's chamber for some time, but then Claude burst through the door like an excited child, Marie clutching at her gown. It was good news, for her beloved François was making his way even now through the Alps to meet our party at Sisteron, in Dauphiny. She swung me around and said that I might even meet my grandfather, the Duke of Norfolk, for he was to accompany the cavalcade. We laughed in relief as she skipped over to the window. I then overheard Marguerite say to her lady-in-waiting that Louise had not told the queen the entire reason for the meeting. King Henry had written to the king bragging about Queen Katherine's pregnancy and telling him not to tarry, but to put his wife in a like situation – the sooner, the better. The remark had rattled the king, for he knew that Queen Claude must give birth to a *dauphin* quickly. If he was in Italy that was not going to happen unless he came to her and did the deed. I had not seen the girl so joyous for weeks, and turning to her secretary, she promised a gift of two hundred livres each year for the repair and upkeep of the church of St-Jean de Moustiers, in Arles. Next to him, the Archbishop of Arles, whose hospitality we were enjoying, bowed in gratitude and suggested something special from his vineyard to celebrate.

Leaving the queen surrounded by her ladies, I asked if I could be spared to see the château. Since we would depart on the morrow, she readily granted my request, and I went in search of my sister. I heard her before I saw her, cursing in the inner court as she tried to untangle dog leashes. At the end of them strained several, snapping lapdogs.

'Well, don't just stand there, Nan,' she cried, 'help me stop these wretches from savaging each other.'

I hurried towards her and separated the growling, trembling little beasts, their teeth bared.

'Why I have to bother with these, I do not know,' said Mary, her cheeks flushed pink with the cold. 'Madame de Châtillon's spaniel hates the sight of Anne de Graville's. Antoinette's dog hates Françoise's bitch, as you can see. As for Bonny – stop, I tell you!' She tugged at the leash. 'I'm not surprised one of them savaged Renée's rabbit to death. Anyway, where are you going?'

I took Bonny's leash from her.

'Will you come for a walk with me?' I asked.

She shook her head. 'You must be moon mad, it is freezing, and I want to return to the warmth of the solar. Besides, I must get these creatures back. Oh, did I tell you I had a letter from Dame Margot? She wrote that Father may have to go to Ireland as Sir Piers Butler refuses to come over to settle the estates of Great-grandfather Ormond, God bless his soul. Sir Piers has already sent his wife over to London to do the business twice in his stead.'

'But what is there to settle? When Grandfather married Dame Margot, her father, the Earl of Ormond had no son, and so she and her sister Anne now stand to inherit the fortune. That was agreed.'

Mary frowned. 'Well, the fuss now is that Piers Butler, as eighth Earl of Ormond, is ignoring that and claiming the Irish estates for himself. Talk about a mess. Anyway, we can discuss this later. We have a very early start for Aix-en-Provence tomorrow and then onto la Sainte-Baume, so do not tarry long.' With that, she pulled up her fur hood and hurried away with the yapping dogs.

• •

As we climbed slowly through the dense forest and up the steep, frozen stairway of ancient rocks, it became obvious that although the route had been repaired, heavy rain had caused further damage. Piles of stones had been made into little altars, there were votive candles and messages scribbled on bits of parchment, and it was clear that many thousands of pilgrims had travelled this way. Shielding my eyes, I gazed across to the distant mountains, and the combination of heavenly birdsong and invigorating air made me feel like I was ascending to paradise itself. The rest of the court had not followed on since this was to be a private visit, and so they had stayed behind to find what lodgings they could – if they could. Now, by the grace of God, on this last day of December, St Sylvester's Day, we arrived outside a wooden door, our pilgrimage over.

As the accompanying monks intoned their prayers, Louise lowered her head and stepped into the dark, holy cave hewn out of the austere rock, placing her lace mantilla over her head. Marguerite took the queen's arm to steady the girl, and several ladies, including my sister and I, entered into the darkness of the cold grotto. Light from the candles flickered on the rock as we knelt in prayer beneath a very dilapidated wooden statue of the Magdalene. I noticed traces of red paint on her hair as it flowed over her once grey gown, and in her hand, she held a jar of ointment. Her shoe appeared worn quite smooth from pilgrim's lips, and no trace of paint survived. Here she had lived, having been set adrift on a boat, to die, from Palestine, with her sister Martha, and her brother Lazarus. By divine intervention, the boat had come to rest on the shores of Gaul, and in later years she had lived here alone. I felt deeply moved to think that we were kneeling on such holy ground, and even my sister, with her black veil covering her hair, looked suitably chaste. As the monks continued chanting, we recited a litany of prayers and

Louise rose to kiss the feet of the statue.

'My thanks and prayers to you, Blessed Mary, are for the safekeeping of my son, whose feet I have washed with tears as you did yourself to Christ our Lord.'

'And I,' added the queen, 'shall erect a statue of François at the entrance to this grotto to remind the world that you have spared his life.'

'To accompany, of course,' said Louise, 'a large donation for the repair of the basilica below. Old Louis promised, but – well – it never appeared.'

The queen flinched, and I placed her fallen cloak back upon her thin shoulders. 'My dear child,' said Louise, haughtily, 'let us never forget that the pilgrims rely on our benevolence. Now, we will hear Mass celebrated and then see that which I vowed to honour. Today, the master of the Dominican friars, Bishop Cajetan, will celebrate the service himself.'

●   ●

The convent offered comfortable, if draughty, accommodation, and the nuns appeared to have stocked it well with good food and a particularly fine white wine – *Clairette-au-miel* – flavoured with saffron. Over a dish of fragrant snails and olives, Marguerite appeared happy to converse with Bishop Cajetan, for as one of the leading theologians of the day, he ensured a lively discussion over an intimate supper. Louise, ever alert, lost no opportunity to speak with this avid supporter of the pope and used various inducements for the papacy to embrace policies favouring French interests. Her agile mind did not rest for a moment, while the queen only talked of her reunion with King François.

I was intrigued to hear the bishop's views as I sat plucking my lute in the corner, but my sister had trouble stifling her yawns, as she languidly stroked Marguerite's little dog. As I finished playing, I began to think about my conversation with Clément and how to carry through my boast. I had no lack of admirers, and here tonight, one seemed to be taking a particular interest. I recalled he was the gentleman on the black horse who had watched me hunt, and I had seen him about the court, immaculately clothed, exuding wealth and self-assurance. I confided my predicament to Mary.

'I thought you had done with such liaisons,' she said, taking the lute from me. She frowned as she turned the pegs to fine-tune it, and then started to strum.

'I have, Mary. Now I desire some amusement.'

She raised her brow.

'All I gained from Clément was a broken heart and tears. Well, if that is love, I am done with it, and I tell you I will never declare my love again so openly. Now I want an admirer who can give me gifts – proper gifts – such as expensive jewellery, a horse, or stuff for exquisite gowns.'

'And in return?' she asked. 'There is always a price.'

'Nothing. Is my company alone not worth it?'

She smiled. 'I would like to see you try and hold a man for no return. It did not work with Clément.'

'You can talk. A man who truly loved me would never have asked for that which I refuse to give before marriage. Anyway, if he is old, will he not be grateful for the flattery of a young girl?'

She stared at me and smiled. 'Well, well, Nan, you will be a Frenchwoman yet.'

'Possibly. But Mary, I am so *tired* of feeling sad. I am young, I am in France, and I want to be spoilt by someone who can afford it and who will lavish attention on only me. Is that such a sin?'

'You used to think so when I felt that way.'

I lowered my eyes, not wishing to remember. 'Well, Mary, what do you think of Comte Louis Nicholas? I am aware that he has been studying me for months.'

'The Comte de Chalon? You are not serious – are you? He must be sixty years old at least and drinks like a fish. Ugh, it would be as bad as having old Louis dribble over you.'

'I mean as a distraction. He is very rich, has various châteaux, loves dogs and hunting, and he is not decrepit like old Louis, even if he does have the same name.'

'Oh, dear Heaven above. Well, he is coming over, so good luck.' She moved away, dipping a curtsey.

The gentleman bowed to me and I saw Madame d'Assigny stare my way, ever vigilant.

'Mademoiselle Boleyn.'

I lifted my eyes and proffered my hand.

He kissed it lightly. 'May I sit with you? I am an old friend of –'

'Oh, I know all about you, sir,' I interrupted.

He smiled, said he was flattered, and sat, somewhat stiffly, besides me. His grey hair appeared sparse, he was of middling height and stout, with broken veined cheeks and nose, but his eyes were lively and penetrating.

Madame d'Assigny immediately arose and walked over.

'Is there anything I can do for your comfort, my dear comte?' She tried to hide the fact that she was prying.

'Not at all, Madame, but I would like to speak with this young lady if that is permissible?'

Madame d'Assigny gave a slight bow of her head and then sat on a nearby stool. She took a glass offered by a page and sat pretending to study the fine, plum wine, one of the queen's favourites.

'Tell me, what do you know of me, dear girl,' said the comte, hands upon his knees. I noticed the flashing emerald rings pressing into his plump fingers.

'That you are Louis Nicholas, Comte de Chalon and that you are a very dear friend of Madame de Châtillon. You have an excellent stable, appreciate fine wines, have been married three times, and now live as a widower.'

He gave a gruff laugh and I noticed that at least none of his teeth were missing.

'You occasionally visit your château in Châlons-en-Champagne,' I continued, 'not far from Rheims, but you live mostly near Amboise. There you breed some of the finest horses and dogs in France, should the king wish to avail himself.'

'My dear lady, I am lost for words that you would take such an interest. I have known Louise de Montmorency for many years, and Marguerite relies very much on her good sense, for she was once her governess. These days, however, I stay away from politics and intrigue and only advise the king on which dogs are sound. I am old and like to enjoy myself without *too* much effort of mind.'

I smiled as he winked at me.

'But please, I am somewhat at a disadvantage. I know nothing of you, except what I have seen: you are well skilled in all the games fashionable at court. Besides singing like a siren, you accompany yourself on the lute, you harp better than King David, and cleverly handle both flute and rebec. You dress with marvellous taste and devise new modes which are followed by the fairest ladies of the French court. However, none wear them with your gracefulness, in which you rival Venus.'

'And is that all?' I was somewhat amused.

'No. When you sing, you sound like a second Orpheus, and would make the very bears and wolves attentive.'

Madame d'Assigny gave a choke as she sipped her wine.

'Bears *and* wolves?' I asked. 'I think you are teasing me, sir.'

'You likewise dance the English dances, leaping and jumping with infinite grace and agility, and have invented many new figures and steps, which are yet known by your name.'

He moved his hand to my own, catching the narrowing eye of Madame d'Assigny, and I politely removed it. He settled back in his chair.

'Tell me of your background and how you came

to be here.'

I told him of my family, the court of Margaret of Savoy, of my passion for music, dancing, and books, for I never tired of reading French literature. I also told him how I loved hunting.

He leant closer. 'Well, I can assure you, I know nothing about books and care even less, but I can talk all night about the chase. You must be aware that here at court if a man or woman, no matter how handsome or beautiful, cannot hunt, he or she is not welcome in the king's company.'

He searched my face, and I found his rapt attention flattering. Here was no mere boy, but a seasoned, experienced man.

'The king has made it an art and a science,' I replied, sweetly, 'and I gather from the queen that he thinks nothing of spending over one hundred and fifty thousand crowns on his sport. As to the chase itself, why I think it is the horses that hunt, for too many gentlemen ride badly, crossing the hounds and breaking their course.'

'That is very true,' said the comte, 'and I would like to ride out with you sometime, but my horses need confident handling. Would you like to try one on our return to Amboise? We could start with one of the more docile creatures.'

I nodded as he devoured me with his eyes. This might prove easier than I thought.

Across the chamber, Mary lowered her fan to pull a face, causing my mouth to twitch.

'I amuse you?' asked the comte.

'Oh, no, sir, I am delighted at the thought of riding your fine horses.'

He sighed.

'Ah, how delightful you are, not at all like the other maids, for there is a lively intelligence in your face. I could not take my eyes away from you when you danced that night in Lyon.'

He put out his hand to touch a strand of my hair, and I moved back.

'Thank you, Monsieur.' I twisted the strand teasingly around my finger, just as I had seen my sister do. 'I enjoyed the entertainment very much.'

'Well, so did I, and I think there might be much that we could enjoy together.'

At that moment Marguerite beckoned to me, and making my apologies to the comte, I rose up to join her. She took my arm and led me over to the window.

'Is he bothering you?' she whispered.

I shook my head.

'Good. Now, Anne, I wish to ask you if you would like to join me on a journey to Hyères, near Toulon, tomorrow? It is some thirteen leagues away, and there is something I wish to do with as little fuss as possible. I would like to take you and a small guard with me. Can you ride over two days?'

I nodded, intrigued.

'Then I suggest you go and get your sleep, for we rise before dawn.'

1516

Racing across the coastal sand, splashing through the frothing waves of the sea, I had never felt such exhilaration. Islands of golden rock, salt marshes and the old monastery of St Honorat, now frequently troubled by pirates, shimmered in the distance. Stone palms bent and swayed in the wind, and the sunlight sparkled on the water as I overtook Marguerite on her horse. Turning in the saddle, I half reared my grey horse and laughed as a gust of biting, January wind whipped away Marguerite's bonnet. She cantered up, clapped her gloved hand to her horse's neck and shielded her eyes.

'Is it not beautiful?' she asked, breathless.

One of the guards retrieved the bonnet as she sat piling

her loose hair back into some order.

My horse pawed the sand, excited by the smell of salt and seaweed, and snorted through its pink, flared nostrils.

'It is so blue!' I cried, gazing into the horizon.

Marguerite, pins between her teeth, nodded.

'And I have never seen such strange-looking trees.'

Turning inland away from the wind, we cantered on along an ancient path shaded by trees, high above the town. Below, the plain of Hyères, with its palms, fig and olive trees watered by rivulets, sprawled out in a haze of sunshine.

Approaching an ancient, fortified building, we dismounted our horses in the courtyard and walked to the gate. It appeared deserted, apart from a few chickens scuttling about, a donkey dozing, and a dog chained to a post. The creature lurched forward and barked at our intrusion as the black cloth that shrouded the opening in the gate twitched slightly to one side.

'Who calls?' asked a voice.

'We are pilgrims,' replied Marguerite, 'and wish for food and water.'

The gate creaked open and leaving our escort outside, we stepped inside the Benedictine convent of Sainte-Clare. A young girl, her eyes bulging above a heavy neck, curtsied as Marguerite asked to see the prioress. As the girl limped away, I glanced about. A large, chipped statue of Christ stood in an alcove, piles of papers lay on the dusty desk and, to our horror, several chickens strutted beneath a table, their shit fouling the red, tiled floor. The smell of mutton cooking pervaded the walls, which were greasy and dirty, and all about was squalor. When the girl eventually returned, she asked that we follow her to the parlour.

'I fear the worst,' whispered Marguerite, as we were led down the dark passageway and into a large chamber.

A woman in black turned.

'My greetings to you, Reverend Mother,' began Marguerite, gently, 'please forgive this impromptu visit but

I have come on behalf of my brother, the king, to see how I may assist you. I hear that you may require support.'

'Most gracious lady,' said the Mother Superior, as she knelt and kissed Marguerite's outstretched hand, 'we were not expecting so illustrious a visitor. You are, of course, most welcome to join me privately for food and wine since we have just attended tierce, and the sisters are about their duties. Please, sit.' She shuffled to a cupboard and produced two expensive Venetian goblets, green stemmed, entwined with gold, and placed them on the table. She poured wine from a dusty wicker carafe and watched as we drank. It was good, very good indeed.

'May we rest awhile?' asked Marguerite. The woman gave a slight bow and an awkward silence fell.

'I would very much like to see the convent,' began Marguerite, brightly, sipping from her goblet.

'May I ask, Madame, if this is to be part of a pastoral visitation? A *visita ocular* has already been conducted by Cardinal Amboise himself, and purification has taken place. As to assistance, I cannot think what you may have heard.'

'With respect, Reverend Mother, that was fifteen years ago,' continued Marguerite, 'but I would still like to see your financial accounts, the register of who is staying here and which priests serve your needs. I am sure all is in order, but there may be some areas on which I can advise you.'

The woman stared, unblinking. 'Then, Madame, I will ask Sister Aloysius to bring them to you.'

Walking through the unkempt grounds of the convent, Marguerite, her brow furrowed, appeared deep in thought. When the ledgers were brought to her, it was clear that little, if any accounts, had been kept. We had met the sub-prioress, the treasuress and the almoness, but they would not speak out, and it was only when Marguerite questioned a young noblewoman abandoned there by her family, that her fears were confirmed; the local priest rarely visited to take confession, and the prioress had no control over her convent. When we were taken up the dark, wooden stairs to their living quarters, I saw that the nuns were allowed personal goods, mirrors and even pets, such as parrots, in their dormitories. These were not simple cells with a bed and a crucifix, but luxurious, velvet draped chambers. We heard they frequently slept together, rather than alone, or sat in social groups drinking and making merry. The parlour was used as the main area of entertainment, allowing male visitors, music, and gossip. Money from relatives of the nuns, deposited in good faith with the prioress, was spent on personal supplies of food, wine, and forbidden books. It was a place forgotten by God. I turned to Marguerite.

'Such negligence and idleness is not new, Anne,' she said, as she pulled on her gloves, 'and what few good nuns there are here, well, they are corrupted by the bad.'

I thought of Clément. He was right – there was, indeed, a vile canker behind the closed doors of such holy houses.

'At Lyon, dear child, I visited the church of Saint-Jean, to pray in peace. As I knelt before the crucifix of the choir screen I saw such a tender sight that my heart broke into pieces. A pretty young girl, a nun, was weeping, beating her breast and rocking on her knees in front of the altar, and I could not help but approach her. She appeared deeply distressed, but eventually, she said she would tell her tale to me and no other, so ashamed was she.'

My eyes widened. 'Go on, Madame.'

'The young woman had been raped by a monk and was with child. She wanted to end her life, but I promised that if she did not, I would do all I could to bring this criminal to justice. Not knowing who I was, she scoffed that I was as powerless as she, but when I revealed my identity, she showered my hand with grateful kisses and tears.'

'And will you?'

'I will keep my promise. But it is very hard. Cardinal Amboise forced through the reform of female houses – partly for their safety – under old Louis, but with no officer nominated in his place, the reforms foundered. Now there is naught but idleness.'

'Saint Benedict says idleness is the enemy of the soul, but what can you do?' I watched a cat chase a chicken around a well. Feathers flew into the air, accompanied by a noisy squawk.

'Oh, in my position there is much I can accomplish!' Marguerite said with vehemence. 'With the agreement at Bologna, I now have the means to ask the *Parlement* of Paris to hasten its reform, by force if necessary. I can make recommendations and put in place those best fitted to the task, removing the prioress. Such failings *must* be corrected, and I will demand a full week's visitation on our return. You will see how privilege brings power.'

As we walked back to the courtyard to join our waiting escort, Marguerite turned and gazed up at one of the windows. A dark figure moved back from the glass.

'Come,' she said sadly, mounting her horse, 'it is almost vespers. Let us ride down to the Franciscan church, and pray for the lost souls in this place.'

* *

On the banks of the River Durance, the great Citadel of Sisteron towered above our convoy as we waited with the mayor and Bishop of Sisteron. Louise tapped her fingers, desperate to see her son, and the queen peered through her jewelled spyglass. It was six o'clock in the evening, and he was late. Then, as trumpets blared and fife and tambour played, King François finally rode into view, surrounded by royal blue banners embroidered with gold angels clasping *fleurs-de-lis*. He dazzled in his white armour, over which he wore a blue mantle lined with ermine, and his horse broke into an eager canter. Children and villagers ran out to watch the sight, cheering and waving at the victorious army, each soldier carrying a blazing torch.

As the king kicked his horse forward his commanders,

such as the handsome Bonnivet, held back their impatient mounts and waited. Marguerite lowered her eyes as Bonnivet smiled and nodded to her husband, Charles d'Alençon, who doffed his cap in greeting. The Duc de Lorraine, a member of the House of Guise, meanwhile, stared at my sister. Louise's eyes blazed with passion as the Duc de Bourbon raised his helm, but he only gazed coldly ahead. Beside him sat her half-brother, René, known as the 'Bastard of Savoy,' and uncle of King François. My own heart leapt as I spied my grandfather, the Duke of Norfolk. Now seventy-three years old, he appeared thinner and more grey-haired than when I had last seen him, and as he shifted stiffly in his saddle, I wondered if he would recognise me.

The king leapt down from his horse and approached Louise's chariot.

'Majesty!' cried Louise, stepping down and smothering his face with kisses. 'I am but a poor mother thankful to see my son safe after all he has endured!'

As she dramatically collapsed, he raised her from her knees, hands about her face, and kissed her fondly again and again.

'Hush, *ma mère*, hush,' he said, smiling at his new title, 'I have returned victorious, as I promised, and with gifts for you all. Tomorrow our entry into Marseille will be the most spectacular ever seen and you will ride in honour beside me.'

When he saw the queen, he reached out his arms, and she flew into them. He embraced her and kissed her tenderly on the forehead, and she clung to his hand, smothering it with kisses, until he laughed, and pushed her gently away to turn to kiss his sister. It was a touching tableau, but as the king put his arm around Marguerite I noticed that his face appeared drawn, and the skin dark beneath his eyes. When Louise remarked on it in concern, he only laughed and whispered it was the result of boisterous night's carousing, including his amusing rescue of a beautiful maid confined to a convent. As he winked at my sister, the queen smiled. It meant nothing. Tonight, at least, he would be hers.

* *

'Where is she? Where is my favourite jewel?' He pushed through the press in the courtyard, his fur cloak thrown over his shoulder, and I watched as he approached the steps of the château.

'Grandfather?'

He paused, his foot on the step, his great hound by his side and threw his arms wide in disbelief.

'Why, by the nails of Christ!'

I ran down the stone steps and bobbed before him. He kissed me on both cheeks.

'Oh, Grandfather, it is so good to see you! I have missed you all so much. How does the duchess?'

We moved nearer to the light of the torches and he laughed hoarsely.

'Never happy, cantankerous fool, still hasn't got over her near-drowning when she sailed to France, but she is well. Now, let me look at you.'

He gave a low whistle as I gazed on his wrinkled, weather-beaten face beneath bushy brows. He looked every inch the seasoned soldier.

'My God, those great, dark eyes remind me so much of your Irish grandmother when she was your age. What a handsome young lady you have become.'

He draped his heavy furs across my shoulders, for the night was very cold, and we walked back amidst the courtiers, dogs, and ladies, to the warmth of the château. Nobles crowded about the doorway as he narrowed his watery eyes and peered about.

'Where is Mary?' He shielded me with his arm from the mass of people. 'Your mother was distraught when she heard of her exploits.'

'You mean my sister?' I asked as we moved inside the warm *salle* with its music playing and crackling fire.

'Who else? The only other Mary – Suffolk's bitch – is back at court, about to drop the devil's spawn. She still wishes to be known as the dowager French queen, conceited brat.'

I smiled, for my grandfather never did mince words.

'You did well, there, Anne, to unsettle her plans. Oh, I heard it all from Madame Louise – I hear everything – she was most impressed with you.'

'Grandfather!' The shriek from across the chamber sounded unmistakable as Mary flew over, all smiles and flushed cheeks. She bobbed in greeting and then pouted at the lukewarm response.

'Well, what did you expect,' he asked, 'a fanfare? You have shamed your family, and you are a disgrace. Your uncle is furious, apoplectic that you have nothing to show for your indiscretion, short-lived as it may have been. Unreliable, he calls it.'

Mary reddened. 'It was not my fault, sir,' she replied, in indignation, twisting the folds of her silver-grey gown. 'I did not seek the king, and yet he forced his attentions upon me. Why, he – he assaulted me!'

'Did he – did he so?' Grandfather's eyes narrowed. 'Well, you would be the first girl in France he ever did, for it is not in his nature to do so, so do not blast *that* lie abroad. Your poor mother is on her bed with shame.'

'At my behaviour or my lack of reward?'

Mary's question went ignored.

'What of Father?' I asked.

'Swept along, as usual, by your uncle. Even I have trouble arguing with him, for his ambition is unbridled. My own son.'

'How so?' Mary and I asked in unison.

Our grandfather rubbed his chin, and his eyes darted about. 'Oh, you know. His pride, his pride will ruin him, particularly since joining the council last year. He is almost as bad as Buckingham. He struts about with far too many retainers and while we both detest Wolsey, making such an enemy of him is rash. He needs to be content with our fortunes and status, but no, no, that is not enough. He wants me dead and out of the way so that he can claim the title as the third Duke of Norfolk.' He sighed. 'Well, I shall retire before long – or die. Had enough of it.'

'You do look tired,' I said.

'I am. I am a fighting man, and do not care to be involved with this –this nonsense. It was your Uncle Howard who wrote to Louise suggesting Mary here might be of use in distracting King François. Hold his attention, keep him from the Suffolk bitch, and so forth.'

Mary's face brightened and he stared at her in contempt.

'That wasn't a compliment. You couldn't hold water in a bucket. He also advised Louise to make use of you, Anne – in other ways.'

'Oh, then I see all now,' I turned to Mary. 'We have one daughter spying and the other used for the king's pleasure. If it was our uncle's idea to keep us both apart – I in Cluny and Mary under the eye of King François – what of you, sir, what was your part?'

'My part? Must I ask your good leave for my actions? By the Mass, I am too preoccupied with war to be embroiled in such matters, although yes, I grant you, had I not insisted that you both stay – only to spite Wolsey, mind, and oust his informers, nothing more – my son might not have interfered and maybe none of this would have happened. But I tell you, that boy with his Howard's spleen is overly ambitious. God's blood I have a brood of hot-tempered children, including your mother.'

Madame d'Assigny called to Mary, and as she left I took my grandfather aside.

'Sir, what do we do with Mary?' I asked. 'I fear the king is sniffing about her skirts again.'

He lowered his voice. 'Remove yourself from her company, Anne, and all will be forgotten by the time she returns to England. Your mother, of course, wants her home now.'

'She forgives her?' I was surprised. 'I bet Father doesn't, seeing he is so wary of my uncle.'

'Your father moves at his own pace and does not like your uncle's overbearing nature. He gets manoeuvred into matters he finds – indelicate. As for your mother, I can swear to you that she knew nothing of my son's plans for either of you.'

'Mary does not know what all the fuss is about,' I sighed. He grimaced.

'Well, she should. All that education and yet she has behaved like a simpleton. Tell me, are *you* happy here?' He perused my face. 'I can take you home if you wish?'

I shook my head. 'No, sir, I am becoming more French than English by the day, and I love the court. Of course, Queen Claude is kind but dull, and we are forever sewing altar cloths, but I provide company for her little sister and help her with her English. I hope to serve Marguerite when we return to Amboise, and so I am truly content.'

'Ah, Marguerite, the wisest woman in the world, of extraordinary complexion. Watch her, emulate her, for to be learned you must be part of the learned set.'

'I try, sir, and when we travel I sit with Marguerite in her litter and listen whilst she composes stories. They are so witty and amusing. Above all, I listen to the talk of Louise, Marguerite, and the queen together for there is much to learn about the world.'

'Good. And you behave soberly, with no dalliances?' He narrowed his eyes again as he searched my face. 'Well?'

'None, sir, I swear! No man will come near me, save for my husband, and you will hear no calumny, but only good report.' It was not a lie, for that is how I intended to proceed. I did not mention the foolishness that had gone before, and never would.

'That is my clever girl,' grinned Grandfather. 'I knew all this would go to Mary's head, but there is still a chance to redeem herself if a match were to be had. They are less lily-livered here than in England about such matters, so maybe we can marry her off here or send her to Ireland.'

'And me?' I asked.

Grandfather touched my cheek and smiled. 'Your father wants Mary betrothed first. We have no suitor for you as yet, but there is time.'

I was not sure if I felt relieved or disappointed.

'Will you ride with us to Marseille?' I asked as people took their seats to dine. He said he would, but not continue to Lyon for he was running out of money.

'King François – that 'boy' as King Henry calls him – owes me nearly nine hundred *livres tournois* in a pension instalment, so I cannot tarry and must return to keep an eye on Wolsey.'

'You will take my letters and gifts home?' I asked.

He nodded and linked my arm through his, patting my hand.

'Come, let me escort my clever grand-daughter to her place.'

The Comte de Chalon bowed his head and smiled as I passed by in a haze of perfume.

* *

Freshly sanded streets lined with garlands, myrtle, and green boughs of oak lay before me as two thousand children, all dressed in white with garlands on their heads, greeted the victorious king. The *entrée* into Marseille proved to be one of the most spectacular sights I had so far witnessed, and true to his word, the king had his mother riding next to him as the great cavalcade processed through the city, admiring the tableaux. The artillery fired a deafening volley, and the crowds roared. Receiving the beribboned keys of the city, the king raised them into the air, amidst a great cheer, and the galleys in the harbour fired their salute. The Counts of Angoulême, Guise, and Laval rode their fine horses behind, followed by every important personage of the court and church.

The queen had an *entrée,* but without the great salvo of guns, for they would have frightened the nervous Renée, and as our chariots followed behind, I noticed that the queen appeared visibly moved. Then as more young girls, also dressed in white, accompanied her to Notre Dame de la Garde, we prayed that she would be blessed with a son.

That night, on the quayside, accompanied by my grandfather and sister, I sat watching a sea combat comprising mermaids and sea gods against pirates and sea monsters. As dusk fell, the many torches and braziers provided warmth from the chill, and the firelight danced on the water. At midnight we retired, but the following Friday night yet more festivities followed, including a good-natured fight with oranges. It was organised by Monsieur Bernadine des Baux, in honour of the three queens and began quietly enough. However, before long, the king and his captains were standing on the tables hurling the fruit at the mayor and the city dignitaries. When the queen, Marguerite, and Louise joined in, all the ladies followed suit, some slipping on the bruised fruit and landing on the floor. Mary hurled an orange at the king, but he deflected it with his wooden shield and instead it hit Signor de Ravenstein, the ambassador from Prince Charles, squarely on the chin. Coquettish, Mary seemed in fine form, as the king drunkenly raised his glass to her. I felt alarmed as I glanced over to my grandfather and saw him shaking his head at such foolery.

The following day, the King of Portugal sent the queen a very strange gift indeed. Standing there on the quayside, peering at the iron crate, we did not know what to make of it. The ugly beast appeared to be wearing very loose, ill-fitting skin, and continually crashed its great horn into the metal bars, making the ladies jump back in fright. All except the foolish Marie, who kicked at the bars in disgust. The king explained that the beast was called a rhinoceros and had it sent back to his menagerie at the Hôtel des Tournelles, to entertain the Parisians there.

The following Saturday we dined at the Abbey of Saint-Victor and then visited Notre Dame de la Garde once more, before leaving Marseille on the twenty-sixth day of January.

We continued our journey to Aix, Salon, Arles, and Tarascon, where Marguerite slipped quietly away with the king, to visit the abbess at the convent of Saint Honorat. She wanted her brother to meet the learned abbess, famed for her verse and prose, and when he returned with her, they spent the evening in her private chamber, where I helped Antoinette de Polignac serve a private dinner to them both. As Marguerite relished the tender lamb, her eyes sparkled. Here, she said, was a convent that was a shining example to them all. However, their seclusion was not to last, for after hearing a commotion in the passageway, Louise burst through the door.

'At last!' she announced, triumphantly, 'that old fox King Ferdinand the Catholic is dead.'

We all crossed ourselves as I thought of Queen Katherine. Who would dare tell her that her beloved father had died when she was about to give birth to King Henry's son?

•   •

Delayed by the fierce Mistral wind, we were unable to continue our journey north along the Rhône River and remained longer at Avignon than we intended, enjoying a riotous dance performed by the Jewish inhabitants. Chambers in the pope's palace had been specially restored for our visit, and as we sat watching the merriment, Louise appeared distracted. She insisted that with Ferdinand dead, the king and Artus Gouffier, his principal advisor, must treat with Monsieur de Chièvres to ensure peace as quickly as possible. They must offer little Princess Louise as a bride to the sixteen-year-old Prince Charles. *Madame la Grande* nodded, pointing out that Chièvres, the most influential man at the court of the prince, and French by birth, would readily agree to subjugate Spain to France. Guillaume Du Bellay, the shrewdest of diplomats, pointed out that he thought friendship with England would be of most benefit and value to the prince, and – more to the point – he trusted King Henry. I thought of the thin, pale boy who now ruled a great kingdom, and did not envy his burden. He did not even understand a word of Spanish, and yet I imagined he would not be easy to fool. In his eyes, he was no longer '*Principe,*' as he had previously signed his letters, but King Charles. I thought fondly of Margaret of Savoy and was glad that he respected his aunt's wisdom and that with her father, they were again working as one towards peace with France and England. Bit by bit she appeared to be regaining her hold over events.

With the wind finally dropped, we sailed by barge along the river, visiting Orange, the Port Saint-Esprit and Montelimar, the king and queen bestowing privileges on the towns as we entered. Our route took our party through Valence, Tournon, and Vienne and finally, on St Matthew's day, we arrived back in Lyon. Here the royal party would remain until the summer, for the king needed to ensure that the conquest of Milan stayed safely in place. He appointed the Duc de Bourbon, against Louise's wishes, as governor, since there were rumours that Emperor Maximilian was about to try to seize the duchy, backed with English gold. All knew he had neither money nor gunpowder, yet he boasted openly that King Henry would assist him. Since the ill-will of the English to the French was no secret, and they no longer dissembled their feelings, the king mobilised his troops yet again. Now, as we alighted from the steps on the riverside landing, by the crowded Pont du Change, the Archbishop of Lyon welcomed our party to his palace for the second time. For myself, I was glad that we could finally stop in one place for a while and rest from the constant packing and unpacking.

⁕ ⁑

As a warm February brought forth blossom and buds to Lyon, Mother wrote to say that in London the river lay so frozen due to the severe winter that market stalls had been erected on the thick ice. From the Palace of Placentia, she watched as the court laughed and skated, enjoying hot chestnuts and mulled wine, before she joined Queen Katherine in her confinement. They had delayed a week before telling her of her father's death, and the queen lay on her bed, heart-broken. The king, however, proved ever kind and solicitous, sending her the latest piece of music he had written to keep her of good cheer, and informing her that King François had agreed to be godfather to the coming prince. Now all the world could do was wait and pray, and enjoy the Feast of St Valentine's Day, with its games of love divinations, feasting, and fun. All seemed to be going well until the beginning of March. A messenger from England rode to the palace in the dead of night, exhausted and hungry, announcing the news that Queen Katherine had, the day after Lent, on St Simeon's day, given birth to a girl. They had named her Mary, after the king's beloved, wayward sister.

⁕ ⁑

Leaving the game of *jeu de mail* in the palace gardens at Lyon, the queen handed her mallet to her page. She was weary of playing, and she missed the king, for he had returned briefly to Amboise to settle in his new horses from Burgundy. Marguerite took her arm and smiled. Tonight, she had promised the queen an intimate supper of a favourite dish of sweet, baked conger eel. The girl seemed to cheer up a little. Louise, however, appeared distracted, having slept badly due to a bad dream that her astrologers could not decipher. She had also lost two games in a row.

'Tell me again, Monsieur Bapaume,' she said, turning to the French ambassador, 'repeat what he said.' She swung her mallet aimlessly at the grass.

I glanced at my sister as I carried Marguerite's little dog. Mary, too, appeared tired, and not her usual boisterous self.

'Madame, King Henry appeared merry and said that since they were both young, boys would surely follow.'

'He is a good actor,' said Louise, turning to the queen, 'and, of course, my son sent his deepest felicitations.'

Marguerite smiled at her sarcasm.

'Oh, girls have their uses,' she continued, 'and you, my dear, I understand are now to be godmother?'

The queen smiled at Louise in reply and took Renée's hand. The little girl appeared most becoming in her new primrose yellow gown, her wooden doll tucked beneath one arm.

'Well, Monsieur, there is time yet. The queen is – how old?'

The emissary's lips twitched in a smile. She knew perfectly well.

'Thirty-one, Madame, I believe.'

Louise gave a slight snigger, and my sister wrinkled her nose as Louise bent down to stroke the archbishop's ginger cat. She liked cats, and this one appeared to like her. The little dog in my arms gave a yap.

'And the she-wolf? I gather from Monsieur de Plane that the French Dowager Queen has given birth at Bath Place to a healthy boy named Henry, Earl of Lincoln.'

'Indeed, Madame,' replied Monsieur Bapaume, 'the king gave his sister and Brandon an expensive gift, but it could not have been welcome news, so soon after his disappointment.'

I recalled hearing how Ann Jernyngham had the honour of carrying the infant at the christening.

'And now we have a mere boy on the throne of Spain – not that he will be accepted with his mad mother, Juana, still alive. She is Queen of Castile in her own right, is she not?'

'Yes, Madame, but sadly incapable of ruling.'

Mary and I fell back a distance as the party continued

down the path.

'*I* hear King Henry cried like a baby on hearing he had a daughter,' said Mary. 'I heard that he was all bonhomie on the surface, yet took himself off hunting as soon as he was informed. Can you imagine? He had burst into the chamber expecting a prince and was met with a mewling girl. None had the courage to tell him beforehand, so he had to save face and pretend all was well. They even had to add double '*s*' to the word 'prince' on the acclamation. That is how certain he had been.'

'King François must have felt the same over Princess Louise,' I added, pushing away the cat as it tried to wind about my legs. I detested cats and stamped hard, causing it to dart away under the bushes. 'But he is no longer concerned that he only has a girl.' I added.

Mary looked at me.

'I have been sworn to secrecy, so do not tell a soul,' I whispered, as we stopped, glancing ahead to make sure that the queen was out of earshot.

'Go on,' she urged.

'Claude has missed three courses. She must have conceived in Marseille, but you are not to say a word in case something bad happens. There is also a rumour that she is to be crowned at last.'

Before I could say more, there was a great commotion and the sound of voices calling.

'What in the name of the holy angels is going on?' Louise turned around, as *Madame la Grande,* followed by her ladies, arrived red-faced and gasping for breath. She looked fit to drop down dead on the spot as she held her heaving side.

'The king! The king is dead! He has fallen from his horse at Amboise!'

*   *

Having been carried inside the château at Amboise, we heard how the king had lain on his bed as Monsieur

Guillaume Cop, his doctor, bled him. Not leaving the king's side, he watched as the priest gave him the last rites, his companions gathered kneeling in prayer. To everyone's horror, the king appeared to stop breathing altogether apart from the occasional, shallow gasp. An hour went by, and then, quite suddenly, with a spluttering cough, he opened his eyes, said he had the most appalling headache, and asked for wine. The king lived, and the bells at Amboise rang out in joy! Confused and stiff, he had tried to sit, but fell back bemused at the sight of the council members gathered about him.

By the time Louise and Marguerite had reached the château, he was up and riding the very horse that had thrown him so violently against a stone wall. Apart from a large swelling and cut on his forehead, he appeared none the worse for his accident. Louise meanwhile, had the unfortunate messenger who had brought news of his death immediately exiled. She would have had him hanged, but for Marguerite's intervention. I, along with the entire court, attended a special Mass in thanksgiving for the king's recovery. As I stood holding my wax taper, I was happily unaware of the dreadful news my sister was soon to impart...

Chapter Eleven

'Time wastes not only our wits.'

The Auvergne

On a hot day in May, every citizen in Lyon turned out to see the great procession, and I gazed down at King François as he made his way to honour the Holy Shroud at Chambéry accompanied by a large band of courtiers.

I watched as the king, dressed as a barefooted pilgrim in black, white and tawny, and carrying a staff, walked with Marguerite's husband, the Duc d'Alençon, across the cobbles. He was on his way to give thanks to God, for Emperor Maximilian had not attacked Milan after all, but instead sat his horse a few miles outside of the city, refusing to fight or budge. The emperor then rode off on a hunting party, abandoning his troops to do as they wished. Yet again, he had made a fool of King Henry and taken his gold for nothing. The Venetian ambassador, Giustiniani, abandoning his plague-infested house at Putney, had even remarked on how gullible the King of England had proved.

Now we stood watching from the bridge over the Rhône, shielding our eyes from the sunshine as the king walked by. Marguerite whispered to me, with a faint smile, that if the shroud was with Margaret of Savoy in Mechelen – and I had seen it for myself – how could it also be in Chambéry?

She then confided that she felt weary of the festivities and pageants and longed to slip away to the quiet church of St Jean to pray. Louise, on the other hand, appeared in fine form since her lover, the Duc de Bourbon, was to be recalled, quite unexpectedly, from Milan and returned to her side.

The sun glinted on the swords of the landsknechts accompanying the Duc d'Alençon as the king disappeared into the distance, and the vast crowds gradually dispersed back to their homes. I looked over at the throng of ladies and *demoiselles*, and saw my sister holding a round, yellow silk canopy over the Comtesse Vendôme to shield her from the sun. As she descended the stone steps, the comtesse then took the canopy herself and Mary, falling some distance behind, beckoned to me. As I approached, her face appeared pale.

'Mary, what on earth is the matter?' I asked.

She gazed down. 'Oh, Nan – I – I think I might be with child.'

I felt my blood run cold.

'I have only missed one course, so I cannot be completely certain.'

'Oh, *please, please*, tell me it is not the king's.'

'Nan, it can only be his, for I have known no other, I swear it.'

'But you said he had done with you, that he never came near you any more.'

'Well, he did. Just once. I did not want him to.'

I stared ahead, trying to take in the devastating news.

'Mary, you once told me that you knew how to prevent such a thing happening, that there were ways to stop such – predicaments. Why did you not take care? Dear God, you are so stupid.'

'I know, I know – I have made a mess of everything,' she wailed.

Seeing her there, so desolate, I curbed my tongue. I suppose she had comforted me much after Clément, but I still felt angry.

'Hush, hush,' I soothed, trying to hide my annoyance, 'take heart, we can always get rid of the thing. There are wise women here at court who know what to do.'

'But I do not want to get rid of it. That would be a mortal sin.'

'Is it not a little late to be thinking of sin?' I asked.

She looked uncomfortable.'

'Do you feel sick?'

She gave a small shrug. 'No, not yet.'

A moment's silence followed.

'Grandfather spoke harshly,' she finally said.

I laughed out loud. 'He will be even harsher now, Mary, of that I can assure you. Anyway, he told me to keep my distance from you,' I added, none too kindly. 'You are a liability. As to Mother, she will die of shame, if she is not dead already.' I began to turn away.

'No! Please do not leave me! I am so afraid.' I turned back.

'But Mary, you might *not* be pregnant,' I said, seeing her panic. 'Do try and calm yourself. If you are, I expect you will be sent away to the country here in France to have the child, and none will be any the wiser.'

'And then what?' she asked.

'How do I know?' I replied, in irritation. 'Anyway, when will you tell Louise? You have some time yet, but you cannot wait too long.'

She glanced towards the king's mother who now stood talking cordially to the queen, her expression almost benign. 'When I am certain, Nan. Then I will tell her, and she will tell her son.'

Her face brightened for her never-ending optimism had now replaced her fear. 'Oh, everything will be all right, you see, for Louise once said that anyone who was once a mistress to the king could expect a good marriage and pension – provided she agreed. I am sure he will help me, for he is very gallant and kind, and cannot bear to see a woman in trouble.'

'You were not his mistress, so is that likely?' I asked.

'Besides, he has a legitimate son on the way.'

'Oh, Holy Mother,' she said, head down. 'Then what do I do?'

'Mary,' I said, turning away again in exasperation, 'why, why must you make everything here so embarrassing for me?'

She grabbed my hand. 'Oh, Nan, if I *am* with child will you write to Mother for me?'

I shook her free, my heart hardened. 'Not I, Mary, this is your mess. You must get out of this as best you can.'

'But where do I go?' she asked. 'I'd need money, an escort, and a horse, none of which I can obtain for my pay has been spent. Dear God, our parents will disown me.'

I shrugged. I was tired of the drama constantly surrounding my sister and wished she would just disappear. She was deluded if she thought that Louise would help, for my sister was not from an influential, noble French family but a girl of little consequence. Besides, her son had long moved on.

As we walked in silence, I felt angry and resentful, knowing that her behaviour reflected badly on me; it was said that where one sister went, the other most likely would follow. No, if Mary had fallen pregnant, I had to think very hard about what to do and hope I could salvage the situation. And then a thought occurred to me that there was someone who might help. Someone not a stone's throw away from where we were standing, who, like me, would be only too glad to see the back of the troublesome girl.

* *

'There – did you feel it?'

I looked up at the eager face in front of me, and removed my hand from the gold brocade of her gown. She looked better than she had for the last few months, for the roses were back in her cheeks. Although initially she'd been afraid, I knew that she wanted this child now, and the fear of childbirth, the pain, and possible consequences were all put aside as she smiled in excitement.

'Now *that* kick is a boy!' said the queen, laughing, and slumping back against the cushions of her bed.

The air felt still and hot as Renée placed her ear on Claude's stomach. Marie immediately copied her and shook her head, tutting.

'For shame, Madame,' she announced, looking up. 'I tell you it is a monkey, possibly two.'

'Go to,' said the queen, pushing her away with a sigh.

She handed me the bowl of cherries that she had developed such a fondness for, and I popped the sweet fruit into my mouth. They had become my favourite fruit, too.

'Oh, how I long to see my baby Louise, for she will have grown so much.'

'We will call him François!' cried her sister.

'We will, indeed,' laughed the queen, 'but first, we must all prepare for tonight, since twelve of my ladies, including you, Anne, are to accompany me to a reception at the Château l'Arbresle, on the outskirts of Lyon. Our new gowns have arrived, and I hear they are magnificent.

Leaving the queen to rest, we spent the whole afternoon in a whirl of excitement, trying on sleeves, shoes, and headdresses, until finally, all had been decided upon, and we made our way, by litter, to the château.

When we arrived, we stood waiting in anticipation for the inspection. Madame d'Assigny walked up and down the line in silence, her brow glistening with moisture. The chamber felt humid, although all the windows had been thrown open, and the scent of early summer roses filled the air. Outside, the sky lay heavy as if a summer storm was about to break, and a bumblebee buzzed lazily about. Eliza Grey promptly swiped it away in a panic, having been stung twice that summer already.

'*Magnifico*,' said Madame d'Assigny, nodding her head in appreciation as she halted in front of the two ladies who were to accompany *Madame la Grande*. 'Monsieur Rozone has excelled himself, *benissimo!*

Each gown had been fashioned in the Italian style, chosen by King François himself, and sent from Milan. They weren't only for his favourite ladies, but for a selection of maids too, and I was one of the lucky ones. Now, he wanted to show off his impeccable taste at the banquet. We had each been asked to think of a device or motto that might be sewn onto our bodice, since this idea had taken Italy by storm, and the king liked to play guessing games with the ladies. I had chosen the Butler family motto: '*Comme je trouve*' – '*As I find it.*' Stitched in silver thread above a white falcon with wings outstretched, it glittered upon a violet-coloured bodice, cut close to reveal my shoulders. The sleeves were gathered, slashed, and puffed, and there were silver stars embroidered all about. Mademoiselle d'Estrac had chosen a gown of green velvet, scattered with knots and hammers, and Madame d'Este a gown of black velvet covered with white, broken feathers. Anne de Graville wore saffron yellow velvet embroidered with the motto '*Musas natura*' – '*Nature inspires the muse*' – in black silk. It was exactly how the king wanted his ladies to appear – flamboyant, daring and very costly.

However, the most beautifully dressed woman was Françoise de Foix. She wore a gown of dark-crimson velvet embroidered all over with gold chains, between which were little tablets of silver engraved with the word '*Sponte*'. She smiled at me, knowing that I understood Latin and the momentous meaning behind that single word.

When we entered the *grande salle*, we were met by rapturous applause and cries of appreciation from the king's friends. He, himself, stood on the dais; the queen, his mother, and sister stood beside him, each dressed in rich, blue Genoa silk and damask. In Italy, blue denoted heavenward aspirations, and the colour could not have been more apt. On Marguerite's gown the words '*Plus vous que moy*' – '*You are more than I*' showed her brother that she acknowledged she was lowlier than he — and it pleased him. Louise had chosen an olive branch guarded by serpents, and the words *'Sagesse, gardienne des choses'* – *'Wisdom, the guardian of all things.'* The queen, slightly open-laced, had chosen *'Nisi eius'* – *'His only.'* *Madame la Grande,* not playing the foolish game, only stood with her hands folded on her black velvet gown, sweating profusely as she perused the company.

As each one of us walked up to the king, we turned slowly to show off our attire. More applause followed as the king nodded in satisfaction. This was followed by such kissing of every agreeable woman on the lips that I felt astonished, having never seen such a thing before. When Françoise swept to the floor, the queen smiled graciously at her, but Louise only scowled as she fanned herself, staring blankly ahead, her lips moving silently. Something, as usual, was irritating her.

As we left the heat of the *salle* to gather outside on the terrace, I turned to Françoise. 'When did Louise approach you?' I asked as she admired the dark, red trailing roses growing by the wall.

She plucked one and held it to her nose, breathing deeply. 'In Lyon. She told me she was in a predicament for she wanted the Duc de Bourbon at her side, and not in Milan as governor. Reluctantly she agreed that if I could join her in persuading her son to return him, she would ensure that he gave my brother Odet the post of governor instead. There were two small conditions.'

'Oh?' I asked.

'My husband and I must leave Châteaubriant and reside permanently at court, and I must ensure that her son refuses me nothing. Did you know that Louise and her lover have exchanged rings? She is besotted with him. Anyway, I did this for my brother, not her.'

'Go on,' I said.

'I succeeded. Bourbon is now foaming at the mouth in anger at having been summoned back, for he is ambitious, too. He wanted the governorship at fifty-five thousand francs a year, for himself, not Odet, for it is no mean sum. He and

Louise had the most terrible row, and he swore that he had never loved her and would never forgive her. In a fit of pique, he admitted it was Marguerite he wants, not a dried-up old fossil like her mother.'

I stared at her. To anger Louise was tantamount to signing one's death warrant.

'She is now poisoning the king against Bourbon, saying that I was his mistress before him. It is not true. You must believe me, Anne, when I say I have never sought Bourbon's affection. He looks with pity upon me, not love.'

'But you are flattered by the king's attention,' I replied.

She smiled. 'At first, yes, but now his passion for me is something near to madness, even he admits as much. I love my husband, but if I do become the king's mistress, it will only be *if* I choose, in my own time, of my own volition. And, as you so cleverly realised, I will brook no competition from any other pretty young woman, high or low, who attracts the king. It will be all or nothing.'

'Well, I cannot thank you enough for your help,' I added, as we walked together in the breathless air.

'Oh, your sister was no serious threat, but well, let us say I prefer a clear field. That is why I was happy to 'assist' you with her departure. I think it is better – for both of us – if she is away from court for a few months. We must thank God she was not with child, as she feared, for King François is not a man to acknowledge bastards.'

'I suppose,' I said, 'for as the king he has no care for consequences.'

Françoise smiled. 'He is fickle – of that, I am sure. Today he has a passion for dark hair. Tomorrow, who knows?'

She was right. He was done with Mary. When her courses finally did arrive, she had suffered badly with a haemorrhage, and lain white as a ghost in her chamber, weak and in pain. My father had agreed that it was better if she retired to the house of Philippe du Moulin, Seigneur of Brie, whose acquaintance he had made in France. The house at Briis-sous-Forges, about eight leagues southeast of Paris, would be comfortable and she would be cared for by the family. Here she was no longer of use.

'Well, a horse and escort were most generous,' I said, watching as she twirled the rose between her fingers, 'and yet I gather Louise has told her she can return to court when she has recovered. I just do not understand.'

'Louise is pragmatic, Anne, like me. Besides, by the time Mary returns, who knows what the situation will be?'

At that moment, the king, surrounded by his family, diplomats, and courtiers, appeared on the terrace and the musicians struck up a tune.

'How dare that woman behave thus?' thundered Louise, turning to her son. 'She might as well spit in our eyes!'

The king smiled into the distance. 'Audacious, *Madame Mère*, I will grant you that. Can you believe the Scottish bitch publicly displayed the great diamond of Naples in her velvet hat at Henry's court? Her brother thinks nothing of giving it away to his older sister.'

'And – *I* – want – it – back,' said Louise, suddenly aware of the Spanish ambassador standing next to her. She walked away, her hand on her son's arm, and Françoise turned to me, inclining her head towards the king, whose eyes fixated on her. It must be serious if he was prepared to offend the watching queen.

'But what of you, Anne?' asked Françoise. 'I see that the Comte de Chalon is very attentive.'

I stared at the gathering crowd and spotted Clément, hovering behind Marguerite. The sky darkened.

'Yes, Madame, but he is away at present, in Orléans, purchasing new dogs for the king. We talk and walk together, in company of course, since the queen has been assured he only wishes to pay polite court to me.'

'Good, it is good for you to practise your charms.'

I laughed. 'Well, I enjoy his company – to a point.'

'Indeed, but take my advice, Anne, and learn the art of

flirtation. To hold his attention, you must give nothing – and *accept* nothing. He is an old man, and flattered that you find him interesting. Let him pay you attention, but keep yourself above reproach. A man will wait forever for what he truly desires, and you must learn to keep him dangling on a hook like a wriggling fish!'

'But I have no intention of making him my lover.' I was shocked.

'No, but do not tell him that. Keep him guessing. One day appear happy in his company, the next bored. Threaten to leave the court and return home one week, and then say you would like to remain in France forever the next. Blow hot and cold. Your sister did not know how to play the game, and once the king achieved what he wanted, well...'

'I must admit, Madame, I am happier with my heart free,' I said.

'Well, a woman must get by as best she can and if that involves a little insincerity, then so be it,' said Françoise.

'But will he not tire of me?' I asked, looking at her lovely face. I did not have her sensual looks and inviting plump body.

'If he does, it shows that you still have much to learn, so you must cultivate your talents. Read, fill your mind with the latest ideas, understand how the court works and listen to those around you. Fascinate with your mind, not just your appearance, for the art of conversation is everything. Flatter, but do not fawn. Make him crave your company above all others.'

'Really, Madame? When we return to Amboise, I am hoping to visit Loche with him, as I love horses and know something about hounds.'

'Good, for that is what keeps Diane and her ugly little husband so content. He is the greatest *veneur* in France, and a mutual passion for hunting ensures they are never apart. Love what your admirer loves.'

'Of course, it depends on whether or not I can be spared

my duties, for the queen's baby will be due in the autumn.'

'Poor girl, she is not strong,' said Françoise. 'She longs for a son, for only then will she be crowned as François' queen. We must all pray for her safe delivery. But come, it is starting to spit with rain.'

As a roll of thunder filled the air, she smiled her charming smile, and I thought how beautiful she looked. At the age of twenty-one, she had brains, beauty, and confidence. When she addressed the king using '*tu*' instead of the more formal '*vous*', everyone noticed her presumption. The meaning of the motto she had chosen was most appropriate: '*Voluntarily.*' Her message to the king could not have been clearer. She would give herself on her terms, in her own time.

The Loire

Life was good at Amboise that August month, for it was a time of peace for France. A treaty had been signed at Noyen with Spain, and at Notre Dame in Paris, the *Te Deum* rang out as the heralds proclaimed the betrothal of baby Louise to King Charles of Spain. The pale young man agreed to pay one hundred thousand *écus* of gold to King François each year until the marriage, and fifty thousand crowns until Louise gave him a son. If he died, she would marry Charles's brother, Frederick.

In the nursery, Queen Claude, now reunited with her child, sang to her in her cot and refused to let the new nurse, Madame Brechenior, remove her. The queen knew that she would soon be confined to her chambers to begin her lying in, and she wanted to spend every minute with her child. However, she felt relieved that little Louise would not go to King Charles until she reached eleven years of age. As Renée jangled the beribboned stick of garnet stones to amuse the child, Louise stared in awe at the mother she hardly knew and began to cry.

When the king returned from Saint-Denis, he wished only for amusement as he awaited the birth of his son. Hosting party after party, and carousing with his rowdy friends incognito around the town, he often ended up in the White Eagle tavern, the worse for wine. At banquets, as his ladies gathered around him, he only had eyes for the lovely Françoise, but still, she did not give him what he desired, fanning his passion to a flame. As I watched her closely each day, I had to admire her assurance, cunning, and seeming indifference. The more changeable she behaved, the more he became her prisoner.

During the day, magnificent tourneys graced the terrace, followed by wrestling matches where everyone bet on their favourites. Then came the masques, and in Marguerite's apartments the night torches burnt out before the dancing stopped. The king's finest young choristers, all dressed in black velvet, sang the praises of little Louise and the child to come, in a motet composed by the talented Monsieur Jean Mouton. I felt extraordinary happiness without the burden of my sister, and we laughed with the exuberance of the young and carefree, too excited to go to our beds. Surrounded by admirers, I teased and flirted – just as Françoise had shown me – knowing that I could drive the old Comte de Chalon to distraction with just a glance. It was the most wonderful feeling to be desired so, and to be free from all the pain, longing, and sleepless nights I had suffered over Clément. The more I refused favours to the comte, the more he seemed to dote, and I enjoyed a new feeling – one I had not felt before. It was the feeling of sexual power.

• •

'But it is beautiful!' I cried, twirling around and gazing up at the white, rounded turrets of the château.

Behind, kicking the golden October leaves, walked Eliza and several other ladies in their riding garb. On seeing their master, two spotted dogs ran forward, barking and wagging their tails in the watery sunshine.

'Down, Caesar, down Cassius,' chided the comte, flicking his hazel switch towards them.

I glanced at his florid face and patted the dogs' heads. 'I see you favour *limiers*, sir, for I understand they are excellent pointers.'

He smiled at my knowledge. 'Indeed, *demoiselle*, they are quick and alert, and I will present this handsome pair to the Duc de Guise on his return from the kennels at the Parc des Loges, near Saint-Germain-en-Laye. The most illustrious Duchess of Ferrara presented these dogs to me.'

I smiled my most charming smile.

'The king is a good judge of dogs,' he continued, 'and, like me, becomes very attached to them.'

'We have English hunting dogs at home, sir, and when I was there, I would care for the whelps. I do understand how important it is to place a kennel well for their comfort.'

The comte appeared surprised. 'Did you hear, my dear, what the king did when his favourite hound, Hapeguai, died?'

I stared at him, puzzled.

'He had gloves made out of his skin.'

'*No!*' I cried, 'that is quite absurd.'

He smiled back at me, his eyes lingering on my face. 'It was good of the queen to allow you to visit,' he said, ruffling the larger dog's ears.

'As you are aware, sir, she is in her confinement now, and only the most experienced matrons and noblest ladies are attending her.'

'Well,' he said, 'let us walk to the stables where I have a docile mount waiting for you. It is a fine, crisp day for a ride, and there is much to show you of the estate. The views from the terrace are quite exceptional.'

As we approached the stables, several horses, bridles held by grooms, stood saddled and waiting by the mounting block. However, in one of the open stalls, a spirited black animal caught my eye, and I strolled over to look. The horse threw back its head with a snort, ears flat, and kicked hard against the wooden half door, making me jump back.

'Hush, now, sirrah, be nice to your visitor. This is Nero,' the comte said, turning, 'and I had him sent from Mantua. In my opinion, Italian horses are superior to French, but he is young and temperamental and needs to learn some manners.'

'May I ride him, sir?' I asked, taking his arm, my eyes wide. I moved nearer to his cheek so that he could feel my warm breath. 'I promise I will not ruin his mouth, for I have ridden all my life and I can handle hot blood.'

'By Our Lady's mantle, no! I have a much quieter animal waiting for you. Besides, Nero is seventeen hands, and you a mere slip of a girl.' He gazed down at my sulky face and pouting lips.

Standing on tiptoes, I kissed him on the cheek, my soft lips lingering and my dark eyes pleading. Madame d'Assigny would have been outraged to see me behave thus.

'My God,' he said, with a sigh, 'I can refuse you nothing in that exquisite gown.'

I quickly stepped away.

'Well, you may sit on him – that is all.'

'You are very kind to me, sir' I said, quite aware of the allure of my costly black hunting gown. I knew I could not have looked more enticing.

'Fetch him out,' commanded the comte to a groom, 'and make him ready.'

As the groom led the fractious horse out, it pawed the cobbles, nostrils flared, and snorted in the crisp air. He was magnificent, with his long flowing mane and coat as glossy as a raven's wing. Eliza, meanwhile, mounted her horse, her whip in hand, and the older ladies heaved themselves into the saddles of the other dozing horses. When all were ready, the comte mounted and took the reins of his horse, warning Eliza to keep her distance with hers, for it liked to kick. Her chestnut horse flattened its ears as he led his horse past. He then turned about to see me already sitting on the black horse and gathering up my reins. As it spun around on the spot, trying to unseat me, I calmly sat still, my feet resting on the wooden footboard of the *sambue*. Half rearing and fighting against the bit, the horse threw its head up and down, and jittered around on the cobbles making sparks fly. Keeping my hands very still, I murmured soothingly and gained my balance until the animal stood quiet as a lamb.

'Well, sir – may I ride him?' I asked.

The comte gave a smile of admiration as we trotted out of the yard and into the open fields.

As we cantered along, the comte pointed out the great vineyards where women and children stood picking the grapes for his cellars, for it had been a good year, promising a high yield. Of course, he said, the grapes here at Loche were not as good as those in northern France, but were fine enough to export. I told him of the grapes in Kent, and we spoke of my home.

After an hour, we stopped our horses to rest, the huge château of Loche rising high above the River Indre on its rocky outcrop, dominating the village below. It's great, square grey walls made it appear like a prison, yet the comte told me that the queen liked it very much, as inside it was comfortable with a pretty terrace.

Our horses refreshed, we continued our ride, and when I spied the open land ahead, I gave my horse his head. As swift as an arrow, I flew past the comte, and, looking back, laughed to see Eliza and her companions fade far into the distance. Exhilarated, I kicked my horse hard, and before long we were galloping at full speed over ditches and heath. I had never ridden such a fine animal and cared not that I had lost my bonnet, or that my hair now streamed behind, whipping in the wind. The comte rode fast to catch me, and before long, we rode neck and neck racing together in the October sunshine. Leaning low, I spurred Nero on, froth flying from his bit, his eyes wild with excitement. On we galloped until the comte threw out his arm to catch my horse's bridle, and brought him to an untidy halt by a stream.

'Why did you do that?' I asked, breathless, 'I was winning!' I clapped my hand to Nero's sweating neck.

'God's death, Anne! He is too strong for you! He cannot feel you on his back. You might have been killed!'

I turned Nero round and round in a circle, his sides heaving. The comte clumsily dismounted and, half running, wheezed over to me.

'Get down now,' he ordered. He appeared angry.

I sat, refusing to move, my long hair falling about my face.

'Or what?' I asked, teasingly.

'Or I will drag you down. Now, drop into my arms.'

I pulled a face and, as he lowered me gently from the wooden seat, I barely reached the middle of his chest. He stroked my hair and sighed, pressing me to his thighs so that I could feel the hardness of his lust. It was horrible, and I deftly ducked beneath his arms to escape the now probing fingers. Then, as he made to move towards me again, I swirled out of his reach. I did not want an old man touching me, so I laughed and played the coquette.

'At home, I ride like a man,' I said, tidying my hair and hoping to shock him. 'I hate the way a woman has to perch on a chair for modesty's sake.'

He stopped in his tracks and stared at me.

'I have an idea,' I said, brightly, alarmed at the lust in his eyes.

'Anne, please, can we not just sit here awhile – alone? The other ladies are nowhere to be seen.'

I glanced about. He was right. There was not a soul in sight and apart from the trickling of the running stream, there was silence. This might prove tricky.

'But I want you to show me Loche,' I demanded, my voice petulant.

'*Now?*

'Yes, now, I want you to show me right now. The others cannot be far behind. Let us ride together, and you can tell me everything you know about the château. I love hearing your tales. *Please?*

He sighed and threw out his arms in defeat.

'Besides,' I added, ' it will be far more comfortable inside.'

'Oh, very well, if we must,' he muttered, as he lifted me back onto Nero, his hand lingering on my soft, leather boot.

He rubbed his thumb slowly across my ankle and squeezed my foot.

'But no galloping away, even if you are an excellent horsewoman.'

As I picked up the reins, I paused and turned my head. A bell tolled urgently and continuously in the distance, soon joined by many more.

'At this hour?' asked the comte, tightening the girth of my saddle.

I glanced at him, relieved as Eliza and the other ladies cantered up.

'Did you hear that?' asked Eliza, breathless, pulling up her mount. 'We must return to Amboise. The queen has delivered her child!'

●　　○

It was a bitter blow. As soon as the baptism was over, the king left Amboise to hunt and sulk in the Touraine with his band of women – except for Françoise. She boldly refused to go, and her indifference must have driven him wild.

Princess Louise now had a sister named Charlotte, in honour of the mother of *Madame la Grande*, with blue-green eyes and downy red hair. Sadly, although the court thanked God for the queen's survival, there were no celebrations during those autumnal days. In England, King Henry rejoiced that his dear brother had been 'blessed' with a mere princess, and the race for a son continued. Louise showed her disappointment, but it was some consolation to her when countless paintings and treasures arrived from Italy and were duly transported in carts up the tower ramp at Amboise, for her to peruse for the royal collection. The king's agents had already scoured Europe for the finest treasures, and heavy trunks of Italian silver statues, gold clocks, goblets, altarpieces, and plate were thrown open before the avaricious eyes of his mother. Artists now flocked to her court, including a new painter from the Low Countries, Monsieur Jean Clouet, who stood with her discussing the merits of the work. In her greed, Louise wanted to keep them all, and there were murmurs of disquiet as courtiers whispered that she wished to carve out the loot of battle for herself. The complaints even reached Paris, and there was much unrest concerning her actions. She only laughed and spread open her arms saying they could grumble all they liked, there was nothing they could do. That's how things would be.

On a chilly day in November, we made our way down the steps of a long, secret passage that linked the Château of Amboise to the house at Cloux. Only King François and Louise held a key, and today, Louise insisted that the queen take the air and greet the new visitor. As Louise descended she muttered to herself about the dowager French queen, for a rumour had reached the court that she was pregnant again, and Louise said she wished her at the bottom of the River Thames. I continued in silence as Renée, holding my hand, enjoyed the adventure but with its low, curved roof and narrow walls, I was glad to reach the end of the damp passage.

As we entered through the small, wooden door to the house, an old gentleman turned and bowed, removing his strange, green glasses with his left hand. Once probably handsome, his long grey beard now straggled to his chest, and his thinning hair touched his shoulders. His face crinkled as he smiled, but he appeared tired, and his right hand hung lifeless by his side as if afflicted in some way. I noticed how letters and documents bulged from the pockets of his long coat, along with various copper instruments.

'Ah, Signor da Vinci, forgive this intrusion, but my son is in Paris and wished to send his regards to you. I trust you and your servants have settled in well and that everything is to your liking?'

'Indeed, most gracious lady, the house is exquisite and you have provided a very grand bed in which to rest my weary bones. The view of the château from my window is most pleasant, and I am grateful for the special services of the cook you have provided.'

Louise smiled as the queen stretched out her hand and the old man kissed the proffered ring.

'Well, I understand that meat is hard to chew as one gets older,' said Louise, 'for I, too suffer from bad teeth.'

'No, Madame, it is by choice. I will eat no living thing that can feel pain, or make my body a tomb for other creatures.'

Louise raised an eyebrow at the absurdity of his comment. 'Indeed, Signor, how utterly amusing, but now tell me, I hear you have travelled far and in the foulest of weather. Thank God your paintings were not damaged.'

'Indeed, Madame, the canvasses were rolled in oilskin, but for seventy-two days, I battled through the rain across Italy, and I fear it has given me a troublesome cough. November was not the best time to travel, but I wanted to set off before the snow set in.'

'I shall send my doctor to you,' the queen offered, concern in her voice. 'He will make you a borage and honey tea.'

I stared at the old man whom the king had met at Bologna and insisted on bringing to his court, for he was known as a great philosopher and inventor of ingenious devices. All King François required in return for the use of his mother's house, and a staggering annual pension of over a thousand *écus soleil,* was the company of his genius.

'My mother,' the queen explained, 'loved this château for

its peace and solitude, away from the court. I do hope you will find the same solace.'

'I hear, *grand-maître*,' said Louise, as she paced around the chamber, her gown brushing against the table, 'that you understand the movement of the planets. Renée here is fascinated by the stars, as you know I am.' She picked up one of the drawings on the table. 'Ah! Locks – you could not have arrived at a better time, Signor, for we must talk of your project of joining the waters of the Loire and the Seine, at Romorantin. You will accompany me, in January, to assess the feasibility of a canal for my new château on the banks of the River Sauldre. My son, who has many happy childhood memories of my home, wishes to make Romorantin the capital of France and move the government to Tours. Amboise is far too cramped, and he intends to build the most magnificent château possible.'

'Indeed, Madame, I am working even now on a project to drain the Sologne area. I am also working on plans to provide accommodation for the travelling court that can be dismantled and re-erected. Housing people is such a problem.'

Louise laughed. 'You mean pavilions?'

'In a sense, dear lady, but made of wood, not canvas.'

Renée gazed about in wonder.

'Aha,' he said, moving to a large cabinet, 'I see the little princess is curious.'

He opened the doors and carefully took out a metal lion, wrought in gold, the size of a small dog. He then placed it on the floor and slowly, turn by turn, wound the springs with a golden key. A soft, whirring sound followed, and the creature began to move, fall to its knees and, to all our amazement, open its mouth and bring forth golden lilies. Renée laughed as each one plopped onto the rush mat.

'Madame Claude,' said the old man, 'may I present this in honour of Princess Charlotte's birth? I gave a similar version to your husband in Pavia.'

The queen gasped and turned to Madame Louise, who tipped her head in agreement.

'Now, Madame, would you care to dine with me? There is always meat for my guests.'

'Alas, we cannot, Signor da Vinci, for much business awaits, but perhaps you would care to show Anne, here, the rest of your inventions? We will, of course, return to speak with you again, as I need to discuss the designs for the children's new bath chamber.'

The Master bowed as Louise proffered her hand and, turning, took the queen by the arm.

'Madame, you have forgotten the lion!' He handed Renée the golden beast and she clutched it in her hands.

The door to the passageway closed behind them and we stood for a moment in silence.

'So, you are Anne,' he said, turning, his face in a kindly smile.

'Yes, Signor, I am one of Queen Claude's ladies and I am assisting Renée with her English, for I am from England myself. I would love to see your work for I enjoy novelties.'

The old man sighed. 'Ah, England, a place, I hear, of damp mists and constant rain, unlike my beloved Florence.'

'Then why did you leave, Signor?' I asked, as he picked up his glasses from the table and rubbed the thick lenses with his hanging sleeve.

'I left, *demoiselle*, because my Medici patron died, and others such as Michelangelo and Raphael stole all the best jobs. I am an old man but I still have my pride.' He held the glasses up to the light, satisfied. 'But come, let me show you my studio. It is still in disarray, so please excuse the muddle.'

Walking through the house, I discovered it was made of two adjoining red-bricked buildings. It appeared small, compared to the great chambers of Amboise, but far more comfortable. There were still boxes and trunks strewn about, and two gentlemen stood perusing the contents of one of them.

'Leave them, Salari, I do not want the fragile charcoals disturbing,' said the Master, pulling his woollen coat about him. These days, he said, he could not get warm.

We passed the kitchen where a woman in her middle years stood at a wooden table before a great stone fireplace, the sleeves of her coarse grey gown rolled up. A strand of dark hair fell from her coif as she wiped her brow and stared at the large cabbage stuck on her cleaver. She glanced up with a scowl.

'And what am I supposed to do with this, I ask you?' she called, banging the cleaver and cabbage down together with a great thump.

I wanted to laugh, for she looked quite comical.

'Well? You are supposed to be the magician.'

'Ah, Mathurine,' soothed the Master, walking to her side, 'do not trouble yourself, for anything you cook will be acceptable, anything at all.' He placed an arm about her shoulder, but she shrugged it away, muttering.

'Soup, pottage, gruel, what sort of food is that for a man to live on? Are you a peasant to live on roots and vegetables?'

As she winked at me, I realised this bantering was good-natured.

'This young lady is from England and wishes to see my work.'

The woman wiped her floury hands on her apron and grunted.

'Ha, as if she could make any sense of your scribbles and calculations! My brother is over in London at present and writes to tell me the French are not wanted there. Is our money not good enough? Well, I worry for him, for mark my words there will be trouble. When are you going to do something useful and fix this old spit?'

The Master smiled, and as I was quickly hustled from the kitchen to continue our tour, she called out. 'Cabbage soup – that is all you are getting tonight!'

Entering the wood-panelled chamber, I stood amidst

papers, drawings, wooden models and dozens of dusty old books. An easel propped by the window held a canvas pinned to the frame, and a dried-up palette of paints rested on the nearby table. Bottles containing oils and brilliant colours filled the shelves, and sticks of charcoal lay in bundles beneath. Papers, strewn across the floor, bore strange letters and writing that made no sense. I opened one of the great ledgers near to me, and shocked, slammed it shut in a cloud of dust.

The old gentleman smiled. 'There is no shame in the human body, my lady.'

I opened the book again and peeped at the drawings before me, horrified. 'But – but these are a woman's form, her secret parts – and here is a child in the womb.' I felt disgusted, and it showed on my face.

'What God created can only be beautiful,' he explained.

'Not the subject, Signor, the fact that – that you have drawn them so. Should not such things be kept a secret for only the physician to know?'

'And how does the physician learn his trade?'

I stared at him. 'Why, from cadavers.'

'Precisely. Which is what I do, recording everything my eyes see. Every vessel, vein, muscle, and sinew so that others might learn after me, for the human body is the most complex machine of all.'

'But you are not a doctor,' I argued.

'Must a man be a priest to pray to God?' he asked, seeing my discomfort.

I quickly recovered my poise, not wishing to appear rude.

'No, *demoiselle*, I see myself as a painter, a philosopher, and an inventor, but more than anything else – I am a soul that yearns to learn life's mysteries. What greater mystery is there than the human body?'

I picked up one of the pots, smelt the contents and drew back. It smelt pungent, of linseed.

'Who is this lady?' I asked, gazing at a small canvas,

resting against a stool.

'That is the wife of Francesco del Giocondo, a very wealthy Florentine silk merchant. I painted it many years ago, and when I am satisfied with the tint of the complexion, I will return it to her.'

'Is she really that dark of skin?' I asked, peering closer, and thinking of my own sallow complexion.

He nodded. 'Indeed, but she is a lady of great charm, and worth taking the extra trouble to get the hue just right.'

Walking about the chamber, I felt intrigued by all I saw and must have asked a hundred times the name of this or that instrument. I was met with great patience and kindness as I spoke of Margaret of Savoy and her wonderful *cabinets* full of curios. I told the Master how she had described to me the different paints and oils used. I then picked up an almanac with illustrations of the phases of the moon.

'Will you cast my fortune, Signor?' I asked, 'if you have time, of course.'

Nearby stood a plaster model of the earth surrounded by the planets fixed on wires. Above, a metal crescent moon glinted and turned as it hung from a ribbon attached to the rafters.

He laughed. 'My dear young lady, I am not a visionary and would not dare presume to tell your future. That is God's secret, but I can tell you of the planets and how, I believe, they influence the course of our lives and our human affairs. Jupiter, for instance, can bring luck, but it is up to you to recognise the opportunity. On its own, it is just – a planet.'

'I was born in May, sir. Is that a good omen?'

'Ah, May, the month of the emerald. Gemini illustrates what it is to be a human being, lively and intelligent. In astrology, it is a star sign that commands others.'

'How so?' I asked.

'Well, people are born under either a commanding sign or an obeying sign. Madame Louise was born under Virgo, like her son, and her daughter Marguerite was born under

Aries. All three are commanding signs. Madame Claude, born under the sign of Libra, is an obeying sign.

'How sadly apt,' I replied.

The Master gave a wry smile. 'Sad? No, she is – although few choose to believe it – much loved by the king. And speaking of kings, to him astrology is a knowledge, or science to learn from. His lucky number is three, which is, of course, the Holy Trinity. Now, let me tell you more of the importance of numbers as we walk in the garden. The ruler for Gemini is Venus and the number five ...'

1517 Paris

The waiting had proved unbearable and leaning out of the casement window, I stared impatiently down as chariots rumbled into the courtyard of the Hôtel des Tournelles. There had been a steady stream of visitors all morning, and I had watched and waited as grooms ran to grab hold of bridles and throw blankets over sweating horses' flanks. Then I saw her: a woman sitting on a fine chestnut horse, pulling off her gloves, and then slipping down into the arms of one of the grooms. She straightened her plum-coloured gown, covered in mud spatter at the hem, and as she adjusted her feathered bonnet, she gazed about, her face in a grimace. She was here!

Pinching my cheeks to give them colour, I left the window, picked up Bonny and, half walking and half running in my excitement, reached the palace steps. Stepping quickly out to the courtyard, my heart racing, I put Bonny down and sank into a deep reverence at her feet. The little dog yapped with excitement, tail wagging. When I raised my chin, the woman broke into a wide smile.

'Anne? Anne, can this *really* be you, my darling, dearest child?'

As my mother brought me to my feet, I fell into her

warm, open embrace. She smelt of lavender, of home, and I could not let her go, all decorum and restraint abandoned. I felt my eyes fill with tears of joy, and I closed them tight as I squeezed her, the buttons on her gown pressing into my cheek. We stood in silence as her arms folded about me, and she stroked my hair. I could not let her go from me.

'Oh, my precious, precious child, my sweet Nan, how I have longed for this moment!'

'Dearest mother,' I whispered, barely able to breathe, 'I should have waited dutifully as I was told, but I could not bear a moment longer. Forgive me, but I had to see you as soon as possible.'

'Ah, Anne, let me look at you,' she said, holding me away from her. 'By the Mass, what a comely young woman you have become and you look so – so grown up! How old are you now, sixteen? You were a small, frightened child standing on the dockside at Dover when I last saw you. But who is this?' she asked, as my little dog jumped up.

I stood staring into her lovely face, thinner than I remembered – for it was four years since we had met – and I noted the dark circles beneath her bright, slanting eyes. She seemed shorter too, since I had grown taller, and escaping from her bonnet, threads of fair hair, tinged with silver, touched her shoulder.

'This is Bonny. Oh, dearest Mother, are you well? I have so much to tell you. Where is Father? How is George? I ho –'

'In time, sweetheart, in time,' she laughed, pinching my cheek. 'I am quite well, everyone is well, and your father is following on behind since he is in Paris on business. Unfortunately, your uncle and your grandfather have stayed in London to suppress the May Day riots, but more of that later.' She glanced about. 'I must say this is a grim heap of stone.' She then perused my face as if she could not believe her eyes, smiling in wonder. 'Ah, you look so elegant, sweetheart, and your gown is beautiful – the colour of winter violets. Do all the ladies dress so well? What is this style of sleeve called – is it French?' Her eyes stared in disbelief as she took in every inch of my person. 'I cannot believe how changed you are, Anne. The shape of your face, your lustrous hair. And your eyes. They were always expressive, but now they are captivating.'

I laughed and turned about. 'The sleeves are my own invention. Do you like them? Best of all, we are allowed to keep the gowns made for us. Oh, you would not believe how lovely the ladies look, for the king insists t –'

'Oh, but where is Mary? I was expecting to see you both together.'

The smile evaporated from my face. 'With Louise's ladies, I assume. Oh, Mother, you are not intending to see her are you?'

There was a pause.

'Mother, please tell me you are not going to speak with her.'

I picked up my little dog.

'Nan, she has broken my heart, and I wanted to bring her straight home, but your uncle would not let me. We have had such dreadful arguments over the situation, but of course, your father sided with my brother. He said I cannot bring her back, and that she is better off staying here.'

'To embarrass me,' I said.

'Please be kind, Nan. Oh, I have pondered long and hard on this matter and wondered if it is impossible to evade fate, our destiny being in the stars. I tried to stop it. I prevented her from going to the court of Margaret of Savoy, fearing her lack of sense, and yet here she is now at a far more licentious court. It will out, you see, such – such –'

'Foolishness?'

'What else? But I must see her, for she is my daughter, too, and she has been very ill. The more they bled her, the weaker she became, but now I trust she has regained her strength. I suffered like she does each month, as a young woman, and I cannot desert her.'

'But Mother, after all the humiliation she has caused you – me – our family. You surely have not forgiven her?'

My mother continued up the steps and then stopped. I stared at her as we entered the *grande salle*.

'One day, Nan, when God willing, you have children of your own, you will understand a mother's love. You will forgive much then, believe me!'

'I will forgive nothing,' I replied.

'Then you and your father have much in common. Come, I am ravenously hungry, and needs must refresh myself. Oh, Nan! I want to hear *everything* you have been up to. I cannot believe how sophisticated you look!'

•   •

As the *Te Deum* rang out, all heads turned as Louise and the cardinals welcomed the slight girl at the abbey doors. The tiny figure glanced nervously first at the proud Duc de Bourbon holding her arm on the right, and then to the Duc de Vendôme on her left. Her pale face was solemn.

Louise stared at the Duc de Bourbon with sheer venom in her eyes, furious that his wife, Suzanne, was pregnant. How could he spurn her affection in this way? And why could her daughter, Marguerite, not get with child? *Madame la Grande* had stayed behind, in Moulin, with Suzanne to be near her pregnant daughter, and Louise seethed at the thought.

Madame d'Assigny knelt as she handed a prayer book to the nervous queen. She then returned to the maids, her eyes watching our every move.

It was just after noon on the May feast day of Saint Bede, as I stood in the Abbey of Saint-Denis watching as Marguerite, the Duchess de Vendôme and Madame de Ranestan lifted Queen Claude's blue train. Before her, down the long aisle, walked the Princes of the Blood, and behind her, the duchesses and comtesses of the court, their coronets dazzling in the light of the torches, candles, and tapers. Every person of title, including English and foreign ambassadors, was present in his finest garb, and flags, tapestries and multi-coloured banners fluttered down from their poles, adding to the colour and brilliance of the abbey. Even the choir-stand, covered in crimson velvet and powdered with golden *fleurs-de-lis*, sparkled in the light.

My mother, striking in a red gown, her hair beneath a black gabled hood, acknowledged Mary and me with a slight nod. Next to her, my father stared blankly ahead, ignoring my sister's smile. Delighted that she had returned to Louise's service at Candlemas, she appeared as lovely and carefree as before her illness, although a little thinner.

Each *demoiselle*, including myself, wore a cornflower blue gown, our hair loose beneath a silver crescent of sapphires. I had now grown taller than some of the other maids, and with my lustrous hair the colour of the horse chestnut and my figure slender as a reed, I knew my parents approved of what they saw. The Comte de Chalon certainly did, and I had finally accepted his expensive gifts. I knew it was unwise, but he insisted, and since I felt jealous of the ladies who wore such things, I accepted a gold and enamel chain, a gold ring set with rubies, and a pearl collar for Bonny. When he presented me with a pair of exquisite peridot bracelets – the stones said to be the hardened tears of a goddess – I could hardly believe they had cost me nothing. It was all so easy, and I knew I would be foolish not to take advantage of such a doting old man. Besides, since I always refused to be left alone with him, what harm could he do? If he did complain, well, I would eschew his company and move on to my next admirer. I knew exactly what I was doing and did not need advice from anyone else, least of all Françoise.

As I stood on tip-toe, all the better to see, Mary Fiennes whispered how unlike the proud dowager French queen the tiny Queen Claude appeared. I agreed. Modest and dignified, she wore a coat of blue velvet with a corset of ermine, a necklace of pearls and a cross of rubies. The Cardinal of Mons officiated the sacred oils, as Louise opened the girl's coat and Marguerite lifted her veil ready for the cardinal's touch. The sceptre, the hand of justice and the ring were given to the girl, and when the crown was placed on her brow a great cheer rose into the air '*Vive la Reine*! God bless good Queen Claude!'

There she sat on her golden throne, amidst a cloud of incense, above the tomb of her beloved parents, tears of joy in her eyes. I looked up, for I knew that King François watched from a balcony hidden behind a metal grille, as with great humility, she received the body of Christ. At last, at seventeen years of age, Claude was now the anointed Queen of France. All she needed to do was to keep her part of the bargain and produce the son she had promised her husband.

• •

At the Hôtel des Tournelles, King François greeted his new queen with open arms. I watched Françoise de Foix smile fondly towards him as we entered the *grande salle* to dine, but he ignored her, for this was his wife's day.

As the many dishes were brought forth, I sat beneath the dais with several ladies, including my sister, in case the queen needed our assistance. I noticed that my mother and father seemed unable to keep their eyes from Mary, yet they showed not a glimmer of embarrassment. Was all so easily forgotten?

As Louise and King François sat on either side of the queen, Marguerite sat next to her dour husband. Her generous heart felt happy for the queen, and she threw back her head in laughter as King François lent over to tell her something amusing. Dressed in her ducal robes, her hair beneath a diamond-studded crown, she looked like an empress. At her feet, sat Marie, a paper crown on her head and her tiny twisted body wrapped in a cloak of gold silk.

After the great feast, the Mayor of Paris presented the queen with a beautiful ermine fur, and as trumpets sounded, pots of coins were flung out into the crowds of onlookers. 'Largesse to the people! Long life to the queen!' A frantic scramble ensued as benches tipped over and people fell onto the golden coins, making the king laugh at the unruly crowd.

I then watched as Clément stood up and bowed low to the new queen. He waited for the noise to subside, before speaking: 'Lady of all virtue and charity, love, peace, prudence, and strength, we pray that your Holy Mother in Heaven and all the saints, send you a son!'

He appeared a little unsteady, and I was glad that I had not confided my passion for him to my mother. There would never be a shred of lewd gossip about me, and so I would have it remain.

The queen smiled graciously and raised her cup to him. She did not notice the dispatch handed to Louise, who, after some moments, flung down her napkin and stood up.

'Tell me,' she said loudly, for all to hear. 'The English – are they – or are they not – in full and loving amity with us?'

King François leant towards her and put his hand on hers, his brow furrowed. 'Why, assuredly, *Madame Mère*, what is reported?'

She sat down again brandishing the letter in his face. 'This! It would seem the diverse hurt to our countrymen lodging in London continues, for thugs proceeded to the house of the French secretary, which they sacked, and caused very great damage there. They would have cut him to pieces had he not escaped up the belfry of the adjoining church!'

The king frowned, as Louise continued. 'Thousands of English artifices have rioted against *our* French merchants, complaining that they have taken all the trade by bringing in better quality goods. Whipped into a frenzy, they have thrown our Frenchmen into the River Thames and damaged their goods and property!' She looked down to read further and grunted in satisfaction. 'Well, at least the king arrested men, women, and children saying that by committing such treason they have broken the truce and the league.' She glanced up, squinting her eyes towards one of the tables. 'I see Sir Thomas and Lady Boleyn are here. I gather her brother, Edmund, as Knight Marshal, showed extreme cruelty in dealing with the younglings, having them hanged and quartered throughout the city.'

'*Children?*' asked Marguerite, blanching, as she wiped her lips with the proffered napkin.

'Rebels,' corrected Louise, 'against our fellow countrymen. I am pleased that the king of England sees fit to deal with this insult to France so harshly.'

My mind turned to Uncle Edmund, a man of little talent, and I wondered if his actions were to try and impress King Henry. Mother had told me how, unlike his dead brother, Edward, he could not gain popularity with the king and was forever in debt, lingering about the court trying to ingratiate himself with anyone of influence.

'He always scared me,' whispered my sister, passing Louise a fresh napkin. 'He would have wheedled himself here if he could have afforded a decent set of clothes, but no-one would lend him the money.'

'Oh, here is a pretty thing,' continued Louise. 'Queen Katherine and the king's two sisters knelt and pleaded for mercy. Swayed by their entreaties, King Henry agreed to stop the hangings and remains as popular as ever.'

She threw the paper down and drummed her fingers on the arm of her chair. The king stretched out his legs and languidly kissed his wife's hand. He did not want to be bothered with such tedious matters. Today, he was the king with his new queen. Later, away from the public gaze, he would play the lover with Françoise. He watched as she danced with her husband wearing the pale green gown he had bought and insisted she wore. Its partlet sparkled with emerald stones, and I saw the king's eyes glaze a little with lust. No doubt he was thinking how lovely she would look without it covering her deliciously plump frame.

'My Lord,' the queen said, causing him to jump out of his reverie, 'I cannot thank you enough, for today has been the happiest day of my life. To voyage together will be my greatest comfort and joy.'

'As king, my love, the people must see how I rule my provinces, but I want the people to see you too, to give them hope after the devastating April frost destroyed their crops. Now we have constant rain, but no matter, in a few days we will proceed to Picardy and Normandy.' He kissed her hand again and raised his glass of hypocras.

'You know I will give whatever aid I can,' said the queen.

I turned to Mary and leant close to her ear. 'Are we travelling *again*?'

She wrinkled her nose. 'You will be, but Louise may return to Romorantin now the pestilence has gone, to supervise the new building works with Signor da Vinci. That means I will be stuck with her on a muddy building site away from all the intrigue.'

'It is strange,' I said, 'but I did not like the château when we visited in January, even though the king loves it. Did you hear how badly the town of Romorantin treated the queen?'

'Yes,' she said, 'and they deserved the pestilence that fell upon them. An *entrée joyeuse* should be just that, a grand celebration with flags and banners. Not a few paltry bits of cloth draped on a dais and a box of raisins for the king's mother. I ask you.'

'Mary, that is a dreadful thing to say,' I said, dipping into the delicious honey and nutmeg pudding. 'Over one hundred and fifty people, including workmen, died in the town of disease. Hardly anyone was left even to build a platform. Of course, Louise is furious over the delay in the work on her new palace. What was the row about over Françoise staying at Romoratin?'

'Oh, you know how Louise hates Françoise, for the woman is so ambitious. Her son housed her at the Pavilion Mousseau, where he lodges his conquests away from prying eyes. Louise was furious, but Françoise refused to leave. One cannot help but admire her nerve, standing up against his mother like that. I have heard how she often arranges to meet the king at some place, and then does not bother to turn up. It drives him mad with desire.'

'But such nonchalant behaviour works, for he is besotted,' I replied.

'Well, Nan, she cannot truly love him, refusing him thus.'

I raised my spoon mid-air and paused. 'Does it matter?'

My time with my mother was short, for she intended returning home on the fifteenth day of May, the day we departed from Paris. Now, walking in the deer park of the Tournelles with Mary, we admired the flowerbeds and hawthorn trees. My mother turned to me as we chatted, and I made sure I had removed any expensive jewellery from my person to avoid awkward questions.

'You know your father is doing very well at court, having received several favours, and as a member of the king's Council, his star is rising. I fear he works too hard. Do you think he looks well?'

'Yes, apart from some grey hairs,' I replied, with honesty. Mary threw a stick for Bonny.

'He is still wary of Thomas Wolsey, of course, and now Wolsey is chancellor the man's ambition is driving the older councillors away. The younger ones are his servants now. Your father will not like that.'

Mother then told us that George – now thirteen years old and a pageboy at court – could already handle a horse at the quintain, and aimed to become one of the best jousters there. So far, he had broken his wrist and knocked himself out cold, but nothing could deter him, for he was impetuous and reckless. For gifts, he had sent me a set of falconry bells from Holland, and for Mary a half mantle.

Mother told Mary and me of the various improvements on the estate, such as the planting of a short avenue of lime trees and the digging of a bigger carp pond. The kitchens had been enlarged, as had the dairy. Dame Margot spent most of her days reading and then forgetting what she had just read. Her new maid, Dorothea, sat with her or accompanied her around the estate to take the air, but she was becoming more quarrelsome by the day.

As to the court, all the talk was of the May riot, and how, instead of enjoying the wonderful celebrations, everyone had remained at the Palace of Placentia, terrified of the angry crowds rioting in the city. Mother said that a John Lincoln had managed to catch the ear of a certain Dr Bell, who was due to preach from St Paul's Cross, in the shadow of the cathedral. Having been convinced by Lincoln that the miserable state of the economy was caused by foreigners in the city, Bell had called for 'all Englishmen to cherish and defend themselves, and to hurt and grieve aliens for the commonweal.'

Children were rushed to the safety of their house as ribbons and streamers fell limp from the maypoles, and their spring flowers lay trampled by scurrying feet. Bells and wreaths were ripped off doorways and shutters as the joyous day turned to ruin. Five thousand troops assembled in the city and Thomas More, the under-sheriff, had desperately tried to placate the crowds.

'We heard about the fury aimed at the foreign merchants,' I said, frowning.

'And are you surprised, Nan? On one Sunday alone six hundred foreigners gathered at Finsbury Heath, shooting at the Popinjay with their crossbows, and taking over the place. London is now overrun with strangers, and it is no wonder that their houses were broken into and their clothes tossed into the river. Carter Lane, Creed Lane, and Ave Maria Lane were completely lawless. It is no longer the London of my youth, but an overcrowded, broiling cesspit of foreigners who take no heed of our English customs.'

I rolled my eyes at Mary as she spoke. All old people felt like that, and it was tedious.

'Well, your grandfather and Uncle Howard did wonders

and seized those responsible.'

'And Uncle Edmund?' I asked, referring to his cruelty.

My mother sighed. 'Gossip. There were many pardons, and Queen Katherine herself begged for mercy, her hair loose as she knelt before her husband like a supplicant. Anyway,' she added, brightly, 'as to the king's sister, Queen Margaret, I will be glad to see the back of her since she is preparing to return from the court in London to her court in Scotland.'

She continued to explain that as a trusted courtier, Father had been appointed yet again as one of Queen Margaret's escorts, ensuring she remained safe from any ill. Spoilt, petulant and jealous, she had been insufferable, but her baby daughter, little Margaret, and Queen Katherine's daughter, Princess Mary, had entranced everyone so much that all was endured. The two women spent every hour of every day sitting with their babes on their knees, giving advice to the heavily pregnant dowager French queen – she still insisted on that title rather than Duchess of Suffolk – whose next baby was due in July.

My sister sighed and threw another twig for Bonny. 'What a pretty scene.' Her voice sounded flat.

'It will be difficult, Mary,' continued Mother, 'but if we can find you a husband, as God intended, you will have your own child one day.'

'Yes, but I see no husband forthcoming, do you?'

'And whose fault is that?' came the reply.

Mary always brought out the worse in her, just as she did with me.

'Not mine!' replied Mary, 'for I never sought the king's attention. It is so unfair!'

I watched as she flounced ahead after Bonny.

'Oh, let her go, Anne, I am too tired for this, the girl has almost put me in my grave. What's done is done. When you are both back home, all of this will be forgotten, and if anything is said, it will not be hard to deny the gossip. Thank God you have more sense and restraint. I am so glad that

Queen Claude took you into her strict care, for she is the most pious of ladies with such a love of learning.'

I sighed. In the precious time we had left, I did not want to talk of the dull queen.

She patted my hand. 'Oh, I cannot believe how you have grown since leaving England. You are still too slight, but move with such grace and lightness that it is quite becoming. When you were little, you were such an odd-looking child, with unruly hair and eyes that were far too large for your face. The old king met you once at Rochford Manor and wondered what hearts you would break with those dark eyes. Do you remember?'

'Vaguely,' I replied.

'Well, now you have grown into a striking young woman. Oh, I do miss you and will be so much happier when you return. I believe that if we can get you an introduction into the English court, as I did, we can start to arrange your betrothal. I hear that you have already attracted attention here.'

My heart missed a beat as I thought for one anxious moment that my sister had told her about Clément – or the comte.

'I suppose it was to be expected with such a lovely singing voice.'

I felt instant relief and smiled. 'Grandfather Howard says I could do well at court, as you did. He always recounts how poets used to praise your vivacity and beauty.'

'Ah, I was so much younger then and intoxicated with life. I danced until dawn and never wearied. I sang, played music and always took the lead in any entertainments, for the world was mine for the taking. I thought the court the finest place to be in the whole world and enjoyed the company of the gentle, Yorkist queen. I've often wondered how she came to love her miserly husband.'

We walked in silence until we halted before a lion chained up in a large, caged pen. It appeared thin, fur-worn and scarred, but these days it was only kept by the king for dog baiting and as amusement for the court.

'Mother, were you ever fond of Father? Did you love him?' I asked, staring at the pathetic beast.

There was a moment's silence as she turned and stared straight into my eyes, unblinking. Horrified, I quickly lowered them in shame. 'Forgive me, Mother, it is just tha –'

'No.'

I looked up in surprise.

'Well, perhaps at first, when we were young. He was good-looking, a fine jouster and was intent on winning me. Later, I was very much enamoured of our young king. I suppose like all the women at court, I adored him, for he was a man of extraordinary charm and generosity. He still is. But it was nothing more than a flirtation, fond as I was. He found me attractive, although I was twelve years older, for I spoke my mind boldly – something rare at court – but that was all. Nothing ever occurred between us. Nothing.'

'Mother, I was in his company at Lille, with Margaret of Savoy, and thought him rude and boorish. He called you a 'Hellcat.' Why would he say such a thing?'

'Fie Nan, may God forgive you! His Grace is a good and perfect prince, and you must never, ever speak ill of him again. He is our king, anointed by God.'

I felt chastised. I picked up a stick and poked it through the rails at the beast. It raised its head with a listless, toothless growl, and then flopped back down again with a yawn.

Then, quite unexpectedly, my mother broke into peals of laughter. 'It is true – I *was* a Hellcat! I would stamp my foot in temper – just like you do – and pout if the king did not dance with me. Yes, he singled me out, and people became jealous, spreading rumours, foolish rumours that are still bandied about to this day. But I was hot-headed and cared not a fiddle what people thought. Perhaps I should have been more aware of the consequences of gossip. Perhaps if Mary ...' She paused and then gave a little shrug. 'Well,

I was married to your father, I was content, and life moved on. I only speak to His Grace these days when we are playing cards, or are together in some other such amusement. We might talk of general matters when he visits the queen's apartments, but nothing of significance. No, it is your father's company he seems to enjoy now, as they both love the joust, and Thomas has an eye for a good horse, as does your Uncle Edmund – just as long as he is not paying for it!'

'What did Father say on the matter?' I asked.

'He never spoke of it, for he knew Howard women were born to be spoilt and admired, not hidden away. Besides, he was flattered that the king enjoyed my company, although he still throws it at me in an argument. Looking at you now, I see so much of myself in you, such boldness and spirit. You must never lose it, Nan, for it is a rare trait to possess.'

'Margaret of Savoy once chided me for being too outspoken. She told me that a woman must pretend to agree with a man and appear to bend to his wishes. I said that was surely dishonest, but she said I had much to learn.'

'She was right,' said my mother, laughing. 'Tell men what they want to hear, but use cunning to do exactly what you want. That is the only way I can handle your father, believe me. But do not be afraid, Nan, no man enjoys the company of a compliant little mouse.'

I thought about this as we walked, and when I looked at her lovely face, she prodded me gently with her beringed finger.

'There is something of Dame Margot in you, too, my darling – I can see it – an ambition and fire. You will not settle for a mediocre life.'

'Unlike my sister?' I jibed, gazing into the distance.

My mother sighed and walked ahead. 'Come now, Nan, try to be charitable,' she replied, over her shoulder, 'she is your sister. Besides, her time here is done – I am taking her home.'

Chapter Twelve

'Loss and possession.'

Northern France

Travelling through France was an established tradition for the monarchy, for it gave the king the opportunity to see his country and check up on his representatives in the provinces. The council dignitaries could meet him and provide entertainment, but it was at no small cost, and I wondered how many groaned at the thought of his arrival. Queen Claude did not wish to burden her people, for there was general unrest throughout France, and in some areas, famine. However, she felt hurt when no effort whatsoever was made. She had recently written to the people of Romorantin saying, somewhat sarcastically, that she would be willing to pay for the bits of cloth they had provided for her last *entrée*. For good measure, she also agreed to pay for all the 'expenses' they had incurred on her behalf over the last twelve years. One could only hope they were suitably embarrassed. However, although exhausted, the queen loved travelling and as this would be her first tour as queen, she acted as excited as a child.

Having left little Louise and Charlotte behind at Plessis-lès-Tours, near Amboise, she now prepared to set out from Saint-Denis, to the northern towns of her kingdom, in Normandy. Marguerite, in the meantime, to her mother's alarm, returned with her husband to Argentan, having suffered some dreadful insult from the king's favourite, Seigneur de Bonnivet. What it was, she would not say, but something very unpleasant had occurred.

Our company included the households of Claude, François, and Louise, as well as seven companies of the king's guard, secretaries, and the chancellor with his seals – in all over five thousand people and hundreds of horses, carts, chariots, and litters. Unfortunately, since no rain had fallen over the winter and spring months, the rivers were too low for the royal barges. However, with the ground hard and dry at least this progress would not be one of muddy, impassable tracks. The queen, ever thoughtful, was more concerned that the dry weather also meant that no fodder and grain could be transported down the cracked river beds, and so the cost of food to the people and horses would prove ruinous.

I have to say that poverty lay far from my thoughts, and I cared little, lost in my thoughts of my sister. We had said our good-byes, made up our quarrel, and she had sworn on her crucifix never to tell anyone about Clément. I believed her, too, for despite being foolish, vindictive she was not. Besides, what was there to tell? Nothing. She knew how much I wanted to remain in France and enjoy the entertainments and admiration of the court. As to the comte, I continued to encourage his attention and his gifts. As I gazed down at the expensive gold ring on my finger I smiled, for how could I resist such beautiful trinkets? If the queen noticed, I would just say it was a present from my mother.

I was still daydreaming when we arrived at Écouen and the magnificent château of King François' close friend, Anne de Montmorency. As we wheeled into the courtyard – a courtyard paved with glittering, coloured stones – I was astonished. How did he acquire such riches? The inside was equally beautiful, a feast of columns, statues, and works of priceless art. It seemed that while most of France suffered terrible poverty, a few enjoyed unimaginable wealth. Entering the château, the king and queen retired to one wing, and Louise to the other. But then something strange occurred. Louise, who had been allotted a bedchamber and suite in another, very private wing, complained that the newly painted walls made her cough, and so she insisted that the king take it instead, leaving the queen alone with just her ladies. This left her son free to entertain Françoise in complete privacy, without prying eyes. I could not understand Louise at all.

As we travelled to Compiègne and on to St Quentin, I was invited to join Madame de Châtillon in her litter. I had the horrible feeling that she might ask me about the comte, but she did not, and I watched as she flicked through her book of poetry, unable to settle. She was not that much older than I and soon to retire to her confinement for her coming child. She gave a sigh and a stretch.

'Are you quite well, Madame?' I asked as she stared ahead.

'Just uncomfortable,' she said. 'I miss Marguerite, but it will do her the world of good to be away from the court for a while.'

I wondered what on earth had occurred between Marguerite and Bonnivet to make her return so willingly with her husband to Argentan. All knew she loathed the quiet of the country. I felt intrigued, but Madame de Châtillon only resumed her reading.

'Madame, may I ask you a delicate question?'

She placed her book down on her knee with a sigh at my interruption.

'Why does the king treat the queen as he does? She is not a fool and is fully aware of Madame Châteaubriant.'

'Ah, you mean the clever Françoise,' she said, quietly, 'but the king is not cruel to Claude and does all discreetly. As to marriage with a king, it is an arrangement to ensure the continuation of the royal line, and nothing else. For that, there must be a son to follow. The queen understands that is all that is required of her.'

'I disagree, Madame,' I said.

She stared at me a moment, clearly puzzled.

'Why must a king have a mistress? Why can he not love his queen and be true to her only? King Louis loved Anne of Brittany.'

'But he had amours,' said Madame De Châtillon.

'Only two,' I said quickly.

She frowned and said only as far as we knew. 'Let us just say, Anne, fidelity is not expected of a king, and never will be. There has never been a queen in the world who had sole knowledge of her husband, and if a woman is fortunate enough to *be* a queen, she must hide her true feelings and show dignity. That is what our queen does and she is loved for it.'

Is she? I thought. Or is she thought a fool? I leant back against the cushions and watched as Madame de Châtillon opened her book again and began silently reading. The discussion was over. But how could the queen – how could any woman - accept a rival like Françoise? I would never endure it.

•　•

And then the rains came. As we reached Amiens in a June deluge, it was to the queen's bitter disappointment that King François left her, and rode with his mother, Françoise and an escort of nobles to St Quentin. Before he left, he did his duty and came to her bed, but after, he had been in a foul mood, forced to face the fact that the finances of France were in a perilous state. There were talks that the eldest son of the Margrave of Brandenburg might marry Renée, but for that, a large dowry was needed, and the king wanted more money for war, not marriage. His mother had soothed him and told him that she would ensure that Baron Semblançay provided whatever he required. If that meant a little creative accounting, so be it. Why, she herself would be demanding four thousand gold lire be released to make the River Sauldre navigable from Romorantin to the Cher. What was the matter of a dowry?

Slightly more appeased, the king now escaped the ever-swelling, travelling court and rode east with his new love, while we travelled north-west towards Abbeville.

Did I miss my sister? No, for I was far happier when she was not around, but I did miss Eliza Grey, for at Amiens she had left our party, having been recalled to the English court. Now, only Mary Fiennes remained with me from England, and I consoled myself with the attention of the young and old nobles alike. The comte constantly sought out my company, but to be frank, by now, I was becoming tired of him. Of course, I was never allowed to be alone with him – or rather, I chose to make sure it was never possible – but he still gave me beautiful gifts. The latest was an exquisite, lozenge-shaped pendant, with a large drop pearl. He did seem to dote on me.

Mother wrote to tell me how Mary had settled back at Hever, and that she awaited a place at court when one became free. Our grandmother, Dame Margot, was with her, repeating the same question she had asked five minutes previously, and they were working on a tapestry together. How dull! She also wrote of a terrible sweating sickness raging throughout England, blamed, no doubt, on all the foreigners filling the city of London. Some towns, like Oxford, had lost half their populations to this dreadful scourge, and many noble persons at court perished. There was even a rumour that my Uncle Thomas had died from it, but thankfully it was not true, and all my family was well. The king, fearing contagion, secluded himself with only three companions at Windsor and would admit no-one. As to the queen, she had been unwell for some time, and there were whispers that she might be pregnant. Wolsey, the king's most trusted advisor, almost died having been ill for a month. It would have been most inconvenient had he done so, for the French ambassadors were about to arrive in Calais to negotiate the surrender of Tournai. By the Grace of God, the good cardinal survived, and I gave thanks in my prayers.

•   •

Without the king by her side, Queen Claude found the *entrées* exhausting, for at each town there were crowds to meet and long speeches to make. Banquets continued late into the night, and I revelled in the attention. Not so the queen, for every morning she felt unwell on rising. She was finally allowed to rest for three weeks at the Château de Gaillon, the summer residence of the Cardinal Archbishop of Rouen.

The king, his mistress and his mother continued down the River Loire to the Château Mauny, one of the homes of Diane and her husband, and enjoyed a few more days of privacy. There, the king received the news that Mary Tudor, the dowager French queen, had given birth to a girl named Frances. When the baby was christened at Hatfield, my Aunt Anne, wife of Sir Edward Boleyn, stood proxy for the queen as godmother. I felt relieved at this news, for hopefully the Dowager Queen's animosity only extended to myself, rather than to my entire family. As for Queen Claude, she stared out at the torrential rain, content; for she now knew for certain that she carried the king's third child. Yet again, she reigned supreme, and no-one could take her place.

By the beginning of September, King François and his mother had re-joined the queen at the Château de Gaillon, and I noticed Louise raise her brow at her son as she studied the fine tapestries and Italian paintings on the walls of the *grande salle*. Such wealth for a cardinal was surely a matter to be investigated. However, nothing could dampen her mood for she was ecstatic that the queen was with child. When I spoke with Françoise, I was shocked to see that her cheek appeared bruised and asked her if she had fallen. She laughed and said no, it was nothing and changed the subject. She told me how the whole visit to Mauny had proved a disaster, for Diane, who was now occupied with her pregnancy, felt too tired to attend the late dinners and the king locked himself away with Françoise, to the annoyance of his hosts and his mother. Louise had raged continually about Suzanne de Bourbon, and the relationship between the Valois-Angoulême and the Bourbons deteriorated further. As Françoise put her fingers to her face, I asked her again what had happened to cause the bruise. She avoided my eyes and gave a little shrug – still nothing. When I pressed her, she finally confided in me that her husband had struck her. I was shocked at this revelation, but she said her attention towards the king had driven her husband to madness, and thus, she deserved it. Besides, he had every right to beat her, although I was not to tell a single soul. I stared at the purple mark, marring her beauty, and wondered what on earth the king would say.

In the meantime, Marguerite, at her own home at Argentan, prepared for the court's visit. It seemed that everyone about her was expecting a child and I knew it made her wistful, for she confided that the fault might lie with her. Although her château was a vast fortress, she was still not certain that she could accommodate everyone and set about finding what hostels she could. When we did arrive, we stayed for two glorious weeks, and the cost must have been ruinous. However, Marguerite was very wealthy – although not in her own right – and she provided excellent food, hunting, and jousts. As I wandered through the *grande salle,* I stared in wonder at the Venetian mirrors in elaborate frames, and the rich ebony cabinets inlaid with gold, silver, and mother-of-pearl. Within these cabinets were inestimable treasures of art, including enamel portraits of the most beautiful women of the court: gems engraved with scriptural subjects, silver filigree work, jewelled medallions of saints and scent-boxes filled with rare perfumes. In the royal apartments, books richly emblazoned were dispersed for the edification of the courtiers, some containing records of the chivalrous deeds of renowned knights of old. How I dreamt that one day I might own such lovely treasures.

As a thank you for playing host, her brother gave her the Duchy of Berry, a gift for her alone with all the income it brought with it. As to Bonnivet, we were still none the wiser as to what had happened, or what he had done to upset her. However, as we watched Louise depart for a wedding in Lisieux, I cared naught for her daughter's troubles. My days were spent busily attending to my duties, perfecting my embroidery and avoiding the attentions of the comte. So carefree were the days that none of us was prepared for the disaster about to fall.

•   •

'How long have you known?' The king appeared devastated as he stood at the door of his mother's chamber.

'A few days,' she said. 'Duprat hastened with the news from Blois. I – I could not bring myself to inform you or Claude sooner.'

He entered, leaving the door open.

They did not notice me as I peered around the doorframe, holding a book I was taking to the queen. I then saw the king throw himself down into a chair and release a torrent of tears, as Louise glanced towards Antoinette de Polignac.

'*Two days?*' he asked, sobbing.

Louise lowered her eyes.

'But, *Madame Mère*, she must know!'

'Today. You will tell her today,' announced Louise. She went as if to comfort her son, but hand paused, thought better of it and tucked it back into her sleeve.

At that moment, Antoinette spied me standing there. 'You, Anne, fetch a fur, quickly!'

I did as she said and on returning, entered the chamber to a scene of tears.

'Poor lamb!' cried Antoinette, 'and she but two years old. What was the cause?'

I handed Louise the sable and she placed it about the king's shoulders with a shiver, before speaking.

'Madame Brechenior said a fever so sudden the child could not overcome it. Charlotte is well, thanks be to God, even though she is frail.'

The king let out another wail, his head in his hands and his lank hair falling through his fingers. Poor baby Louise had died, and as I stood, horrified, I feared that the queen would collapse from shock when she heard the news.

'You must tell her yourself, my son,' said Louise, twisting the cross at her girdle.

'Does my sister know?' he asked.

Louise shook her head.

'Then I will go to my wife now,' said the king, rising.

He stared at me as he stumbled past, his eyes blurred with tears. 'You – follow,' he commanded, as he walked down towards the queen's suite. When we reached the outer door, I could hear laughing inside. My heart pounded. The men-at-arms jumped to attention as an usher opened the door, and I saw that the queen and her ladies were playing hood-man blind. Her face lit up at the surprise visit as Gillette bumped into her, making Marie laugh.

'Leave us,' said the king to the women. They curtsied deeply and retreated out of the door, Gillette pulling the scarf from her eyes. 'But not you,' he said, turning to me. 'Sit here outside.'

As the silent girls disappeared down the gallery, I sat on the bench and waited. It was not long before I heard the most dreadful wail. Poor Queen Claude! I jumped up, just as the door opened.

'Fetch Dr du Puy, quickly!' the king cried.

However, Louise had already sent for him, and he arrived as the king spoke, holding a bowl and towel in his hands. He was followed by a gaggle of nobles and ladies, headed by Madame de Tournon. I strained my head to see the queen collapsed in the the king's arms, and I watched, alarmed.

All was commotion as she cried, her little dogs adding to the noise with their yapping. I saw the king carry her to the bed, stroking her hair, and admired his tenderness. He cared nothing for his tears but covered her face with kisses as Dr du Puy prepared to bleed her. Anne de Graville took charge, taking the bowl from him.

'Come,' she murmured.

'Hush! Think of the child you carry!' begged the king, 'please, be calm for the sake of the prince. It is God's will, God's will. Come, drink this, sleep, my love.' He took the cup from the doctor, but as she drank, the queen voided the potion onto her gown.

Madame de Tournon pulled the king gently away. 'Ah, sire, she needs rest, please, let the doctor tend to her.'

The king, in anguish, turned away.

I had never seen anything so dreadful before and wished only that I might vanish. Dear God, how could she survive this terrible blow? As for Louise, although she had appeared strong, when she entered the chamber, she dissolved into grief, weeping, beating her breast and raising her eyes to Heaven. Was it an act or genuine grief?

That night, as the town bells slowly tolled, Queen Claude knelt at her *prie dieu* and wept silent tears. All of her ladies, even Diane, had been dismissed, and she sat alone with Marie, her dwarf, clinging to her knees. When I entered with Renée, she rose up and gathered her sister to her.

'Oh, my darling, I must go to Charlotte. I must return home.'

Chateau d'Amboise, The Loire

'But what am I supposed to do about it?' the king asked.

We were finally back at Amboise, and I watched as he sat lounging in a chair, his long legs on a silk stool, his lank hair ruffled and his night robe draped about him. He hated formal gravity and thought nothing of appearing thus. He had also not slept well and suffered a throbbing headache. Sadly, Louise's shrieking was not helping matters.

'I do not know, but something has to done!' she cried, staring at the queen. 'I am surprised you hid your true feelings so well.' She looked back at her son as he belched and grimaced. 'Are you ill?' An expression of alarm was on her face.

The king shrugged.

'You know, *Madame Mère,* how fish sits ill with me but I could not resist the trout.'

Louise moved to his side and entwined her fingers in his dark hair. He took them in his hand and kissed them. The queen sat open-laced, fondly stroking the green stuffed crocodile that had been given by the Venetian ambassadors as a present for Louise and Charlotte. Beside her, on the table, lay the book I had brought to her – Sir Thomas More's *Utopia.* I had hoped it would distract her, but it did not. She murmured only of little Louise as her listless eyes filled with tears. I handed her the cup of warm milk, picked up my embroidery yarns and sat in the corner of the chamber.

The king rose up, yawned, and put his hand on the back of his stiff neck. His greyhound padded towards him, and he fondled its ears.

'I am as angry as you are, *Madame Mère,* but we must bide our time. Bourbon is holding a rival court – that much was evident from what we saw at the christening. Five hundred gentlemen waited on him. Why, his wealth exceeds mine, did you see the great master's work adorning his walls?

'See it? I nearly choked on it,' said Louise, hatred in her face. 'You might be godfather now to his precious son, but it is as if he were king, not you, sovereign in all but name. Cousin or not, I will not tolerate such an insult to the house of Angoulême!'

The king's face darkened as he walked over to the window and gazed out onto the terrace. He bore an expression I had not seen before.

'No château in France,' he mused, 'including Blois or Amboise, can rival his with its Italianate gardens, terraces, fountains, and parks. They call it the pearl of the Sologny river. Pheasants, partridges, francolins – he has a stock far greater than mine and nowhere can equal Moulins. And the way he greeted me, did you see?' He turned to see his mother pacing about, fuming. 'He overreaches himself,' he continued. 'Surrounded by the finest gentlemen swathed in gold chains, he was, as you say, a king greeting his subject.'

'Moulin is a fortress,' muttered Louise, 'and he can raise any number of troops. *That* concerns me more than his gardens and collection of game.'

The king turned. 'He even presumed, *Madame Mère*, to ask me for the money owed him from the last campaign.'

As I threaded a new silk Mary Fiennes entered, curtsied deeply, and joined me on the bench.

'There is trouble brewing,' I whispered, as she picked up her piece of embroidery, a silk cap for baby Charlotte.

'I know,' she whispered back. 'Louise wants revenge on the Duc de Bourbon for refusing her advances, but the duc cares nothing for her threats. There is even talk that if his wife Suzanne died, he would try and seize Renée next.'

'A royal bride?' I asked.

'So it is mooted. His immense wealth, and his relationship to the king, seem to justify his claims to the hand of the girl whose childish imagination he has deliberately fostered and captivated.' She handed me a few strands of red silk. 'Do you think she carries a prince?' She glanced at the tearful queen.

I leant in towards her. 'After the terrible shock she has had,' I said, 'who knows what she is carrying? The child might be deformed, or a half-wit. Still, Dr du Puy thinks all is well. She certainly looks big enough to be carrying a boy, but then she is so swollen and dumpy who can tell?'

'Well, her sister is a great comfort to her. Do you miss

your sister?' she asked.

I shook my head. 'No, not at all, but I miss Ann Jernyngham.'

'Well, Nan, I just wish that my family would hurry up with finding me a match. I'm twenty years old and want to have a family and manage a household.'

'So do I, but how terrible to lose children so young. I know it is expected and I lost all my brothers, except George, but it is still heart-breaking. The queen does not seem able to recover from her loss, although it has been three months now.'

'At least you already have an admirer, Nan, for the Comte de Chalon is becoming more attentive to you as the weeks pass.'

I stared at her, then laughed. 'Oh, really Mary, he is just a foolish, old man – isn't he?'

The look on her face unsettled me, but then we sat talking of our families, and I told her mine were locked in some land dispute with Sir Piers Butler. However, my father was happy, for he had finally been granted his licence to export wood from his mill of Rochford, in Essex.

As we continued our sewing, Louise picked up the book on the table by the queen, flicked through it, and threw it down again.

'What of King Charles or whatever he calls himself?' she asked the king. 'According to the Treaty of Noyon, if Louise died before the marriage could take place – which she has – then he is bound to marry Charlotte or Renée. That way you keep Milan, and he can have Naples. He must also continue to pay the one hundred, thousand *écus* of gold to you, each year until the marriage. With Cardinal Wolsey agreeing to marry the little Princess Mary to your forthcoming son, we are in a strong position.'

'*Madame Mère*,' the king said with a sigh, taking a seat, 'we were discussing Bourbon. As you know, Charles is in Spain and is aware of the tragic situation.' He glanced at the queen. 'Really, I do think a little tact at the moment would be considered welcome.'

Louise raised her brow as the queen continued her sniffing. 'Politics, my son, cannot be put on hold due to sensitivities.'

I glanced at Mary before we both lowered our heads again.

'To return to Bourbon, Madame, I will bring him down when I am ready, and I will use his most mortal enemy, Bonnivet, to do it.'

I wondered what Marguerite would think of this plan.

'For now,' he said, rising up, 'I must dress, go to St Martin of Tours and pray for a son, for terms or not, everything is in the hands of God.'

He kissed his wife's hand, bowed to his mother, and with his hound by his side approached the door. He then stopped and turned. 'I intend staying till Martinmas,' he said, before walking sadly away.

After he left, we sat in silence, and I pondered on the fate of the Duc de Bourbon. It was true, he did own entire provinces and was vastly wealthy, but as Constable of France, he was also a very great soldier who had raised a valuable army for the king in Italy. Surely François owed him a considerable debt? I felt myself shiver, for there seemed to be a very fine line to walk when dealing with the pride of kings and princes. In England, the premier duke was Buckingham, and he too, according to my mother, was not liked for his great wealth and pride. But King Henry was young, amiable, full of bonhomie and enjoyed rewarding his nobles. Not so Louise. She intended to bring Bourbon to his knees.

* *

Having delivered the queen's gift of an embroidered pair of gloves to Louise, I returned to her as she walked with Signor da Vinci in the gardens at Cloux. The Master had shown a touching kindness to the queen since the death of baby Louise, and she enjoyed her drawing lessons with him. For her comfort, he had given her a tiny prayer book, bound in red velvet with golden clasps, which had been specially illuminated in Tours. I was thinking of the little book as I rounded the corner, my dog bounding ahead through the fallen leaves. The air felt crisp, and a slight mist rose above the ground as I walked, lost in thought. I then heard someone softly call my name. I looked around at the gardener and his assistants and realised it was coming from behind a tree.

'Anne!'

The voice was that of Clément. I stopped and turned, making a polite dip in reverence as he appeared before me. So, he was back, the last person I wanted to see.

'Anne, have you seen this?'

I stared blankly at him.

'This!' he said, impatiently, waving a pamphlet at me.

'Why can you not leave me alone?' I said. 'I still do not wish to speak with you.'

'But this, *this* will put all Europe in a roar,' he replied, his eyes shining.

I gave a shiver in the cold, but this time I declined the use of his cloak. Instead, I folded my arms across my russet-coloured gown.

'Walk with me, please,' he urged. 'I thought of you when I received this, for I knew it would interest you.'

'No, you thought of Marguerite,' I corrected. 'I will do, because she is not here.'

'And I know why she is not,' he said.

Damn him! He knew I could never contain my curiosity.

'So you will speak with me after all?' he teased.

I raised my brow in disdain. 'That depends on what you have to say,' I said.

'Marguerite was attacked,' he said, pushing aside a low branch.

I stopped walking and stared at him. '*Attacked*? By whom, when?'

'By Bonnivet. I was with her, as you know at Argentan, and overheard her talking to Madame de Châtillon. Marguerite, Louise, and the king had visited the château to hunt, and when Marguerite retired Bonnivet silently lowered himself down through a trap door in his chamber, into hers. He then crept across the chamber and climbed onto the bed. With the bed drapes drawn, it was too dark to see who was trying to kiss her. Of course, she screamed, fought back and scratched the man across the face. As she pulled at the drapes, light entered, and he ran from the chamber, blood pouring down his cheek. It *was* Bonnivet.'

'Are you sure?' I was aghast.

'There is no doubt. Madame de Châtillon heard her cries and chased the man away, in her nightgown. She then comforted the frightened Marguerite. But, listen, you are not to breathe a word, Anne, to anyone – and I mean it. You do not speak to the girls or any man, or you will be sent from the court in disgrace for spreading gossip.'

'I am not a child. I *can* be discreet.' I was offended by his remark and asked if she was hurt.

'Bonnivet is a fool, but no rapist. He admires women too much. She was more startled than anything. He came off worse, I believe.'

'Will he be arrested?'

'No, for although that was Marguerite's first thought, Madame de Châtillon advised that she says nothing. That way the matter would never come to light and her good name besmirched. It also gives her great power over him should she ever have to use it.'

'But she was innocent!' I cried.

'Anne, you know how the court works, you of all people. When is a woman ever thought of as the innocent party? We know she is as pure as the angels, but others will create tittle-tattle and rumours. They will say she encouraged him, that there is no smoke without fire.'

He was right, for I had been taught that the greatest

glory of a woman was to be least talked about by men.

'Poor Marguerite must be very upset by the whole incident,' I said. 'She being the king's sister. As to Bonnivet, he must be insane to put himself at such a risk. He could be exiled or hanged.'

We walked on a little, and I stared down at the paper in his hand. I asked what it was.

'A tract. An important tract. The other girls are too stupid to understand or care, but you are not. If you wish to be ahead of them, it is in your best interest to know about this.'

We moved to the quiet of a bench and waited for the gardener to amble away, his wheelbarrow piled high with leaves.

'And?' I glanced down.

'A paper from Germany, in Latin. The professor of theology there, at Wittenberg, a Martin Luther, pinned a disputation on the 'Power and Efficacy of Indulgences,' to the church door, just before All Saints day. He criticised the abuse of them by Pope Leo who needs money to build his cathedral in Rome. His opponent is a German Dominican friar and preacher, named Johann Tetzel, who claims that the pope's indulgences are so powerful that even if a man ravished the Virgin Mary, he would be forgiven.'

The image of Bonnivet trying to attack the king's sister flashed through my mind.

'But Clément, we have always paid for Masses for the dead and for prayers to be said for those who suffer in Purgatory. We pay, and the pope releases their soul. It has ever been thus. How else do souls fly to God, but through the priest or pope?'

'No, *think*, Anne. If the pope can empty Purgatory, why has he not done so once and for all?'

'I do not know, but I believe the release of souls is worth a penny.' I stared at him in his dark, burgundy doublet and wondered who had paid for it. He certainly did not earn enough for such a garment.

'Yes, worth it if he *could* release them, but he cannot! Can you not see, Anne?'

I frowned in annoyance.

'Well,' I continued, 'it is an attack on the pope's authority since he decreed the practice.'

'Exactly, now you understand, but it is not a serious attack because at present it is only meant to provoke a debate.'

'Why?'

'He is pointing out that indulgences are increasingly taking the place of both contrition and confession. Listen to this.' He turned the pages of the pamphlet in his hands, and I noticed that it was heavily annotated as he read: 'He preaches like a heathen who teaches that those who will deliver souls out of Purgatory or buy indulgences do not need repentance and contrition.'

'Does this Luther not believe in the church's doctrine?' I asked.

'Yes, he does. He says he remains a 'papist,' believes in Purgatory, and does not believe that his '*Theses*' represent a break with established Catholic doctrine.'

'Then he is a fool,' I retorted, annoyed that Clément had captured my interest. 'Besides, have not these things been discussed a great deal already? What is so different now?'

'Why now, Anne, a challenge has been issued that cannot be ignored.'

'Has Marguerite seen this?' I asked.

'Of course, as has her brother, but it concerns him not, for he already controls the church and he is lazy where doctrine is concerned. He leaves that to Marguerite. However, the *Parlement* of Paris is afraid of the huge power this gives the king, and when some members complained, he had them arrested.'

I smiled to myself. King, Church, *Parlement*, why were they always wrangling?

'Why do you seek me out, Clément?'

He shrugged his shoulders. 'I miss our conversation, that is all.' He put his hand over mine and held it there, but I jumped up from the bench.

'No, please. I will be polite to you, as manners demand, but do not think for one minute that I have forgotten the pain you caused me.'

His face appeared suitably embarrassed.

'Is that a gift from the Comte de Chalon?' he gestured to my gold chain. 'You should keep away from him.'

'Why, are you jealous? I can assure you that nothing improper has occurred, sir, and unlike you, he asks for nothing but my company.'

'But you do not love him, surely?' He searched my face.

'That is not your business. Besides, I have done with love. Now I love things – beautiful things – expensive things – and I intend having them. Is that so very wrong?'

'Be careful, Anne, he is no boy.'

'Like you?' I asked imperiously. 'Now, I have duties to attend to. As to this Luther fellow, it is nonsense, for nothing will come of his ramblings.'

With that, I called Bonny, picked her up, and with a swish of gown, flounced away, pondering on the frightful fate of Marguerite.

●   ●

On a cold December day, King François rode to Notre Dame, in Paris, to ratify the treaty made with King Henry to uphold the marriage of the king's daughter, Princess Mary, to his future son. At the Hôtel des Tournelles, he swore the oath and agreed that the treaty was to be concluded in 1520, in a meeting at Calais. All the queen had to do was produce the *dauphin*. Now, as we sat in her chamber at Amboise, we watched the rain pattering against the rattling windows. It had been too wet to go hunting, and as the wind whistled eerily outside, even the crackling logs in the fire and the fine tapestries could not keep the chamber warm.

I watched as Louise, Anne de Graville and Madame de Châtillon sat deep in conversation and then glanced at the queen, wrapped in mink furs. She had been unwell, and so throughout Advent, the church had released her from all her duties of fasting and abstinence. She must keep her strength up – although she could keep little food down – and was existing on vegetable broth, a few truffles and artichoke hearts. I feared a dull Christ-tide ahead.

It was a quiet scene as Mary Fiennes, Gillette and several of the other ladies helped me sort the queen's books into those to keep and those to return to the royal library at Blois. Only the dwarf, Marie, was proving a hindrance by messing up my neat piles. Over one and a half thousand books, along with rare manuscripts printed on vellum, were stored at Blois, and the cost must have been inestimable. The queen was constantly sent books from all over Europe and the Middle East by French diplomats, and they soon mounted up on the desks in her chambers. As I picked each one carefully up, I admired the gold-tooled red morocco and intricate gold clasps; there were books in Greek, Hebrew, and Arabic. One of the loveliest, '*Les Heures de la Reine Anne de Bretagne*,' I had read myself.

The talk amongst the ladies was of Martin Luther, and it soon became apparent that Madame Louise, the queen, and Anne de Graville disagreed with Madame de Châtillon. Then, as Françoise entered the chamber to join the conversation, she beckoned me to join her.

'The king, you will be pleased to hear, has threatened to cut off the head of my husband if he strikes me again.'

'Good,' I said, 'and so he should. Your husband has an unforgivable temper.' What I meant to say is not if I cut it off first. I then watched as she curtsied low to the queen and joined the circle. Although the queen was aware of Françoise and the king, she bore no grudge, and only gazed with pity. Just as she had with my sister. Louise was another matter altogether, but she had to accept Françoise for her son's sake.

'But I say we must support the pope in all things,' continued the queen, staring at the company, 'for does he not exhort the king to lead Christian princes in a crusade against the Turk?'

'Yes,' said Louise, 'and just to make sure, is he not sending your husband Signor Raphael's great painting of *The Holy Family* as a bribe to influence him?'

'You know as well as I, Madame,' said the queen, 'that the king has already touched upon his great inclination for the union of all Christendom, his ardent desire to free the Holy Land, and his obligations to the pope. He has offered to serve him in person and put himself and his kingdom entirely at his disposition.'

'But he is also interested in hearing of reform,' said Madame de Châtillon. 'Has he not said he welcomes scholars with new ideas, for he wishes intelligent men to freely visit his court?'

I knew that of all the women at court, Madame de Châtillon stood closest to Marguerite in her beliefs. Like her, she believed in traditional Catholic practices of piety and attachment to the Virgin Mary and wanted the monasteries to return to the strict rules set out when they were established.

'Unless,' countered Louise, 'they interfere with his prerogatives.' There was general nodding as Françoise rose up and pulled a drape across the window to block out the draught. She shivered and when she sat again, I moved to her side.

'Madame,' I said, 'this Luther fellow still regards himself as a papist.'

'And where did you hear that about him?' asked Françoise.

'Oh, I have heard of his *Theses* from Clem –'

'You have been speaking to him?' She was alarmed. 'Anne, did you not heed my advice?'

I looked down, annoyed. 'Madame, I did not seek him out. He – he approached me while I was walking.'

She sighed. 'Well, that maybe, but there is nothing for you to hear or know, Anne. These monks come and go with their foolish ideas.'

'But surely,' I said, refusing to be spoken to like a child, 'does Luther not say that a soul cannot fly from Purgatory just because a coin tinkles on the collection plate?'

'And did you also hear that from Monsieur Marot?'

'No, Madame, I can think for myself.' It was not entirely true, but I had thought much about my conversation with Clément, and I had recently read the works of Jacques Lefèvre d'Etaples and changed my previous opinions.

'Anne, the king has to please the pope, so I do not think this indulgence argument will come to anything.'

'But –'

'No, let us change the subject.'

I felt frustrated as she opened the book of hours at her girdle.

Louise stood plumping up the queen's cushions. How differently Claude compared to the strong, healthy Diane back at her château in Anet, now in her confinement.

'Well, the Christmas festivities will be soon upon us,' I ventured, brightly. It was the only safe thing I could think of to say. I was wrong.

'There can be no joy with the death of little Louise,' said Françoise, 'and of course, the loss of Suzanne de Bourbon's son. For such a magnificent christening to have ended in a tragedy must be unbearable. *Madame la Grande* is desolate, and so François has insisted she be godmother to the queen's new baby.'

'Do you think *she* put a spell on Suzanne's son?' I forgot all caution as I looked towards Louise. 'You know how she hates her.'

Françoise glared at me. 'Do not *ever* say such a thing,' she whispered back. 'Are you not aware of the harm you could do? King's mother or not, many hate her and would see her come to ruin.'

Nothing I said was right today. After a moment's silence, I tried again. 'Madame, my sister writes and tells me that the celebrations in England are cancelled due to the Sweat. It seems the court is quite depleted since many have returned to their country estates, including my parents. The king has locked himself away in solitude.'

'I am more concerned for Queen Claude than King Henry,' said Françoise.

'But why would you care a pin for her?' I stared at the woman who had stolen the king's heart.

'I have no quarrel with the queen. However, you know how weak she is and may not survive the birth. Her confinement will begin soon, and the holy relics to ensure a safe delivery are on their way as we speak, including the Holy Cord which bound Our Lord. Fifty-one nurses and midwives have been selected, and yet I fear after the sorrow of losing little Louise, Claude may not be strong enough to bear the pain.'

'Do you think she might die?' I whispered. 'The doctors have bled her so copiously over these last few months that she now has a horror of them coming anywhere near her.'

'And can you blame her?' asked Françoise. 'She has promised in the presence of her priest that if her prayers on the tomb of the holy friar François de Paule are answered, she will have the child named after him. She and Louise revere this humble man.'

'Louise,' I said, 'has made sure that everything is as perfect for the queen's lying in as possible. She has ordered tapestries of the greenwood to be hung in the chamber, and the huge bed has a canopy and curtains made of the finest red silk, decorated with swans. Even the coverlet is lined in squirrel fur. I have heard there will be six doctors, five surgeons, ten barbers, an apothecary, and her astrologer. But which women will attend her?'

'Madame de Brissac and Madame de Bouyan. Older ladies chosen by Louise.'

'Oh, it must be wonderful to feel so precious,' I said, the feeling of envy creeping into my heart. 'To have the very best, whatever the cost. If I were queen, I'd own the most precious books and works of art, and employ the finest musicians in Europe. Everyone would dance to my tune.'

Françoise grimaced. 'I would not be queen for any known thing, for if a queen does not produce a son, she is in a perilous position. The people's love is fickle and can quickly turn to hate, blaming her for threatening the peace of the realm. A kingdom must have a king.'

I thought this foolish, for the queen was adored, and it must have shown on my face.

'You only see the riches, Anne, the display and queenly status. Not the reality of the situation. The queen is not as content as she pretends and it is an unhappiness I have contributed to.'

'Well, I would give a king a palace full of princes,' I said, watching as the queen arched her aching back. 'We have always had boys in my family. I said as much when we spoke on this very subject at the Regent's court. Besides, Howard and Boleyn women are strong and carry babes well.'

Françoise raised her brow as she held my gaze. 'Why, I do believe you would do anything you set your mind to. However, since you never will be a queen, the discussion is rather pointless.'

1518

The entire court stood to listen as King François raged. It was a dreadful start to the New Year at Amboise, as two members of *parlement* quaked before him in the council chamber. We heard him accusing them of trying to undermine his authority and so, against their advice, he was going to grant Baron Semblançay unlimited power over France's finances. When he stormed petulantly out of his chamber, shrieking that there could be only one king in France, everyone in the gallery flew out of the way. He bellowed that if the members wanted to speak with him again, they could trot after him like lackeys. The two men ran after him, pleading that since the Loire had flooded that would not be possible, and so, turning, he ordered them to leave his court by six the following morning or be thrown into a pit for a year. As they stood shocked and humiliated, I heard Louise's mocking laughter. Her son cared not if they thought him a tyrant and hurried off to the library to peruse his New Year gifts. Everything from gold clocks to tennis racquets had been presented to him, including a crossbow from my father. My mother had sent me a mantle lined with miniver and my sister had sent a pair of green woollen stockings. Although subdued by the scene, I was well content.

But good news came, too, for we heard that after a long labour, Diane de Brézé had given birth to a healthy baby girl, called Françoise, in honour of the king. She recovered quickly and was soon back at court, ready to attend to the queen.

●　●

On the second Sunday of Lent, the king galloped into the courtyard, dismounted, and flung his wet cloak at a groom. In the fading light, he hurried into the château, past the saluting guards, and ran towards his wife's chamber. He had only just returned from hunting in the Touraine and, dishevelled, collided with the nurses and midwives as they rushed back and forth with bowls of hot water and towels. The great crowd of nobles, courtiers and ambassadors bowed low and swept to one side.

'Is it true?' he cried, 'is it true?'

A great clapping ensued as the king's mother burst out of the chamber, triumph on her face. 'France has a *dauphin*, thanks be to God, a *son*! The queen has asked me to tell you that he is even more beautiful than yourself.'

The king immediately burst into weeping and threw

himself into her arms.

As the door opened further, we all stood craning our necks, trying to gain a glimpse of inside the chamber, but there were too many nobles, ambassadors, and courtiers blocking the way.

'Oh, Mary,' I said, as we turned and hugged each other.

The girls laughed as Diane squeezed through the throng.

'Diane?' I asked in concern, reaching for her hand. 'What ails you?'

'It is nothing, Anne,' she said, wiping tears from her eyes.

Puzzled, I watched her slip through the excited crowd.

'Well,' said Gillette, above the noise, 'the queen has now done all that can be expected of her, let us hope she survives the next few days.'

When I returned with Renée, the queen lay white as milk in her bed, her hair neatly plaited beneath her cap. Beside her stood the most beautiful cradle I had ever seen, decorated with a dolphin and swathed in curtains of silver and gold tissue. As Renée peered at the new baby, the ladies bustled about, and the chamber felt so hot from the roaring fire I feared I might faint. When the queen saw me, she beckoned. Although exhausted, she could not hide her pride.

'See, Anne,' she said, 'how beautiful he is, like his father. My little François, my gift from God.'

I leant towards the cradle and saw the tiny babe with its fair wisp of hair, tightly swaddled. He looked adorable, with rosy skin and a tiny, pink mouth.

'Madame, he will grow to be the most handsome boy ever,' I said.

'Oh, yes, he will, and my love for him is already overwhelming, but did you see Diane? It was so selfish of me to recall her to my side. I must let her return to her new babe as soon as possible, for the poor girl longs to hold her.' She tried to lift her head but fell back, and Madame de Brissac gently took the rosary from her hot hands.

'The queen suffered a difficult labour and must rest,'

whispered the governess. 'The king has requested that no more visitors come without his express permission, for she needs quiet, poor lamb. Such crowds in here have been an abomination.'

When I looked back the queen's eyes were shut and as Madame de Brissac took the hand of Renée, we quietly left the chamber.

A salute from the artillery signified the event to the more distant quarters of the town, making the windows rattle. The firing continued without intermission for upwards of an hour, and so great was the uproar, what with the pealing of bells and the shouts of the populace, even the thunder of heaven itself would not have been heard.

As Bonnivet — now the new French ambassador to England — took horse to give the news to King Henry in England, I could only imagine how devastated he and Queen Katherine would feel. Mother said Henry doted on his little daughter, but she was not the son he craved, and now God had shown his favour to François. It was a bitter blow, all the more so when he heard that François had mocked him, saying he would get no son on his ugly, old wife. She was thirty-three years old. It was galling, but then, as part of the Treaty of London, the agreement was now finalised and signed, betrothing Princess Mary to the Dauphin of France. Queen Katherine did not want the match, begging her husband to reconsider, afraid that this union with France would weaken ties with Spain. However, Wolsey had worked tirelessly for a French alliance, and since he wielded the power, Mother told me he thought nothing of sacrificing Katherine's daughter. However, for the moment, Wolsey had other matters to worry about, for three of the king's pages had died of the Sweat and yet again Henry fled the court in panic.

* *

On an April evening, every prince, noble and ambassador in France attended the church of St Florentine, at Amboise, for the baptism of the new *dauphin*. Signor da Vinci had been given the task of designing the festivities, and he did not disappoint. Now, having worked tirelessly with a team of workmen for weeks, the delighted king promised him a private banquet of his own, in June, in the comfort of his own home at Clos-Luce.

As the heralds from Savoy, Brittany, Normandy, and Dauphiné sounded their trumpets, the little *dauphin* was carried from the church in triumph by Lorenzo de Medici, the pope's nephew. The king wore his new, closed crown and beamed with pride as a thousand torches lit up the magnificent tapestries in the courtyard. Meanwhile, Marguerite, her mother, and the royal princesses walked behind. Françoise, to everyone's surprise – for she was not of the royal family – walked with them, as the great procession made its way down to the town square to show the people their prince. As the king took his babe in his arms and held him up beneath the triumphal arch, a roar of approval filled the air. He possessed all he desired.

A long night of entertainments followed in the covered courtyard of the château. I had never seen such inventions – one appeared to be a machine that shot forth fireworks into the night as if by magic. The artist had even designed the menu and chosen the food and wine, bringing in the best cooks from all over France. Dancers from Italy performed an intricate and athletic dance of immense grace and skill called *Les Danses des Planetes*, and there were magical plays and orations. Clément recited a poem he had composed for the Dauphin and blessings rained down on the baby.

As the gaming tables were brought forth and bowls containing gold coins and dice placed down, the queen, yawning, beckoned me to her side.

'Anne, your father is here,' she said.

I curtsied low as he stepped down from the dais, looking pale and preoccupied.

'Father, it is so nice to see you again,' I began.

Taking off his bonnet he let out a great sneeze and blew his nose into a kerchief, for he had been suffering from a heavy cold.

'Is it?' he looked at the contents of the cloth. 'Come here, I wish to speak with you, Madame.'

He took my arm and manhandled me through the crowd of courtiers, before sitting down at one of the empty gaming tables. I was puzzled by his demeanour.

'Why, Father, whatever is the matter?'

He stared blankly at me. 'You know very well, young lady.'

At that moment, the queen rose and beckoned me to her. Whatever my Father wanted to say would have to wait – but I had the feeling it was not good news…

Chapter Thirteen

*'Love charms not with the eyes,
but with the mind.'*

The Loire, Chateau
d'Amboise and Angers

The commotion and noise outside the queen's chambers made everyone start, as the door flung open and a nobleman sank at the queen's knee, bonnet in hand.

'Make way! Make way!'

The choirboys ceased their singing as she handed baby François to Diane, an expression of alarm on her face. What on earth had happened?

'Dearest Majesty, forgive the intrusion, but it is the king.'

The queen turned white as Anne de Graville bustled the group of singers out of the chamber.

Madame de Tournon stepped forward. 'What has happened, sir?'

'Speak!' cried the queen.

The nobleman looked up, avoiding her eyes. 'Madame, there … Madame, there has been a grave accident. The king is not harmed, just badly shaken, but it has caused the death of several bystanders.'

'My God!' the queen cried, hand to her throat.

'It was just a game, Madame. The king had a mock town

built of wood, erected in an open field, and surrounded by a moat. Four great artillery pieces were put to guard it. The Duc d'Alençon, with a hundred men-at-arms, stood stationed inside the construction as it lay besieged by the Duc de Bourbon and Monsieur de Vendôme. Fleuranges, with four hundred men and assisted by the king, tried to come to his aid. Of course, the cannonballs were filled with air, but during the attack, something went badly wrong.'

'Should I go to him?' The queen waved the gentleman back onto his feet.

'No, Madame,' said the nobleman, 'he is at Romorantin and wishes to be left to recover.'

'Is Françoise with him?'

'Madame Châteaubriant *was* there with him, yes, but there occurred some unpleasantness between her and Madame Louise, and she returned home to her husband, riding sixty leagues in bad weather in her hurry to depart. The king was on his knees begging her not to leave.'

'What unpleasantness?' asked the queen, displaying her gentle dignity.

'I gather, Madame, that the king's mother did not make her welcome, and now there is a rift between the king and Madame Louise. His sister is having to act as a go-between since they are not speaking.'

I glanced at Eliza, trying not to smile, for I could just imagine the king trapped in bed as Louise paced up and down, railing against his mistress. I also admired Françoise in daring to leave the king in such a way. She had no fear of him at all.

'Why is he always doing this to her?' whispered Mary. 'One day he will kill himself and then where will we be? God help us all if Louise takes over as regent for the Dauphin.'

'He cannot help himself,' I said, 'for he is young and reckless, more so now he has an heir.'

'I hear people at the English court are saying he doesn't have a son, that it's all a lie,' said Mary. 'They are sending ambassadors over to see the child for themselves.'

I turned to look at her, astonished. 'And what did they think they saw at the baptism, Mary? An ape?'

* *

I could not believe my eyes. Such audacity! The most esteemed place, next to the king – Queen Claude's place – had been given to *her*. I knew that if I were the queen I would not have suffered such shame, and yet she did not appear offended, just grateful that the king had recovered from his accident. As to the king, he could no longer deny his passion for Françoise, and the affair now lay open for all the court to see. His close-cropped hair was immediately copied by his courtiers, and his burns were healing nicely leaving only a faint, red mark across his forehead.

As I stood there observing the scene, the queen sat talking with the new bride, Madeleine de la Tour. She was just sixteen years old and a distant relative of François. Her bridegroom, Lorenzo de Medici, ruled Florence. The king adored her and had given her a gift of ten thousand gold crowns and a beautiful manuscript of music. How I envied the sparkling diamonds about her neck! In response, Lorenzo's uncle, the pope, gave the king and queen so many treasures, including an enormous state bed, that it took thirty-six horses and carts to carry them back to Paris. I did not know if Louise received anything, but from the expression on her face, it was clear that she could barely hide the contempt she still felt for her son's mistress as she sat between Bourbon and the Duke of Urbino. I gazed about in wonder, for Signor da Vinci had again produced a magnificent show, and had even designed a new uniform for the king's Swiss Guard in blue, gold and white.

When the dancing began, seventy-two ladies disguised in the Italian and German style took to the marble floor. The queen was unable to dance herself, for she had still not fully recovered from the birth, but my father, avoiding the gathering dancers, came to my side. His face appeared grim and his voice sounded hoarse.

'Anne, can you please explain why the Comte de Chalon is allowed to pay such court to you? Françoise de Foix has informed me of the situation.'

So that was what he wanted to talk to me about.

'You mean she spied upon me,' I said. 'I would have thought she had quite enough to occupy herself with at present, without concerning herself about me.'

'Most likely she does, but she does not wish you to be gossiped about.'

'As she is?'

'Anne, you would do well to heed her, for she is a woman much raised.'

'And do you agree to her supplanting the queen in the king's affections? For I do not. Look at her pride!'

He gave a loud sneeze. 'Don't try and change the subject.'

I told him I could not think what he had heard, for I had not behaved inappropriately with the comte, in any way. I explained how he only spoke to me in company, and always with the permission of Madame d'Assigny. He grunted and wiped his nose.

'Besides,' I continued, somewhat puzzled, 'such conversation is expected, Father. We are encouraged to converse politely and entertain those nobles who find favour with the king. Honestly, I am eighteen years old, and I can manage my affairs without *her* help.' How quickly I had forgotten her previous help with my sister, or her advice.

'And what affairs are you referring to?' he asked.

I remained silent and brushed back the hair from my shoulder.

'Well? And who gave that to you? Come, let me see.'

I twisted the ring from my finger, and he gazed at the fiery stone set within fine, Italian goldwork.

'From him?'

'No! I am not like Mary. I cannot be bought with

trinkets.'

'And do you know the value of this "trinket"?' he asked. 'It would keep a labourer for a year in food, ale, and rent. So, I ask you again. Who gave it to you?'

'My sister,' I lied. 'It was a present to me from Mary before she left. King François gave it to her.'

He stared at me, scrutinising my blank face and I steadily held his gaze.

'Did he now? Well, since the ruby denotes sexual favours, I find it quite appropriate, don't you? Ha, at least she got something out of him.' He stared at me in silence and then spoke. 'I am sorry, Anne. You are a modest girl, but take care. You know very well that if such expensive gifts were offered to tempt a young woman, it would only lead to one expectation, and thus place her in an impossible position. You do nothing without my leave. I am sure Madame whatever her name is, is vigilant.'

'Madame d'Assigny, Father, and she is very strict.'

'Yes, yes. Look, I know you are brighter than Mary, but men such as he – well, you understand my meaning. Believe me, I know the French court, but all you need do is apply yourself to serving Queen Claude. Nothing else need concern you.'

I told him I had nothing to be ashamed of, and asked if I was to remain in France.

'I see no reason to bring you home yet, Nan, just as long as the peace signed between France, England, and Spain holds, which it should.'

'Marguerite is very kind to me,' I said, desperate to change the subject.

My father sneezed again. 'She is an extraordinary woman. No, it is Louise I am wary of, for she has an unbridled temper and a violent, domineering disposition. She is the most feared woman in France. And she likes to hoard money.'

I did not say 'like you'.

'Steer clear of that Françoise woman, too,' he added.

'Louise hates her, so do not be seen talking with her.'

As I watched the dancers, I asked about home, anything to get off the subject of the comte. My father told me he was very concerned about Dame Margot. His mother, he said, had taken to wandering about the estate at Hever, thinking she was at Blickling. George, Mary, and my mother were staying at Allington with the Wyatts, since Tom Wyatt had recently returned from Cambridge, and they were there to celebrate his betrothal to an Elizabeth Brooke.

'Oh,' I said, in surprise, although I knew of our Kentish neighbour, Lord Cobham. Somehow I never imagined the unruly Thomas marrying anyone. I asked if Thomas liked her.

My father shrugged. 'He made no objection since with her father's money and a planned career in banking, he has a good future ahead of him.'

Banking? Had the imaginative, sensitive Thomas changed so much from when I last saw him?

Father went on to tell me how the Sweat had returned, and the king and queen had fled in panic to the mid-shires to hunt. The king was seen to treat his wife with great tenderness and love, and they were both delighted – as were the council – to find that she was pregnant again. So much for King François' tactless jibe.

'The comfort of the realm,' continued my father, 'demands a son, and this time they are both certain that come November, a boy will fill the royal cradle. He is fuming that François got there first.'

'Well, I shall pray for a happy outcome,' I said, 'for it is my ardent hope.'

'Incidentally, I had a despatch from Margaret of Savoy,' he said, turning to me.

I asked if she was well.

'Indeed, for she is reconciled to Prince Charles, and I hear he is to issue an edict from Saragossa authorising her to sign all documents in his name, giving her full power as though she was ruler again. Her father, Maximilian, was happy when he heard of Charles' renewed confidence in his beloved aunt.'

I said I was glad of it, for she was wise in her rule.

'Oh, and Charles' sister Eleanor is about to marry King Manuel of Portugal, and Isabeau has given birth to a son.'

I said how I recalled Isabeau being such a sweet girl and hoped that King Christian did not treat her harshly. Poor Margaret had cried in apprehension when the girl left to join him.

'I'm not surprised, for he's a mad man. But that is royalty for you. Now, you must excuse me. Mark what I said.'

As I watched him re-join the other ambassadors, I thought of the comte and felt my blood freeze. I had told a blatant lie concerning the ring, and I would now have to confess to the priest. How tedious that my father had heard all from the meddling Françoise.

When the queen beckoned me to her she appeared truly happy. She cared nothing for Françoise, for now that she had given the king a son, none could touch her. I offered the napkin to her, as required, and then sat back on my cushion, thinking to myself. Now I was a grown woman, attractive and talented, and many nobles cast their eyes in my direction. Why should I not enjoy the riches the court could offer?

* *

Walking aimlessly through the gallery at first light of day, the jangle of harness in the courtyard below caught my attention. Looking out of the window, I saw the king mounted, his hounds gathered around, and his nobles ready to do his bidding. With his crossbow slung across his back, he held his courser in check as it pulled against the bit, desperate to be away. His archers stood ready in a long procession, and the *limiers* quietly wagged their tails, straining at their long leashes, ready to sniff out the quarry.

Amongst the huntsmen and women, I noticed the Comte de Chalon, and quickly stepped back as he glanced up to the window. When I peered again, he was taking a spear from one of the grooms, inspecting the tip and nodding. Françoise tripped lightly down the stone steps, and the king's eyes lit up as a wide smile split his face. She looked captivating in her grey velvet hunting gown, a plumed Venetian bonnet tipped to one side and her hair netted in a silver caul, as she mounted her horse.

Marguerite smiled as she handed her brother his golden horn, and he kissed her hand. She was not hunting today, but keeping the queen company, and she walked over to talk to Louise, who was mounted on her courser. There was a light breeze, and the white plumes on Louise's bonnet fluttered around her face, making her appear younger than her years. After some minutes, she ambled her horse over to Françoise, and as she spoke, I saw Françoise start a little. Louise moved closer to speak again. Whatever was said, Françoise did not like it. She gathered her reins and trotted over to the king, leaning in towards him. He put his hand on her arm, concern in his face, and she frowned as they spoke for some moments. Finally, she turned her horse about and trotted back towards the stables. The king gazed after her, disappointment now in his face, but as the horn blew he trotted away, followed by the ladies and nobles. What had happened?

Puzzled, I sat down on the nearby bench, the guards staring impassively ahead. I still had some time to myself before I attended the queen, so I opened my French book of fables. However, I could not concentrate, concerned at the curious scene I had just witnessed. When I finally settled to read, the noise of someone striding heavily along the wooden floorboards of the gallery disturbed my peace, and I looked up.

'Bitch!' came the cry, as Françoise appeared, bonnet in hand, shaking her long hair loose. She brushed the courtiers in her way aside, like annoying flies, her ladies behind barely able to keep up with her angry steps. 'Bitch, bitch, *bitch*!'

I jumped up and curtsied low.

'Did you see that?' She turned to me. 'Did you see that – that woman?'

The ladies gathered into an untidy huddle.

I shook my head as she sat down on the bench, and pulled off her gloves, flinging them to one side.

'God's *teeth*, I despise her as much as she despises me.'

'Whatever is the matter, Madame?' I tried to hide my interest, for I always loved gossip.

Françoise waved her women away and waited until they had disappeared down the gallery. 'Louise is the matter. She said I may think I am the sweetheart of the king – *for now – but she will do everything in her power to prevent my brother, Thomas, from being appointed Marshal of France and Odet continuing with the government of the Milanese duchy.*'

'Forgive me, Madame, but is it because of them that she hates you?'

She tugged at the plumes on her bonnet, as if pulling at Louise's hair. The broken feathers drifted to the floor.

'Of course. She did not sanction either post, but more to the point, her precious son had already agreed to *my* requests over hers.'

'Did you tell him?'

She shook her head. 'François will hear nothing said against his mother. Nothing. God, she was insulting! I told him I could not continue to hunt today due to a headache. I said there was nothing to be concerned about and insisted he went without me.'

A moment's silence followed before I spoke. 'Madame, my father spoke to me about the comte.' I had not meant to blurt it out, but it was too late. I had.

'Then you know I discussed the matter with him,' she said, 'for I do not think it appropriate for a man such as he to pay court to you.'

'Court me? But Madame,' I said, 'there was no need to

inform my father of any such thing, for I can handle the situation myself.' I wanted to say it was none of her business.

'Anne, my dear girl, you have no experience of life, and this flirtation with the comte must now cease.'

'But I am not a child,' I replied between clenched teeth, 'and besides, he gives me beautiful gifts jus –'

'Gifts? Then you did not heed my words,' she interrupted. 'In fact, you seem very loathe to take any of my advice on any subject.'

'Madame, I really cannot see the harm in it. Have you not done as much?'

She turned to face me and I knew I had spoken too boldly. 'Yes, I will not deny it, but I received gifts from the king only when I chose to accept them. When I was prepared to accept the shift in the balance of power and become his mistress. Are you ready for that with the comte? All men expect some return on their investment, even our dear Admiral Bonnivet.'

'*Bonnivet?*' I asked, puzzled.

'When the king found out, he did not like the rivalry one bit, I can tell you,' continued Françoise. 'He was so jealous. Well, it did him good.'

I stared at her.

'Oh, did you not know? Marguerite made a fool of herself with him. It is me he desires.'

I thought of poor Marguerite, so in love with Bonnivet, and wondered if my sister had told the king after all.

'Madame, I *swear* on the blood of Christ that nothing has occurred, or ever will with the Comte de Chalon. I do not even like him anymore and long to be rid of him.'

'Then what do you think you are doing accepting these expensive presents?' She flicked her finger up to my emerald earrings. 'And what do you think he is doing offering them to you?'

'Pleasing me,' I said, my voice petulant.

'No, silly girl, he is striking a bargain. There will come

a point when he wants more than your company, and you will not be in a position to refuse. You have already accepted the payment.'

I gazed ahead, feeling indignant. Had the present of a brooch from Clément been no more than a bribe?

'Suppose he asks your father for your hand in marriage?'

'Oh, really!' I was shocked. 'He is too old. My parents would refuse and, besides, I would not be able to bring him any great fortune.'

'He would not need your dowry, for he is very wealthy – a tempting match, I would say. One to please your family.'

'I doubt it. Anyway, my father wishes me to return home to England, not stay here in France. Hopefully, he will find me a rich, *young* man like Madeleine de la Tour's husband. He looked so handsome, and I envy her having everything she desires, from gowns and horses to priceless jewellery.'

'Really?' asked Françoise. 'And do you envy her lying with a man who most assuredly has the Italian disease? I doubt it will prove a long marriage.'

The great pox. I was not expecting that revelation.

'So – so what am I do?' I asked, shocked. 'Must I give back the comte's gifts?' I thought of my lovely bracelets and could not bear to part with them.

'Yes, you must, and I have already asked Madame de Châtillon to speak with him.'

'What?' I was mortified. 'Who else knows? Not Madame d'Assigny I hope?'

She shook her head. 'Anne, I know you think I am interfering, and I understand that Clément once hurt you, but this is not the way to behave.'

I watched as she tidied up her hair and arose, having no idea why she insisted on interfering. It was true, she had been sympathetic over Clément, but somehow I found her insincere. I also had the feeling that, for all her kind words, she saw something in the Boleyn girls that she did not quite like.

'Come, Anne, we must attend the queen. At least you have taken my mind off Louise.'

As we walked together, she tucked her arm in mine and leant her head closer.

'You have much to learn, Anne, and you must let me help you, for there is a very specific way to handle a man that takes skill, cunning and daring. If you allow me, I can teach you many things to keep a man bound to you forever. French things…'

I was not sure if I wished to hear such things from the king's mistress, but my curiosity overrode my hesitance.

'Go on.'

'Well, for instance, to make a man responsive to the spur, you must manage him so adroitly that he knows not what to make of you. The most confident man *must* be reduced to despair, and the most down-hearted allowed a ray of hope. It is a skilful game.'

'But I do not possess your beauty, Madame.'

'True beauty is suspect. As *Madame la Grande* says, it is the most prejudicial and least valuable grace that God can bestow on a woman, for it inevitably muddles the sentiments. You do not have to possess beauty to be thought beautiful.'

'You speak of charm,' I said, intrigued.

'Yes, because charm is a form of witchery, a woman's knack, as it were, of enveloping all around her in an invisible net. Like all other arts, true charm is a gift of nature. But you must charm with your mind.'

'And I can use such charm, Madame, to obtain my desires?'

'Most assuredly, but you must refuse trifles, for you do not need to be bought and paid for by any man. Accept them, and you will be beholden to your admirer, giving away your power. Just imagine, if you can use your allure to constrain a man to your will *without* accepting his gifts – make him yearn for you, but give nothing – until you wish to – well, I think that would be a very good trick, don't you?'

• •

On the sixth day of June, Queen Claude made a grand entry into Angers, the capital of Anjou, meeting up with the king, who had returned from hunting. That night, we enjoyed a vast banquet at the château of René de Cossé-Brissac, governor of Anjou and Maine, the planning of which had taken a month to complete. So impressed were the royal couple that they decided to stay for two months and the cost almost broke the duc, since every evening he provided some entertainment, from tennis to a bear fight, a water pageant to jousts.

The beautiful summer days were spent walking with the queen, playing boules, or reading on the terrace surrounded by her dogs. There was some alarm when we heard that in England, smallpox and measles had caused the deaths of servants at Bisham Abbey, Berkshire, where Princess Mary lodged, and prayers were offered that she remained safe.

The king disappeared hunting with Françoise, now his *maîtresse-en-titre*, and they rode away quite openly. Meanwhile, Bonnivet – the scratches to his face made by Marguerite now only very faint – along with the other ambassadors, started for England on their peace embassy, the most splendid that ever left France. The French were pleased with the alliance; but would it last? As for Marguerite, always busy, she was happy if her brother was happy.

The only one not happy was the Comte de Chalon, who fell into a great melancholy and left the court to return to Loche to cool his ardour. According to Madame de Châtillon, he felt he had been made a cuckold of, for when he asked if he could approach my father for my hand, I made my feelings very clear. To put it plainly, I told him I would rather cast myself into the River Loire, and he scuttled away, red-faced and hurt. Yes, I had behaved unwisely – possibly unkindly – but Madame de Châtillon told me the matter was not to be discussed ever again. Did the queen know?

If she did, nothing was ever said. I knew she did not want me to leave her service and return to England, so perhaps she had been aware of the matter. Well, the least said the soonest mended. I was not sure if I felt relieved or not, for I had enjoyed the attention. And I had been amused by the fact that the more uninterested I behaved, the more attentive the comte became, just as Françoise had said. Now, there was little else to do apart from reading the lives of the saints, sewing and admiring the new baby. I had hoped that Marguerite would allow me to accompany her more often on her charitable visits, but she did not.

As I reluctantly returned my lovely gifts to Madame de Châtillon, I felt sad that I still owned nothing much of any worth. I sulked as I watched the noble ladies with their expensive jewellery, fine furs and sumptuous gowns parading their wealth before me, and my heart yearned even more for such gew-gaws.

Brittany

That early August, after Lammastide, we sailed down the Loire and visited most of the Breton towns, including Saint-Malo. However, the most important entry was that of Nantes, the capital of Queen Claude's Duchy. Although her mother, Anne of Brittany, had visited before, the queen had been too young to accompany her, and so this journey fulfilled all her dreams. We were lodged at the great château of the Dukes of Brittany, and as I assisted to dress her in a coat of blue velvet, its diamond buttons glittering, I could see her immense happiness. She had produced a *dauphin*, the Breton people adored her, and the king smiled magnanimously to all.

When she reached the gate of the Basilica of St Nicholas, in the heart of the town, a young girl presented the keys, and an immense cheer rose into the air, startling the pigeons on the church roof. Other gifts were showered upon the queen, such as a beautiful, intricate heart made of gold, but fearing she would burden her people, she insisted it was melted down by the Master of the Mint and the gold put towards the town's taxes. Although it was a kind gesture, I did wonder what the poor artisan would feel seeing his work go back into the furnace. Louise flatly refused to give up her gift of twelve silver-gilt cups, and they were hurriedly packed away for her to peruse later. Either way, the cost of the banquets, fireworks, sanding of the streets and strewing herbs and flowers had cost the town dearly.

Nine days later, the king had had enough and, booted and spurred, left again with Françoise, Marguerite and a small band of friends for the Abbey of Mont Saint Michel. At first, Françoise said she wished to stay behind, and the king had to plead with her to mount her horse. He said he wanted to be there to celebrate Michaelmas, and besides, he had no intention of facing Françoise's husband who was busy in Nantes collecting taxes. To his utter delight, she condescended to go. As to the queen, she had bid him a fond farewell, and he kissed her tenderly, his hand resting on the front of her gown, satisfied that she was carrying another child. He would catch up with her in Paris, and I watched her as he cantered out of the courtyard, waving his bonnet in the air, exhilarated by his freedom. I would much rather have accompanied his party, but I, along with a very small group of ladies, travelled instead with the queen and Louise along the river, two hundred miles to Château du Plessis-sur-vert, near Dreux, west of Paris. This beautiful château, tucked away in the quiet of the green woods, allowed both Louise and the queen the rest and privacy they now craved, away from ceremonies.

As the green leaves began to turn golden brown, the château became more of a peaceful, private retreat, and we spent our days walking the dogs and listening to the musicians play the latest compositions. As September melted into a drizzling October, we were also able to visit Diane de Brézé at her splendid château in Anet, and while there, we heard the sad news that Suzanne de Bourbon had given birth to stillborn twins. Diane, holding her babe close, wept with compassion, and even Louise kept her thoughts silent for once. The queen, meanwhile, felt fearful for the precious child she was carrying and having been sick as usual, spent most of the days in her chamber playing cards with Marie.

When the messengers arrived with their despatches, my sister wrote to me with the news that she, George – now a squire in the royal household – and my parents had attended the magnificent celebrations at York House for the betrothal of Princess Mary and the Dauphin. She described how Bonnivet had stood proxy for the Dauphin, and the little princess had appeared dressed in a gown of gold cloth with a black cap covering her red hair. The princess's godfather, Cardinal Wolsey, presented Bonnivet with a diamond ring which he then placed on the young girl's hand. She behaved impeccably throughout the ceremony but mistakenly believed that Bonnivet was the Dauphin, asking:

'Are you the Dauphin of France? If you are, I wish to kiss you.'

The celebrations organised by Cardinal Wolsey – who had negotiated the payment of one million gold crowns to King Henry – were on such a grand scale that everyone present had never seen such extravagance. Queen Katherine appeared very large with her forthcoming child and had to retire due to fatigue. However, the dowager French queen danced the night away with King Henry, still very much in love with her Charles. She was back in her brother's favour, married to the man she adored, and dazzling everyone at the court. No place had yet been found for my sister, but she said she was not in the least bit bothered for she had the most exciting news ever.

Paris

'Well, who is it?' asked Mary Fiennes, as we walked in the crisp November air. We were back in the stink of Paris, at the Hôtel des Tournelles, the king having recently received the delegation of English envoys at Notre Dame, to sign the Universal Peace.

We followed the queen as she walked in the distance, through the arbours in the garden, all her little dogs, including Bonny, running ahead. As she pointed out to her gardener where she wanted to place the new rose bushes, I turned to Mary Fiennes.

'Carey – a William Carey.' I pulled my cloak tight against the chill. In the distance, I could barely see the deer park through the mist.

'And is your sister happy with the match?' asked Mary.

'I do not know for certain, for she has said very little about the matter in her letter, which is odd. I suppose that at twenty years old she will be an old maid if she waits much longer and so is content. I am not far behind, at nearly nineteen.'

'Anne! I am twenty-three, so how do you imagine I feel? But, do you think this Mr Carey knows about – you know – what happened here in France?'

'Nothing occurred,' I said, sharply, causing her to halt. I glanced at her crestfallen face. 'I am sorry, but all the talk at the moment is about weddings. I do wonder what my parents have planned for me.'

'Your time – our time – will come,' said Mary, as we continued past gardeners raking the soil. I watched as Bonny snuffled through the sodden leaves.

'At least you have all the men here, young and old, constantly admiring you and staring at you, unlike me.'

'Do I?' I asked. 'Last Valentine's Day when I tossed hemp seeds into a bowl of water, they revealed no letters of a name.

Nothing. And I do so wish to be the lady of my own house.'

'Well, St Katherine's day is almost upon us, so we will both pray to her as our last hope.'

I laughed as Bonny ran towards me, and as I picked her up, removing bits of leaf from her fur, she smelt of wood smoke. It reminded me of Clément when he had once wrapped me in his cloak.

'I hate this old palace,' said Mary, wrinkling her nose.

'Not as much as Louise does. I gather she finds her apartments here far too inadequate and has persuaded her son to find her a grander residence with a magnificent garden on the banks of the Seine. Thus, she continues to empty the treasury.'

At that moment Marguerite appeared, hurrying across the terrace, a paper in her hand. Dressed in red velvet, her cheeks flushed with cold, she held a sable muffler close about her neck.

'Where is the queen?' Her cold breath swirled as Mary and I curtsied.

I pointed to the arbour and Marguerite hurried ahead. Something was afoot and we both quickly followed, eager to find out.

The ungainly queen turned to see Marguerite.

'Ah, dear sister,' she said, smiling.

Marguerite kissed her on both cheeks. 'Madame, this despatch has just arrived and I wanted to inform you immediately. It is Queen Katherine. She has given birth to –'

'Oh!' the queen cried, her face bright.

'No, Madame, it is – was – a girl. However, by the will of God and to the king and queen's great distress, the babe only lived a few short hours, dying the very day we signed the peace.'

I stared at Mary and we crossed ourselves as the queen's face crumpled.

'Oh, poor Katherine!'

Mary turned to me and whispered. 'That is a bad omen

for France and England.'

'Nonsense,' I said, for I hated superstition.

'Well,' said Mary, 'Louise's astrologers *did* predict she would have a girl, but they did not predict she would lose it before her saint's day. Saints in Heaven, what if she does not conceive again? Six pregnancies and all to show is two dead daughters and three dead boys.'

'Princess Mary is healthy,' I said. 'Anyway, should the King of England die without an heir male, his daughter is to inherit the kingdom and marry the Dauphin when he attains his fourteenth year. It is all signed and sealed.'

'That is a long way off, Anne.'

'Mother tells me it is Katherine's constant fasting and kneeling on cold stone that has made her weak. But I am sorry for her, truly I am, poor lady. What could be the cause?'

'A myriad of things, as you know,' said Mary, taking Bonny from my arms.

'Are you afraid of having a child, Anne?'

I tickled Bonny beneath her chin and glanced at Mary's pale face. 'No, for I will put my trust in God.'

'Much good has that done Katherine,' came the reply.

I paused a moment and a dreadful thought came into my mind. 'What if it is *his* fault?' I asked.

Mary laughed as Bonny licked my fingers. 'Don't be so absurd, Anne. He gets children upon her with ease, but she either cannot carry them, or they are too weak to survive. That weakness comes from her, not him, so the fault is hers alone.'

As we wandered back to the Hôtel I could not help but muse on how the crippled Queen Claude had produced a strong, healthy boy, and yet Queen Katherine naught but a single girl. The problem, indeed, must lie with her.

• •

The cobbled courtyard lay covered in mud, snow and ice as the crows hopped along the crumbling walls. We were residing at the Hôtel for Christmas and although it had been decorated with festive greenery, wreaths, and ribbons I thought of old King Louis, decaying like this old palace, in his grave. I loathed this place, for it was forever cold and draughty, and I longed for the warmth of the south.

As Christmas drew closer, we sat by the blazing fire busy sewing shirts for the poor as they huddled outside the gates in their meagre sacking and rags. I sighed with utter boredom. Carollers added some cheer as they sang in the courtyard, and gifts arrived by the cartload – everything from pies to peacocks – as the snow continued to fall.

Claude occupied her time with her babies, while Louise attended to state business, leaving her son to enjoy the constant round of celebrations, jousts, bear-baiting, and banquets. He spent most of his days out in the icy, Paris streets, cavorting with the English courtiers who had stayed on for the peace celebrations. King Henry's favourites, Mr Carew and Mr Bryan, behaved despicably, throwing eggs, stones and other such trifles at the people in the streets, encouraged by King François, who found it highly amusing. Clattering through the narrow, cobbled lanes, faces muffled, they had tipped over carts of goods, frightened the cattle at the market and leapt their horses over barrels of beer. However, for once, the people did not complain, for every day the fountains ran with wine on the street corners and bread was provided in abundance.

On the twenty-second day of December, the celebrations in Paris culminated with a banquet at the Bastille Saint Antoine. This entire fortress, with its eight enormous towers, moat, and eighty-foot high walls, had been transformed by Signor da Vinci to a magical world of stars and planets. Real trees had been planted in boxes, buffets loaded with gold plate, and a huge, fire-breathing salamander took pride of place in the centre of the *salle*.

I had dressed with particular care, for we were instructed to impress the English guests, and Madame d'Assigny had fussed over our gowns and hair more than usual. Oh, I knew I was not the prettiest girl present in my cream gown, but I had carefully studied the ladies at court and made a note of those with style. Copying Françoise, I had placed a black, French hood trimmed with pearls farther back on my head than usual, showing more of my lustrous hair, and it suited my oval face and long, slender neck. I had used the slightest touch of rouge to brighten my complexion and shaped my eyebrows neatly with wax. My elegant, long sleeves fell over my slender arms, hiding my odd finger, and my bosom had, at last, developed. I wore no neck chains or ornaments, for, in truth, I now owned nothing much worth showing. But it worked to my advantage for such a lack of adornment made me stand out.

At four o'clock in the afternoon, the trumpets sounded, and the king entered the *salle*, accompanied by the English ambassadors, papal legate, bishops and French princes – two hundred and fifty guests in all. Queen Claude stood dressed in cloth of gold, lined with sables and glittering with jewels, and the English guests were left in no doubt as to the power and wealth of France. Their English clothes looked positively shabby compared to the silks and satins of the French, and for the first time, I began to compare them myself. The English women, who had accompanied their husbands, appeared to wear ill-fitting gowns and old-fashioned gabled head-dresses with long lappets, more suited to the previous ten years in style. Neither the men, nor the women, smelt very clean, while the French women – wearing expensive Ethiopian perfume – had taken such care with their hair, jewellery and cleanliness that the result was – it has to be said – far more appealing.

When the feasting had finished, the musicians struck up a stately pavane, and the king danced first with his sister, then, as Françoise watched, he approached the queen's ladies. The girls simpered, giggled and hid their faces behind their feathered fans as he chatted first with the French ladies and then to Mary Fiennes. I stood a little way off, elegant and composed, refusing to blush, aware that several gentlemen were smiling in appreciation. When the king turned to me, bowed and held out his hand, I made a perfect, deep reverence. Strange to say, I held no hatred for him and his treatment of my sister, partly because I was not sure whether to believe her story or not.

'*Mademoiselle*,' he said.

At that moment, at the Bastille, I felt something change inside my heart. This is what I had waited for, and I felt every eye in the *salle* cast upon me as the king, towering above my slight frame, his coat of white satin, embroidered with gold and covered with compasses and dials, led me out onto the wooden floor.

I had been close to King François many times, but had not danced with him before, and although not good-looking, he did possess great charm – and a crown. As his eyes held mine, I understood – just a little – the thrill a woman felt when the king paid court to her. As we placed our opposite hands together, turned and hopped, the king matched me in grace. As courtiers stared in admiration, including Françoise, I realised that this is what I desired the most – to be the centre of attention, to be lauded and admired by those in power. When I caught the eye of Madame d'Assigny she nodded in approval, for I was her charge, and she had trained me well. Polished, elegant and finished I had become an adornment to any court. When I sat back down, exhilarated, she walked over to me and whispered '*bravo*,' pleased with what she had witnessed.

The king, meanwhile, had taken the hand of another lady, and I saw Françoise, goblet in hand, appear unconcerned. She knew she had his heart, he was her slave, and I pondered on the secret things she had told me to make him so. Even my sister Mary would have been shocked, for some of the acts Françoise had described were condemned by the church as mortal sins. And yet these practices worked, for of all women she held his heart captive, and no matter how sharply she spoke to him, he begged for more. As I watched her laugh, I could only marvel at the power she held over her lover.

Chapter Fourteen

*'I can create a noble, but only God
can create artist.'*

1519 Paris

I could not believe he was dead. The man I had so admired had, they said, died from a surfeit of melons. Louise sat, frozen-faced, a black candle in her hand, as we prayed in the chapel. From where I sat with the other ladies – except for the queen, who had retired to rest – I could imagine the busy workings of Louise's mind as she clenched and unclenched her jaw. We heard that Emperor Maximilian had received the last sacrament that third day of January, having announced that he wished his heart to be buried next to his first wife, Mary of Burgundy, in Bruges. He had been ill for some time and hoped the clear air of Innsbruck would aid his recovery, but it did not, and he died not quite sixty years old.

His daughter, Margaret, suffered great anguish, for there had already been much affliction during her life, having lost her two husbands previously. She had adored her father, although she found him impossible at times, and I thought back to the homely scenes I had enjoyed in their company at the Château d'Antoing, when I had served at Margaret's court. The emperor had always had time to notice me, although I'd been a mere child, and for a while, I had felt fondly towards him. I knew I must write and send my condolences, for this would be a terrible blow to her.

The news of his death from the German bankers, however, cheered King François, for when I glanced across to where he sat, whispering to his love, he appeared oblivious to the priest intoning the prayers. With Maximilian's death, he now revived his hopes of winning the much-coveted imperial crown, a crown that would give him sovereignty of Spain, Naples, the Indies, Austria, the Low Countries, Flanders, Bohemia, and Hungary. Prince Charles, adamant that it had been his grandfather's will that he alone succeeded to the imperial dignities, insisted that his grieving Aunt Margaret now do all she could to aid him. Louise and her son cared nothing for a dead man's wishes, and as Charles's rival, the king now began winning over the German princes by every means in his power. His mother had already leapt into action the moment she heard Maximilian lay ill, and spent a great deal of money in bribes, eager to benefit from the immense wealth and power the title 'King of the Romans' would bring.

At the end of the prayers, she took her son's arm, ignoring his mistress, who was forced to follow behind with her ladies and Louise's dwarf, Cosima. Louise had made up her argument with her son since the disagreement was Françoise' fault, not his, and she wanted matters to be pleasant before she left for Cognac.

After I had left the chapel, I proceeded to the crowded dining *salle*, where I saw my father. He had now arrived in Paris in his official role as ambassador from the English court, and beckoned me to him, goblet of wine in hand.

'Sit, sit,' he said, moving aside a little.

'Congratulations, Father,' I said as I sat beside him.

'Thank you, Nan,' he said, pouring a little wine for me. 'This post has been a while coming, but the king knows my worth. I said as much to Artus Goffier as he lay in his chamber sick with gout and –'

'Oh, please tell me more about my sister and her

betrothed,' I interrupted. I cared nothing for Monsieur Goffier's gout.

'If you insist,' he said, pushing away the stone flagon. He then went on to explain that William was about the same age as Mary, of a good Wiltshire family, an intimate and distant cousin of the king, and prominent in the local gentry. Mary seemed rather enamoured of him, for he was a decent young man and well-liked, and he felt the same about her. If the family could just agree on the financial arrangements, the matter would be settled.

'But he is not wealthy, is he? I asked. I could not endure hearing that she liked him *and* that he had money.

The answer did not soothe me, for my father said although William was not rich at present, he was well placed to make his fortune. He had recently entered the court as Esquire of the Body to the king and so had a good career ahead of him. More importantly, he was well connected, being a first cousin to Sir Henry Percy, son of the Earl of Northumberland. They appeared quite close, loitering about the court together as young men did.

'Is William handsome?' I asked, hoping he looked like a gargoyle.

My father shrugged. 'How should I know what you women find appealing? He is tall, well built and has good teeth. The king enjoys his company, for he is a good gambler – although forever in debt – witty and most importantly, trustworthy.'

I felt my heart sink, for he sounded better than she deserved. 'Are *you* pleased, Father?'

He replied that frankly, he was glad to get rid of her, but my grandfather was not happy. He said a younger son was not fitted to marry the granddaughter of a premier duke. However, as a member of the privy chamber, William was close to the king and, he believed, could be of use. Having held the post, himself, he knew William could obtain positions and favours for our family. So, yes, he was well satisfied.

I stared down at my hands. It just did not seem fair that Carey should be handsome *and* have a promising career ahead of him.

'So, where will she live?' I asked, not wishing to know.

'She will share William's lodgings at court for a while, but after that, I must give it some consideration. Possibly Hertfordshire at a family property.'

I asked how Mary was finding the court, and he said she was doing surprisingly well and appeared more settled now that she was betrothed. She occasionally served as one of seven gentlewomen to Queen Katherine, but the queen found her a little too exuberant, as did Lady Willoughby. The queen liked to give Mary advice on how to please a husband. I tried to hide a smile, certain it would not be the same advice Françoise had given to me, not from the saintly queen.

'I know, I know, ironic, isn't it? The queen should concern herself with delivering a healthy son, not giving out nuggets of wisdom. Anyway, these are unsettled times,' said Father, changing the subject and gazing about the *salle*. 'If King François succeeds to the imperial crown, he will be the wealthiest ruler in Christendom.'

'Is it likely?' I sipped the Gascony wine, which tasted particularly good.

'It is possible. Letters had been received from the King of England promising King François all his power to obtain it for him. However, the pope believes that Charles would be a much more fitting ruler than François.'

I told him that I had heard that King Henry coveted the title for himself.

'Of course he does,' said my father, 'but he does not have the money to pay the ruinous bribes, unlike François. Taking me aside the other day, he declared: 'By my faith, my kingdom is worth six million gold florins, and I will spend three million just to be emperor.'

'Then his chances are excellent.'

'Well, Nan, they will have to elect an emperor favourable to universal peace, and competent enough to protect Christendom. I would back Charles.'

'But not King François?'

He said he was a diplomat and would not comment. However, he said that when King François took him aside to a window, just the other day as he came from Mass, he told him his whole mind. He said his lady mother desired the title for him more than he did himself.

'Well, it is good that he trusts you, Father, but what do you think of him as a man?' I was intrigued. 'I did not care for him much at first.'

'I find he speaks openly, which is good, but he is indolent and allows his mother to attend to business. The people are much enraged at his exactions and he is happy to empty the coffers. As to his incessant gambling ... it is a pity that such a rich country should be ruined by a man who allows himself to be surrounded by licentious ministers. I suspect his throne is shakier than he might suppose.'

I said I knew that he would rather hunt than attend to his affairs.

'King Henry is the same, Nan, and at twenty-nine years of age should know better than to leave the cares of state to Cardinal Wolsey. The man is a mere servant and used to say, 'his Majesty will do so and so,' then subsequently, by degrees, forgetting himself, he has commenced saying, 'we shall do so and so.''

'Cardinal Wolsey was very kind to me when we were in Lille,' I said. 'He explained how to play tennis.'

'Well, he would not have time for you now, for he is held in very great repute, seven times more so than if he were pope. He has a very fine palace where one traverses eight rooms before reaching his audience chamber, and they are all hung with tapestry, which is changed once a week. In his private chamber there is always a cupboard with vessels to the amount of thirty-thousand ducats, according to the custom of the English nobility – which, of course, he is not.'

'I thought him very handsome,' I continued.

'Perhaps he is to women. Or boys? Who knows?'

As the servers brought forth the various dishes, my father helped himself to the veal whilst I sampled the excellent vegetable pottage. I asked when he was leaving for Cognac to report on the dauphin, my spoon in hand.

'In a couple of weeks, around Mardi Gras. You will, I assume, remain with Queen Claude?'

'I will, Father, although I wish that Marguerite had taken me into her service instead. She promised me she would, although she does allow me to serve her in little ways. Queen Claude, as you know, has been very unwell. All I seem to do, day in and day out, is hold a silver bowl to her chin for her to vomit into.'

'Well, at least she is young, unlike Queen Katherine,' said Father, glancing around. 'Between you and me, I cannot see Katherine having another child. Not at thirty-four. Even François has described her as old and deformed.'

I waved away the offer of more wine, saying the king must be in despair.

He then leaned in closer and said he was, but before too long we would know who was at fault.

'How do you mean?' I remembered my conversation with Mary Fiennes on this very subject. He then told me the king's mistress was full-bellied.'

'That Bessie Blount girl?'

'The very same. Accomplished, well-educated and of a good family, she left the court immediately to avoid upsetting the queen in her pregnancy. Of course, she might have a girl, she might die – or she might give the king a healthy son.'

When I pointed out it would be a bastard, my father cupped his hand as he spoke in my ear, for the noise from the crowded *salle* cut across our words.

'But we would *know* that Katherine was at fault. We would know for sure that she either cannot hold a male child in her womb, or breeds weakness in it. The king's conscience would be clear.'

'Clear to do what?'

My father broke off a piece of bread.

'Make Bessie's child his heir.'

I asked if he could do this, over the right of Princess Mary.

'Most assuredly, but it is unlikely. Without a legitimate heir, the realm is at risk, for certain nobles will seek to take the crown, including one in our own family.'

Intrigued, I asked who.

'Your Grandfather, old Norfolk,' he whispered. 'Do not repeat this, but he holds some hopes of the crown, although he would, of course, pass it to his son. Then there is the Duke of Buckingham, and it is thought that were the king to die without a male heir, he might easily obtain the crown. Finally, Suffolk has great hopes of the crown in right of his wife, the dowager French queen.'

This was news to me and I felt shocked. 'Impossible!'

'The other danger is the Duke of Albany. King Henry is very anxious to prevent his return from France to Scotland since he is next in succession.'

When I asked where Bessie's child would live, he said Windsor seemed the most likely place and that Elizabeth Stafford's boy, Henry, was to be his companion. I asked of Queen Katherine, and he said she would be packed off to a convent. As I sat staring ahead, I realised I had been unaware that matters had become so serious.

'Poor Katherine, Father. Surely there would be war with Spain since Charles would support her if she were sent away? Tell me, is it true that everything Spanish is out of favour in England? I hear the court is quite mad for French ways and fashions.'

To my surprise, he said not entirely. Some of the courtiers, including Carew and Bryan, had returned to England after their horseplay here and offended many with their bragging and bad manners. Brown and Hart had been at variance; the latter being sore hurt on the head, and not likely to be whole before Easter. Young Gifford was very ill due to cavorting with harlots, and Wolsey was on a mission to close the brothels. Father admitted he, himself, had been rather vocal in agreeing to a purge of these intimate young fellows, but now we had worse for they had been replaced by Wingfield, Jernyngham, Weston, and Kingston. Old farts, my father said. At least Wolsey and my father agreed on that. Interestingly, although friends with Carew and Norris, William Carey had not been listed in the complaints and had the sense to distance himself from the trouble.

'Well, Father, I hope this Bessie has a daughter. Then, if Katherine has a son, that harlot can go to devil!'

My father drained his goblet and wiped the wine from his mouth. 'Ah, my dear Nan, ever the optimist.'

I asked him if the meeting would still go ahead between King François and King Henry, and he replied that he was there in France to arrange it, hopefully for the end of June or the beginning of July. With the king absent, my grandfather, as Lord Treasurer, would remain in England as governor.

'And I will see Mother?'

'Yes, and Mary, George, and the Howard clan. Not my mother, though, since she is becoming more insane by the day.'

I threw back my head and laughed. 'Oh, George must have grown so. I have presents for him if you would take them? Ribbon for his garters and two dozen arming pointes.'

'He will like that. At fifteen he is already taller than I and more athletic! He has proved diligent in his studies, is talented at music and is very much like your mother – proud and petulant, but he will grow out of that once he gets a wife.'

I asked if I had any suitors, for I felt desperate to know my future. He beckoned to the page again and held out his goblet. Once filled, he drained it and rose.

'Let us get Mary out of the way first. Now, I must return

to Sir Richard Wingfield. He has been hunting the heron with the king, and no doubt has some interesting gossip.'

He kissed me on both cheeks and as I watched him go, I thought of my dear, darling brother and how much I longed to see him again.

●　●

'Mary – dead? But that is impossible!'

As I put the letter down, the litter swayed causing the queen to hold her side, and wince in discomfort. We were on our way to the Château of Saint Germain-en-Laye for her confinement, and as I sat opposite her with Renée, the princess sat reading, engrossed in some chivalric tale.

'Madame, it is but a rumour,' said Madame d'Assigny, placing her hand on the queen's knee.

'The Princess of Wales is but two years old,' said the queen. She then gave out a piercing cry and slumped forward. As her litter came to a standstill, the ones behind halted too, and Dr du Puy sprang forward producing his smelling salts.

Queen Claude began to sob. 'The baby – I feel quite dreadful!' she cried, as Renée clutched her hand.

'We must stop here at this village,' said the doctor, glancing around, 'here at the Porte de Neuilly, and let the poor queen rest. Quickly, girl, find a house!'

I scrambled out of the litter and ran into the first dwelling I came upon. It appeared dilapidated and poor, and the woman inside shocked as I burst through the wooden door. As my words tumbled out, she wiped her hands on her dirty apron, her eyes wide and her hair dishevelled. As I signalled towards the meagre fire, she poured more water into the iron pot hanging there. By now, Dr du Puy and Madame d'Assigny were half carrying the queen into the house, struggling towards a straw mattress. Guards were placed outside as the commotion had disturbed the villagers, and they hurried to see the cause of the noise.

'Is it coming?' I asked, as beads of sweat formed on the

queen's brow. She shook her head.

'It is not like the other times. But I can barely draw breath, and I have a pain high up – here.' She pointed to the top of her stomach.

'Are you bleeding?' I whispered.

As the other ladies entered carrying velvet cloaks and cushions, the woman in the corner stood transfixed. She had probably never seen such finery, and certainly not in her humble cottage.

'Here, to make the queen more comfortable,' said Gillette, flicking away bits of straw and smoothing down the fine cloaks to lay the queen upon.

Queen Claude clutched my hand tightly as the villagers crowded around the wooden shutters. Dr du Puy slammed them shut, cutting out the light.

For the next two hours, we watched as the queen lay there, breathless, while Dr du Puy listened gravely, an ear to her stomach. As her legs appeared to swell and her head ached, he became more deeply alarmed.

'Where is my François?' Queen Claude turned her head to the doctor.

'We do not know, Madame, for he is sporting six leagues away.'

As he spoke, to my surprise, my father entered, for on hearing the news from the messenger he had ridden out from the court to the village.

'Sir Thomas,' said the queen, trying to raise her head, 'please, tell me, is the Princess Mary dead?'

'No, Madame, I have had no such despatch, and gather she is in the best of health. It is you we are concerned with.'

He stared around in distaste.

'I will find the king, but Madame, you cannot stay here. Artus Goffier has lodgings nearby, and although he has no chimney in his chamber, there is an oven for warmth. Later, if you are strong enough, you must be conveyed by water to Saint-Germain-en-Laye in a closed barge. If not, you must remain at his house.'

He then fumbled in his leather pouch and turned. 'You, woman, for your trouble.'

She stared vacantly at the gold écu in her palm. I am not sure she knew that the Queen of France lay before her.

By nightfall, the queen lay sleeping on a soft bed with pillows of down at the house of the *grand-maître* of France. Rumours flew back to the court that she had died, then delivered a girl, but she lived, and soon appeared out of danger. The following day, Dr du Puy felt she was recovered enough to travel, and as we slowly sailed down the river, we still felt terrified she might yet lose the child.

Three days later, on the last day of March, Queen Claude gave France another fair-haired prince. The only blemish appeared to be a disease of the eye which had occurred with her other babies. As to the birth, since she had employed the best matrons in the land to assist, banishing the doctors from her sight, it had proceeded smoothly. King François did not return until later, for on the evening of the Feast of the Annunciation he had ridden out some eight leagues to hunt. He was overjoyed at the news, and my mother wrote to tell me that while King Henry was outwardly pleased, inside he was devastated, knowing that his manhood had become a joke throughout Europe. When asked to be godfather to the child, he petulantly refused unless it was named after him. Queen Claude agreed to name the babe Henry, Duke of Orléans.

When Marguerite fell ill, King François, terrified it might be contagious, ensured his sister did not visit his wife or baby. Fortunately, Marguerite recovered and was eventually able to see both and bring her gift of a golden cup. As to the christening, on his mother's advice, the king postponed it until the babe's eye had improved. My father, in his role as ambassador, would act as sponsor, and wrote from Poissy, a league from St Germaine, to say that Wolsey had sent one hundred pounds to pay for the nurse, the rockers and gentlewomen of the queen's privy chamber. When the christening did take place, my father presented to the queen, in King Henry's name, the salt, the cup and the layer of gold, which were much praised. King François was greatly pleased and said whenever it should be the king's fortune to have a prince, he would be glad to do for him in like manner. It was a generous gift indeed.

•   •

We remained at the château of Saint-Germain-en-Laye throughout April and into May, enjoying a late Easter Sunday while the queen recovered from the birth. King François, sporting his new beard, proved very attentive and gave his wife an exquisite cloak lined with mink, and a pair of purple velvet, jewel-encrusted slippers. A solemn procession ensued in honour of the queen's safe delivery, attended by the king and his mother, and as the ecclesiastics carried the Holy Cord with which Our Lord was bound to the pillar, we proceeded to the chapel to place it on the high altar.

When the king later informed the queen that Madeleine de la Tour had died in Italy, two weeks after giving birth to a little girl named Catherine, we were all shocked. When her husband died, too, within a matter of weeks, the queen wept at the thought of the orphaned child. As I recalled how jealous I had been of Madeleine, I felt ashamed, for we could never know what the future holds. But further bad news followed when we heard that the daughter of Françoise had also died. Sick with grief and inconsolable, even the king could not comfort his mistress. Was this God's punishment to her for taking the king away from his wife?

Some days later, we were listening to a new setting for the *Magnificat,* in the cool of Louise's private chamber. Her eyes were closed in ecstasy, and Marguerite's were moist with tears as the voices of the singers filled the air. The queen watched as I arranged the May blossoms in a large, golden jug and the hot sunshine poured through the open windows. As I cut the sprigs and handed them to Marie Darcille, I recalled my father mentioning that Thomas Wolsey had written to him to say that the king was considering appointing my father either treasurer or controller at court. However, although my father had asked Wolsey to sue for him, he feared he might not gain either due to Wolsey perceiving some fault in him. Concerned, my father told the king he only wished to serve him, and that he would never ask for a higher place if he could gain either, for, unlike the proud Howards, he had no further ambitions. He had told Wolsey that if being in France was a hindrance, he would return immediately and Wolsey would always have his support. However, having the French king's ear, he stood in a position to do much good for the cardinal if he would do the same for him.

As I stood wondering if Wolsey believed him, the king entered, his fool Triboulet padding behind. King François looked dreadful – unshaven and heavy-eyed. He mopped the back of his neck and loosened the collar of his shirt in the heat. Something appeared to be wrong. Louise put her hand up to stop the singers, and as they bowed low, music sheets in their hands, we ladies rose and curtsied.

'Is it true, my son?' Louise glanced at Antoinette de Polignac.

The king sat down and pinched his closed eyes. He shook his head sadly as the queen moved to his side and laid a comforting hand on his shoulder. As his fool settled at his feet, the king raised his bloodshot eyes to his wife. He had not slept.

'I can make a noble,' he said, his fingers over hers, 'but only God can create an artist. Yes, it is true. The man I called 'Father', my dear Leonardo, died at Cloux, on the second day of May.'

The queen stared in disbelief as we all crossed ourselves, and the king continued.

'He had been struggling with shortness of breath for some while, but when he began to gasp, he knew that his end could not be far off. At sixty-seven, he was a very old man, and since he had studied the human heart many times, he knew that his own was failing. His pupil and assistant, Giovanni Melzi, remained with him and when he summoned Father Guillaume, the Master insisted on kneeling by his bed to make his confession. Knowing that the end was near, a servant rode to find me, but the news did not reach me in time, and I only arrived at Amboise the following morning, having exhausted a relay of horses over the forty-eight leagues of the journey.'

Louise moved forward and offered him a goblet of wine, which he emptied. She returned to her chair and gazed out of the window, fanning herself. The heat today seemed to be one of many things that irritated her.

'Go on,' murmured the queen.

'When I arrived, I knelt, devastated, for hours, covering his cold, stiff hand with endless tears and kisses. The most brilliant light in the firmament has been extinguished, for there has never been a man born in the world who knew as much as Leonardo. I will honour his wish to be buried at St Florentin's church, in Amboise.'

Louise stood up. 'Oh, really, François,' she said, sighing in irritation, 'what will become of my Romorantin project now?'

I felt horrified by her callous response and paused, jug in hand.

Her son rose, pushing Triboulet away with his foot, and turned away to the fireplace. His eyes were full of tears for his mother's words had saddened him. When he finally spoke, his voice sounded choked. 'Leonardo once said, "I thought I was learning to live, but I was only learning to die." Well, I am losing all my friends, for now, my tutor and *grand-maître*, Artus, has died and thus Bonnivet has lost his brother.'

'My half-brother, René,' said Louise, lowering her fan, 'can be the only choice to replace him. But really, what of Romorantin?'

'I will apply the plans to Chambord instead,' replied her son, his voice weary.

'But –'

'And that is my final word.'

*   *

It was a boy – a beautiful, healthy boy.

Sitting on a stone seat in the open gallery, Bonny at my feet, I stared at the words in front of me. A cool breeze wafted through the stone arches and proved a welcome relief from the heat.

The letter had come from my sister, who wrote that Father had received secret confirmation that King Henry had visited Elizabeth Blount and his new son at the Priory of St Lawrence, at Blackmore, near Chelmsford, in Essex. This was the 'Jericho' that I had heard of long ago, where the king liked to conduct his affairs, not far from the beautiful residence of Newhall. I knew my father had sold the property to the king four years previously, and with its extensive hunting grounds, the king had paid handsomely for it. However, Mary wrote that although Father had heard news of the birth from Wolsey, who was to be godfather, it would not be officially reported. It was not even commented on at the French court, and I suspected it might have had something to do with the imminent elections for the imperial crown. After all, the child had been conceived in adultery – hardly the action of a Christian prince.

Mary went on to write that the boy had been given the surname of Fitzroy, and the king now spent his days hunting in Essex, happy that this finally proved he could sire a healthy, male child. I thought how sad that the bells could not ring out in celebration, followed by banquets and jousts, and how although the king must have been elated, he could not share his joy with the world – or his wife.

I read that Bessie would not be allowed to return to court, but would be married off to some rich noble as soon as possible. Mary thought the whole matter very exciting, for the king would be forever beholden to her. As the mother of his son, she would have manors and riches for life. I thought Mary was naïve to think Bessie would be of any further interest. No, Bessie would be quickly forgotten, for she had given the king the proof he wanted. What more use could she be?

As to Queen Katherine, Mary found her kind, if not rather opinionated, and described how she was no longer attractive, but short and dowdy and forever on her knees. Her lovely, golden hair had turned dull, but her fresh complexion and grace gave her an immense dignity of bearing. She appeared much older than the king, but he still seemed genuinely fond of her, and they enjoyed riding out together. She also wrote that our mother seemed content to have her and George at court and that she and William Carey were very happy. She told of how she had been singled out to dance for the queen, and Katherine was so impressed she had asked her to entertain the king at the next banquet. All in all, she had made a very good start, and many were impressed by her talent, sweet nature and manners. Even the king thought her charming and frequently spoke with her. I bet he did. The only person who found her irritating was George.

I screwed the letter up in my hand in frustration and threw it down. Bonny patted it playfully with her paw. Why did everything always turn out right for Mary, no matter how she behaved? I gazed out onto the shimmering parkland and sighed, for I knew I must return shortly to the dull Queen Claude. She wished to play a game of boules, and I was to make up the number of players. As I picked the discarded letter up off the gravel, a group of gentlemen, their hunting dogs at their heels, rounded the stone pillar. One of them took off his bonnet and bowed.

'Mistress Anne, good afternoon to you.'

'Is it?' I asked, as Clément picked up my excited dog before she was eaten alive by the others.

As he tickled her chin he waved his friends on. 'I will join you later!'

'I suppose I must congratulate you,' I said, rising and taking Bonny abruptly from him. She was mine, not his. 'You have achieved that which you have so long yearned for.'

'Thank you. I am honoured beyond words to be appointed Marguerite's new secretary.'

'Well, you had better find the words since that is why she has employed you.'

There was a moment's pause.

'I am fortunate, Anne, for my persistence and optimism has paid off. Let us say that good hope patiently fed me in the forest of long waiting.' He replaced his bonnet and smiled expectantly.

'I would rather not,' I said, unsmiling.

'Then tell me, Anne, have you read my *petite epistre au roy*? I believe it led to my appointment.'

'I have glanced at it,' I said, grudgingly. 'It was written to appeal to the benevolence of the king.'

'Of course,' he said, 'for I, the poor rhymer, the plaintive and even supplicant, must naturally place the king in a position of superiority.'

'I have also read your poem in praise of Marguerite. A beautiful flower, indeed.'

'And?'

'It shows some virtuosity, but both are – sycophantic.'

'Praise, indeed,' said Clément, with a faint smile.

We began walking across the gravel in silence just as the queen, Louise, and the other ladies came into view. I waved at Mary as she trotted behind, holding a blue sun canopy over the queen.

'Have you thought much more about that Luther fellow?' I put Bonny down and watched her as she ran towards the group. 'I hear his writings have reached Paris.'

'If there is anyone left alive to read them,' said Clément. 'The sickness there has been overwhelming since April.

Anyway, the pope is refusing to listen to him, and he will be excommunicated if he's not careful. It is not a breach he wishes, but he still seeks to modify all that is against the teachings in the New Testament. He has been warned that he may be called to Rome to account for himself.'

'I gather,' I replied, 'that a German Catholic, Johann Eck, is championing the pope's cause.'

Clément smiled. 'Then you know as much as I do.'

'Tell me, sir, do you talk much with Madame de Châtillon?'

'Why?' he asked.

'It has been noticed how outspoken she has become on religious matters. She says that Louise plans to make a saint out of Brother Francis de Paule. Affronted, she asked how Louise could do that since he wasn't even a priest. It has caused something of a stir.'

'Louise can do it because she will pay the tax to the pope and thus buy Brother Francis his sainthood. Erasmus scoffs at such prayers to saints and relics as does Madame de Châtillon. But she should take care of her tongue, as should the Duchess of Nemours. The duchess may be Louise's half-sister, but that will not save her.'

'Well, *I* believe in them,' I said. 'I prayed for my life to the Blessed Virgin when I once crossed the Narrow Seas in a storm.'

'Indeed, and those prayers reached her ears, for you are safe here. Now, forgive me, Anne, I must catch up with my companions to complete a bet, and then I am for the cooler shade of the garden to write. Look – the queen is waiting for you.'

He bowed and made to kiss my hand, but I only turned away to join the ladies.

•   •

It was a bitter blow. On St Thomas's day, after a great thunderstorm, letters reached Louise, informing her that King

Charles of Spain had been elected Emperor Charles V, King of the Romans, at Frankfurt, on the twenty-eighth day of June. François had not yet returned from Melun, just outside Paris, where he had been hunting that fortnight past, and although publicly his mother expressed her congratulations at Charles' election, my father said she would have had any other emperor than him. It was true, for as poor Bonnivet and Fleuranges stood uneasily before her, she stormed up and down the audience chamber, incandescent with rage. She was most angry with Fleuranges, for, as Marshal of France, he had failed miserably on his mission to Germany. The queen sat quivering as he explained how, due to the plague, the electors had pushed through the decision as quickly as possible, and that they had had no choice but return to France. When he had the audacity to say that no-one in Germany had wanted her son and that King Henry had thrown in his hand at the last minute, Louise became apoplectic. Bonnivet bravely stepped in saying that the English gold angels could no more work miracles than the gold crowns of the sun, and that no-one wanted the king of England either. Sadly, neither comment pacified Louise.

When King François did finally return, he tried to save face, muttering to Marguerite the understatement that he did not like the result. But she had her own concerns having just heard that Bonnivet had ridden off to the baths in Plombières, in the hope of a cure from the dreaded 'French Disease.'

To the queen's dismay, no sooner had the king returned than he left to hunt again in the forests of Fontainebleau with Françoise and his close friends, leaving his mother to deal with the outcome of the election. She had spent vast sums of money in bribes, and in opposing Charles, her son had made an implacable enemy. Now, she had the enmity of the people too, and the Venetian ambassador wrote that the king and his mother were universally hated for they had begged, borrowed and plundered in every direction. When objections were raised about the taxes, the result was hanging or flogging. Poor Queen Claude appeared horrified, but there was nothing she could do except pray and beg for leniency.

On a personal level, I was glad to hear that Charles had named his 'very dear lady and aunt' as governess of the Low Countries. Margaret of Savoy had served him well, and through all her trials and tribulations, she now reigned supreme once more in Mechelen. I felt immense pride in having served such an honest, noble lady.

The Loire

Back at Blois, the magnificent new wing with its astounding spiral staircase stood almost complete and added much space and light to King Louis' old château. Its construction was a marvel of Italian taste and skill, its beautiful stone carved balconies lit at night by flaming torches. I spent many a day assisting the queen as she superintended the formation of the gardens to match the building's splendour. She did not want to modify them, but rather to keep them the same as she recalled in her childhood, just as her parents knew them, with divided layers for flowers or herbs. Her great love was the fruit trees, and she loved to supervise the picking of fruit, which she found indispensable to her health. However, she took as much care of the artichokes as the apples and grapes.

As I held the various plants that were to be potted, Renée carried the soil for the beds in a pail, back and forth, along the path. I watched fascinated as flowerbeds of interlacing patterns – designed to be seen from small, raised mounds – were dug out and filled with favourite flowers such as blue irises and roses. Sometimes Marguerite, carrying a silk canopy against the sun, would join us and she proved very knowledgeable on plants. She insisted that flowers must not only be cultivated for their attractiveness, but for their use as flavourings for food. She particularly adored violets.

In the cooler evenings, as we walked beneath the shade of the orange trees, she spoke to me of books, poetry and religious matters, including Luther. Thanks to Clément, I was able to hold an intelligent conversation and surprise her with my knowledge of his controversial theses. I felt absolute joy in her company as we meandered together across the new terraces, our little dogs trotting behind. I resented it when *Madame la Grande* decided to join us, for I wanted Marguerite's attention all to myself, and I knew *Madame* would not agree with our religious opinions.

• •

As the summer turned to a riot of gold autumn leaves, the vineyards bustled with activity, and the harvests were gathered in. That September, before the Feast of Michaelmas, the king had yet another accident when a branch hit his head while he was out hunting, almost blinding him. It was more than the queen could bear. She had not felt well again, and with her husband recovering in his chamber, Louise in bed with gout and herself sick, the Feast of the Assumption passed quietly. However, once recovered, all three hosted the Venetian ambassador, and King François took deliberate pleasure in showing off his children. Much was made of the happy family scene and news of it must have made King Henry sick to his heart, for King François had been blessed with two fine boys and a girl. Henry's sister, the dowager French queen, had just delivered another little girl, Eleanor, and now she and the duke had three children. My Uncle Howard too, had just been given a daughter, called Mary.

When we heard the news that King Henry had decided to give his illegitimate son a large household of his own – far more lavish and expensive than that of his daughter – we were somewhat shocked. Poor Queen Katherine complained, and the king stormed off in anger, dismissing three of her Spanish ladies to punish her. It was a dreadful way to behave.

As the days wore on, it also became apparent that the meeting between King François and King Henry would not take place this summer after all, which was a disappointment, for I longed to see my mother again. Wolsey wrote impatiently to my father saying he must stop dragging his heels, speak sharply to the *grand-maître* and the king's council, and hurry the affair along. My father was not pleased with the rebuke.

When the Bishop of Limoges died unexpectedly in his chamber, the court quickly moved to Amboise. The English ambassador present informed King François that, to be on the safe side, the sending and receiving of any gifts to England was banned, for fear of contagion. He also informed Queen Claude that Queen Katherine had insisted that her husband shave off his beard, although the two monarchs had sworn a solemn oath not to remove them until they met. King François was most affronted to hear that the queen had daily made great complaint against it, and desired Henry to put it off for her sake. To calm matters, Louise hurriedly stepped in replying that the King of England had a greater affection for her son than any man living and that their love was not in their beards but their hearts. Such words of diplomacy could not have been matched, even by my father.

On the tenth day of December, fearful that the sickness might yet reach Amboise, the royal party decided to journey southwest, fifty leagues to Cognac. As the childhood home of King François and Marguerite, it was held in great affection, and as our barge sailed down the Loire on a damp, winter's day, they sat together sharing some great joke with Bonnivet and the Duc d'Alençon. It was rare that her husband accompanied her on such journeys, but this time he had insisted. As to Bonnivet, the waters at Plombières had worked, for he appeared in fine spirits again, and I wondered if that was why the duc had decided to accompany his wife – to keep an eye on them both. Whatever had occurred previously – and no-one knew for certain – Marguerite was not able to hold any grudge against Bonnivet, and besides, her brother relied too much on his good counsel. She knew better than to come between them, but she was not thrilled by the company of her husband. Meanwhile, the queen sat with Louise and the two dwarfs, Marie and Cosima, wrapped in mink furs, for although the queen had been advised to stay behind, she had wanted to accompany her husband. Renée stroked my little dog, perched on her knee, and waved to the curious villagers standing on the banks of the river beneath the steel grey sky. As I turned around, I saw Françoise. Her husband had been sent away on yet another diplomatic mission and she appeared pale and subdued as she sat with the other ladies. No doubt the loss of her daughter still grieved her.

Our first stop was Chambord, three leagues from Blois, to inspect the building progress and although still a construction site, it was clear that the finished château would be one of exquisite taste – and unimaginable expense. The recent rain had turned it into a site too muddy to walk through – even on wooden planks – but I could still see that when finished, it would be the largest château in the Loire, with over four hundred chambers.

After the king and his sister had spoken with the master builder, we continued our journey down the river. There had been talk of staying at Loches, as the guest of the Comte de Chalon, and I was relieved when it was decided against for I did not want to be in his company again. Instead, we sailed down the River Vienne and arrived at Châtellerault. There we spent Christmas, hosted by the Duc de Bourbon, for the king wished to enjoy the superb hunting on his estates and the best wine cellars in France. Renée appeared to have a permanent smile on her face, for she had developed a fierce passion for the handsome duc, and he, in turn, paid court to her. When we departed, I had great hopes for the coming year, for the meeting between King François and King Henry was now to take place in June, and I would finally see my family.

Chapter Fifteen

*'The first point of wisdom is to discern
that which is false.'*

South-west France, 1520

As we entered the magnificent château of Admiral Bonnivet, four leagues from Poitiers, on a cold St Genevieve's day, Mary Fiennes asked 'Greenwich?' The courtiers began their usual scrabble for accommodation, each hoping to grab the best chambers. However, this imposing edifice had more chambers than days in the year, and so could easily house the travelling court. Work had only begun four years previously, but now almost complete, it boasted a grand, central staircase adorned with sculpted decoration in the Italian style.

'Help me,' said Mary, the heavy furs slipping from her arms to the floor.

'But why did my sister not confide in me?' I asked as we knelt together, gathering up the pelts. 'Apparently, she and William were secretly promised before any formal agreement had even been reached. They were already sweethearts.'

'Well, what did you expect?' said Mary, 'You were hardly charitable towards her. Why should she tell you anything?'

'It is not fair,' I said, 'not only is she to marry him on the fourth day of February, in the presence of the king, but she is happy with him.'

We hurriedly stood to one side as people pushed by.

'She always manages to get out of trouble,' I said, 'like a cat with nine lives. How does she do it?'

Mary gave a slight shrug. 'Perhaps because she is a kind, sweet girl, Anne.'

'Meaning?'

'Nothing.'

'Apparently, Mary, she is to wear a new robe of silver damask lined with crimson velvet *and* new slippers to match.'

'How wonderful,' said Mary.

'No, it isn't,' I said, curtsying low, as Louise, hobbling from her gout, and *Madame la Grande,* walked past.

'Well, the king would be expected to be present, being a kinsman,' said Mary, her voice muffled behind the furs.

'Only distantly.'

'You said William descended from King Edward. I thought you enjoyed such pomp.'

'Well, I would if it were me, but it's not me. It's *her* and she doesn't deserve it.'

At that moment, a group of ambassadors appeared through the crowd.

'Still sulking, Anne?' asked my father, brightly, as he strode past, a large sheaf of papers beneath his arm. I bobbed as Mary giggled.

'*And* I am not allowed to attend the ceremony,' I added, as we followed behind him. 'I have to stay here to tend to the queen.'

'Is she sick?'

'No, Mary, but she has missed this month's course – again.'

'Mother of God, no. That poor girl. I swear the king will be the cause of her death. Has she not done enough?'

As we entered the queen's chamber and silently unpacked her gowns from the baskets, Marguerite told her how she and her brother would be visiting the faculty of theology at the university when they reached Poitiers. She was hoping to distract him from the antagonism between Bonnivet and the Duc de Bourbon, for when the king asked Bourbon what he thought of Bonnivet's château, she heard the constable reply that 'the cage was too big for the bird.' When the king claimed the constable was jealous, Bourbon only laughed, saying he could not envy one whose ancestors had once served him. As the tension increased, Louise only watched and bided her time.

● ●

'I just do not understand,' I said, as I stood in the courtyard at Cognac, holding the bridle of the grey horse. 'You have succeeded in arranging the meeting between King François and King Henry near Calais.' I felt cold as I stood in the fine, drizzling rain and watched my father mount.

He checked the papers in his leather despatch bag. 'Wolsey is behind it,' he said, rummaging inside, 'I am sure of it. He has become all-powerful since his appointment as papal legate – basically the pope's representative in England. He told the king I am too cautious and so Sir Richard Wingfield – old-summer-will-be-green – has been instructed to take my place as ambassador here as he is more optimistic. Am I not optimistic? Ah – there it is.'

I was not sure how to reply as he closed the bag.

'As to King Henry, he said he would not be satisfied unless he sent one of his 'trusty and near familiars' in my place to do the business. I thought I *had* proved to be trusty.'

I told him he was too suspicious, for he, of all people, knew that the business of kings could never be trusted to just one man. He said he thought it might be Bonnivet, since he and Wingfield were old friends. But there was something else that put him ill at ease, regarding Wolsey. He had kept my Uncle Howard idle for months, achieving nothing worthwhile since the May Day riots. Then, out of the blue, he had appointed him Lord Lieutenant of Ireland.

'To what end?' I stroked the horse's nose.

He explained it was to settle the dispute between Butler and Kildare. Kildare had quarrelled with Wolsey, and my uncle had to go and restore order. He said the damned country must be either conquered by the sword or governed through the Irish chiefs. It was all very awkward, for on a personal level we still had the family quarrel with Piers Butler, the self-styled Earl of Ormonde.

'That old argument?' I recalled my sister's conversation about this matter. 'It has been dragging on for six years.'

'I am aware of that fact, Nan, but I will not let the matter lie since I have a stronger claim to the title through my mother and her sister. Far more than some warring Irish cousin.'

I said I thought the matter had been resolved, for although Grandfather Butler died without male heirs, was it not stipulated that the title and lands could rightfully go to heirs general – and thus pass to my father, as he said, with the stronger claim?

My father snorted. 'Yes, but it isn't resolved, since Butler has seized lands that are rightfully mine, under Brehon, or Irish law. Unfortunately, Wolsey wants to keep him placated since he is useful to him in Ireland, so God alone knows how it will turn out.'

'But w –'

'It is not your concern, Nan, and I am sure your uncle will come up with something.'

'So when do you leave?' I released the bridle as the horse shook its head.

'Not until late March. I cannot even attend my own daughter's wedding, for when old Wingfield arrives at Calais I must speak with him first and get him up to speed on the situation.' He took up the reins and raising his leg, tightened the girth on his saddle. His horse blew out its sides and shifted position. 'Perhaps they want me back in England for the Emperor Charles' visit to the king and Queen.'

'If he survives the voyage from Spain, for he is such a

feeble boy. I have spoken with him, Father, and he is so *dull*.'

'Yes, so you keep bragging to everyone, but he is not stupid. He is determined to reach the ear of King Henry before King François does, and they are in secret talks as we speak. The emperor knows the great desire of both kings to meet him, for they are hoping to make arrangements which will benefit their subjects.'

He turned his horse about as the rain fell heavier. 'Now, for the love of God, Nan, go inside!' he called, over his shoulder, as he trotted away. 'I must ride with this despatch, but will return later!'

I pulled my cloak close and watched him disappear through the gates of the château. As I gazed up at the grey-stoned turrets, the rain resting on my eyelashes, I realised that although I was not close to my father, I did not want him to leave France. King François had appeared to like him, and although Father could be irritable and cautious, I felt he was respected here at court. As to organising the meeting between her son and King Henry, Louise herself said that he had executed his charge most virtuously. He had persuaded her that Calais would be far more convenient for the meeting, than Paris, and she persuaded her son to agree. That was not a man of little influence.

●   ◦

As I walked, I glanced at the girl sitting on the velvet-clothed saddle, humming a tune to herself. Her ladies followed behind, hoods up against the chill. Renée, wearing a warm riding robe of burgundy wool and a jaunty cap, sat lost in her thoughts as we entered the deer park at Cognac.

I, meanwhile, thought of my sister. Her wedding had not been a grand affair, but the king had graced it with his presence, as had a few of his close friends. However, the chapel at Greenwich Palace, having been rebuilt and newly decorated, proved a splendid setting overlooking the River Thames. Mother wrote that the day had started a little foggy, but once it had lifted, the low, winter sun shone on the wedding party. Mary had appeared quite resplendent in her new robe, carrying a posy of winter violets. She had worn her hair crimped and loose about her shoulders, with pearls woven through the strands. William, sporting a doublet of grey damask decorated with spangles, had a cold and could not stifle his sneezing, which irritated my Uncle Howard. As various aunts flapped about the bride, my brother had appeared very pleased with himself, for he seemed to like William, and saw him now as an older brother. William's family were present, including his sisters, Margaret and Mary – Eleanor and Anne were both nuns at Wilton Abbey and thus could not attend – and his brothers John and Edward stood witness.

Mary undertook to obey her husband, and when William gave her the wedding ring, he declared that he endowed her with all his worldly goods. Mother described the ring as engraved gold, with a small, table ruby – which had greatly pleased Mary – although Mother thought it not of great worth. Typical. I would insist on a large emerald stone, as green as the Irish grass. William had also given Mary a wedding pendant, in the shape of a lozenge with four drop pearls, suspended from a chain of woven links. I had, rather grudgingly, intended sending her a gift of a new pair of gloves, but it would have to wait until the sickness had abated and the ban on sending gifts lifted. The king had made an altar offering of six shillings and eightpence, and afterwards, in one of the chambers, they held a small wedding feast. So – the deed was done. Mother said she had sighed with relief to know that Mary was now William's responsibility, and she could turn her thoughts to finding me a husband.

'Why are you sad, Anne?' asked Renée.

Her voice made me jump and I turned smiling towards her.

'Is it because your father is leaving the court?

'Not at all, princess, I am never sad,' I replied.

She stared solemnly at me, her head to one side.

'Yes, you are, I can tell. But, you do not have to lead me around like a child. I am nearly ten years old.'

'I like to,' I said. 'Now, speak to me in English. I was thinking of my sister, who has just married.'

'I know. I gather your father was very cross at not returning home in time.'

I laughed.

'I am going to marry the Duc de Bourbon,' she said, brushing aside a bare, winter branch.

'Bourbon already has a wife.' I halted the palfrey as Bonny barked at a squirrel. 'And at nearly thirty, he is too old.' I thought for a moment of the serious, reserved constable who imagined slights at every turn. The man of whom King Louis had once said 'stagnant waters frighten me.'

'No, he is not,' said Renée, patting her horse's neck, 'and anyway, she might die.'

'Oh, Princess, that is a wicked thing to say,' I said, trying to hide a smile. 'However, the king has already sent a power to Germany for the conclusion of your marriage to the son of the Marquis of Brandenburgh.'

'Oh.' She was quiet for a moment. 'Is a marquis higher than a duc?'

Nothing ever disturbed this child's sunny nature for long, and she asked me when I was to be betrothed.

'When my parents have negotiated a good match,' I said.

'But I want you to stay here!' she cried.

I smiled at her, for I loved France and the French court but I was not sure if I wanted to be here forever, away from my family. And now my father must return.

'What *is* the matter?' persisted Renée, as my face clouded.

I shook my head. 'Nothing, princess, nothing at all. Now, let me watch you ride ahead and I will walk behind.'

That evening, a great feast had been arranged by Louise to welcome the court to her beloved Cognac. The theme was ancient mythology, and a man dressed as Mercury greeted

Queen Claude. Before long, all the gods on Mount Olympus descended from a mock cloud made of painted paper, wood and wire, and took the hands of Louise, Marguerite, and *Madame la Grande* in a stately pavane. A ballet by nymphs followed, and then – to her utter delight – a giant Apollo carried Renée on his shoulders. After a mock battle, Vulcan announced that there would be fireworks outside on the river, and everyone followed the royal party to the barges. A thousand torches blazed, and each barge had been fashioned into a different sea creature, such as a dolphin, a mermaid or a swan, paddled by several oarsmen. I sat with my father, for this was the last night I would see him before he returned to England, and watched the sky light up with falling sparks of gold, blue and red. The river appeared to be on fire as we sat, our faces illuminated by the glare, enjoying the hot chestnuts.

As the yellow dawn appeared, we said our goodbyes, knowing that the next time we met, in June, we would enjoy a family reunion. I would be able to meet William Carey and see George for the first time in eight years. I might even see Tom Wyatt again and his new wife, for now, they were married. How strange that when we last met, we were just children.

● ●

We were back at Blois by Lady Day, enjoying a warm spring of blue skies and meadows bursting with wildflowers. The nights became gradually longer and lighter, and one evening I was asked to join the queen and a few of her ladies, including Françoise, in the *Salle des Etats*. The Spanish ambassador, Don Prevost, had just finished his audience and as we sat in attendance, the new ambassador, Sir Richard Wingfield, entered. He gave a sweeping bow and knelt before the queen as she sat on her throne beneath a golden canopy. She was now open-laced and very ungainly, but she waved him to his feet with a kind smile, for he appeared to have difficulty rising. Louise, sitting next to her, began by saying how much she valued the friendship of England. Wingfield turned to face her and said he trusted this friendship would continue. Louise replied that matters could not have come in so good a train unless God had put his hand to it and that when the two princes met, they would only act for the weal of Christendom. It was a pretty speech, and we all clapped. But then Louise's demeanour changed. She arose, spread her arms out, and asked if, in truth, Queen Katherine had any true devotion to those present around her. Wingfield appeared a little surprised and answered there could not be a more virtuous or wise princess than the queen, his beloved mistress. Her only comfort in this world was to do the king's will; and, moreover, he considered her to be entirely affectioned to the said assembly and the marriage between Princess Mary and the Dauphin. Louise walked up to him and stared him full in the face. For one dreadful, tense moment, I thought she might slap him. Wingfield, however, kept a pleasant face, but it was clear she was taunting him, for it was well known that Queen Katherine hated France and had done everything in her power to ally England to Spain through her nephew Charles.

To my surprise, Louise then smiled. 'Well, that is good. And is your queen with child yet?'

'Madame, I do not know of such a condition,' replied Wingfield.

'Well, then I trust God to send her fruit in time,' came the reply. 'After all, when your king has a son – or two – they and the dauphin will be brothers.'

It was a strange thing to say, for any hope that the queen might yet have just *one* son was rapidly fading.

'My son,' she continued, 'has consented to delay the interview with King Henry until the last day of May, and hold the tourney on the fourth day of June; but as his queen will be eight months into her pregnancy, he cannot extend it further. As my son agrees to give the *premier honneur* to the

King of England by entering his territories, he hopes he will also be met in a liberal spirit.'

'Madame, such graciousness will be reciprocated in full measure.'

As one of the servants came forward with a tray of wine and wafers, the king burst into the chamber. Louise's face lit up like the sun and the queen rose awkwardly, smiling as he took her hand. He ignored his mistress and threw his bonnet down onto a chair.

'Ah, I wanted to see you, ambassador. I have just returned from the chase. Now, tell me, what do you hunt with in England, spear or crossbow?'

He took a goblet of the proffered wine and drank quickly.

Before Wingfield could straighten up from his reverence, the king proceeded to give a detailed description of the boar hunting in France, comparing his mode of hunting and hawking with that practised in England. Wingfield stood politely listening, and I knew that my father would not have been so patient.

When Louise finally interjected, the king took it in good part and sat in the window seat, his long legs sprawled in front. He apologised for boring the ladies and picked at his nails.

'I have heard, Sir Richard,' said Louise, 'that the interview between King Henry and the Emperor Charles, is to take place *after* that of my son and your king. I am content. With France encircled on three sides by Charles' borders, I need England to stand with me – with my son. However, I am concerned that the meeting with your king and my son is very unpopular with the nobility and people of England. Is that report true?'

'No, Madame, and I can assure you, as will the Duke of Suffolk, that the meeting will take place only *after* your son has met with him. That is for certain.'

'Good,' the king said, looking up. 'I do not want Spain interfering before I have shown my mind to King Henry.

I wish to make him entirely devoted to France. I have your solemn oath on this?'

The ambassador, with hand on heart, gave a bow of his head and turned to Louise. 'Madame, the purpose of my king meeting with your son is to make such an impression of entire love between the two monarchs that the resulting bond can never be dissolved.'

I felt puzzled. That is not what my father had told me. He had said that the emperor was desperate to reach the ear of King Henry first, implying that he would trick King François by breaking the Treaty of Noyen.

'Well,' said Louise, brightly, 'to other matters. Since you have not seen him yet, I wish to present the dauphin to you. He waits in the nursery, along with the Duke of Suffolk. Ladies, please carry my gifts. I have new coifs, coverlets and a woollen dog for my precious grandchild.'

The king remained seated, inspecting his nails again, and as we rose and took the boxes of gifts off the side cupboard, I pondered on the lie I had just heard from the ambassador's lips. Surely, I should say something? As we followed the queen out of the door and across the gallery, I wondered about the man I had not seen for so long and if he would remember me.

When we finally entered the nursery on the other side of the château, the queen held out her hand to the Duke of Suffolk. As he bowed and kissed the diamond ring, I noticed that he appeared to have lost weight, but he was still well-built, with a golden beard and a very fine suit of black velvet. The queen moved to the ornate bed, covered in ermine, where little François lay.

'Hello, my darling,' she said, as Madame Montreuille lifted him.

I curtsied low and wished the duke good-day, a box of gifts in my arms.

'Mistress Anne Boleyn, sir,' I said.

He gazed at me as if I were a bad smell but said nothing.

Could he and his wife still be angry with me after all this time? Either way, I fell affronted at his rudeness. The child, meanwhile, smiled and immediately starting babbling and holding his plump arms out to his mother.

'Madame,' said Wingfield, acknowledging the duke, 'he is as joyous as ever I saw a child.'

'And without blemish,' said Louise, whipping off the child's silk shift so that his pink skin lay quite bare.

'I can see, your highness,' said Wingfield, 'he is as fair a babe as can be, and as large for his age.'

'As is his brother,' said Queen Claude, proudly smoothing her baby's hair.

The Duke of Suffolk nodded in approval.

'Now, Sir Richard,' said Louise, taking the babe in her arms, 'if you would go with the duke here to discuss business, I will speak to you again at supper. I wish to amuse my grandchild for a while...'

As they both filed out, I lingered a little. Louise picked up a bone rattle from the table and stared at me.

'Yes?' she said. 'Is there something you wish to say?'

I asked where I should put the gifts, and she waved to the table. 'Now, all of you go, please.'

The ladies trotted out.

As I watched her turn away, Françoise took my arm, and we left the nursery together.

'What is the matter, Anne?' she asked. I said it was nothing, but she was not convinced.

'Something has upset you,' she said.

'I hate that man.'

'Which one now?'

I replied Suffolk. I cared naught for Sir Richard Wingfield.

'And that is your complaint, the cause of your sullen face?' she asked.

'No, Madame, it concerns the visit of the emperor.'

'To François?'

'To King Henry.'

'And what have you heard?' she whispered, with a mischievous grin.

'Madame, my father tells me that the emperor is bent on seeing King Henry before King François, not the other way round.'

'When does he plan this?'

'I am not sure, but very soon, for he is intent on visiting England on his return from Spain, under the pretext of visiting his aunt whom he has never met. King Henry is in full agreement.'

'Oh, I bet he is,' she replied, with a slight smile. 'What exactly did your father say?'

I told her that when King Henry wrote to King François to desire him to defer the time of the interview, he took great care not to disclose the real reason; Father said he must not know the state of friendship between the emperor and himself and the thing must be kept as secret as possible. King Henry desired to see the emperor above all things and please Queen Katherine, who daily prayed to God for the meeting. She was desperate for a Spanish alliance, and still wielded some influence with her husband.

'But England is betrothed to France through Princess Mary,' said Françoise, 'What harm can Katherine do?'

'Madame, my father tells me that King Henry will offer the princess to the emperor instead.'

'That I do not believe, Anne,' said Françoise, as we walked.

'Madame, I can assure you that Wingfield has not played straight with King François. My father would have told him the truth.'

'Then he is a poor diplomat,' she said, taking me over to the window. 'A diplomat tells a foreign king only what he thinks he should know.'

We gazed out at the courtyard and watched the king striding across the cobbles with his companions, his dogs gathered about his feet.

'Six years ago I would have informed Louise,' I said, as she waved. The king blew her a kiss. 'I would not have been able to resist the urge to –'

'*Mêler,*' interrupted Françoise.

'Madame, I have no desire to meddle, but while I am at this court, I still wish to be of use to Louise. Should I not tell her what I know?'

'To what end? If it is in the hope of favours, it did not work well for you last time. If to feel of some importance…'

'Both, I suppose, although I must admit my wish to ingratiate myself is now overcome by caution.'

'Then praise be to God, for you have finally grown wise,' she smiled, squeezing my arm. 'You know as well as I that Louise is dangerous. She will not thank you for information she did not ask for. Besides, we cannot stop the emperor meeting King Henry first, so there is no point in telling her.'

'Perhaps,' I shrugged. 'But at least Louise would know that Wingfield is not trustworthy.'

'I expect she already does, Anne, for who knows what your father has said? Is that what is eating you up, the fact that your father has been replaced by him?'

I glared at her. 'No,' I lied. 'Will you tell the king, Madame?'

She shook her head. 'Not I, for there is nothing to be gained by it.'

No, not for her family, I thought.

'But as to the meeting, Anne, we can only trust that King Henry will not listen to any proposal prejudicial to France.' She halted and looked at me. 'How old are you now?'

'Almost twenty, Madame.'

'*Twenty.* My goodness, I am surprised that your family has left you here for so long, unlike your sister. I hear that she has married quite satisfactorily.' She leant in close and whispered. 'You are right not to speak of what you know. Keep your own counsel and be discreet. Now, I must join the king at the stables and help him choose which Neapolitan horses are to be given as gifts to the English nobles.'

I watched as she walked away, wishing she had not mentioned my sister. I was sure she was just as glad to see the back of Mary as I was, but I still disliked Françoise's air of condescension. As to meddling, it was all very simple. Sir Richard Wingfield had taken my father's place, and I did not like him. If I did tell Louise all I knew he would have to explain himself, and that would not bode well. Not well at all.

• •

Having celebrated Easter at Blois the court – apart from Marguerite who had returned to her estate near Alençon with her husband – travelled four days to Paris, to the château at Montreuil, for Whitsun, where the preparations for the meeting between François and Henry now continued in earnest. As I sat on my bed, grooming my dog, the door of the chamber burst open.

'Quickly, we have been asked to attend Claude immediately!' cried Mary Fiennes, her eyes wide.

'Whatever is it?' I jumped up.

'It has finally arrived – the most beautiful stuff you have ever seen. Oh, Anne! We are to have the most exquisite gowns made for the meeting.'

I closed the door, leaving Bonny scratching frantically behind, and as we hurried down the gallery, my rose silk gown rustled with every step. Beautiful gowns never ceased to entice me, and as we entered the *grande salle*, a steady queue of seamstresses brought forth bales of silk, sarcenet, damask, and velvet. I watched as the billowing gauze and tissue were thrown over the long trestle tables, and could not believe my eyes. Louise had insisted that we outdo the English court in dress, and so thirteen bales of cloth of gold were also carried in and spread out across the trestles. There were also charts showing the order of procession, and drawings of all the chariots and litters. It would be the most spectacular event ever witnessed, and every moment brought me closer to seeing my family.

Queen Claude sat on a raised chair dangling her feet and perusing the sketches and drawings held in her hands. Marie Darcille, standing on a box behind, peered over her shoulder as the queen's embroiderer, Monsieur Bernard, stood to one side holding a card of colourful silk threads.

'Ah, there you are,' she said, smiling, as we curtsied.

Next to the queen stood the *grand-maître*, a sheaf of papers in his hands. The latest numbers for the queen's train were nearly two thousand persons, including chaplains and bishops, and around eight hundred horses. No wonder he appeared exhausted. Diane de Brézé handed a sample of velvet to Madame d'Assigny, who took the cloth of purple and rubbed her fingers across its luxurious pile.

'I'm afraid,' the queen said, 'that my robe will have to be loose to accommodate my ever-expanding girth! How wonderful that my beautiful François is designing it himself.'

'Madame, you will look every inch a true queen,' said Anne de Graville, as we murmured our approval.

'Anne,' said the queen, glancing up at me. 'You must act as my interpreter. I hear Queen Katherine is bringing twenty-five gentlewomen and just over three thousand others in her train, and it is imperative I do not forget the ladies' titles and insult them.'

'Of course, Madame,' I said. 'I will check the lists myself, and I will also mark those who require special attention, for it is as well to know who is deaf, short-sighted or dull!'

I thought of how proud my mother would be to see me in such an important position.

'Exactly,' said the queen, 'and I expect Queen Katherine will also be making frantic notes of who is who. But tell me, sir, what of gifts?'

'Majesty,' said the *grand-maître*, 'your husband has arranged for you to present Queen Katherine with a litter of cloth of gold lined with sables, along with mules and pages.

Madame Louise is to give Cardinal Wolsey a jewelled crucifix worth six thousand crowns, and your husband is to give him gold vases amounting to twenty thousand crowns. I have to add that I do fear the cost will be ruinous.'

'Not *more* taxes?' asked the queen.

I hated to see her enthusiasm squashed.

Madame d'Assigny walked over to the plans on the trestles and perused them. With a total French retinue of five thousand, yes, there would be a heavy price to pay, a burden to the poor. She turned around, her brow furrowed. 'Majesty, none of this expense was desired by your husband,' she said, almost apologising.

'That is true, Madame,' said the *grand-maître*. 'He wished to save what money is left in the treasury for his future campaigns, and wrote to King Henry that they should meet as equals, in private, without needless cost and ceremony. However, King Henry, encouraged by Wolsey, wishes to dazzle your husband and felt insulted that by suggesting so little an effort, he held King Henry in low esteem. King François – encouraged by his mother – has no choice but to match the show. If he does not, France will look the poorer.'

Queen Claude turned back to the plans. 'The burden always falls on the poor,' she said, 'but at least the destruction of so many buildings by the recent storm has led to the availability of wood for fires. Do you see how God cares for his creatures? Oh, but perhaps I should not wear such an expensive gown.'

'Madame,' said the *grand-maître*, 'you are to represent France in all its wealth and glory, as Madame Louise insists. It is expected of you. Besides, you are not the cause of the expense. It is the other ridiculous constructions that are bleeding the treasury dry. But, we must leave the matter to Baron Semblançay. He always manages to find the money.'

'Well, it is too late now,' said Madame de Tournon. 'Pavilions, statues, tents – even a chapel are to be erected. I hear King Henry is bringing over a palace constructed of oiled canvas, wood, and glass, to be reassembled on-site, near the ruined castle of Guînes. In front of the archway, a magnificent thirteen-foot, tiered fountain is to spout claret, and behind the castle, a nine-hundred-foot tiltyard has been built. Not to be outdone, your husband has charged Monsieur Galliot de Genouillac to erect a sixty-foot high tent in gold and silver, furnished with turkey carpets, and a life-size statue of St Michael, carved in walnut. What you wear will be but a fraction of the cost.'

I caught Mary's eye, and we smiled. I cared not a jot for the treasury, and neither frankly did she, just so long as we had our beautiful new gowns to attract the young men.

The queen smiled. 'Then so be it. But what about the food and wine? Thousands of people over two weeks of festivities need feeding. How will it be organised?

'With tickets, Madame,' said the *grand-maître*, 'since security will be a problem, although all vagabonds are to be banned on pain of hanging. The problem of accommodation is being dealt with, as we speak, and over three hundred tents are in the process of construction at Tours. The timber will be transported from Rouen, by packhorse, to the site and those who cannot find accommodation – well, too bad, they must sleep in haystacks.'

The queen let out a laugh and then realised he was serious. 'Well, I must ensure all my ladies have their signed passes, too. I do not want any embarrassment occurring should they be stopped.'

'Madame, I can assure you, everything has been thought of, and Admiral Bonnivet will outdo all that Cardinal Wolsey has devised.'

'It does sound splendid,' said the queen, 'and, I agree, we must look our finest. Now, I wish to have my closest ladies in green and white, to honour the English king. There will be several changes of gown, but I want those ladies around me to be of the same colour and hue. The other noble ladies may wear whatever they wish, depending on their status.'

The *grand-maître* appeared to stifle a yawn, for he had little interest in women's fashion and he had much to organise. Seeing his face, Claude kindly dismissed him.

The seamstresses continued scribbling their notes as more cloth arrived and Mary and I, along with the other ladies present, helped to unroll the bales. The queen then rose and with Madame d'Asigny's assistance began pinning notes to the various colours.

I smiled at Mary as we unfurled the silver tissue and crimson velvet.

'I cannot believe we have been here seven years,' I said. 'The English court will seem so strange. As to King Henry, I wonder if he will remember seeing me at Lille when I served Margaret of Savoy?'

'I doubt it, Nan, but it will be interesting seeing all the people we have heard so much about over the years. People like Queen Katherine and Cardinal Wolsey, and of course, our families.'

'They say, Mary, that there is a new world in England, a sobriety after the purge of boisterous, young courtiers from the court. I hope there are some young men left. Who knows – there might even be the chance of a romantic flirtation. I would very much like to see how they compare to Frenchmen.'

'From what we have seen, they appear to have coarser manners and are careless with their cleanliness,' she replied. 'Anyway, I doubt we will get the chance to leave the queen's side. But I do intend to have some fun.'

'Then so do I,' I whispered. 'So do I ...'

●　●

By the middle of May, the court had left Paris and continued north through rain and storms. The rivers lay swollen and the tracks muddy, as the litter carrying Queen Claude swayed and lurched from side to side. As the mules stumbled and brayed, Renée rode her horse next to mine, and

we discussed the coming celebrations. She was upset to see
the poor ragged folk picking through the broken remains of
houses devastated by the storm. They had lit small fires, but
in the damp there remained only dwindling wood smoke.

As our cavalcade slowly ambled past in silence, I became
aware of the grumbling, and even the sight of their 'Good
Queen Claude,' could not cheer the people. None ran out
as they used to, with pies, milk and home-made gifts, but
instead stood sullen-faced in the spitting rain, arms folded
tight around their chests to keep warm.

Arriving at the Château de Rambures, the queen
appeared quite unsettled, and we hurried her inside to the
warmth to rest. Such travelling when pregnant was not easy
but she had no choice. Besides, she was looking forward to
meeting Queen Katherine, although she knew her condition
would cause her rival distress. If only Queen Katherine could
greet her with a full belly, too.

While the queen slept, the king disappeared with
Françoise to enjoy a day's riding in the forest of Crécy-
en-Ponthie. On his return, he held a meeting in his
bedchamber with all the great personages of the realm
assembled, including Sir Richard Wingfield. Louise stood
by the king's side, gazing steadily at the company, while
four ladies, including myself and Françoise, remained apart.
The king informed the audience that he had been advised
of King Henry's departure from his manor at Greenwich,
and his progress towards Dover. En route, the Archbishop
of Canterbury, William Warham, had entertained the king
and his vast party at his beautiful palace at Charing, on the
banks of the River Medway, in my home county of Kent.
The king – like his father before – loved the palace so much,
he wanted it for himself, but the land lay under the control of
the priory at Canterbury. This appeared to be one palace he
could not possess. As I thought of the meadows of Kent filled
with swooping skylarks, cowslips, forget-me-nots and daisies,
I felt nostalgic for England. Of course, France was beautiful,

but Kent still held a special place in my heart.

King François said that he intended to outdo the archbishop, and entertain the English king as 'the prince of the world whom he esteemed, loved and trusted above all.' He urged his nobles to receive the English in a friendly manner and avoid bringing any evil-advised persons to the momentous meeting. He was about to leave the chamber when a messenger appeared, and kneeling handed the king a letter. He stood to read it, then raised his hand to stop the murmuring and called Wingfield to him. His pleasant expression had turned cold.

'So, the emperor landed in England after all. You assured me that they would only meet *after* I had met King Henry. Is that not so?'

'Majesty,' said Wingfield, 'I am at a loss what to say and can only relate that which I was a party to. I am sure that nothing he or his council asked of King Henry was of importance.'

'*Importance?*' asked Louise. 'Is not Queen Katherine the aunt of Emperor Charles and therefore, as family, would she not have insisted on England's support for Spain?'

The ambassador stared at his shoes as Louise stepped forward and placed her hand on her son's arm. She appeared surprisingly calm.

'Well,' she continued, 'whatever he said, there is nothing to be done now. We must be content in the knowledge that there will be no further delay for the planned meeting with my son.'

'None whatsoever, Madame,' Wingfield bowed his head. 'All is prepared and once you are ready to depart, the journey to Ardres will take just over a week. A little longer if the rains continue.'

As I caught Françoise's eye, she raised her brow at the scene that had just unfolded.

• •

I placed the counters on the board and watched, with Renée, as the queen moved one to the next position. We were enjoying a game of merels, and as we played, the ladies sat sewing. A young gentleman stood strumming the lute, accompanied by the voice of Anne de Graville, and the dogs lay dozing by our feet. It was a homely scene until Sir Richard Wingfield entered and bowed stiffly, bonnet in hand. His leg appeared to be bothering him as he straightened up. The musician stopped playing his lute, and Anne's voice trailed away.

'Madame,' said Sir Richard, 'I have just returned from the church of the Jacobins, where the Bishop of Amiens sang High Mass for the king. I must tell you that when the hautbois and sacbuts played together, it was as melodious a noise as ever was heard.'

'And, sir?' Queen Claude looked up.

'Madame, the king asked me to bring you news of the meeting with King Henry.'

'Ah, yes,' said the queen, rearranging the cushion behind her back. 'The one that was going to take place *after* the one with my husband. I assume that is the one you are referring to, sir?'

Wingfield tipped his head slightly and I enjoyed watching his discomfort.

'Go on,' said the queen.

The man cleared his throat and began. We heard how the emperor had landed at Sandwich, in England, beneath a cloth of estate depicting a Black Eagle fringed with gold, followed by a vast company of Spanish nobles. Cardinal Wolsey had greeted him with great ceremony, and the ships in the harbour shot out salvos in greeting. The next day, they had progressed to Dover Castle, where Emperor Charles kissed all the noble ladies present on the mouth, in the English fashion. King Henry then hurried over from Canterbury to meet him, and once the niceties were out of the way, the two rulers sat down to business. The magnificent cavalcade then returned to Canterbury amidst banners, flags, and streamers, and there the young emperor met his aunt, Queen Katherine, who cried on seeing her nephew for the first time. As her husband showed him the relics of St. Thomas à Becket, the bells from the cathedral rang out in celebration. Queen Katherine appeared overjoyed and insisted that as this was a family reunion, her nephew must speak in private with herself and the king only, much to the discomfort of Wolsey. We also heard, to our great amusement, that at a banquet that evening, the emperor laid eyes upon his once future wife, the dowager Queen of France. He could not hide his immense disappointment at finding her as lovely as the portrait he still possessed, and he petulantly refused to dance.

'Let me read it,' said Queen Claude.

Wingfield handed the paper to her.

'Oh, ladies, listen:

'Watching him sulk, the Dowager Queen, dressed in a gown of silver tissue, danced and swirled about — taunting him with her beauty and vivacity!'

I smiled, thinking back to when Emperor Charles had told me in the library at Mechelen that the artist had lied in his portrayal of Mary Tudor, that no-one could be as attractive as her picture, and he did not want her for a wife. No wonder he felt devastated, seeing her in the flesh.

'I wonder what he thought of his uncle, King Henry,' said the queen.

'If I may speak plainly, Majesty,' said the ambassador, 'I gather neither were impressed by the other. King Henry, obviously older, towered over the thin youth and both thought the other pompous.'

'And his Aunt Katherine?'

'He said he thought she appeared old, but he sympathised with her lack of a male child and advised she tried to please

God with more pilgrimages and fasting.'

'And what else was spoken of?' asked the queen.

'Majesty, the young emperor tried to persuade King Henry and Cardinal Wolsey not to meet with your husband, but King Henry refused to listen. He has promised to meet the French king and said the emperor must have confidence in his conduct. I must add this proves my king is an honourable man, with no guile or trickery, and stands by his promises. He and Wolsey are pro-French, regardless of what is reported, and England does not seek war. I can assure you, the meeting will ratify once and for all the Treaty of London.'

'Amen to that,' said the queen. She moved another counter on the board and, thanking the ambassador, waved him away.

When he had left the chamber, she signalled to Anne to begin her song again, and the soft notes from the lute filled the air. She then sat back, a faraway look in her eyes.

'What troubles you, Madame?' I asked.

She sighed. 'Oh, Anne, I feel a great heaviness in my heart for Queen Katherine. What offence can she possibly have committed that God should punish her with no male child?'

I looked down at the board and moved my counter. 'Madame,' I said, smiling triumphantly, as Renée clapped in delight. 'God knows a great many things that we do not.' I had won the game.

Standing on the hillside between Guînes and Ardres, six miles from the English-controlled Calais, I gazed down in the setting sun at the hundreds of courtiers in King Henry's entourage. Could anyone be left behind in England? All around, on the hillsides, hundreds of peasants and commoners had also gathered to watch, not caring about the risk of being caught and hanged. Louise, Marguerite, and *Madame la Grande*, sitting next to Queen Claude, peered at the great cavalcade below as Anne de Graville and Diane waited in attendance. Behind them stood a great many titled and noble ladies. The queen shielded her eyes and tried to make herself more comfortable, for in just over a month she would give birth. She turned to Marguerite and said how relieved she felt that Marguerite had joined them in time, having first dealt with a terrible fire at her estate at Montreuil. I cared naught for that, for I was desperate to see my family. How slow the hours seemed!

'You will see them soon enough, Anne,' the queen said kindly, noticing my restlessness.

I gave a faint smile and thought of my sister. I was not sure how I would feel seeing her again. Rather uncharitably, I hoped that William Carey would not prove good looking after all. But George? Oh, how he would have grown!

Below, on the grassy plain, the sun continued to glint off the turrets of hundreds of tents, giving the appearance of a golden valley. The sight was almost blinding in its brightness and the workmen, on both sides, must have worked for weeks in the rain erecting the beautiful pavilions. When two massive cannon shots rang out, the French and English processions moved slowly forward from either the Guînes or Ardres side, resplendent in plumes and gold chains. First marched the *prévot de l'hôtel* with his archers, and then the marshals of France; the *grand-maître* with the king's steward and officers, all in cloth of gold; the *Grand Seneschal*, who conducted two hundred gentlemen, some in cloth of gold, some in crimson and others in coloured velvet, and the king's pensioners. Next, the Swiss on foot, all in new liveries, with rich plumes and plenty of drums and flutes, trumpets, hautbois, clarions, and sackbuts. After them, the king's gentlemen and chamberlains, followed by the Constable de Bourbon in cloth of gold frise, set with jewels, his horse barded, bearing a naked sword before King François. I noticed Louise, unsmiling, devour him with her eyes as she took in every detail of his magnificence as if compiling an inventory.

King Henry approached King François, attended by Cardinal Wolsey and his Yeoman of the Guard, dazzling in cloth of gold and silver, laden with jewels. He was also accompanied by the Dukes of Buckingham and Suffolk, the Marquis of Dorset, and the Earls of Northumberland, Talbot, and Salisbury. The king's archers, around two hundred in number, followed behind with halberts. Next came some four hundred gentlemen, all dressed in velvet, either black or crimson, and all wearing massive chains around their necks. Then the mace bearers, trumpeters in green and white damask, and heralds, all with the arms of England. The king himself rode a Neopolitan courser, trapped in gold and silver, and it was impossible to decide which side appeared the most impressive.

I could not see King Henry clearly, but he did appear broader than when I had last seen him in Lille, and he now sported a beard. Queen Katherine had been overruled after all. King François, although striking in cloth of gold himself, appeared very swarthy in comparison to the ruddy-faced Henry.

As a great fanfare rang out, the two kings then galloped their coursers towards each other, before pulling up sharply, sweeping off their velvet bonnets and embracing each other. They then swiftly dismounted and withdrew to a great pavilion with Cardinal Wolsey and Admiral Bonnivet. Marguerite gazed towards him, her expression pensive.

'Good,' said Louise, rising, 'now we will leave them to their talks. I believe that on Sunday, my son wishes to pay his respects to Queen Katherine and the dowager French queen, at Guînes. That meeting I would very much like to see. At the same time, King Henry hopes to pay his respects to Claude at our camp, and we will entertain him and his court accordingly.'

She took the queen's arm and helped her stand.

'Now,' continued Louise, 'let us return to the litters and

then to our chambers to rest. We have over two weeks of late-night carousing ahead of us. Hopefully, we will have time for the very thing we have troubled ourselves to come here for.'

I felt the tone of her voice did not bode well for this ruinously expensive event.

• •

As King François rode away on a mule with the Dukes of Vendôme, Bourbon, and Lorraine to pay his respects to Queen Katherine and the dowager French queen, I wondered what he would think seeing again the woman he had once tried to seduce. Knowing him now as I did, I knew he would bear no malice, but take what had happened in good part. After all, who could not admire the English king's defiant and brave sister?

Meanwhile, intent on impressing King Henry, Louise had insisted that only the most beautiful ladies greet him on his arrival at the queen's lodgings, before escorting him to the king's lodgings to meet Queen Claude. I, of course, along with Mary Fiennes and the other girls, was not among that number; that honour was allotted to Françoise, Diane, and other ladies from King François' *petite bande*. These titled ladies were the finest the French court could offer, and no expense in their dress and jewels had been denied them. But I cared nothing for this, for I was impatient to see my mother and family as they accompanied the king, and nothing could dampen my excitement.

When the trumpets blasted, we knew that King Henry had arrived at the French camp. As the ladies chatted with excitement, another fanfare sounded and, accompanied by the Dukes of Buckingham and Suffolk, he appeared, magnificent and imposing, at the entrance to the king's lodging. The French ladies moved aside as Louise, dressed elegantly and simply in black velvet as a widow, swept to the floor. Standing at the back, almost hidden with the other young ladies, I peered over the heads in front of me and stared at the king. So there he was – the most powerful man in England. He instantly raised Louise and kissed her fondly several times on both cheeks.

'Well, what do you think?' Mary whispered. 'Is he not handsome?'

I could not speak, only stare.

King Henry, wearing a double mantle of cloth of gold with jewels and goldsmith's work and a beautiful collar, appeared exuberant, full of bonhomie and charm. He was still the man I remembered and did not like – I would never forgive his insult to my mother – but his auburn beard suited him, and his powerful frame dominated those around him. Yes, he had put on a little weight, and his sunburnt face appeared rather fleshy, but he exuded vitality and power. When he glanced around at the French ladies, he briefly caught my eye, but there was no recognition – not that I expected it – and yet, foolishly, a small part of me felt disappointed. Well – I was no longer the gaudily dressed young girl he had first seen in the Regent's retinue, but an elegant young woman wearing a beautiful, verdant green gown, its neck edged in a band of gold passamayne. A French hood, edged with gold, complemented my hair and a simple gold chained adorned my neck. How could he possibly remember, and yet why did I feel sad that he did not?

'He *is* dazzling,' I whispered back.

'Madame,' said King Henry, in perfect French, 'Everything has been done to my pleasure. You do me great honour when, in truth, the honour is all mine!'

'Sire,' said Louise, 'I have longed for this meeting and prayed for your safe conduct here. France now awaits your desires, your comfort, and weal.'

'Dearest Madame, I trust my own queen and my sister, Mary, likewise, honour your son at my camp in Guînes.'

He then proceeded to kiss Marguerite, elegant in violet-coloured velvet. She smiled and blushed. Louise then took his arm and led him along the walkway to the beautiful *salle* where Queen Claude sat waiting on her throne, holding Renée's hand, surrounded by the noblest ladies of the French court. Her canvas pavilion had been turned into a palace lined with panels of cloth of gold and silver, all embroidered with *fleurs-de-lis*. The queen herself sat in a robe of cloth of gold, her hair glittering with jewels and wearing on her breast a fine diamond. As the English king bent down on one knee, bonnet in hand, she rose awkwardly to greet him. Staring at her great belly, he rose, and bending very low, kissed her fondly. She appeared like a tiny doll next to his great height, and everyone in the pavilion burst into applause.

'Good friends, French and English all!' he cried. As he held her in his arms how he must have wished his queen was as fruitful. He then kissed each noble lady present.

After all the formalities, he spoke with Queen Claude privately for a while and she invited him to rest before dining. In the meantime, while the musicians struck up a tune, the accompanying English guests took their places in the adjoining tent. When all was ready, the trumpets sounded and the king, with our queen on his arm, followed by Louise, Marguerite, and Madame de Vendôme, entered. Queen Claude insisted the king sit beside her, beneath a golden canopy, and when all were seated again, I searched the guests at the long tables. However, although the pavilion was full of English courtiers, it appeared that many of the noblest English ladies – I assumed those who could speak fluent French, such as my mother – had remained with Queen Katherine, presumably to entertain King François and his guests. Those I did recognise, like Eliza Grey, had accompanied Mary Tudor when she married King Louis, but I still felt deeply disappointed. Again.

I gazed about at the ladies' fashions and thought that compared to the French ladies, the English were not well dressed in their cumbersome Spanish gowns. I also noticed sweat stains beneath their arms and stains on their linen. They could at least have taken more care.

'What is the matter?' asked Mary, as the pages brought the first meat dishes to our table. The other girls twitted and blushed as the king raised his glass goblet to them.

'Nothing,' I said, sulkily, taking a sip of sweet wine. 'I just hoped my mother – or at least somebody from my family – would be here.'

'You will see your family later, just as I will,' she countered. 'I cannot wait to see my two brothers.'

'Yes, but when? We have been here several days already and watched nothing but endless processions, at the end of which we all retire to either the French or English side.'

'But Anne, the tourney is taking place tomorrow. After the combat, we will be free to mingle. Can you not wait a little longer?'

'No, because there is a rumour that it might be cancelled due to the high winds, so that will be another day stuck here in the French camp with Queen Claude. Look at the size of her. She looks fit to burst.'

'Something else is bothering you,' said Mary. 'I know that look.' She cut into the veal sausage.

'It is my sister,' I said. 'I am concerned that François will sniff around her skirts again. Having a husband will not deter him, neither will the proximity of my father. It did not bother him before.'

'Would it bother *you*?' she asked.

I shrugged and looked up at the glittering company. King Henry appeared much taken with Queen Claude, which flattered her, for she was not used to male compliments. As he gently brushed back the strands of hair from her face, there was something very touching and unexpected in the gesture. I noticed the auburn, downy hair on the back of his hand and the immense diamond rings on his fingers. I thought him more handsome than King François, due to his fair colouring and hair the colour of autumn leaves. His high-bridged nose and small mouth were attractive, but his eyes were too small beneath the sandy, feminine brows. And he was not at ease. The French king had a charisma that, for all his pretended bonhomie, the English king did not possess. He laughed, but his eyes were restless, flitting to the next woman who caught his eye, demanding attention.

Louise, of course, smiled when he spoke with her. When the conversation turned to the Duc de Bourbon, he asked how such a subject could afford to wear an enormous, priceless pearl around his neck. A pearl fit for a king – or the richest man in the kingdom. Louise, knowing full well that Henry coveted the pearl for himself, only nodded. Well, somehow, when the time was right, I expected she would make sure he obtained it. Henry, meanwhile, appeared peeved.

'Why, Madame,' he said, his voice high, 'if I should have such a noble at my court, I would not risk leaving his head on his shoulders.'

'As you say, my lord, as you say,' said Louise, 'but do you not have an equally troublesome duke in the person of my Lord Buckingham? I gather he has been so rude here he is to be excluded from the jousts. My son even prophesied to me that the man will die a traitor's death. Do you not agree?'

'Madame, he is hot-tempered and proud, I will grant you that, but I have no quarrel with him.'

Yet, I thought.

When the musicians were ordered to play, King Henry rose and asked the queen to dance. It was a mere formality, for she politely refused due to her ungainly size, and he eagerly took the hand of Marguerite instead. I stood watching as he showed off his immensely skilled footwork and wondered what it would be like to partner him and have everyone's eyes on me. After all, I had danced with King François, so why not King Henry? Besides, as one of the best dancers at Queen Claude's court, I longed to show off my steps. When I *was* asked to dance a galliard, it was with an elderly, English gentleman who trod on my slippers and almost ripped the hem of my gown. As the dance progressed, I smiled at the king, but he turned away, for he only had eyes for the English girl he partnered, a girl named Anne Browne. Buxom and attractive, she appeared to have his undivided attention.

When the dancing finished, I returned to the queen and asked if she required anything. She said no, but wondered if the king would think her rude if she retired and asked Louise to continue as hostess? I did not say so, but I felt sure that Louise would be only too glad to pack her off to bed.

'Madame, how did you find talking with King Henry?' I asked as she picked at a bowl of grapes.

She stopped chewing and fixed her crooked eyes on the king, who had now taken the arm of another lady. 'Sadly, I fear this is no more than a charade, for he has no true confidence in my husband. Oh, he did not say as much, but I could glean his meaning. He did say he enjoyed my company and found me of great political intelligence, which perhaps he was not expecting.'

'But what of the man?' I persisted.

'In truth, Anne?' she asked, barely above a whisper. 'Why, I have never met a more egotistical, proud, self-opinionated young man in all my life. Boastful and conceited. I truly pity Queen Katherine ...'

Shivering with cold, I took my place with the rest of Queen Claude's ladies. Still, the discomfort was worth it just to wear a beautiful crimson gown with its low shoulders. I had dispensed with the little cape for it looked far more attractive without. Mary Fiennes had done the same and shuddered. So far, the wind had kept away the rain, but the dark, looming clouds still threatened to spoil the event, and I wondered if the whole tournament might be cancelled yet.

Our procession from Ardres into the English camp had proved magnificent, and when our litters arrived, we entered a fantastical meadow of green and white striped tents. Each appeared to be connected to the other via long galleries and, on top of the tent poles of one crimson pavilion, the king's beasts proudly stood. I gazed up at the great canvas banqueting house before me and admired its archway, roundels of Tudor roses, swags and pillars. It even had a moat. Looking away from the palace, through an ornate arch, I saw that a great tiltyard had been erected, dominated by the Tree of Honour upon which the combatants would place their shields. At first, it was thought too windy to couch the blunted lancers, but now the wind had dropped a little.

The plan was that the two kings would hold against all comers. The supporters for King François would be the Duc de Bourbon, Alençon, and eighteen gentlemen; for King Henry, the Duke of Suffolk, my uncle, Thomas Howard – making his last appearance before he set sail for Ireland – and eighteen others.

The marshal below our stand called out the rules for all to hear: 'Each gentleman shall fight in the order in which his name has been entered. Any man disarmed so that he cannot complete his courses must be content with what he has done for that day. If the horse bolts, it is but fair that the comer shall have a fresh start. If a challenger strikes or kills the horse of his opponent, he shall not run again that day, without the ladies' leave.'

Queen Claude and Queen Katherine had already received the homage of the knights and now sat in a glazed gallery, hung with tapestries. As they sat talking, I was clean amazed that Queen Katherine had tactlessly chosen to wear an ugly Spanish headdress at such an important event. It was a dreadful *faux pas* and one that would surely be noted by the ambassadors, for even if she did hate the French, it was a foolish thing to do. I noticed that unlike her husband, she had not aged well, although she certainly was not ugly as some reports had suggested. Mother said that once she had been very attractive. Of the two, I felt the younger Queen Claude dressed with more elegance in cloth of silver, while Queen Katherine appeared overdone in violet, black, and crimson velvet, laden with heavy jewels.

I leant forward, eager to try and catch a glimpse of my mother and family.

'Are they there?' asked Mary.

'I cannot see,' I replied, 'too many heads are in the way. Oh! Oh, yes, I can see my mother. She is there – there in the tawny coloured gown!'

I resisted the urge to stand up and wave, for I knew it would be seen as undignified, and I watched as she chatted to someone whom I thought might be the Duchess of Buckingham. My aunt, Lady Boleyn, Sir Edward's wife, sat nearby with Lady Guildford, and I also recognised the Countess of Stafford. Mother appeared well and animated, tapping her hand on her knee, impatient for the tourney to start. Always beautifully dressed, she had an innate sense of elegance, unlike those ladies around her. No gentlemen sat with them, and so I expected my father and George would be down at the lists. As to my sister, I had no idea where she might be.

'I think Queen Katherine appears rather jaded,' said Mary, 'particularly compared to the dowager French queen. It is obvious that she is the real star today.'

She was right, and it was shrewd of King Henry to use his finest ambassador to impress the French, instead of his wife, for Mary Tudor dazzled in silver damask. She had arrived in a magnificent litter of gold, embroidered with lilies and bearing the monogram of '*L*' and '*M*' supported by a porcupine, the emblem of King Louis. I thought it was a ridiculous display. She was simply the Duchess of Suffolk, yet the French cheered her and cried out hysterically for their '*Reine Blanche, Reine Blanche!*' as if she were still married to their old king, and not the duke. How she revelled in the adoration.

I turned to see Louise of Savoy, sitting with the Duchesses of Nemours, Bourbon, and Longueville, talking to Marguerite. She was not impressed by the giddy girl before her and glanced nervously below for King François. When he appeared, the crowd roared with approval, for he rode his favourite courser, 'Dappled Duke', draped in purple satin embroidered with corby feathers. His challengers surrounded him, all mounted in coats of silk. King Henry rode out on a similar courser trapped in gold tissue, with waves of gold laid on russet velvet – a device to show that he commanded the Narrow Seas. Next to him rode Sir Henry Guildford.

As each king came to do reverence to Queen Katherine and Queen Claude, the English queen stood up and placed her favour upon the raised lance of her husband. One day, I thought, I would do such a thing myself with a knight, and he would carry my scarf for all the world to see.

As the tourney progressed, the two kings bore themselves valiantly, especially King François, who shivered spears like reeds and never missed a stroke. Sparks flew, and the French king even had his plume cut clean in two. At one point, he gave King Henry such a blow it threw him to the ground and killed his favourite horse from under him. King François only suffered a black eye, but it was enough to cause his queen to shriek. Fleuranges, Bonnivet, and Bourbon rode bravely, but in truth, the English rode just as well, apart from the Duke of Suffolk, who had injured his hand and did not ride well. As my uncle reared his courser, caparisoned in gold and azure, and cantered past, helm carried beneath his arm, my mother stood to applaud. My Aunt Jocasta did the same when my other uncle, Edmund, entered the lists, and I must say, he handled his horse superbly, unseating his opponent to great cheers from the English spectators. Fortunately, apart from King Henry's horse, there was only one fatality, the rider being French. The jousts lasted for three hours, and Marguerite became alarmed when she heard that Bonnivet had been kicked by King François' horse. Fortunately, he was not badly hurt. Then, when the heralds sounded '*disarmy!*' the trumpets sounded the end of the tourney, and we were free to enjoy the revels.

Stumbling out of the seats, I made my way as quickly as

I could towards where my mother stood, fastening the clasp of her cloak. As she descended the steps, I jostled against the ladies as they tried to exit the stand all at the same time.

'Mother!' I cried, squeezing my way through, 'Mother!'

She turned, a wide smile lighting up her face. 'Nan, my darling girl!' She kissed me fondly and then held me away, at arm's length. 'I miss you so much and long for you to return home. Your father, of course, will not allow it, not while we are on good terms with France.'

'But will the peace last, Mother? Surely all this show is but empty posturing?'

She took me aside and held my face in her hands. 'Shush, shush – enough. Let me look at you.'

I gazed at her and noticed the shadows beneath her eyes.

'I know, I know, too many late nights. But you, you are so slender. Are you eating enough?' Her face showed concern.

'I am very well, Mother,' I said, 'but tell me, is George here? If so, I am not sure that I will even recognise him!'

'I believe he is down with the horses, and he has grown into a very handsome young man indeed. You will see him shortly.'

'Who else?' I asked.

'Well, your grandfather, the Duke of Norfolk, has remained in England, to keep the country safe in the king's absence, aided by Bishop Fox. Both, God forgive me, are so old they could drop dead at any moment and then where would we be? Anyway, the Wyatts are here, since Sir Thomas is acting as Knight Marshal to maintain order.'

'With Tom?'

'Yes, and he is looking forward to seeing you again.' She turned and her face fell a little as my aunts, Anne and Alice, approached.

'Lady Aunts,' I said, dropping an elegant curtsey.

Both looked as if they had seen a ghost and there followed much hugging and kissing. None could believe how I had grown – and I thought how much older they appeared in their gabled headdresses since I'd last seen them.

'By my trowthe, Anne,' said Lady Shelton, 'you are so – so elegant! I cannot believe this is the same, pale young girl I last saw at Allington. Do you recall our visit?'

Lady Alice then walked around me, admiring my gown. 'Are you not cold, dear?' she fussed, 'with your shoulders so uncovered?' She began plucking at the velvet fabric. 'You will get a quinsy of the throat in this unseasonable weather. Where is your cloak? And the enamelled chain I sent you, did you not like it?'

'Why no, I mean yes, it was lovely,' I blustered, 'but Queen Claude prefers her ladies not to wear too many jewels, and over-adornment is no longer in fashion here.'

'Fie, one can never wear too many chains, particularly on such an occasion as this. Is that not so, Elizabeth?' As she played with the tasteless gold links at her neck, I already wished someone would attach a heavy stone to them and throw her into a pond. 'No, dear child, I can assure you, English ladies know how to dress with taste.'

My mother raised her brow as Lady Anne lifted out my gossamer veil.

'Do all the French ladies wear them like this?' Her voice sounded surprised. 'Surely placing the hood so far back on the head, revealing the hair, is considered rather, well – immodest?'

'No, really, Aunt Anne, even Queen Claude approves, although at first, she preferred the old style Breton hood. This is the fashion now, and Queen Claude loves to be in fashion.'

I already found them both irritating and could not bear the way they spoke to me like a naughty child.

'Well, I find French ways quite mystifying,' said Lady Alice, 'although the younger ones at court are all for French this and French that. As to manners, have you seen how over fond of wine the French ladies are? I hope you have not acquired such a bad habit. And have you kept up your music?

I cannot wait to hear you play for me. Will you play later? When we dine together you mu –'

'Alice, please, I must speak with my daughter alone – if you would be so kind?'

I tried not to smile as my aunt's face fell.

'Why – why, of course, Elizabeth, if that is what you wish. We will see you later with Thomas. Oh, I cannot believe what a charming young lady your daughter has grown into. Now, I must go and find my husband. Come, come.'

We watched the two of them go, and I burst out laughing. 'Oh, Mother, what absolute busybodies.'

'Indeed, but you have not asked me about your sister,' she said. 'Are you not eager to meet her new husband?'

'Not particularly,' I replied, with honesty.

'Then do I perceive you are still not friends?'

I told her we had parted on reasonable terms, but that, in my heart, I could not feel happy for her.

She turned her face to me. 'Nan, what happened in France must stay here in France. Mary is now a married woman, so any foolishness must be forgotten for our family's good name. We have influence at court, position and some wealth. People will always try to destroy that, if they can, with gossip and rumour.'

'But surely William has heard?' I asked. 'Someone is bound to say something.'

'Yes, Nan, but it will not be you. And you are not to discuss the matter with George, who will tell all and sundry. Do you promise?'

'Mother, I assure you, I will not repeat her behaviour to a soul, but how *could* she embarrass our family in such a way?'

'Try to be understanding, Nan. This is a new start for your sister, and, God willing, she will be a mother as soon as William has done his duty.'

'Well, I do marvel that her follies have turned out so well. How pleased I am for her.'

'Are you, Nan? It sounds to me as if you are jealous.'

I burst into peals of laughter. 'Of Mary? Oh, you jest!'

However, as we walked, I pondered on her words. I felt angry towards my sister, and in my heart, I knew I resented her happiness. But was it really jealousy?

'Mary is loved by everyone, Nan. She has a nature that is warm and affectionate. Much can be forgiven her, for she is kind.'

'And I am not?' I came to a halt. I was tired of hearing Mary's virtues.

My mother put her hand out and gently touched my cheek. 'My dearest girl, you have mettle, fire, and passion that she will never possess. But it makes for a difficult nature, and life will always have its drama for you. I should know, for we are not unalike. You feel things keenly and have a hot temper, and I worry that you will not be content with life as Mary is content. As to feeling jealous of others' good fortune – I understand that too.'

'But why did you bring her home?' I asked.

'She needed me and I could not abandon her. I would have done the same for you.'

As we continued to walk in silence I decided it best to change the subject. Anything but talk of my sister.

'I have seen the king,' I said.

'Yes, we heard he paid his respects to Queen Claude. Do you still not like him, Nan? You were but a girl when you first saw him.'

I screwed up my nose. 'He has grown attractive enough, Mother, but he is quite fleshy. However, I was surprised at how tender he was to Queen Claude, not that she likes him much either. But, how did the meeting with King François and Queen Katherine go?'

She told me how the banquet itself went well, although it was delayed because King François wished to kiss every attractive lady in the chamber before proceeding.

'Including you, I hope?' I did not ask if he'd kissed my sister.

'But of course! He did *not* kiss Lady Wyatt and several of the large matrons fluttering around Queen Katherine in their hideous gowns.'

I had to say I was not surprised.

'There were a great many guests, and dinner was served solely by Englishmen, except for the French cupbearer. King François sat in the centre of the chamber, opposite Queen Katherine. He was polite to her, of course, charming in fact, but she did not pique his interest one jot, for he could not take his eyes off the dowager French queen. She flirted with him outrageously. Even Cardinal Wolsey joined in the saucy banter, and he a churchman.'

'One would think she is still the queen of France,' I said.

'No, what she is is King Henry's most priceless possession. He cannot show his queen off since all the jewels in the jewel house could not make her appear young and attractive. So, he uses his sister.'

'Well, it has been a vast event to organise,' I said, as we walked.

'Yes, Nan, but Wolsey has the energy of ten men and never rests. He has, however, still taken the time to enjoy the company of the Duchess d'Alençon, insisting she become his *filleule d'alliance*.'

'Marguerite, his adopted daughter?'

'Indeed. However, I am not sure what will be gained from all this expense. King Henry is not as confident as he appears and already suspects treachery from the French. Even at the very first meeting, Nan, both kings felt there were too many soldiers attending, all prepared and ready for trouble. You see how they mistrusted each other?'

'Well, it is a shame the weather has spoiled things,' I said. 'A large French pavilion blew down the other day, and the mast broke. Then the Duc d'Alençon's tent caught fire and burnt down.'

As we reached the end of the tilt barrier, we strolled towards the arming pavilions and around to where the destriers stood. Steam rose off their flanks as the grooms removed the protective metal chanfrons and bridles from the horses' heads, allowing them to shake out their manes, drink deeply and eat their hay. Dozens of competitors still half in armour, their brows glistening with dirt and sweat, stood at the booths, cups of ale in their hands. Their voices were raised as they relived the jousts and argued over the results. A short distance away, a tall young man lifted the caparison off one of the horses, his hair falling over his eyes. He swept it back and then quickly darted to one side as the horse, ears flat, bucked and kicked out.

'Bastard!' he cried loudly, as my mother and I stood there trying not to laugh.

He turned around, frowning. 'Nan – is that you?'

I ran forward and threw myself into his arms. He swung me around, lifting my feet off the grass as he whooped and laughed.

'George put me down, I cannot breathe!' I cried, my voice muffled against his chest. He immediately dropped me and held both my hands. 'Oh, George, you have grown into a man!'

'Well, it would be quite something if I had grown into an ape!'

I laughed at him, enchanted by his deeper voice.

'But, let me look at *you*, sister.' He stroked his chin as he appraised me. 'Well, I suppose you have turned out reasonably attractive, in a foreign sort of way. A bit too sallow, not much meat on you, but passable. I am not sure about the affected accent, though.'

'Oh, George,' said our mother, 'what a thing to say to your sister.'

'He is being deliberately mean,' I said, pretending to be insulted.

'Of course I am,' he said, turning to her, 'but I love her as my life. However, I know that unlike our sister Mary, she will give back as good as she gets.'

He smiled the wide, generous smile I remembered from my childhood. 'You were always sharp-tongued and fearless, Nan. Do you recall when we raced our horses at Hever, along the Gallop Path, and how nothing was too high for you to jump?'

'On my beloved Ciara! Is she well, do you still ride her?' I asked.

'She has put on weight and is too small for either of us now,' he said.

I gazed up into his fresh, handsome face and large brown eyes. He had my mother's features and smile, and like me, our Father's pointed chin. I could not believe my impish little brother had grown so handsome.

'Oh, Christ's nails, Nan, have the aunts seen you yet? I've spent every minute avoiding them. If they do see you, they will say you are too thin, too pale, too French, too –'

'Late! Too late, George, for I have just escaped their clutches.'

'Tom is here,' he said, pulling me to him again.

I placed my hand against his chest and looked up at him.

'He cannot wait to see you again.'

Mother then announced that she must go and find Father and that she would see us both later at the masque. After watching her walk away, George and I sat down together on a hay bale.

'Is Tom enjoying married life?' I watched him roll down the sleeves of his shirt.

'Between you and me,' said George, 'he finds his wife rather tedious. I do not think it is a happy match.'

I jumped up. 'So, she is not witty and fascinating like me?' I was secretly pleased. I had liked Tom and could never see him settling with some country mouse. 'Well, we French ladies are far superior to English country maids.' I twirled about, holding out my arms to show off my beautiful, embroidered sleeves.

'She is no simple maid, Nan, you know her family. Lord

Cobham is a wealthy man and the Wyatt's were content with the match. Sadly, Tom was not.'

'Well, more fool him for accepting her. How spineless. But, George, you are not much younger than Tom. Has Father no betrothal in mind for you yet?'

'I have no idea,' he said, as I sat back next to him, 'and it must be said, no interest. However, until I make the loving voyage of matrimony, I am content to sample everything on offer, even the mutton at the gates.'

I could not imagine my little brother with doxies but refused to appear too shocked.

'Well,' I continued, 'perhaps Father is waiting to rise higher still in favour so that we can marry into some noble family.'

'Perhaps. Have you met William Carey yet? I like him very much. He is a good jouster and will be appearing as one of the Comers later in the week. He escaped the purge of young courtiers, but I must say, the king's good intentions did not last long for he soon grew tired of life without his irresponsible, amusing friends. Our cousin, Francis Bryan, is the worse, he behaves like the very devil.'

We then spoke of a hundred things, from my time in Mechelen with Margaret of Savoy to my attendance on Queen Claude, in France. Fascinated by my conversations with Marguerite, he sat listening intently, chin on hand, as we discussed the new religious ideas sweeping through Europe. We spoke of Martin Luther, and he told me how Father had begun to take an interest in his writings and that he was in correspondence with Erasmus.

'I cannot wait for you to return,' he said. 'The court is the only place to be, and you will love it. It has the best horses in the world, particularly the Spanish ones, and Sir Henry Guildford allows me to ride them. I hear King François covets King Henry's *Morello* Neapolitan courser.'

'I expect he does, George, and I thought the joust thrilling. It was touching to see Queen Katherine give her favour to the king for she still loves him very much.'

'She does and they behave fondly towards each other in public. Of course, privately, I hear it is another matter. But forget Queen Katherine, what of you, Nan? Have you had any secret dalliances in France? Have you given yourself to anyone? Go on, you know you can tell me anything.' He gave a cry at the sharp slap and stood up, grinning, hand to his reddening cheek.

'That was for your impertinence, George Bullen. No man has touched me, unlike Ma –' Her name was almost out of my mouth and I quickly lowered my eyes.

'There's no need to look so secretive, Nan. I do know.'

'Know? How?' I felt horrified.

'Ann Jernyngham.'

'*Ann?* But what has she said? Oh, George, this is frightful. Mother is convinced that no-one knows anything.'

He gave a grin. 'What is there to know? She told people how Mary had outrageously flirted her way through the French court, conquering all. Hardly surprising when you know how giddy she used to be.'

'Yes, but to end up with not even a gold chain from King François –' I stared at his face and paused. 'Oh, holy angels above, George, you did not know.'

He gave a low whistle. '*King* Francois? Now that she did not say. Well, well, our pretty sister and that lascivious French dog.'

'Shush, George, you must promise me that you will discuss this with no-one. Promise me now, I mean it.'

He put his hand on his heart and sighed. 'For you, Nan, anything. I swear I will tell no man or woman, on my life.'

'Mean it, George. It is for our family, for no calumny must touch us, not if we wish to marry well. Besides, I promised Mother, who does not know that you know, so please be on your guard.'

'Did the affair last long?' he asked.

'No, it was a fleeting thing, over before it began, and she

gained nothing.'

'Not even a good horse?' he asked as if that was all that mattered. 'But, you did not answer my question. Have you given your heart to anyone?'

I shook my head, for I would never tell of my love for Clément. It was a secret that would stay deep within my heart forever, a secret to be kept even from my beloved George.

'No, but that is not to say I have not learnt a great many things from the French ladies. Why the things I could tell you, quite shocking.'

'Such as?' he asked.

'I am not telling you, for Françoise de Foix has revealed secrets far too saucy for your tender ears.'

'Oh, please. I doubt there is anything you could tell me that I do not know already, for I am no fumbling virgin.'

'George, you are outrageous!' I cried.

'Perhaps I am, but I do wish you'd introduce me to that ravishing girl with the strawberry blonde hair. The one with the palest of complexions.'

'Ah, you mean Diane, the wife to the *grand senechal* of Normandy. Well, I can tell you now George, you would have more success with Queen Claude's dwarf!' Instead of pouting, as Mary would at the tease, George laughed heartily and put his arm roughly about my shoulder.

'Oh, Nan, my darling, how I have missed you! Come, tell me more about our naughty sister and the king of France.'

●　　●

King Henry insisted on visiting Queen Claude again, this time wearing an ancient Greek visor with a beard of gold wire, a golden cloak and a short tunic. The theme was the life of Hercules, and a long train of courtiers and maskers, all in elaborate costumes, followed behind. As he proudly held his sister's hand, the company processed towards the queen as she waited in the banqueting pavilion. She smiled graciously, noticing how the Duc de Bourbon devoured the dowager

French queen with his eyes. When I looked at her myself, she stared blankly through her mask of beaten gold. She was playing Hebe, the goddess of eternal youth, to perfection, as she turned away with an imperious swish of gold tissue.

Nearby, Louise stood, stiff-backed, her mask that of Urania, goddess of astrology, her headdress a half crescent moon and circlet of stars. My face itched beneath a mask depicting Circe – the goddess who turned anyone who insulted her into beasts – but I dared not loosen the ribbon to scratch. Instead, I stood in my gown of white damask, the sleeves embroidered with animals, and watched as the three of them sat on the dais.

The main maskers processed around the chamber first. It started well, with one of them dressed as Hercules in a lion-skin of cloth of gold to match the buskins on his legs. But then others followed, such as Alexander, Hector, and Julius Caesar, glittering in tinsel satin, Turkish robes, and bonnets. They were followed by Judas, David, Joshua, Charlemagne and – of all people – the dead Prince Arthur. Before long, the whole masque appeared to have little to do with Hercules and more to do with showing off the king's magnificent physique.

When the ladies processed forward, dressed in Milanese and Genoese gowns, I saw that one of them was my sister. Mask or not, I would recognise her anywhere although I had no idea whom her mask depicted. She looked buxom, for her gown was low; her sleeves were banded and puffed, and her hair hidden beneath a Milanese bonnet. As she moved to the side, my eyes settled on the two young men beside her. I could not see their faces due to their elaborate masks, but one was wearing an expensive black doublet, glistening with spangles and beads of jet.

Queen Claude then insisted that the king, his sister, and everyone removed their masks. Applause ensued as guests feigned surprise at their partners, and even Louise began laughing. I was glad to remove the restricting papier-mâché from my hot face and smooth down my hair. When my sister recognised me she waved her hand excitedly, and since the queen had asked that we ladies now mingle and speak with the guests, I knew I could not avoid her. I was right, for she fell upon me in a swoop.

'Oh, sister, is this not wonderful? I am so pleased to see you again. Have you missed me, sweetheart? I have missed you.' She kissed me on both cheeks, her mask in one hand and a plumed fan in the other.

'And who are you supposed to be?' I asked.

'Why, Melpomene, of course,' she said, with a smile. 'The Muse of Singing.'

'I thought she was the Muse of Tragedy or some such thing,' I said.

'No – no there is nothing tragic about me, Nan, for I have never been happier. Come, come and meet William, your new brother-in-law! He rode so well in the jousts.'

When we reached the group of gentlemen, she took the hand of one of them. He turned, and I saw, to my great disappointment, that William Carey was not ill-favoured. As he bowed and reached out to kiss my hand, I saw a gentle face with twinkling eyes and the beginnings of a beard. He stood tall, broad, and elegantly dressed. As resentment filled my mind, I told myself I was being foolish. He was not rich and hardly noble. I could do better.

'Mistress Anne, it is my great pleasure to finally meet you,' he said, his voice well-spoken and soft. 'I have heard so much about you from Mary. You are as lovely as I hear talented and I look forward to seeing you dance, for your reputation precedes you.'

'Thank you,' I straightened from my curtsey, not wishing to be charmed by this young man. 'Is your own family here?'

'Yes, somewhere in this vast gathering,' he said, as Mary put her arm protectively through his. 'But forgive me, I am being rude. May I introduce you to my first cousin, Sir Henry Percy, son of the fifth Earl of Northumberland?'

The gentleman turned, mask beneath his arm, and

bowed low. My heart missed a beat.

'This is mistress Anne Boleyn, my wife's sister,' said William.

'My lady,' he said, as I stared down at his handsome face.

He must have been about eighteen years old, tall, with copper-coloured hair that fell about his ears. His black velvet clothes were costly and covered in spangles, fitting for the son of the most powerful noble in the North of England.

'I am honoured to meet you, sir, but tell me, who do you depict?'

'Do not laugh, but I am supposed to be Ares, the god of war.' He glanced about. 'Truthfully,' he whispered, leaning in close to my ear, 'I should be wearing nothing more than a Grecian helmet, but I did not wish to frighten the ladies.'

I burst into laughter and he smiled, showing straight white teeth.

'Have you enjoyed the festivities, Mistress Anne?'

'Indeed, sir,' I said. 'Every day there is some new amusement. King François has ridden to visit Queen Katherine to attend a similar masque to this. I watched him leave, his ladies all dressed in horned headdresses and plumes. Quite remarkable.'

'Well, Cardinal Wolsey has certainly created a spectacular show, and he has worked tirelessly for months. He seems to need very little sleep. I had the honour of being a page once in his household and saw for myself the energy of the man. But please, forgive me leaving you so soon. I must find my father. I believe he is with the Duke of Suffolk.'

He bowed at Mary and me, and I watched as he made his way through the crowd. I turned to William Carey, wishing it was he who had left instead, but felt I must make some effort at polite conversation.

'What a very pleasant young man,' I said, trying not to sound too impressed.

'Yes,' came the reply, 'and promised to one of the Talbot girls, Mary, I believe.'

I gave him a sweet smile. 'And who, brother-in-law, are you disguised as?' It was all I could think of as he stared at the mask in his hands, its golden ribbons trailing.

'Oh, I am Caerus. Not a very important god, but one of opportunity and luck.'

'Which is fitting,' said Mary, proudly, 'since William is so very lucky at cards. Is that not so, sweetheart?'

Her husband reddened and smiled. 'Well, the king seems to think my presence brings him luck, so I am happy to oblige. Your father agrees and –'

'Oh, Nan,' interrupted Mary, excitedly, 'did you hear that Father has named two ships in our honour? One each in our name! Oh, and have you seen George yet? Let me go and bring him to you.'

As she disappeared in a waft of dizzying scent I stood in silence, embarrassed by her exuberance.

'Mary is a lovely young woman,' said William, watching her flit away, 'and I am very fortunate that your father saw fit to join our two families.'

'Indeed,' I stared ahead, 'and she is so very – generous.'

William's lips twitched in a faint smile. 'If you mean by generous she helps everyone, then yes, she is most generous. She has a soft heart and cannot bear to see anyone in need. Everyone loves her.'

'Oh, they do, they do,' I agreed. 'The problem is that she is happy to love them all back – being such an affectionate creature. She turns no man away.'

'As I said, a generous soul.'

He refused to be goaded or ask questions, and I felt annoyed when Mary returned with George. I wanted to find out just how much William knew about his loving wife.

'Well,' said George, wiping the sweat from his brow, 'I thought I'd seen it all, but have you seen the monkeys covered in gold leaf?'

I pulled a face in disgust for I hated the creatures.

'King Henry, to his guest's utmost annoyance and his

own mirth, is encouraging them to jump all over everyone. It's absurd!'

'He is absurd in that ridiculous garb.'

'He is the king, Nan, and can look as ridiculous as he wishes.' He glanced around. 'I must say, the French women do not need ancient masks to look like goddesses.'

'Oh, look away, George, look away. The French ladies are far too fastidious for you, unlike the English with their poor manners. Why, they – we – are appalled at how the English pass around the *same* cup to drink from. When I return, I shall never do such an ill-mannered thing.'

'Well then, Nan, the sooner you forget your foolish French ways, the better.'

'George, you have no idea what you are talking about. French manners are the m –'

'Oh, stop it, you two,' interrupted Mary. 'Really, can you not wrangle somewhere else?'

I looked at George and he rolled his eyes. We loved to banter and Mary never had the wit to understand how we found it amusing, even when we were children. I put on a mocking face just as Mary Fiennes approached in a fluster.

'Oh, Anne, I must speak with you,' she whispered as she took me to one side.

'Whatever is the matter?' I asked.

She was just about to tell me when a pleasant, lanky youth in a green doublet and hose appeared before me.

'Tom?'

My interest in Mary's news was now quickly forgotten, so she turned to speak to my brother instead.

'Thomas Wyatt!'

The youth took my hands and kissed me on both cheeks. His dark blue eyes and light brown hair were just as I remembered them, but his voice, like my brother's, sounded rich and deep.

'Why, Anne, how wonderful to see you again!'

I smiled at him, astonished at how handsome he had

grown. 'And you, Tom, have grown taller than Father! When did that happen?'

He laughed. 'It *has* been quite a few years. Now, look at us both, all grown up. I have been hearing of your progress and was most interested in your travels.'

'Not enough to write,' I said, feigning displeasure. 'It was quite unneighbourly.'

'Oh, you know me, Anne.'

'I know the old Tom. Are you still writing verses? You once said you would write something for me.'

'No, my father wants me to enter a banking house or some such thing. Frankly, I would rather be at court. I need the inspiration to write, and I have none.'

'I know, Father told me. But do you not write love poems for your new wife?' I asked, rather unkindly. 'Anyway, where is she?'

'Elizabeth has not accompanied me here. As to my scribblings, she does not care for idle verse'

I asked what she did care for.

'The house. She is a good housekeeper.'

'Thomas, have you changed so much from when we used to talk as children at Hever? You had such passion and dreams, and yet here you are, barely seventeen, married to a housewife. My God.'

'That is unfair of you, Anne. Elizabeth is just, well, not very intellectual. She is a plain soul who, hopefully, will give me sons. Besides, if I obtain a place at court, she will remain in the country. I would be content with that.'

'Well, you won't get sons on her from a distance,' I replied.

He stared at me and frowned.

I looked about and sighed. 'Oh, Tom, it seems all around me are settling for contentment. It is not what I desire.'

'And what do you desire, Anne?'

I thought for a moment. 'I want to marry a man of distinction, power, substance, and influence. A man I admire, feel passionate about – not someone in their dotage. Here in France, I have seen the beautiful things money can buy and now I want them for myself. Marguerite has them – the finest horses, gowns, and châteaux. She has shown me many things I now desire for myself.'

'She is of royal blood, the Bullen's are not,' he said. 'Besides, we all want things we cannot have. I want to own Arab horses.'

'But who is to say I cannot have my desires, Tom?'

'Who, indeed,' he said. 'Still, if you think such riches would make you happy. I am not sure they would, for there has always been a restlessness and disquiet about you, unlike your sister. She was always the contented one, whereas you –'

'What, Tom?'

'You were always dissatisfied, always wanting more. And do not think I've forgotten that you stole Mary's place at Mechelen. As the eldest sister, that was her chance, her moment, yet you wanted that place for yourself. You cared nothing for her disappointment, thought of nothing but your desire.'

'There is nothing wrong with ambition,' I said. 'Besides, I was the better choice and time proved Mary could not be trusted.'

When he asked what I meant, I just gave a mysterious smile.

'Why, Anne, you are just as infuriating as ever. Tell me about your adventures. You must have a dozen suitors in France, and do not deny it.'

'Oh, I have,' I replied, 'but none that are worthy of me.'

He laughed as the musicians began tuning up their instruments for the Saltarello. I loved this dance and took Thomas's hand. We made our reverence, and I thrilled to the smiles of approval. Mary might attract the eye with her comeliness, but I, too, commanded attention with my poise and grace.

'Your sister has married well,' he said, glancing back

towards her and William as they joined the dance.

'Perhaps,' I said, 'but I was glad when Mother recalled her from France.'

'Oh?'

'Oh, nothing,' I said.

'You are being very intriguing again,' said Tom, as we held hands.

The drums struck up their beat and we began the dance.

'Well, Anne, it is our gain and France's loss, for Mary is impossible not to like. The sort of girl one might forgive anything.'

'Yes, one might. Except me, Tom,' I said, smiling. 'Except me ...

•   •

'Take cover! We are under attack!'

Mayhem ensued in the tiltyard – now turned into a temporary chapel – as ladies screamed and scrambled to hide beneath the benches. The great roaring, whistling noise seemed to come from nowhere and caused panic and mayhem. Who was attacking this solemn event?

Cardinal Wolsey, who had been celebrating the Mass – his first in several years – turned about in confusion, as the French and English choir boys suddenly dropped down in their stalls to hide, covering their heads. Renée began to cry, for she hated bangs and loud noises, and hid her face in the queen's gown as the guard encircled her and the royal ladies. No sooner had the noise died away, and everyone stopped coughing in the acrid smoke, when, with a great whoosh, we saw an enormous firework in the shape of a salamander – the emblem of King François – streak across the sky from the French side, spitting flames and sparks. It had been discharged by mistake as had the other noisy rockets. However, although the French thought it all highly amusing, the English present did not and it did nothing to alleviate the tension.

After the Mass, as gifts were given on that twenty-third day of June, King Henry presented King François with a collar of precious jewels, diamonds, and pearls. King Henry received a magnificent bracelet in return, and the queens exchanged sables, jewels, horses and litters. The first stone was also laid for the foundation and erection of a beautiful church to be called *Notre Dame de l'Amitié*, or Our Lady of Friendship, to be built at the expense of the two kings. They also agreed to build in the valley a very handsome palace, promising to visit each other there once every year. No-one was fooled by this outside show of enthusiasm, and it was said the two kings hated each other cordially. Yes, they had wrestled together, embraced, exchanged compliments, but out of all the expense and show, one wondered what exactly had been gained apart from a friendship forged between Queen Claude and Queen Katherine. They had taken great joy in discussing their children, the English queen remarking how precocious Princess Mary was, and how she had grown very fond of her new governess, the Countess of Salisbury. The French queen confided her fear in Queen Katherine for her coming confinement, and Queen Katherine promised to pray for her safe delivery. It was hardly of any political note.

That evening I watched the fireworks – minus the already spent salamander – with my parents sitting on either side. My father appeared distracted, but Mother told me it was to do with the ongoing family feud with Piers Butler. I was to take no notice and enjoy the celebrations. The next morning, as I said my tearful goodbyes to my family, I realised I did not want to take my leave of them, particularly George and Thomas. It had been wonderful seeing them both again, and I would miss their company. Much as I loved France, my heart now ached to return home with them.

* *

It was St Lawrence's day, a day which could not have been more apt, for the saint had been renowned for his almsgiving to the poor, just like Queen Claude. She now lay exhausted, having given birth to a girl whom she named Madeleine, at Saint-Germain-en-Laye, at ten o'clock on the morning of the tenth day of August. Marguerite would be her godmother and supervise her education. The king, who was in Paris with Françoise when he received the news, sent his wife a beautiful brooch of golden lilies as a token of his affection.

When she had recovered, we returned to Amboise. My mood was unusually melancholy as I sat with the queen's ladies, embroidering baby gowns. I had not been able to settle since seeing my family and sighed as I held up my work to inspect the intricate stitches. The columbine would have to be unpicked, for I had not concentrated, and the petals were poorly executed. Feeling mightily sorry for myself, I pulled out the bits of blue thread. With Mary Fiennes departed, things were not the same, particularly when she had finally managed to tell me her news. In Guînes, she had been sought out by a very distinguished gentleman by the name of Sir Henry Norris. I remembered how well he had jousted, and she had delighted in telling me he was Keeper of the Privy Purse and very well thought of by King Henry. Norris was so enamoured of her that he intended asking her father for her hand in marriage on his return to the English court. Was it not the most wonderful thing? she had asked. It was not, for at the same time, Eliza Grey, who had returned briefly to enjoy the celebrations in France, had herself captured the heart of the young Earl of Kildare. Handsome and intelligent, a lover of art and books, he had accompanied King Henry in his retinue to France and immediately sought Eliza out. Having already made his acquaintance at court, she now accepted his proposal of marriage, delighted at the prospect of becoming a countess. How could I possibly feel happy when everyone, including Clément, would see that I was the only English girl left in the queen's household without a suitor? I felt utterly dejected.

As I continued with my dull task, the talk turned to King
François. Madame d'Assigny commented on how unhappy
he was. Not with the queen for giving him another daughter,
but with King Henry. And we all knew why. Back in July,
on their return from the festivities, King Henry and Queen
Katherine had met with Emperor Charles and his aunt,
Margaret of Savoy, at Gravelines, in Flanders. How I wished
I had met her again myself! King Henry had provided a lavish
dinner at the Staple House, in Calais, and built a temporary
banqueting house for their entertainment. King François'
friends had attended incognito, and he had instructed them
to find out all they could. All they could discover was that
the emperor had promised the English king that it was in his
power to have Wolsey elected Pope. He would also do much
to stop the spread of the new, religious ideas sweeping across
Europe. King François cared nothing for either.

However, Madame d'Assigny said Louise had not
appeared perturbed, for her astrologers reported that during
the entertainment the torches were snuffed out in a squall
of bad weather, and the thrones for King Henry, Queen
Katherine, and Emperor Charles lay overturned in the mud.
This, they assured her, was a good omen for France, and
King Henry's hope of friendship with Spain would, likewise,
lie in ruins. Besides, with the state of the coffers empty due to
the expense of the meeting, France was in no position to go
to war. As a result, King François remained sulking in Paris
with his lover.

I cared little for King François and his obsession with
war, and felt more and more morose as the afternoon wore
on. The summer had begun to fade, and another year would
soon be coming to an end. I missed my friends and supposed
I should have made more of an effort with the other French
ladies, but I preferred to spend my time with the English
girls. Now they were gone and I felt lonely. As the women
chatted mindlessly on, I looked up as a messenger bowed
and handed me a letter. I broke the Bullen seal and began

to read my mother's script. My uncle, over in Ireland, had taken to his bed due to terrible sickness in the English Pale. He was so concerned, he begged leave to send his wife and children into Wales or Lancashire, to remain near the sea till the disease had ceased. My mother wrote that she was beside herself with worry and had asked Wolsey to intercede and bring him home. As I continued to read news about home and general snippets, I then gave out such a gasp all the ladies turned towards me. My mouth open, I dropped the letter to the floor in complete amazement. I was about to be married!

Chapter Sixteen

'With pride comes disgrace.'

The Loire

Queen Claude stood up and walked over to her pet linnet, chirping in its cage. She put out her hand as it hopped towards her on its perch, and when she turned, she appeared perplexed.

'But why did you not confide in me sooner, Anne?'

It was true. Once I had read the actual details of the letter, I felt so disturbed I kept it secret for days. Finally, I had to talk to someone, and that someone now sat before me, concern in her face. Thank God she had granted me a private audience, for I felt close to tears.

'I did not know what to think, Madame, for I understand he is against the match.'

'But your father has good reason, from what he has told me.'

'Yes, Madame, for he wants to have the Butler lands for himself.'

'Let me understand this correctly. Your great-grandfather, Thomas Butler – the seventh earl – died six years ago and with no male heirs, left his Irish estates to your grandmother Margaret and her sister. But due to years of war in England, you say the Butlers were too busy to run the Ormonde estates.'

'Indeed, my lady. However, although Thomas Butler, as absentee Earl of Ormonde resided in England, he was kept informed of Irish affairs by a network of agents.'

'Meanwhile, Anne, the estates were managed by a cousin, Sir Piers Butler. In effect, he did all the work. Is that correct? So, when Thomas Butler died, Sir Piers assumed – quite understandably – that as the next earl, the Irish estates were his and seized them.'

I nodded and explained that it had proved a foolish assumption and was challenged by Sir George St Leger and my father – sons, respectively, of Sir James St Leger and Sir William Boleyn. Both were descended from the third earl's elder son, whereas Piers was descended from the second earl. Thus, they had a prior claim. Sir Piers answered that the title could only descend from heirs male, not heirs general.

'A tricky case, indeed,' said the queen.

'As my grandmother, Margot, did not wish for the title,' I explained, 'my father claimed it through her – along with all the lands and revenue – and he is supported in his claim by King Henry. The crown does not recognise Sir Piers' claim.'

'Then if King Henry wishes it, I do not see the problem,' said the queen, returning to her chair. She signalled to me to sit.

'Madame, as you know, my uncle is in Ireland acting as deputy. The English and Irish lords there only obey King Henry when they require something from him, so the king must look to the English nobility to assert control. Matters there are fractious, with a great deal of unrest, and my uncle wishes to return home as quickly as possible. However, he cannot until some order is established by someone he trusts. Someone he can appoint as a deputy in his place.'

'And who can blame him, Anne, I hear it is a devil of a place.'

'Madame, Sir Piers has proved invaluable at handling his warring kinsmen, something no outsider can accomplish. My uncle knows he is useful to the English government in keeping the peace and has gained his trust and friendship. He agrees with Wolsey that Piers will guard English interests in the Pale.'

I explained that my uncle had come up with a solution to keep everyone content by writing to Wolsey, saying that if I married Piers' son – my cousin James Butler – I would be allowed to take the title Countess of Ormonde, instead of my grandmother. The title would then be passed to my children. However, all the lands and wealth would remain with the Butlers, not the Boleyn's, since Wolsey wished to keep Piers appeased.

'I see – hence your father opposing the match,' said the queen, nodding. 'Tell me, how far has this matter progressed?'

I told her that my uncle had spoken to Piers and the Irish Council, and everyone in Dublin desired to see the match.

'Madame, James Butler is at present at court, in Wolsey's household, as a hostage, in case his father should do anything to displease the king. I have met him, but only very briefly, at Tournai. I recall he was a personable young man, with pleasant manners. Of course, it was a long time ago, and I do not know how I would feel now, but I would be content to meet him again.'

The queen twisted the gold ring on her finger, no doubt thinking of her beloved François, and sighed. 'Women will always be used as pawns for the greater weal of politics.'

'That is true, Madame, and yet, if I do find him agreeable, I cannot believe my father would spoil my chance of becoming a countess.'

The queen then explained that it might not be up to him. As I was the daughter of an officer in his household, King Henry had a customary right in the disposal of my hand. If he now agreed that this was politically the best solution, my father would not be able to object.

My face brightened.

'Well,' said the queen, 'there is still a great deal of negotiating to be done before anything is finalised. You can now only wait on events and pray for a happy outcome. With God's grace, all will turn out for the best.'

Although I smiled, inside I felt concern, for patience was not my virtue.

'Tell me, Anne, why did you not come to me sooner? You know, surely, that you may approach me in confidence.'

I was not sure how to reply. Although the queen had always proved kind and generous, I could not feel anything other than duty towards her. I would much rather have confided in Marguerite, but she was not at Amboise, and I suppose I felt with my friends gone, I had no-one to talk to. I could not say this, of course, but thanked her for listening. My audience was at an end.

During the next few days, I wrote frantic letters to my mother, sister, and George concerning James. I wanted to know everything about him, and when the betrothal would take place. Of course, I had always known of my family connections in Ireland and was aware that the country had long been divided into two factions, the Geraldines and the Butlers. The Earls of Kildare and Desmond were the heads of the Geraldines, and Ormonde the head of the Butlers. The Geraldines were of Irish blood, with no allegiance to the English government, whereas the Butlers were mostly of English blood and loyal to the crown. How genuine that loyalty was, was debatable, for in truth the king's law was rarely obeyed and Sir Piers did as he chose, without any licence of the king.

My mother appeared unwilling to write much but insisted she would do all in her power to ensure my inestimable joy and comfort. Nothing would, or could, be forced upon me. Besides, it might take as long as a year to sort out the issues, so I was not to concern myself too much for the present. Somehow her words left me feeling more alarmed than comforted. And yet was this not what I had longed for, to be married and supervise my own household? However, now that the matter had been raised, I was not entirely sure that I wished to live in Ireland, away from my immediate family. At thirteen, I had been sent to the Low Countries, at fifteen to France, and now, in my twenties, I might be sent to Ireland. It felt as if I would live my life permanently in exile, away from those I loved most.

The letter from George – when it finally arrived – proved useless. He wrote how James had a reputation for being good at cards, although not a gambler, and was followed everywhere by a white greyhound. Was that it? Why could a man not notice the important things to a woman? I cared not a jot if he was followed by a greyhound or a lunatic and screwed the letter up in frustration. Thankfully, it was my sister who wrote to tell me all I was so desperate to know. The ever kind Mary went to great lengths to find out as much as she could by paying a visit to Cardinal Wolsey's household, at York Place. She wrote that on the pretext of delivering a message, she was able to see James at first hand. He appeared to be in his early twenties and when she inquired of him, was informed by the other wards that he was a very pleasant young man, both wise and discreet. He had accompanied his father, Piers, around Ireland, learning how to raise and command the Ormonde army and before long, gained such respect from his men that, despite being young, the Butlers would only obey him or his father.

Lingering around the door to the cardinal's chambers, Mary had observed that James was not as tall or slender as her William. He was well built, with a slight limp, and known as James 'On Bacagh' – the lame. Oh. He had straight, reddish-brown hair worn to just below his ears, and was clean-shaven, with a ready smile. All in all, he did not have a displeasing face. When she spoke with him, introducing herself as my sister, she discovered that he had been born in Cork, had three brothers, Richard, Thomas, and Edmund – Richard being very handsome – and sisters. His mother was a very strong woman who appeared to acquire and build castles at every opportunity. James himself knew about as much as

I did about the proposal, but was putting it far from his mind for the present while he made his way at court, under the guidance of the good cardinal. So, there we had it. God bless Mary. At least now I knew he was young, popular, a man of authority – and limped ...

Northern Central
France, 1521

'A siege! A siege!'

At four o'clock on a dark afternoon on the Feast of the Epiphany, Diane de Brézé's husband, as King of the Bean, led King François, his boisterous friends and the entire court along the narrow, icy streets of Romorantin. As the cry filled the air, we made our way to the lodgings of the Comte de Saint-Pol, brother of the Duc de Vendôme.

We were staying at Louise's château to continue the Christmas festivities since, with the River Sauldre flooded, she had not wished to travel overland to Blois. The court, no matter how inconvenienced, must come to her. On hearing the noise, the comte and his friends quickly battened down the doors of the pretty red-bricked house. Then, from the upstairs balcony window, they began to throw down eggs, plate, candlesticks, and anything else they could find, onto the cobblestones below. When they ran out of things to throw, somebody by the window heaved a huge, burning log out of the casement. It hit the king's shield, but although he tried to deflect it, it struck his head, causing a bloody gash. The siege was immediately stopped, and the king's surgeon summoned. Although he tried to make light of his injury, King François appeared somewhat disorientated and was carried to his chamber as the crowd stood silently in shock. What had started as a joke had ended in serious injury, and when we returned to the warmth of the château, the other ladies and I tried to calm the distressed queen. It did not help that she was suffering from toothache and as I prepared a poultice of ivy bark, honey, and wine – a remedy Dame Margot had taught me – I hoped it might provide some relief.

When the queen heard that her husband must endure an operation to cut away the skin on his damaged scalp to avoid infection, she fainted clean away.

Matters then took a turn for the worse, for by the Feast of the Conversion of St Paul, her husband lay in serious danger. The surgeons had accidentally touched on a vein, and he bled so profusely that it weakened him almost to the point of death. This was the third time that Christmas he had faced his mortality, having been thrown from a horse on frozen ground and then survived being trapped in a burning hamper. As to the log, he refused to take any action against the perpetrator, much to Fleurange's alarm and accepted full responsibility for the accident.

Before the month was out, he was sitting up in his chair, head bandaged, discussing with Lautrec and Bonnivet his plans to venture an army into Italy and seize Milan. He also declared war on Emperor Charles, who on provocation, prepared to invade northern France. Marguerite appeared horrified at the thought of war again, but there was little she could do, and her brother only sneered when he heard it reported abroad that he was either dead or blinded. The King of England offered his condolences, enquired over the state of his health and sent the English ambassador, Sir Nicholas Carew, over from court with presents. The magnificent rubies did little to amuse King François, for the accident had taken a toll on his health and left him deeply depressed.

Marguerite showed her sisterly concern and asked me to go to the library and find the most recent books to entertain her brother as he convalesced. It was a task I enjoyed beyond all others, as I pored over crates of incoming works from across the world in Louise's magnificent library.

It took over two months for the king to fully recover, and with his head shaved, he felt so self-conscious that he insisted all his courtiers do the same, including the ambassadors. The Italian ambassador was so appalled he announced he wished to terminate his position immediately, but the English ambassador, Sir Richard Jernyngham, was fortunate enough to be recalled home before he lost what little hair he possessed. When he was replaced by the much younger Sir William Fitzwilliam, the latter was forced to comply.

Queen Claude, meanwhile, left with Louise to visit Notre Dame de Clery, to the south of Orléans, to give thanks for her husband's recovery, while the king stayed behind to hunt the deer with Sir William. King François began to grow his hair longer, to hide the scars from the stitches, and I must say, it suited him and the rest of the court right well.

His sister had been so pleased with my efforts in finding interesting books for her brother, that, quite unexpectedly, she asked if I would like to join her household permanently. With one of her ladies departed home, a post had become vacant. She said she had spoken to the queen, who had agreed to release me since Renée required less of my time. I was astonished! To be out of the pious queen's company and into Marguerite's intellectual circle was my greatest wish. It was the most wonderful present.

So far, these early months were proving to be happy. The plans for my betrothal continued apace, and I was soon to spend my time in the company of the most fascinating woman in Europe. Everything appeared to have turned out perfectly as the court made preparations to journey with the king north to Champagne, to inspect his army.

Only one thing disturbed my peace of mind. I heard that the Duc d'Alençon had been given command of the vanguard of the king's army – and the man who had accompanied him was no less than Clément. He had ingratiated himself with the duc as well as Marguerite, and desperate for adventure and glory, desperate to write of war, he had left Romorantin without a word of farewell to me. Why I expected him to, I did not know. Since his appointment as Marguerite's secretary, I had barely spoken to him, and with the passing years, my passion for him had long passed. But I could not help think of the first time I met him, and what might have been. He had taught me a great deal about the New Learning, and because of him, I had been able to contribute to discussions with guests and other ladies. Such knowledge certainly gave me an advantage. And yet, how could a poet have ever given me the life I desired, or one of which my family could be proud? He would always be a servant, relying on the whims of the court. No, my destiny did not lie with him, for I was about to become a countess.

• •

'How dare he, the matter shall not rest here, for by the Creator of souls his words shall cost him dearly!'

As Louise stormed back and forth across the long gallery of the Archbishop's Palace at Troyes, Madame de Taillebourg attempted to place a cloak about her shoulders. It was instantly cast off to the floor. One of the ladies stooped to pick it up.

'*Madame Mère*, dearest of all mothers, calm yourself, please,' said Marguerite, rocking her little spaniel in her arms.

'Why must I? Such an insult! Well, now he has no excuse, none whatsoever.'

I turned to one of Marguerite's ladies as we stood in the rays of April sunshine pouring through the dusty glass windows.

'Why is she railing thus?' I whispered.

'Suzanne has died unexpectedly,' she whispered back. 'After sixteen years of marital bliss, the Duc de Bourbon is heartbroken and cannot be consoled. To add to his misery, since he has no male heir, the crown is entitled to claim all the estates acquired through his now-dead wife.'

I asked why this should affect Louise.

'She told him the only way he would be allowed to keep his inheritance is to marry her. However, the duc refused her, yet again, saying he detested her before and still detests her, and besides she is fourteen years older. Furious, Louise ordered Chancellor Duprat to push her claim through *parlement*, and the king agrees since it would keep the duc's huge wealth in the family. Now Bourbon faces ruin, for Louise intends to seize his estates through a malicious lawsuit, citing the fact she was Suzanne's first cousin and so more closely related to the duc.'

'Poor *Madame la Grande*,' I watched as Louise hobbled with her stick down the gallery, her ladies trotting behind her furious figure. 'Losing her dear daughter and already in failing health.'

Marguerite passed her dog to one of her ladies. 'What can I do?' She stared about as we stood in silence, not daring to speak, and gave a long sigh. 'Come, ladies, I need to take the air. Let us join the queen in the gardens.'

We dutifully followed Marguerite outside until we found the queen. She was dressed in a plain, grey gown and apron and stooped as she tied a length of string around one of the plants. She straightened up and smiled as we approached.

'Dear sister,' said Marguerite, 'the archbishop has gardeners, you must not concern yourself with such trivial matters.'

'But I enjoy it,' the queen said, handing the ball of string to Diane, 'although I do miss Renée helping me. Still, it is better that she is at Blois.' She smiled at Diane, who despite her size due to her coming child, appeared as lovely as ever. 'It is such a shame the winter frost at Blois destroyed the precious fig tree brought back from Italy.'

'So I heard,' said Marguerite, frowning.

The queen began to take off her apron.

'Well, we must thank God we are past Easter and enjoying the spring,' said Marguerite. 'Did you not think, sister, our entry into Troyes was the most splendid affair? One hundred beautiful ermine to line our litters was most generous.'

The queen agreed and said that since the town has proved so generous, she had asked her husband to grant a new charter by which the town could hold a free fair and market for fourteen days in October. She then paused, apron in her hand. 'What is the matter, Marguerite?' she asked.

'Oh, my mother is in a rage over Bourbon refusing her hand again,' she said. 'She will not let the matter rest, and I fear they are making dreadful enemies of each other. Plus, she is making a fool of herself.'

'Does not love addle every female brain?' asked the queen. 'However, he could do worse than marry the king's mother.'

Marguerite bent down to stroke the palace cat, and I watched as it swirled about her, enjoying her caresses. She said it did not help that her mother's gout was causing her so much pain and ill-health.

'Madame,' I said turning to her, 'my father says Buckingham's pride knows no bounds, much like the duc, although he retired from court this year past, to enjoy his wealth at Thornbury. Why does pride corrupt so?'

'For that, we must look to the Bible,' said Marguerite. 'Corinthians tells us that if pride stems from self-righteousness or conceit, it is sin, and God hates it because it is a hindrance to seeking Him and his love. It is far better to be lowly in spirit and among the oppressed than to share plunder with the proud.'

'Pride,' added the queen, folding the apron, 'is giving ourselves the credit for something that God has accomplished. Such nobles think that all their achievements and wealth come solely from themselves.'

'So pride is self-worship,' I said.

'That is very astute,' said Marguerite. She then asked me to walk privately with her in the gardens, for she had something to discuss with me.

Leaving the queen to finish her task, I accompanied her down the path bordered with blossoming trees.

'As you know, Anne, Charles, having now been crowned emperor in Germany, has announced that he wishes to settle the problem of Martin Luther – that troublesome monk – once and for all. To that effect, he has summoned Luther to attend an imperial assembly at Worms, in Germany. Luther is there as we speak, and must renounce or reaffirm his heresies.'

I tugged at a long blade of grass.

'It is my observation, Anne,' she said, avoiding my eyes, 'that you seem destined to find yourself in the company of those interested in his teachings.'

I stopped walking. 'How do you mean, Madame?'

'First Clément Marot, then your father and now James Butler.'

Surprised, I asked what on earth James had to do with Luther.

'At present, nothing more than a passing interest.'

'Then, Madame, you know more than I,' I said. 'I am astonished that –'

'Anne, it is no criticism, but when I take a young woman into my household, I am interested in her welfare. I am aware that your parents are discussing the details of your betrothal to this young man, and while I cannot interfere in any way, I am naturally concerned.'

'Is interest in Luther so very dangerous then?' I asked as we resumed walking.

She told me while the man himself declared he was bound by scriptures and his conscience was captive to the word of God, he did not trust either the pope or church councils. He complained that they had often erred and contradicted themselves, and he challenged the absolute authority of the pope over the Church. He maintained that the Holy Father's doctrine of indulgences was in error since it was not found in scripture.'

'So, Madame – the real danger is in denying the pope's authority.'

'Indeed, although there is no doubt that the church needs reforming.

'But how do you know about James?'

'Anne, I am in regular correspondence with your Cardinal Wolsey, and James is in his household. It is to be expected that he should write to me of him since his future betrothed is residing in mine.'

Of course. I had forgotten how Wolsey had been enchanted with Marguerite at the meeting at Guînes, taking upon himself to be her only confessor throughout the celebrations. They had, it seemed, become close acquaintances.

I said I felt sure neither James Butler nor his family denied the power of the pope. If he was interested in reform, then yes, it was no more than my own father's interest. I asked her what her spiritual confessor, the Bishop of Meaux, thought of Luther. She said he condemned him, as she did. He agreed there must be reform in the light of the Bible, and had done much for improvement in his diocese by restoring discipline and the art of simple preaching. Having visited many churches, he noted that most priests did not reside in their parish and that their attendants were hardly trained at all. He had invited Jacques Lefèvre d'Etaples, who lived in Meaux, to work with him, since it was the writings of Lefèvre that influenced Luther. At present, the bishop was translating the New Testament from Latin into French to enable people to understand for themselves that which the priests read during the Mass. Of course, the doctors of the Sorbonne were not pleased with such an idea.

'Madame, I can understand the university's alarm, for it undermines the priests,' I replied.

'Indeed, but then there is also Guillaume Farel, a friend of Lefèvre who teaches grammar and philosophy in Paris. He is so disillusioned he wishes to break from the church altogether. There are others, too.'

'So this group of men wish to return to the theology of

the early Church,' I said, as we stopped to sit on a bench in the herb garden.

'They do, Anne, and I want to protect them.'

'Against the Sorbonne?' I was surprised.

'I am the king's sister,' she said, gazing ahead. 'We need reform for the sake of France, and through me, such ideas can reach the ears of my brother. As you know, unlike your own King Henry, François has no interest in theology whatsoever. But he does have faith and is simple in his beliefs.'

I said surely as a Christian king, it was his duty to protect his country from heresy. She said we both knew he would rather hunt the boar than heretics.

'That is true,' I laughed.

'I must admit, Anne, I do miss Madame de Châtillon now she has left the court to give birth. Sadly, I believe she will not return, for she fears her thoughts on reform compromise me. However, I am delighted you are able to join my household, and you already know my other ladies. Amongst them, Louise de Daillon speaks well of you – although she can be prickly – and Antoinette de Bourbon is extremely witty, with an absurd sense of humour. Françoise de Silly is charm itself. All are good conversationalists, and that is why I enjoy their company.'

I felt delighted. I knew that scholars, preachers, and friars all freely visited the ladies in Marguerite's apartments and the thought of being allowed to hear their opinions and read books banned by the Sorbonne thrilled me. As we sat enjoying the warm sunshine I thought back to Louise, and I asked Marguerite what would happen to the Duc de Bourbon. She replied that her brother would defend their mother, but that the time for revenge was not ripe. He needed the duc's military prowess at present, although the duc was peeved that Marguerite's husband has been given a military command in the north to defend Champagne. She admitted it was only her secretary she missed, although she wished her husband no harm.

'Anyway, Anne, if Bourbon will not have my mother, then he – he…'

'What?' I saw the alarm in her eyes.

'There is talk that if my mother is too old to give him an heir, then he must take me for his wife, and my husband seek an annulment.'

I asked on what grounds.

'That our marriage is fruitless. Perhaps not the best of bets for the duc after all.'

I made to speak, but Marguerite raised her hand. She said her brother knew she would do anything he commanded, whatever her personal feelings, for that was the price she paid for privilege. *Madame la Grande*, of course, was horrified by the thought. Marguerite then turned away as if gathering her thoughts.

'Come now, Anne, let us speak no more of this at present. This evening I have planned a supper with a discussion on the works of Guillaume Budé, and I would be delighted if you would join me. It will not be a late evening, for tomorrow we depart early for Dijon, as my brother wishes to meet his generals.'

As we rose and walked back to the archbishop's palace, a messenger bowed and handed Marguerite a letter. When she finally spoke, her face appeared serious.

'Well, well. I see that thus far it is proving a hapless month for ducs.'

As she nonchalantly handed the paper to me and walked ahead, I read the words myself. The French ambassador wished to inform Marguerite that the premier duke in England, the Duke of Buckingham, had been arrested at his home in Thornbury, in Gloucestershire, while working in his garden. When I read further, my blood ran cold:

> *'The king has dismissed the Lord Lieutenant of*
> *Ireland, Thomas Howard, and appointed another in*
> *his stead because he was the son-in-law of the Duke of*

*Buckingham. Two of the duke's nephews have already
been detained.'*

I must write to my father immediately. Would my uncle
be arrested, too?

●   ●

Nervously searching the crowd, I stood in the shade
of the palace of the Dukes of Burgundy, at Dijon, and
watched as the bronze field pieces rumbled past across the
cobbled courtyard. Behind them, marched the Swiss on
foot, their captains on horseback; all were in new liveries,
with rich plumes and plenty of drums and flutes. Other
soldiers carrying crossbows, pikes, and halberdiers sang as
they wheeled into view, while the ladies of the court waved
their scarves. I looked up to see Louise, Queen Claude, and
Marguerite admiring the colourful parade from a balcony. It
was a pretty scene, more to show off the cavalry and high-
stepping horses than anything else. Still, I knew the queen
had a horror of war and losing her beloved husband, and
wondered how she felt watching Françoise standing beside
him in the courtyard. Wearing his favourite colours of
mulberry and pale green, the king kissed Françoise's hand,
saying she was his sweetest general but that to honour her,
her brother, Odet, would command his army. Blushing, she
played the coquette to perfection. Poor Queen Claude. Signor
de Bayard, adjusting his sword, laughed, threatening to retire
if no longer required. King François, knowing he was the
bravest soldier he possessed, let out a great roar of laughter
and clapped him on the back, causing his hound to bark.

'Tell me,' said the king, turning to Montmorency, 'what
is our present situation?'

'Your army, majesty, advances as we speak to join the
Duc d'Alençon at Rheims. He has twelve thousand Swiss
and expects four thousand more to join their number. The
Admiral of France, Seigneur de Bonnivet, waits in Bayonne

with two thousand men-at-arms, and twelve thousand Landsknecht. I will serve you by commanding the defence of Mézières against the imperial German army.'

'Sire,' said Philippe de Chabot, 'the *Grand Seneschal* of Normandy intends to be in Lyon by July.'

'And my good brother Henry, what are his thoughts?'

'King Henry,' said Montmorency, 'has heard that you intend waging war on the emperor and this displeases him since he wishes for peace between Christian powers. He will do all he can to dissuade both the emperor and yourself from entering Italy.'

'I *will* have Milan,' said the king, feeding his hound a morsel of meat. 'Old Louis had it, he was invested with it by the old Emperor Maximilian. It is mine by right.'

'Majesty,' said Montmorency, 'King Henry loves you above all other princes, most esteeming his amity and constant dealing.'

'Does he?' asked the king. 'Well, King Henry may act as a friendly mediator, but not as an arbitrator, for I will not bind myself to him in such a fashion or suffer his meddling.'

As I turned away from their talk, I finally saw the ambassador, Sir William Fitzwilliam, pushing through the crowds, and quickly made my way toward him.

'Oh, thank God, Sir William,' I said, bobbing in greeting. 'Thank God I have seen you. May I trouble you for a moment?'

'Of course, Mistress Boleyn.' He took off his bonnet and smoothed his hair. 'Whatever is the matter?'

'Sir William, I have been so worried. Can you tell me, please, if my uncle has been recalled from Ireland because of the Duke of Buckingham? Is he to be examined? No-one will tell me what is happening.'

He appeared surprised. 'Recalled? Why not at all. I heard a rumour, but, no, your uncle is not to be questioned. Cardinal Wolsey – who does not want him back in England yet – told me himself, so please be assured it is true.'

'Oh, thank God and his saints,' I said, closing my eyes in relief. 'This whole affair with the duke is quite dreadful.'

Sir William agreed that it was a travesty of justice, although they did say that not one of Buckingham's ancestors ever died in bed. I asked if that made a man a traitor and what was his own opinion of the duke.

'Well, mistress, when I was asked the same question by King François, I had to admit I thought him high minded. The king replied he himself judged him so full of choler that there was nothing that could content him. I had to agree, but I still think his arrest is unjust.'

'And yet, sir,' I said, 'I hear he is a very dear friend to Queen Katherine. He, of all men, proved kind to her when she first came to England.'

He pointed out how that could prove his downfall since Wolsey maintained he was plotting with Spain against England. Wolsey hated the duke and would never allow the king to be merciful, so he doubted Queen Katherine could save him should he be found guilty.'

'Can he do that?' I asked.

'Mistress, Wolsey rules England.'

'So the duke has been arrested due to his intrigue?'

He said it was one reason, yes, but that he also stood for the imperialists. However, the duke bragged openly that if anything but good should happen to the king, he, the Duke of Buckingham, was next in succession to the crown of England. Others reported the duke had foolishly arranged to have the cardinal assassinated.

'Wolsey,' he continued, 'promised to sit on his skirts, but the duke only treated this threat as a joke. Well, the cardinal never forgave him for deliberately spilling water over his slippers. No, one must be very careful with our great cardinal, for he is lofty and sour to those that love him not. Of course, to those men that seek him, he is as sweet as summer.'

I thought of the poor Duchess of Buckingham, half out

of her mind with worry, and recalled the time I had met her at Thornbury, at the marriage of her daughter to my uncle. I was but a child at my first grand occasion, and it seemed so long ago. Still, Heaven be praised, my family would not be involved with the duke's disgrace if it came. The sound of drums, hautbois, clarions, and sackbuts brought me back to the moment.

'Do you think King François will really go to war?' I felt more at ease.

Sir William picked at the black feather on his bonnet. 'All I know for certain is that the emperor wants Italy and so does King François. I also know King François cannot afford it, and his mother is against it. There is even talk that men have still not been paid from the last campaign. However, Louise has instructed Semblançay to find two million livres, and the king himself is borrowing heavily off every man in Burgundy.'

'King François thinks King Henry is meddling,' I said, repeating what I had heard my father say.

'The French king has been informed that if he does not accept Henry's mediation, England will ally with the emperor. The pope wants Wolsey to arbitrate.'

I pointed out that if he did not, England would be at war with France. He said it might not come to that, for King Henry remembered what the last war against France cost him. Still, my father thought we might be able to negotiate a truce.

'How is my father?' I asked.

'He appeared well when last I saw him at Greenwich. He is much pre-occupied with your coming betrothal to James Butler, although he does not seem amenable to the terms so far. What are your thoughts on the matter? Does it please you?'

I was not sure what to say, for until I met James again I could not be certain how I felt.

'My mother is content,' I said.

'That is not what I asked,' said the ambassador, a smile dancing around his eyes. 'What of you, what of Anne Boleyn?'

As I gazed ahead at the dwindling cavalcade, I could not help but wonder about my feelings, although in truth, I had thought of nothing else. What if I did not like James? Mary's match with William Carey had been a love match, and I wondered if I could hope for the same. As I clapped at the last of the prancing horses, I turned to Sir William and smiled.

'Why, sir, how could I not be content with the prospect of becoming a countess?'

•   •

Buckingham was dead.

A messenger carrying the news rode to Louise, at Dijon, as she lay in bed, suffering from gout, surrounded by charts and astrological forecasts.

While the other ladies quietly plied their needles, I stood at the foot of her bed, holding a cloth containing a paste of goose fat. Marguerite read out to her how the duke had spoken in his defence for an hour, confuting the charges brought against him with great eloquence. At the trial, all present were so affected that no-one dared pass sentence. However, my grandfather, the Duke of Norfolk, having been forced to reside over proceedings, had tears streaming down his face when he pronounced death. They had been friends for thirty years. Buckingham then fell upon his knees, and desired the lords that they should ask the king's grace to be good and gracious unto his wife and to his children; and as for his own life, he would not sue. As a result, my grandfather informed the king he himself intended to resign the Lord Treasurership, all duties except Earl Marshal, and retire to Framlingham. He had had enough blood-letting and was an old, broken man. As for King Henry, on the thirteenth day of May, the day Buckingham was condemned, he fell ill with tertian fever and rode to Eltham Palace to recover.

Some say it was brought on by guilt and regret, for the duke's death was universally lamented by all in London, and Queen Katherine felt bereft.

'Buckingham was a fool,' said Louise, wincing as she moved position, 'and I cannot agree with the emperor when he said that Wolsey – the butcher's dog – had pulled down the fairest buck in Christendom. The duc was ever against an alliance with France.'

Marguerite, casting the despatch aside on a chair, pulled the cover down from her mother's legs and I began to apply the plaster gently to her red, swollen toe. It appeared three times its normal size and looked very painful.

'Thank you, my dear,' she said, observing me closely as I worked. 'Dr du Puy has offered me little comfort, and yet your hands are so cool and gentle.'

I said nothing, but continued, hiding my little finger as best I could. This slight deformity still bothered me, although now I had learnt to disguise it better with sleeves and cuffs.

'Do you recall,' asked Louise, 'when you first came to court, mistress? You were such a bold little thing – ambitious, too – and not afraid to speak with me. I have watched you grow over the years from a rather pale-faced child into a charming young woman. I am glad that you are serving my daughter, it was a most generous gesture from our queen here. Tell me, is it true that you are to become a countess?'

'It is talked about, Madame,' I replied, as I wrapped the poultice carefully around the joint, 'but nothing is agreed upon as yet.'

She cried out in pain as I raised her foot on to a cushion, before flicking her hand at me to leave.

'Poor Mama, let me try and distract you,' said Marguerite. 'I hear Madame de Châtillon has delivered safely of a boy she has named Gaspard. Now she has three Coligny boys, how wonderful! Diane, of course, is in her confinement as we speak.'

'Then we must send gifts,' said Louise. 'What of my son?'

Her daughter replied he had enjoyed hunting at Saussey, and on Whitsunday cured many sick people there.

'Then why can he not cure my wretched gout?' Louise raised herself on one elbow.

'Because, as you are well aware, *ma mère*, gout is not the King's Evil. Anyway, when he dismounted from his horse, the poor folk were so in awe of his glittering cassock of gold frieze, they could barely come forth. He must have appeared like a god from antiquity. Incidentally, where on earth are we going to put that hideous, equestrian statue of François?'

'Sister, dear,' said the queen, looking up from her needlework, 'it may be a dreadful likeness, but the magistrates at Dijon felt it was an admirable gift, and my husband could not be rude to them.'

'It can sink to the bottom of the sea, for all I care,' said Louise, 'and I am certainly not having it at Romorantin. The artist has given my son an absurdly long nose.'

'Well, I am delighted by my gifts,' said the queen, brightly. 'So many beautiful gowns as well as fifty-five ells of white cloth embroidered with flowers.'

She was right, for gifts and gowns amounting to over eight hundred livres had been presented to her, and I had received an exquisite gown of burgundy velvet, with a matching French hood studded with pearls.

'Shall I open the casement, *ma mère*?' asked Marguerite, 'now the rain has stopped?'

'What?' Louise lay back on her bolster, 'and catch my death from a draught, on top of my gout? This is the worse spring weather in a long time. No, order the chamberer to make up the fire. I cannot get warm.'

Marguerite then turned the talk to the latest news on Luther. She described how he had entered the presence of the emperor, who inquired whether the books printed in his name were his and whether he would withdraw them and recant? Since they were condemned by the pope they were heretical. Luther admitted they were his.

'The result being?' Louise peered through a glass lens at the chart in her hand.

'The result,' said Marguerite, 'is that the emperor, the electors, and princes ordered all his books, wheresoever found, to be burnt, and that he be punished as a notorious heretic.'

Louise put down her glass and stared at her.

'I have heard,' continued Marguerite, 'that amongst other follies, he believes any layman in a state of grace is competent to administer the Sacrament of the Eucharist, that marriage may be dissolved, and that fornication is not a sin.'

Her mother snorted in derision and the queen asked if it were true that King Henry had written a soon to be finished work, entitled *Asserto Septem Sacramentorum*, or the *Defence of the Seven Sacraments*, defending the supremacy of the pope.

'I believe so,' said Marguerite, 'for he says he is so much bounden unto the See of Rome he cannot do too much honour to it. He then ordered Luther's works to be burnt at St Paul's Cross.'

'Ah, but did he write it, in truth?' asked Louise. 'It smacks of Wolsey's work, who is desperate to be the next pope, with all the glory that entails. Leo is ill, all can see that, and yet, if Wolsey but trusts him, my son would secure the seat for him at the first opportunity. He commands the voices of fourteen cardinals and the whole Orsini faction in Rome. Let but the King of England and my son remain at peace, and they would make popes and emperors at their pleasure.'

I smiled at this, for Sir William had confided to me that Wolsey stated he only desired the pope's crown 'to exalt their Majesties,' and not for personal gain.

'Oh, *ma mère*,' said Marguerite, her face clouding over, 'we have stumbled upon the subject of war. If *only* Henry and François could overcome their differences, for I believe they love each other as brothers. There must not be, there cannot be war. Erasmus, and other such good men, are firm on the matter. He says the Englishman is an enemy to the Frenchman, simply because he is a Frenchman; but these things should not be. The Rhine, the Pyrenees and the Narrow Seas should not divide the unity of the Church.'

'Prettily said,' murmured Louise, 'and yet I fear Wolsey may say one thing and do another. I asked Fitzwilliam if it were true that all the English scholars in Paris had been asked to return home. He said he did not know, but that the last time his servants passed that way, the greatest gentlemen's sons were there still. I said I should be sorry to see war with England, and he said there was no war, but as great a love as could be, as long as my son maintained the amity.'

'And Wolsey?' asked Marguerite.

Louise said the cardinal told her he knew nothing of the matter, and they were doubtless scholars who wished to revisit their homes and relations. All of them, at the same time? Louise thought not. Wolsey said he was quite content for the ambassadors to remain safely in France to prove there was no animosity.'

Having finished my task, I dipped in reverence to Louise and returned to where the other ladies were seated. Were English scholars leaving France due to the possibility of hostilities? I had heard nothing from my father to that effect.

Antoinette de Polignac ceased her sewing. 'I do not think the problem can be resolved,' she said, passing my book to me. 'I fear so for my husband, Claude, for he never did quite recover from his wounds at Marignano seven years ago.'

I placed my hand over hers and told her there was still time for negotiation, and that King Henry in England was determined to bring peace to Europe. 'Neither side wants conflict and so, we must put our trust in princes.'

'If that is your considered opinion,' whispered Antoinette, 'you are naive.

•   •

As the rain lashed down and parts of the country were reported to be close to famine, life at Dijon continued unperturbed, with entertainments, banquets and even a bear-baiting in the palace courtyard. When it proved too wet to ride out, I read with Marguerite, played chess, and sang before her accompanied by my lute. When she offered to take me around the palace to see the beautiful Bourbon treasures, I felt honoured to spend the hours in her company. She was so lively and joyful, compared to Queen Claude, and I knew that when the time came to leave her, as surely it must, I would feel deeply saddened.

As to the queen, when she announced that she was with child yet again, King François appeared so delighted he held a supper party in her honour and did not invite Françoise. As the queen enjoyed his undivided attention, his lover sulked in her chambers. But this time it was clear that the queen herself did not appear as content as her husband, for each pregnancy brought another risk to her already weakened health.

When Louise congratulated the queen and brought her a bowl of fresh strawberries, I wondered if she might finally be softening towards the girl. After all, she had done everything Louise could have hoped for, giving France a full nursery and providing genuine love and affection for her beloved son. It comforted Claude when she heard that Diane de Brézé had safely delivered a girl, named Louise, in honour of her husband, Louis.

As Diane recovered at Anet, Marguerite and I busied ourselves selecting a gift from the many received so far. We chose a bale of blue velvet to cover the cradle and golden bells for a rattle. As the queen looked on, I knew she missed her children at Blois and longed to return.

When Sir Richard Jernyngham arrived back in France, he told Louise that King Henry remained at Richmond, locked away with my father and the council, considering his next political move. He would not come to court at Greenwich on account of the pestilential fever, which was rife there and throughout London. That dismal, cloudy summer, Mary and William returned to Rochford for a while and were later joined by George, who fell ill. He soon recovered, to my parents' relief, but all were in great fear that it might be the Sweat.

•   •

At the beginning of August, as famine raged in Normandy, we heard that Cardinal Wolsey had arrived at Calais to preside over a conference to put an end to the fighting that had broken out, fighting which had increasingly involved French and imperial forces. King Henry desired this meeting because of the evils of war, but he also knew he would eventually have to declare for one side or the other. However, although he said he desired peace, it was reported that he was excited by the prospect of war.

Wolsey rode in great pomp in a litter accompanied by my father, who, along with the other ambassadors, was given strict instructions to stick doggedly to the treaties of Noyon and London, and not to open ancient quarrels. By these treaties, England was bound to France by the marriage alliance of Princess Mary with the dauphin, and the emperor bound to a marriage alliance with a Princess of France. When Wolsey was met by the imperial ambassadors at the waterside, the guns of the ships in the harbour and of the town, fired salutes. The French ambassadors arrived on Sunday, and they all proceeded to the Staple Hall, where the conference was to be held.

The talks dragged on, and although sick, Wolsey refused to say who the aggressor was. His Holiness the Pope announced that as long as King François was ruled by his mother and Admiral Bonnivet, his word was not to be trusted and that he must not proceed any farther with his army. I was more interested in the fact that I heard that Wolsey had taken James Butler over to Calais in his train and kept him close in his sight at all times. Did he fear he would escape back to Ireland, to his father? What then would become of our betrothal?

With matters at a stalemate, Margaret of Savoy stepped in and wrote to King Henry saying she desired above all things a perfect understanding between the two princes. Only she called for neutrality. She also wrote to Louise offering her help but was ignored. Concerned, Margaret then advised the assembled States at Ghent to prepare for an attack, and twenty-two thousand troops were raised on the outskirts of Mechelen. As I thought back to that beautiful, peaceful city where I been so happy, I could not imagine it preparing for hostilities. And now, the country I had called my home was also considering war with England. If the scholars were truly fleeing Paris, there was every chance I, too, would be recalled to England.

• •

As the horses made their way up the precarious, winding streets to the great *Cathédrale Saint-Lazare,* I felt unwell. I had never become used to travelling and still fell sick with the motion. We had travelled sixteen leagues, the last two along the River Arroux, to Autun, southwest of Dijon, and as our litter made its way up the steep cobbles, I could barely keep my seat.

Passing through the ancient gate, I saw ahead of us the cathedral, perched high on a hill that had been occupied since Roman times. It was the Roman sites that King François – taking a short break from his martial affairs – and Marguerite now wished to visit. The king's librarian, Guillaume Budé, had arranged to meet them both here and show them the Roman amphitheatre and imposing remains of the Temple of Janus. The queen and Louise, however, wished to visit the Abbaye Saint-Andoche, a former Benedictine nunnery, and the Abbaye Saint Jean le Grand. This would be a private visit, and since we ladies would not be required, we would be free to visit the *Place de Terreau,* in front of the Romanesque cathedral, to see the magnificent fountain. However, all I wanted to do was lie down with a cool cloth on my face.

That evening, after the viewing of theological books in the great library – many of the priceless tomes chained to the table – the bishop produced a magnificent supper at his palace, in honour of the king and queen. The court sat in the *grande salle* enjoying spinach and veal tarts, poached eggs in custard and a hundred other succulent dishes. As we sipped at the highly concentrated Burgundy wine, seasoned with herbs and sweetened with honey, I noticed that the queen appeared sad as she gazed down the long table at the vast expanse of food. Knowing her as I did, she was, I imagined, concerned that as famine continued to spread through the country, with no bread or corn to be found, we sat feasting.

'Quite scandalous,' said Louise, leaning towards the bishop. 'You will, of course, dismiss the abbess for the sinful life she lives at Saint-Jean. Such disorder. Drinking, dancing, gambling. My daughter and I were deeply shocked.'

'Madame, great as are the evils of the Church, the remedy is worse than the disease.'

'Meaning?'

The bishop replied that there was none suitable to take her place, at present, and besides, she came from a powerful family who did much for the town. 'The notables in Autun do not wish to antagonise them.'

'My Lord,' said the queen, leaning forward, 'while we found good order at the Abbaye Saint-Andoche, life at Saint-Jean is an abomination. I can assure you that when we return to Blois, I shall be recommending certain reforms. Do you not agree, Sire?'

King François sat engrossed in some conversation with Marguerite and ignored her.

'Sire?' she repeated, loudly. The king looked up and waved his hand airily towards her. He said that whatever she wished would be done and resumed speaking to his sister.

When the dancing began, and the king took his wife's hand in a stately pavane, Marguerite beckoned me to her, her face downcast. I asked her what the matter was.

'Oh, Anne, the emperor's forces have crossed the French border. They have plundered and massacred all in their wake – including women and children – and are now laying siege to the city of Mézières. My husband, meanwhile, commands forces at Attigny, between Mézières and Rheims, where my brother is about to join Bourbon and his army.'

'And you fear for your husband?' I asked as she took a paper from her sleeve. I recognised the writing as she unfolded it. It belonged to Clément.

'I fear for my brother, for Monsieur Marot has sent me this letter from the camp at Attigny concerning conditions there. Listen to what he writes.'

As I looked at her worried face, I recalled how Clément had once written to me of war. Well, those days were long gone. She cleared her throat.

'In the summer, the drums and trumpets gaily sound, but in a few month's winter will come, women and children will flee, fire will destroy all, even the enemy will be pitied. That pitiless Serpent, War, has darkened the air and I ask prayers of you, Princess of France, that Peace, the sacred daughter of Jesus Christ, may descend on French lands.'

She looked up, a tear in her eye. 'Oh, if anything should happen to my dear brother!'

'With God's good grace, all will be well,' I said, as she blew her nose. However, I knew there was some other matter troubling her. 'Tell me, is it true that the churches, abbeys, and priories in Paris have been stripped of their wealth to pay for this war?'

She proffered a thin smile and nodded. The cost had proved great, not only in human life but in treasures. Treasures that should not have been melted down and destroyed. Her mind was in great torment, for her mother ordered this, and she was finding it hard to reconcile her mind to these actions. Louise was desperate for money, for

France was bankrupt, and she was using any means she could to obtain it.

'Oh, Anne, I am in great need of advice and comfort and must seek out my spiritual advisor, Guillaume Briçonnet. With this in mind, when the king journeys to Rheims with his army, I shall travel to Meaux.'

* *

It was subtle at first. A look here, a glance there, a seat at the refectory table taken when I tried to sit down. With Marguerite in conference with her spiritual advisor, and her brother visiting the royal abbey of Saint-Denis, in Paris, I was now able to relax and enjoy the peace of the bishop's palace at nearby Meaux. Standing on the ramparts, I looked down on the herb and medicinal garden as the late September sun glinted on the trees. Several other courtiers also strolled, taking the air, and I smiled as Louise de Daillon swept past. However, she avoided my eyes as she linked arms with Madame de Nevers and pointed to the view in the distance. I wondered if I had done something to upset her? I could not think what, as I picked up Bonny and moved to the edge of the battlements. Below, I watched Louise as she walked with her ladies, a spaniel in her arms, and the queen trotting behind. The girl appeared paler than usual, and I knew she suffered from morning sickness again.

As I stood engrossed, I heard my name. I swung around to see Françoise, and she laughed.

'Have a care! I did not mean to make you jump.'

I was surprised. I thought she would be with François, but evidently not. Perhaps he felt that visiting Saint-Denis to pray before war was best done without his mistress in tow. She looked as captivating as ever in cream velvet, edged with mink, her hair piled beneath a caul of sapphires.

'I have been watching you,' she said, folding her hands on her gown.

Puzzled, I put Bonny down and watched as she

scampered away to chase the leaves.

'And I have observed how they are treating you.'

Still unsure what she meant, I remained silent.

'Oh, nothing much at first,' she said. 'A furtive look, a conversation that ceases when you approach a group of ladies. Well, I suppose I am used to such things and pick the signs up easily.'

I then understood her meaning. I had not imagined the coolness towards me, although at first, I thought it was because Marguerite had singled me out, favoured me in some way.

'People are fickle,' she said, 'and I am under no illusion that if anything happened to François, I would be banished. The imperial army is, I hear, besieging Tournai, and he plans to ride there at the head of an army to relieve it. I pray daily for his safety, for matters for me could change in an instant. Now matters have changed for you.'

She was right. I was an English woman, and if negotiations collapsed, my country was most likely to go to war against France. No matter how much I might feel myself part of the French court, I was not. And if I thought myself held in some esteem by Marguerite, it mattered not. In the end, I was English and not welcome. I gazed down at the party below. There was still the possibility of a truce since the delegation at Calais continued to seek a solution. But if not ...

'Where would you go should anything happen to the king?' I asked.

'Back home to my husband in the country,' she replied.

I bent down to stroke Bonny as she bounded back to me, tail wagging, and told Françoise that I, too, felt uncertain of my future. I did not know if I was to be married, return to England, go to Ireland or remain here. The decision on my betrothal just dragged on and on.

'Well, Anne, you cannot stay here if hostilities continue. The emperor is withdrawing his ambassadors, and I do not think it long before my Lords Worcester and Ely will depart from here. In a few days, we leave for Saint Germain-en-Laye and then on to Calais if the queen can bear the travelling. Do you not think she looks rather jaded at present? It must have been such an effort for the king to get another child on her.'

The comment, although true, was spiteful, for the queen had never been anything but kind and tolerant of Françoise.

'Now come, Anne, will you walk with me? I, at least, am happy to be seen in the company of an English girl.'

When I returned to the palace, a letter from my father – written from the imperial court at Courtray, not far from Lille – made my heart almost stop beating. He wrote that it was imperative that I left France, for the king wanted the marriage between James and myself finally solemnised. The reason why it had become so urgent was that Sir Piers Butler, much troubled with gout, could not stir in the cold weather, let alone ride out to keep the peace. Since his men in Ireland refused to move without him, or his son – whom they respected as 'right active and discreet' – he wanted James back to maintain order. Wolsey had already written to the king from Calais, saying that on his return he would talk with him on how to bring the marriage to a speedy conclusion. Besides, finalising the negotiations would be a good pretext for delaying in sending James back to Ireland sooner. So, at least now I knew I must leave France as soon as possible. What I did not know, as yet, was that the wheel of fortune was about to spin full circle and I would see again the lady I held most dear in all the world, next to my mother.

Chapter Seventeen

'The sky goes all the way home.'

Calais

Our journey had proved slow as the litters progressed north through the November fog and drizzle. Now, in the warmth of the hall of the English Merchants of the Staple, in Calais, my eyes searched about. And then I saw him.

'Father!'

He pushed his way through the expectant crowd of people waiting for news. All seemed to be the usual confusion.

'Anne, I do not have much time, but I can speak for a moment. Are you well?'

'Indeed, Father. Oh, Father, tell me is J –'

'How long have you been here?'

I told him just a day, having travelled by way of Beauvais, Amiens, and Crécy. Louise, Queen Claude, and Marguerite had arrived already, and the rest of the court were gathering, as he could see. He said he knew, having already spoken with Louise. As he took my arm, and we stepped aside into an alcove, I felt desperate to ask the one thing on my mind.

'Anne, you must know the conference here is not going well,' he said, voice lowered, 'and the situation is unlikely to develop into a peaceful settlement. The imperialists will not negotiate without the authority and assistance of the pope, and each side is more concerned with ancient right, historical precedent, and diplomatic convention than agreeing on a truce.'

'So what do you think will happen?'

He said he knew not, for the quarrel was between King François and the emperor, and King Henry could only back one of them. The pope had even advised his nuncio to keep procrastinating, and so they went round in circles.

'Well then,' I said, my face serious, 'we must pray for a solution. Tell me, who else is here?'

He glanced about at the crowds and nodded his head towards a group of gentlemen, shaking out their wet cloaks.

'Docwra, Worcester, Ely, More, Wingfield – most of the ambassadors have returned. Even Erasmus is here somewhere.'

That was not what I meant and I felt I could wait no longer.

'Oh, Father, please tell me – is James Butler here in Wolsey's train?'

He nodded as he took off his fur cloak and placed it over his arm.

'And may I meet him?' I felt my heart racing with excitement.

'No.'

I stood staring at him. 'But – but why ever not?'

My father avoided my eyes. 'Because the cardinal does not wish it. Listen, I like it no more than –'

'Than who, my mother? Or perhaps James does not care for the match?' I felt my irritation rising as my father gripped my arm.

'I have no idea what he thinks, Anne, but I do know that your Uncle in Ireland, Sir Piers, Cardinal Wolsey and the king are pushing for the conclusion of this affair.'

I pulled my arm away and asked him again if James was with Wolsey. My father rubbed his chin. 'He is.'

'Then can your daughter not at least meet the man she must marry?'

My father looked uncomfortable.

'Nan, the cardinal is not a man to cross, and he has his reasons. I will introduce you if you insist, but you are not to seek him out yourself. I know full well how impatient you are, so I must have your solemn oath on this. Do I have it?'

I folded my arms and leaned back against the stone pillar, staring up at the wooden rafters. The cold seeped through my winter gown and into my bones. I sighed and mumbled my promise. Why must he always speak to me like a child?

'Good, then take that sour look off your face, for I have some news that will please you very much. The cardinal, having visited Bruges for crisis talks, has ordered Thomas Docwra and me to return to the emperor's palace, the *Princenhof*. The articles of agreement are not to the emperor's satisfaction. So, in two days' you will accompany me to Oudenarde and then onto Bruges to see Margaret of Savoy.'

I turned my head. 'Are you serious? When was this arranged?'

'When she heard you were coming to Calais she insisted on me fetching you, despite her preoccupation with the present situation. Marguerite is happy for you to go.'

'But that is wonderful! I yearn to see Margaret again and have so much I wish to tell her. How long will we stay?'

He replied not long, for he was presently waiting for news from Italy, Navarre and the northern front, before returning to England.

'Oh, I must take my little dog, for she was a gift from Margaret and she will be so delighted to see her again.'

'You will do no such thing.' My father replaced the velvet bonnet on his head. 'You will be back here in a few days, and I'll have no extra encumbrance.'

'But I —'

'Enough, Anne. Come, let us go and find something to eat. I have had nothing in this flea-ridden hole since last night, and that was stale. Tomorrow, you can meet your betrothed.'

* *

Unable to stem my curiosity a moment longer, I peered around the door. Sitting at a large desk in the Staple Hall, holding a clove-studded orange to his nose, sat the cardinal. Although I had seen him at the meeting at Guînes, a year ago, he now appeared fleshier and somehow grander in his scarlet robes. An important man, indeed. A tower of papers lay before him, and he sorted through them with one hand, tossing them onto different piles. A servant moved forward with wine to fill his glass, but he took the silver jug from him and waved him impatiently away. He appeared to have much to do, and although the work of the day was not scheduled to start for another hour, Father told me he liked to be well briefed before he went into the council.

Across the hall, a crowd of ambassadors and dignitaries began noisily arriving from their lodgings. As they gathered about, documents held beneath their arms ready for the long afternoon ahead, the cardinal rang the silver bell on his desk. I moved back as a young man appeared from a side door. I peered around again and saw he had hair as red as a fox's pelt and a florid complexion. Was *that* James Butler? He certainly appeared as my sister had described. He stood dressed in an expensive suit of black, wool cloth. The collar of his shirt, embroidered with black stitching, was clean and tidy. He wore no adornment, no brooch or chain. Heavily set, he had the physique of a soldier, rather than a courtier, but he was not unattractive. However, he was not quite how I remembered him at all, all those years ago at Tournai, for he now appeared much broader. He took the proffered note from the cardinal, and with a slight bow, turned to leave the chamber. I stood back, hidden, as he hurried past me down the gallery. His limp seemed quite pronounced, but he managed to walk briskly enough.

Following discreetly at a distance, I watched as he entered the dining hall and approached a swarthy looking gentleman.

He handed over the paper with a bow and then sat down on one of the benches. As he looked about, I knew that if I stayed any longer, he would notice me, and so I thought it best to return to continue my packing. I had not broken my promise to my father, but I had seen the man I might yet marry – and I was not sure what to think.

I hardly slept all night, tossing and turning. From what my sister had said, James Butler sounded a decent young man, with a reputation for being good-mannered. He was of a similar age as me, but dare I hope I might find him acceptable? What if he did not like me? Sitting on my bed, I nervously watched as the young chamberer wrapped the last of my gowns in linen and lifted it into the basket. The bulk of my wardrobe would be sent on separately to England since I had acquired quite a few beautiful shoes, hoods, and veils – most of them gifts from the queen or Marguerite. As I sat, I watched Bonny pouncing on the stockings on the floor, growling and daring them to fight back. She always made me smile. When a knock sounded on the door, I knew it must be my father, and as the chamberer abandoned her task and let him in, he appraised me.

'Do you have anything plainer?' he asked. 'Less French?'

I gazed down at the low shoulders, and gold edged bodice of my dark green gown. I shook my head, for everything was now packed away, save for a few travelling clothes and a gown for meeting Margaret of Savoy – my best.

'Well, when you get back to England you will have to throw off your French ways. Everything French is out of favour now, so don't flaunt it.'

'Did the talks go well?' I asked, ignoring the comment as we walked down the gallery. Outside the rain made the window panes rattle and the torches flicker.

'Six goddamned hours we have been in there, six hours,' he said. 'Gattinara challenges King François' rights to Milan, and Madame Louise has begged Margaret of Savoy to reconcile the emperor with her son. All to no avail. The duchess has now demanded that England joins her and declares war against France immediately.'

I said matters must be bad, for I knew that the duchess was advocating peace.

'Well, Nan, she says the French have broken the terms of the treaty of Noyon, but you know she has ever been pro-English – *'la bonne Angloise.'*

As my father ranted on, my mind wandered; I was far more concerned with the meeting about to take place. My heart pounded, and my hands felt hot as I wiped them against my gown. In vain, I tried to steady my breathing. When we reached the door of a chamber, just off from the chapel, Father strode in, and I curtsied to the man standing there. A matron I had not seen before sat in the window, her hands resting in her lap. She rose and dipped a bob.

'Good even, James,' said my father. 'As we are all, by some happy chance, in the same country, I have brought my daughter, Anne, to meet you.'

He moved over to the table and poured two glasses of wine, handing one to James. The young man took the glass and bowed to me.

'May we speak, sir?' asked the young man.

My father nodded and handed a glass to me. I felt tempted to down the contents in one desperate gulp.

'I am honoured to meet you, my lady,' said James, his brown eyes hovering over my slight frame, his voice tremulous with a distinct accent. As he moved towards two chairs, I tried not to stare too hard at his limp.

'And I, sir, am honoured to meet you,' I began brightly, 'although we have met before, at Tournai. I rode in the train of Margaret of Savoy, having been placed at her court. I fell from my horse in the procession, and you and your friend came to my rescue. I was with a girl with red hair. Do you recall the incident?'

He appeared puzzled. 'Should I, my lady?'

'Well, it was eight years ago.' I felt a little irritated for he could at least have had the good grace to pretend. So much for his good manners.

'I hear you have been some years in France,' he said, his voice flat.

I told him that I loved France with its beautiful châteaux and gardens, particularly around the Loire valley. An awkward silence followed.

'My grandmother,' I continued, 'has told me much of Ireland, of Kilkenny Castle and the beautiful River Nore. She says it runs fast and deep.'

'Did she tell you of the cold and rain, my lady?' he asked. 'I am afeared that after the warmth of the south of France you will be much disappointed, for the summers are short and the winters long and harsh.'

We sat in silence again as my father wandered over to look at nothing in particular down in the courtyard. This was not going well.

'Do you enjoy music, sir?'

I was met with a blank expression.

'My lady, I care nothing for such pastimes, nor do I have the time. I am more concerned with keeping the peace in Ireland than enjoying the frivolities of court.'

'But sir,' I said, 'a court education is not frivolous. Surely it is the supreme academy for nobles of the realm, for it is a school of vigour, probity, and manners. Music is an integral part of the court.'

'Is it, my lady? I care not, provided I am kept informed of royal policy.'

I told him I had heard that Ireland was a difficult country to rule. He said it was, for there were more than sixty regions inhabited by the king's Irish enemies. In these regions, there were more than sixty chief captains, who lived by the sword. He then fell silent, and I felt desperate to say something.

'Sir, I love to hunt and ride,' I finally offered.

'Good,' he said, 'for we have fine horses in Ireland.'

I waited for him to elaborate, but he did not. Nothing.

'My grandmother says they are very well-bred.'

As he stared down at his glass, I noticed his nails were short and bitten. Was this proving as much of an ordeal for him as it was for me? And then he looked up at me.

'I must tell you, my lady, that I wish to return to Kilkenny as soon as matters are settled, for my place is at my father's side. I trust that would be agreeable to you?'

I offered a stiff smile, not knowing how to reply. After the sophistication of the French court, I was not sure that Kilkenny – seventeen leagues of bog and mountain – appealed one bit.

My father turned around but I had no idea what he might be thinking. He moved to pour himself another glass of wine and downed it, before sitting back down. I waited for James to speak again, encouraging him with a smile, but he just sat there, staring at his shoes. In the end, I felt exasperated. Why could he not make more of an effort? He appeared thoroughly bored.

My father slapped his knees and stood up.

'Well, that is done,' he said, trying to sound cheerful. 'You two have now met. As you know, matters are still to be decided, but the cardinal is keen to progress the match as quickly as possible. I trust you will not mention this meeting to him, as we agreed?'

Appearing relieved, James stood up, bonnet in hand, as my father walked to the door.

'You have my word, sir.' He then bowed towards me, his cheeks reddening, and I curtsied low. 'I wish you good ev'n, Lady Anne.'

As I rose up, he leant close and spoke quietly in my ear. 'My lady, I am fully aware, as you must be, that this marriage is proposed with the express intention of reducing distrust and violence in Ireland. It is hoped to be a contract that will bring peace between houses. However, I can assure you that I seek this – this arrangement – no more than I think you do. Still – we must do as our betters bid.'

The matron in the corner stood as my father took my arm and we left the chamber. We then made our way to his lodgings, and once inside, I slumped down on to a chair. He handed me a glass of hypocras, his face solemn.

'Here, you need this.'

'By God, I do,' I said, my hands shaking. 'Look at me.' I held out my trembling fingers.

My father stood there, expectantly. 'Well – what did he whisper?'

'He does not want me,' I said, my voice petulant. 'How dare he! What is wrong with me? Well, I'll not have him. He is not as I remember and the prospect of becoming a countess is fast losing its appeal. Will I be forced?'

'No,' said my father, turning, 'for the matter does not suit me either. He is a decent boy, but we can do better, regardless of your uncle's plans.'

'But why does the cardinal not want us to meet?' I asked.

My father shrugged. 'He knew you would not care for James. He has been following your progress most carefully, through Marguerite, and from what she had told him knew that it would be an unsatisfactory match. He hoped to have everything signed and sealed should you prove difficult and your mother unable to beat any objection out of you.'

'That she would never do!' I cried. 'Anyway, why did *you* agree for me to meet him?'

'I know you, Anne,' he said, 'you would have sought him out yourself, oath or not. It's what you young women do these days, no propriety as in your mother's time. But it *has* confirmed what I hoped. Neither of you appear enthusiastic about the match, and that strengthens my case.'

'But if Wolsey, the king, and the Irish council insist, what then?' I suddenly felt cold.

My father sat down and loosened the neck of his shirt. He rubbed his tired eyes and yawned, feeling his chin. His beard needed trimming.

'I am not sure, as yet, but by the Mass, I can promise you

this. You will not be marrying James Butler.'

A long pause followed.

'You must be tired of travelling, Father,' I eventually said.

He agreed, saying he feared he was becoming too old. Fitzwilliam was only young, but already weary of the whole game and begged to be sent home. His servants were sick, his clerk likely to die, and he couldn't make head nor tail of the cyphers used in the despatches. Since there was a constant interception of letters and breaches of confidence, Father said he had better work them out – and fast.

'I hear Louise is spying on him,' I said, 'forever eavesdropping on his every word.'

My father moaned and closed his eyes.

After a few moments of silence, I spoke.

'Father, what if James and I had liked each other, what then?'

He opened one eye and looked at me. 'Liking or loathing would not be allowed to get in the way of what is best for the Boleyn's. You know that, Anne.'

'But my sister was allowed to marry a man she loves,' I replied.

'Does she?' came the reply. 'You would not think so from the way she enjoys the recent attention of the king.'

       •   •

Travelling by way of Gravelines and Dunkirk, we cantered along the North Sea coast towards the Cistercian monastery of the Abbey of the Dunes, in West Flanders. I had left Bonny in the capable hands of Anne de Graville, but since I had never been parted from her for any length of time before, it felt strange not having her with me. I felt sad, too, that Margaret would not see her gift and how she had grown, for I remembered well the day she presented her to me and how I had spent all day choosing a name. Now I had to put her from my mind as we rested our horses and enjoyed a decent meal, before continuing along the coastal path to

Nieuwpoort. It felt good racing Thomas Docwra and my father along the dunes, the biting cold wind seeping through my muffler, as our two escorts straggled behind. I recalled the last time I had galloped along the coast, with Marguerite, looking down on the plain of Hyères, in the south of France. How long ago that seemed.

Now, having travelled twenty-five leagues, we finally reached the west side of the city of Bruges, entering through the *Smedenpoort*, or Blacksmith's Gate. Although it was busy with merchant's barges unloading their wares, Bruges no longer enjoyed the trade it once had. Only twenty years before it had been a key trading centre in north-west Europe, exporting Flemish cloth all over the continent. Now the cities of Antwerp and Ghent were far more prosperous.

As we clattered over the bridge, the River Dijver flowing below, I looked up at the city walls still lined with banners from the cardinal's visit in August. They now hung limp and somewhat battered by the wind. Thomas Docwra trotted his horse beside me and told me how the cardinal had proceeded in great state, his company including many nobles. The emperor himself had waited to greet him and all in all, there had been over one thousand horses. Entertainments followed, all paid for by the emperor, in return for the hospitality he had enjoyed at the cardinal's expense at Canterbury, the year before. These were followed by interminable and tedious discussions.

In contrast, our progress was a sober affair as we trotted towards the *Princenhof*, the former residence of the Dukes of Burgundy, in the Rue Nord du Sablon. A carillon of bells rang out, reminding me of St Rombouts, in Mechelen, and a flight of starlings scattered into the air. As we approached the narrow, painted houses with their stepped roofs, weathervanes and intricate brickwork, I smiled at the housewives sweeping the leaves from the steps of their dwellings. How familiar it all seemed, so clean and tidy, unlike the French towns and villages, knee-deep in mud and offal. I would have liked to have stopped and visited the *Grôte Markt*, for as carts carrying cloth, wine and pelts rumbling past, today appeared to be market day.

Sadly, I knew time was short, and I trotted on behind my father, our escort following until we approached a great, sprawling palace. As we halted outside its arched gateway, the guards asked for my father's papers, and I lowered the hood of my cloak to gaze up at the stone shield carved with the arms of Burgundy. We then walked our horses through the gate and across the courtyard to another archway. This was the entrance to the *Princenhof*, and it appeared to be attached to a rather impressive chapel. We turned our horses to the stone steps and dismounted, and I noticed that the hem of my travelling gown was badly stained with mud. As our escorts led our horses to the stables, I attempted to tidy my straying hair.

'Time enough for that, Anne,' said my father, pulling off his gloves. 'We have private lodgings at the back of the palace, at the Hôtel Vert, where you can change before your interview.'

I followed my father and Thomas Docwra up another set of stone steps, to a beautiful walled garden with an ornamental trellis and pond. In the mid-morning mist, a gardener busied himself pruning a hawthorn bush. But there was no time to stop as we hurried through the gardens to our lodgings on the Rue du Markcage. Inside, the hôtel, once the residence of the Count de Charolais, appeared comfortable enough, with Flemish tapestries lining the walls. The heavy, iron candelabra were already lit, and great shadows danced about the wooden rafters of the vaulted ceiling, giving the place an eerie feeling. A large, Flemish woman, her fair hair bound in thick braids, bade us follow her up the stairs.

'Here,' said my father, opening the chamber. 'Your bags will be brought shortly. Your meeting with Margaret is at three of the clock this afternoon, so you have time to prepare yourself. Refreshments will be sent up privately, and I will be in the chamber just down the hall, should you require anything.'

I peered inside and a young Flemish girl, her white coif and apron clean and crisp, bobbed in greeting. I turned and asked if my father would eat with me.

'I cannot.' He walked over to the window to look down. 'Thomas and I must prepare our brief for the meeting tomorrow, although he is complaining that he feels feverish. I will leave you and will return later.'

As he left I sat down on the bed, lay back and closed my eyes.

* *

Sitting outside the door, I knew I looked my best, although having fallen asleep, I had left myself little time to prepare. I had chosen a dark blue gown, its sleeves of blue lined with cream silk, and a simple French hood. I wore no jewellery, except for a single strand of white pearls about my neck. My long hair fell over my shoulders, burnished and brushed to perfection. I could not have chosen better, but oh, how nervous I felt! My father stood with his hands behind his back, fiddling restlessly. And then it came.

'*Entrez!*'

In that very moment, I was back at Mechelen, a child, about to have my first meeting with Margaret of Savoy. As the door opened, my father swept in and approached the woman sitting at her desk. He kissed her outstretched hand. 'Most gracious lady.'

'Ah, welcome, Thomas, are you well? My sincere congratulations on being appointed treasurer.'

'My thanks, dear lady, I am well, although Docwra has fallen ill. Now, may I present my daughter, Anne, to you?'

Margaret rose as I sank gracefully to the floor, not daring to raise my eyes.

'My goodness! Can this lovely woman be the young girl who first came to my court all those years ago?' She walked

towards me and raised me, and I smelt her familiar, sweet
perfume. 'My dear child, how you have grown! Thomas,
what a charming creature your daughter has become, thank
you for bringing her to me again. She was ever-delightful
before, but now – why, I can hardly believe my eyes.'

When I looked up, I stared into the brown eyes of the
duchess. I had been but a child when I last saw her, and
I could see that she, like myself, had changed. Now in her
early forties, plumper of face, her golden hair showed a few
grey strands beneath her white coif, but she appeared as
elegant as ever in her black velvet gown, a golden girdle at her
waist. The skin around her eyes was more lined than before,
but she still had the most delightful smile. I kissed her hand.

'Why,' she said, gently holding me away from her, 'you
now match my height, although I do not have your willowy
figure. As you can see, my waist has thickened out but well,
that is what age does. Oh, I cannot believe what an elegant
lady you have become. Please, sit here with me and let me
look at you. Thomas – please.'

I took the chair beside her while my father poured three
glasses of wine.

'You were ever the most willing of all my young girls,'
she said as I sipped the Burgundian wine. 'I was so pleased
to receive your letters.'

I thanked her for the gifts she had sent over the years,
and when I told her the most pleasing gift from her was
my dog, she appeared surprised. She asked if I still had the
little bitch.

'Ah, what was her name now – it began with a 'B?''

I reminded her, and she laughed.

'That was your fault, Thomas, you insisted I find your
daughter a puppy of her own. You would not give me a
moment's peace until I did.'

My father smiled politely but I knew he was not
genuinely amused.

'Ah, Anne, when my little dog Bella died, I could not

bear to replace her. I am so happy that your dog has proved a faithful companion.'

'Madame, I would have brought her to you,' I said, glancing at my father, 'but it was decided to leave her behind. Do you still have your parrot, Patou?'

'Ah, my devoted, green companion,' she said wistfully. 'Sadly, no, he died, as did my guinea pig.

We then spoke of the court, and I said I had always missed the homeliness of her household and her gentle guidance.

'And did good people find you?' she asked, a mischievous look in her eye. I recalled the words she had said at our parting.

'They did, Madame, for Queen Claude proved ever wise, gentle and loving.'

I then asked who might still be with her that I remembered, but she said all had long gone. The Countess of Hochstrate had retired, and Madame Symonnet had returned to Calais. The girls I knew had returned to their families or married. We both felt sad that dear Beatrice had died.

'Now, I hear, you too, Anne, are to be married?'

I glanced at my father.

'There is a proposal, Madame,' he said, 'but I am not happy with the terms as yet. Still, the cardinal is pushing for it in the hope of settling some difficulty in Ireland.'

Margaret then asked of my music and I told her I still had the beautiful lute she had given me. She appeared delighted.

'Ah, do you recall what I once told you, Anne, in the schoolroom? Never stop singing and playing, for it is a jewel beyond price and measure, more than any princely thing on earth.'

We then spoke of my time in France, and of Amboise where Margaret had been brought up as a child. Of Louise and Marguerite, and a little of King François, but only a little. She complimented me on my perfect French and apologised that she had never learnt English. Too many other pressing matters, she said.

'Tell me, are your lodgings comfortable?' She turned to my father.

'Madame, they were good enough for the cardinal, so yes, I thank you.'

'Ah, the cardinal,' she said. 'Such wealth. The men and women of Bruges visited his lodgings just to see the plate he brought over from Calais, and to drink his wine. I visited him several times, and he entertained Gattinara, Berghes, and others with singers from his private chapel. He visited me privately and on one occasion, spoke with the Emperor Charles and myself the whole day, not returning home until very late in the evening.'

'But has anything been achieved?' asked my father. 'Sir Thomas More is convinced there will be peace between France and the Empire.'

'Thomas, he is wise and discreet, but you must know that the emperor has empowered me, and my advisor, Berghes, to arrange a treaty of marriage with England, and ratify any stipulation for war against France which it might contain. Of course, were Chièvres still alive, he might have advised differently.'

'Wolsey fears a truce will be all he can obtain,' said my father.

Margaret nodded. 'Perhaps, but none of us can agree on for how long. The French king has abandoned Tournai and has ravaged and destroyed the Habsburg region of Artois. However, he says he will consent to halt his army for three days if the emperor does the same.'

'But Madame, who will make the first move?' asked my father. 'King François is encamped near Cambrai and is proving very difficult to treat with. First, he wants one period of truce, and then another. How can one treat with such a man?'

'Thomas, although Wolsey promises that King Henry will never fail the French, I can assure you he will. The

Emperor Charles intends to marry Princess Mary of England. He will not change his mind for he sees well what the cardinal wishes to do with him, regarding France. That is to say, asking things so unreasonable that neither he – nor I – could agree to them either for his honour or advantage.'

My father rose and refilled Margaret's glass. She asked if we would be returning to England. He replied we would, and it had been suggested that the other ambassadors return at a later date – but not all at once. Worcester and Ely must withdraw separately, and Wingfield must stay until he could be replaced.

'We will, of course, return briefly to the Staple Hall to return the horses and then proceed to the port at Calais.'

'Ah, Anne,' said Margaret, stretching out to take my hand, 'how I wish you had more time to see this beautiful city. The windmills that encircle it are quite a sight, as are the great ramparts and the inner canals. The *Grôte Markt* is just as busy as the one in Mechelen. Do you remember?'

I said I did and asked her if there was a *Begijnhof* in Bruges.

'But of course, in the south of the city. At Mechelen, you used to buy my ribbons and lace from the pious ladies when they visited the court at Christ-tide. It all seems so long ago and when I look at you, I know I am getting older. Plus, my aching knees tell me it is so.'

'Dearest lady,' said my father rising from his chair. I stood up. 'We have taken too much of your time already, and must leave you to your next meeting, for I gather Lord Berghes will be along shortly. We must return to our lodgings and hope that Docwra is well enough to travel.'

Margaret rose and took me in her arms. 'Dear child, my blessings go with you. I will always be interested to hear about your progress, and I hope you will be as happy at the English court as you have been in France. You must now return home and go with my deepest affection.'

I kissed her fondly on both cheeks, then kissed her hand.

'Madame, you will be forever in my prayers.'

As my father took my arm, he turned. 'Why, if the world lay in the hands of such as yourself, Madame, there would be no earthly troubles in all the realms of Europe.'

•   •

'Anne – I – I am so sorry. I have been dreading your return.'

As the grooms led our horses away to the warmth of the stables at the Staple Hall, at Calais, I pulled off my muffler and turned to see Anne de Graville. She was standing in a muddy puddle, her face white.

'What has happened?' I asked, walking towards her. I gave out a great sneeze for I appeared to have caught Thomas Docwra's cold.

She lowered her hood and shook her head. 'Oh, Anne, it happened so fast,' she mumbled, 'before I could stop her.'

'What? What has happened? Where is Bonny?'

Anne stood wringing her hands. 'She ran off, not long after you left. She scratched and scraped at the door of your chamber, and when I opened it, just a little, she shot out. I cried out to people to stop her, but they just stood mute. I then watched her disappear fast as lightning down the main staircase, but could not see where she went. I made the guards go out and look for her, but although they checked the building and surrounding areas, they could not find her. I sat up all night hoping she would return to eat, but then dawn came and nothing, no sign of her at all.'

'But where else did you look, where else did you try?' I asked, my expression frantic. 'Oh, God, Anne, my poor Bonny, what if she is trapped or injured? How dare you lose my little dog!'

As I sneezed again Anne took off her cloak and placed it around my shoulders.

'Did – did you check all the chambers?' I asked, in terror. 'And the kitchen. What about the bakehouse? Oh,

Anne, we must look immediately, how *could* you be so careless!'

As we walked back, my gloves and whip in my hand, I thought I might die of sorrow. How could I return home now, without the one companion who had never left my side since coming to France? Had I not spoken of her to Duchess Margaret, not two days past?

I turned to see Anne's desolate face. I had trusted her completely, and yet I knew how quickly Bonny could wriggle away. I also knew that she hated being left alone, even for an hour, and so this was all my father's fault. Had he let me take her with me, she would not now be lost.

Anne de Graville turned to me. 'Perhaps, dear Anne, it is for the best, for she may not have settled in England.'

I knew this was untrue since Bonny would have been content wherever I happened to be. I could hardly speak, for I was incandescent with rage. I wondered if Bonny might be hurt somewhere, or even worse, had she been attacked by one of the hunting hounds?

As if reading my mind, Anne spoke. 'Nothing has been found,' she said. 'If the dogs had attacked her, the *grand veneur* would have reported it. You know the law on attacking ladies' lap-dogs.'

As we returned to the hall, I knew there was little I could do until I had seen Marguerite and told her the situation. Perhaps she would send out more servants to check farther afield. Either way, I knew I could not blame Anne, for it had just been the most dreadful accident.

That night, I wandered Calais alone, searching and calling Bonny's name until dawn. Only when the birds began their dawn chorus, did I wearily return to the Staple Hall and my chamber. As I closed the door, I stood crying and shivering with cold. I then bent down and picked up my little dog's blue leash and sat on my bed. The sight of her white hairs scattered about on the coverlet broke my heart and, covering my face with my hands, I curled up into a ball and cried myself to sleep. I would not – could not – leave Calais without her.

* *

I knew she insisted on such a place wherever she travelled, for she often wished to enjoy complete peace: a private sanctuary away from the court, a refuge from its constant demands. As the usher opened the door, I saw her seated, head down, a paper in her hand. Dressed in a loose, black velvet robe trimmed with white ermine, her fingers twirled a strand of hair as it lay loose about her shoulders. A fire blazed, and her spaniel lay curled in a ball on a floor cushion at her feet. I gave a low curtsey and a sneeze.

'Ah, Anne, please come in,' said Marguerite, pointing to a chair. 'You look tired and unwell. Now, forgive the informality, I am just reading a letter from my spiritual advisor. But it can wait.'

Her little dog looked up and wagged its tail and I felt my eyes prick with tears. Marguerite glanced at it.

'My dear girl, I am so sorry to hear about Bonny. I have sent servants out to look everywhere they can, but so far they have reported nothing. Please, do not despair.'

I thanked her as she asked me to sit.

'Anne is very upset,' she continued, 'for she feels responsible. She said she has never seen you so angry before.'

'It was not her fault, Madame, but tomorrow I must leave with my father for home. I cannot bear to abandon Bonny, to think she might still be here, trapped and lost somewhere. I feel desolate.'

'Anne, we will do all we can to help. If she does appear, we will, of course, return her to you. Please try not to worry. Come now, let us talk of brighter matters. I gather your betrothal is to be finalised, and so you must be very excited.'

I said I could feel nothing at present, so numb was my heart. However, I had come to regard France as my home, and I would miss her, Queen Claude and Renée very much.

She said she would miss me, too, for she had fond memories of our conversations. Now, a new life lay ahead of me, and, God willing, I would one day enjoy a family of my own. She smiled in sympathy as I sneezed again.

'Now,' she said, rising and picking up a large book from a nearby table. 'I would like to give you a parting gift, a wedding gift if you like.'

I stared at the dark blue, velvet-bound book in her hands.

'I was wondering what to give you, but since you have a great love of music, I think this is most apt. Here, take it with my blessing.'

I took the book from her hands and opened it, my finger tracing the cream silk marker.

'But – but this is exquisite,' I murmured, quite overcome. As I turned the pages, I saw before me the compositions of Loyset Compère, Antoine Brumel, Jean Mouton and Josquin des Prez. All were Franco-Flemish composers whose work I admired, and the sacred and secular pieces of Masses, motets and *chansons* danced before my eyes. This collection of music was priceless and surely fit for a queen.

'As you are aware,' said Marguerite, 'these great composers are now all in their graves – except for Jean Mouton – but I truly believe des Prez, not long-buried, was the greatest composer of our time.'

I said I felt quite overcome, for I particularly loved the work of Mouton and putting him in charge of the musical festivities for the meeting at Guînes last year had been inspired.

'Well, he was my mother's choice,' said Marguerite, 'for she is blessed with the greatest of musical taste. Now, you must promise me that you will add more works to this book, and so continue to study and expand your library of music.'

At that moment, the queen entered, fat, ungainly and open-laced. Only three months off giving birth, she appeared to be the most cumbersome I had ever seen her. Putting the book down, I sank in reverence, but she quickly raised me.

'Ah, my dear, I am so sorry to hear of your little dog. Renée will be so upset to hear she has gone missing, for she loved the dear little thing so much.'

I said I would always think fondly of the girl and remember her in my prayers.

'Now, I, too, have a small gift of thanks,' she continued, as she handed me a black velvet pouch.

When I opened the drawstring and took out the contents, I beheld a beautiful, silver falcon, wings outstretched in flight, holding a *fleur-de-lis* flower in its beak. A perfect, round emerald glinted from its eye. The queen explained that she had intended to give it to me as a New Year's gift, and that it had been made in Paris. I was so touched that I felt unable to speak as she pinned the brooch to my gown. The dark burgundy set off the silver to perfection.

'Thank you,' she said, 'for all the service you have done me, for cheering me when sad, and for helping Renée with her English. You have proved a delightful companion to her. We will all miss you very much.'

I kissed her cold hand. 'God bless you, my lady, and the coming child.'

Marguerite then moved forward to kiss me on both cheeks. She wished me great happiness but I could not reply for fear I might lose my composure.

'Now,' said Marguerite, brightly, 'I must return to my letter, and the queen here must rest. I am sure you wish to say goodbye to various people, so you are excused for the rest of today. It only remains for me to bid you God speed and a safe journey. We, ourselves, will shortly be returning to Amboise.'

Picking up the book, I gave one final curtsey and walked towards the door. As I opened it, Marguerite spoke.

'Anne, please rest assured, we will do all we can to find your little dog.'

Averting my eyes from the squalor, I stared into the distance at the fort defending the harbour entrance of the port. Although banners and streamers hung from the tower, there was nothing brave or gay about them. They just looked dismal in the November mist, as did the caravels that bobbed in the dark water, sails furled.

Turning, I watched as a great wooden crane swung into the air, lifting crates of French wine onto our waiting carrack – *The Bethany*. As I saw my father fumble through his papers and documents, cursing when one blew away, I wondered if the wine was bound for the English court.

On the dockside, bells clanged, and sailors hauling the ropes of the square sails shouted out to each other as the vessel swayed and creaked on the water. A dead cat floated past, bloated, as the filthy water slapped against the mossy stone below, and I was glad that we had prayed at the *Église Notre-Dame* for a safe crossing. I recalled with horror the last time I had sailed on the Narrow Seas and felt deeply apprehensive. To return to England in the winter was surely the worse time of year to travel. Would I endure a dreadful voyage again? Would I reach England safely?

Coughing, I anxiously looked around at the crowds of merchants and travellers. All life appeared to be here, including the harlots as they stood, sunken-eyed and diseased, waiting for custom. Beggars sitting on the filthy cobbles, their coats torn to shreds and offering no protection against the bitter cold, cursed and spat as it began to rain. Inside, my heart was breaking. How could I possibly leave, not knowing what had happened to my dog? I had spoken barely a word to my father, for I blamed him entirely for my loss, and I would never forgive him. When he offered to buy me a hot pie from one of the traders who approached with her tray, I shook my head, refusing to speak.

Leaving him to fight off the seabirds that had descended

upon him as he attempted to enjoy the steaming, hot crust,
I wandered over to the edge of the stone wall and gazed out
to sea. Apparently, on a clear day, one could see the Kent
coast. My home.

My father called out to me. 'Come, Anne, it is time
to leave!'

I noticed he was covered in crumbs as he descended
the wooden walkway, bags slung over his shoulder. Greasy
rats scurried out of his way, and two men grumbled as they
picked up my heavy chest of belongings by its rope handles.

'Anne, will you come along now!' he cried, turning.

I stood rooted to the spot. I was not ready. I refused
to leave without my dog. After some moments, my father
walked back to me and took me roughly by the arm.

'For the love of God, will you board the boat, or I will
leave you here. What's done is done, and I will not endure
this incessant, miserable face a moment longer. I'll get you
another damned dog.'

I alighted, reluctantly, onto the waiting carrack and we
made our way to the open decking in the middle of the boat.
There, I sat on my wooden chest, huddled inside my cloak,
as the sailors climbed up the rigging and unfurled the ship's
masts. Shouting and calling to each other, all was noise and
bustle as preparations to cast off began. When the bell finally
sounded, we began to drift slowly away from the stone steps,
bit by bit, swaying and lilting. And then I saw her. Jumping
up from the chest, my eyes wide, I ran to the wooden rail.

'Anne! Anne, I am *here*!' I called.

As I frantically waved, Anne de Graville hurried down
the mossy steps, the hood of her cloak falling from her head.
In her arms, she held my dog.

'Anne, I have her, I have Bonny! Look, she is safe
and well!'

My little dog began frantically barking, but Anne had
the leash wound tightly about her hand and held her close.

'*Bonny!*' I leaned over the rail.

'Fitzwilliam – we will send her back with *Fitzwilliam!*' shouted Anne. 'Do not worry, she will be safe this time, I promise!'

'Thank you!' I cried, 'Oh, thank you, thank you!'

Sinking to the deck and clinging to the rail, I watched as Anne, Bonny, and Calais, with its castle and church tower, receded slowly into the distance. Soon, I could barely see them at all, and I turned my face up to the falling rain. As it gently touched my cheeks, I lowered my hood and thanked God for finding my precious dog.

Before long my thoughts turned to those I was leaving behind. Although François was king, it was the women in his life – particularly his formidable, terrifying mother, Louise – who truly ruled. The queen had given the king the sons he needed, and I hoped she would survive the coming birth. I would miss her gentle dignity, courage and fortitude. She was a daughter of France and never once doubted it. As to Marguerite, how I had loved the hours spent listening to her views, for she had awakened in me a great love for God's word. I would do all I could to emulate her, reading, learning and doing good works where I could, as a good Christian woman. Of all women, she whom I had once disliked, would be as a shining light.

When I pictured the lovely Françoise, I wondered how long she would remain the king's mistress. The very opposite of Marguerite, she was cunning, ambitious, daring and immoral, and yet I had learnt much from observing how she handled the king: No matter what demands and ultimatums she made, she knew he would always return to her side. It was an extraordinary power that surely could not last.

I smiled when Clément came to mind. What a child I had been, swept away by his exciting words, flattered by his attention. But although I had said I would never forgive him, I knew in my heart I would always hold him dear. Not so the Comte de Chalon. I had behaved cruelly with the confidence of youth, not caring a whit for his feelings, and I felt glad that I would never have to face him again.

Now, as the moment of leaving France arrived, I felt mixed emotions. Seven years had elapsed since a small girl of fourteen, awkward yet eager to impress, had arrived at court, quite believing she could talk, smile and charm her way through anything. All I had cared about was to please whomever I needed to please, keep myself above reproach and concentrate on my education. And what an education it had been. I had travelled, met artists, writers and poets and seen at first hand the machinations of court life. Now, if I did succeed in obtaining a place with Queen Katherine I knew that my French manners, poise, and sophistication would set me apart from the other English ladies. So must I really throw these off as my father had advised? Surely I was still an English woman, born and bred, a Boleyn and a Howard? No, I wanted to flaunt my education and my experiences, for I had finally grown into the young woman I had always wanted to be, confident and assured. My sister might be happy with her William, but I was destined for a far better life than she – whatever that might be.

As I stood and gazed out towards the grey, rolling sea, I sighed in contentment. I caring nothing for the rain. Nothing mattered any more. My little dog would soon be joining me, and as I looked up to the lowering sky, I smiled. I was sailing home – sailing back to England – and my heart sang with joy.

The End

Acknowledgements

Mr Peter Harvey for assisting me with French translations and for his editing work. Mr Hugues Marion for his patience over many months translating books on Queen Claude from French to English. Pamela Bridge for her translation work on Claude's life. Professor Robert Knecht for kindly assisting me in my research. Professor Kathleen Wilson-Chevalier, the American University of Paris. Cynthia J. Brown, Professor, Department of French and Italian, University of California.

Eliane Viennot, Université Jean Monnet (Saint-Etienne) & IUF. Dr David Potter, School of History, University of Kent for information on early, modern France. Dr Stephen Tyre, University of St Andrews. Renée Davray-Piekolek, Conservateur en chef, Musée Carnavalet, for information on maps of old Paris. Pierre-Gilles Girault, Conservateur, Château Royal de Blois, France for his assistance. Anne-Sophie Bessero, at the château-musée de Gien. Dick Wursten for his kind assistance and information on the early work of Clément Marot. Hernán Buteler Bonaparte for pointing me towards the Butler Society Journals, and also to other society members for information on James Butler. And finally, Claire and Tim Ridgway for helping to get these books out to the world.

Author interview

Why write a book about the years Anne Boleyn spent in France?

The reason for me writing this book, apart from following on from the first, was because little has been written about Anne's seven years at the French court. I wanted to know more about the world she lived in and how the things she experienced affected her later opinions and behaviour. By the time she and King Henry had met, she had already led a full life, well versed in the ways of the court.

As we know so little of Anne's time in France. Where did you begin?

When I started this book, there was not a great deal of information on this period of Anne's life. However, it made sense that if Anne served Queen Claude, as one of her young ladies, she would most likely have been where she resided. So, it was to Claude's life I first looked and I began by researching books and papers about her. I then had a timeline of events and could slot Anne into them. I also needed to know where King François, Marguerite, Louise of Savoy and the people around her were at any given time. Thus, little by little, using books, journals and state papers, I was able to piece together a chart and see where the key players resided from 1514 to 1521, and what they were up to. I also plotted their movements on a map of France, so that I had a visual reference.

Did you just consult books and papers?

No, not at all. I felt it essential to actually visit the places Anne would have known. The châteaux of Blois and Amboise, Loche and others along the Loire valley gave me a feel for the countryside, the buildings and the opulence Anne must have experienced. Paris, Amiens and Marseille were also visited and my travels gave me an idea of distance. I knew that the court travelled extensively, but when I plotted my map, I was surprised to see just how much of France Anne probably experienced. In fact, her journey's with Claude took her from Calais all the way down to the south of France. This was no mean feat at a time when travel was difficult, even using the rivers. Interestingly, it has been assumed that because Claude was constantly pregnant, she did not travel, but from contemporary journals, it appears she did.

Why Clément Marot?

It is actually thought that Marot had a passion for the lovely Anne d'Alençon (as well as a fondness for Marguerite) and wrote fifty-five pieces inspired by her. However, I felt he was just the type of man who would have appealed to the young Anne Boleyn. In my novel, it is she who captures his heart and I like to think that maybe he had Anne in mind when he wrote the poem at the front of this book. On the subject of romance, we can only speculate as to whether or not Anne did have liaisons, and so for the sake of a story, I have imagined her relationship with Marot and the Comte de Châllons. Only Anne will ever know the truth. I do believe she learnt a great deal about love in France – very likely from observing Françoise – and that what she learnt affected the way she was later able to handle King Henry.

*Would Anne really have been interested in what
was going on around her?*

It would have been expected, for Claude's ladies
would have had to talk intelligently to ambassadors and
guests. Whilst in France, she would have been kept fully
informed of life in England, particularly when her father
became ambassador to the French court. No doubt she
was useful to him, being so close to Claude and hearing
what was discussed. Of course, we can never know private
conversations that occurred, but I am certain that the events
I have written about would have been discussed. The New
Learning sweeping Europe, for instance, would have been
the talk of the day.

How true is this account?

Although a novel, I hope that this journey of Anne's is
believable. All the characters actually existed and must have
influenced her to some degree. I certainly think they shaped
her later evangelical interest regarding the bible. All of the
events I have written about did actually occur, (the only
difference is that for the sake of a story, I have placed Anne at
the centre of the action.) I have kept to the correct dates and
time frame wherever possible, and used known conversations
where possible.

And finally…

Anne's years in France honed her intelligence and wit,
and she had much to offer long before she ever met King
Henry. By the time she did meet him, she had attended
two European courts, and led a life that other English ladies
could only dream about. Confident and cosmopolitan, she
was no green girl, and it is no wonder she went on to capture
the heart of a king.

About the Author

Originally from Derbyshire, Natalia trained as a graphic designer and illustrator, before deciding to become a museum curator and fulfil a passion for all things historical. Working with collections ranging from toys and military objects, to Royal Crown Derby China, she is now retired and divides her time between London and Derbyshire.

In her spare time, Natalia likes to walk in the Derbyshire countryside, research the Tudors, and travel abroad.

This is her second novel. Her first book, *The Falcon's Rise*, covered Anne Boleyn's earlier life.

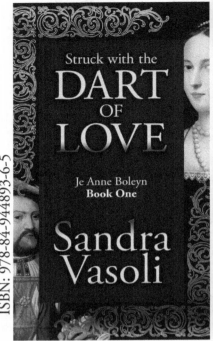
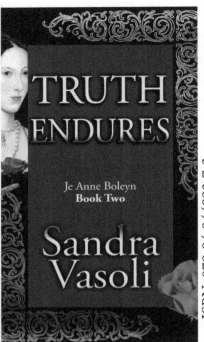

In a love letter to Anne Boleyn, Henry VIII wrote: *"It is absolutely necessary for me to obtain this answer, having been for above a whole year stricken with the dart of love, and not yet sure whether I shall fail of finding a place in your heart and affection…"*

Sandra Vasoli's Je Anne Boleyn series is a compelling memoir, narrated in a richly detailed, authentic voice, which depicts one of the most exceptional women in the history of England: Anne Boleyn. It is at once romantic, eloquent, and insightful. Through the series, the reader will come to know Anne as an intimate friend.

"This is a beautifully written, first-person account of Henry VIII's courtship of Anne Boleyn. The first book begins at their first real exchange, and ends at their marriage." – **Janet Wertman**

"I love that Sandra Vasoli's Je Anne Boleyn novels have the feel of a memoire. It's as if I've sat down with Anne herself to hear the tale of how she came to be the king's love and executed queen. Vasoli fills her tale with rich detail, yet it is extremely readable. Without giving away too much, I can say that I really enjoyed the way Vasoli ended her heart-rending saga." – **Adrienne Dillard**

ISBN: 978-84-946498-3-7

Jane Parker never dreamed that her marriage into the Boleyn family would raise her star to such dizzying heights. Before long, she finds herself as trusted servant and confidante to her sister-in-law, Anne Boleyn; King Henry VIII's second queen. On a gorgeous spring day, that golden era is cut short by the swing of a sword. Jane is unmoored by the tragic death of her husband, George, and her loss sets her on a reckless path that leads to her own imprisonment in the Tower of London. Surrounded by the remnants of her former life, Jane must come to terms with her actions. In the Tower, she will face up to who she really is and how everything went so wrong.

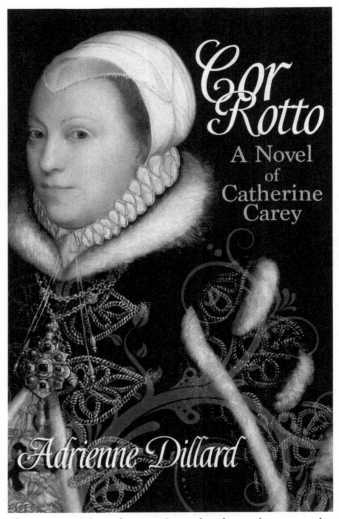

Cor
Rotto

A Novel
of
Catherine
Carey

Adrienne Dillard

ISBN: 978-84-937464-7-6

Fifteen year-old Catherine Carey has been dreaming the same dream for three years, since the bloody execution of her aunt Queen Anne Boleyn. Her only comfort is that she and her family are safe in Calais, away from the intrigues of Henry VIII's court. But now Catherine has been chosen to serve Henry VIII's new wife, Queen Anne of Cleves.

Just before she sets off for England, she learns the family secret: the true identity of her father, a man she considers to be a monster and a man she will shortly meet.

This compelling novel tells the life story of a woman who survived being close to the crown and who became one of Elizabeth I's closest confidantes.

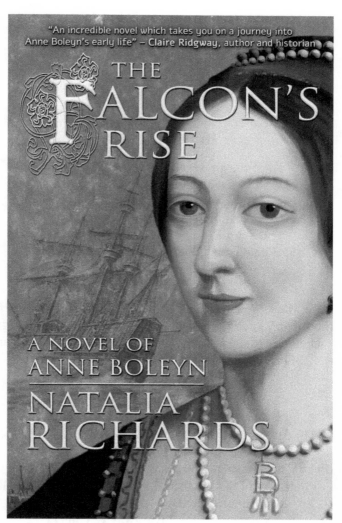

ISBN: 978-84-946498-8-2

"An incredible novel which takes you on a journey into Anne Boleyn's early life" – **Claire Ridgway**, author and historian

THE FALCON'S RISE

A NOVEL OF ANNE BOLEYN

NATALIA RICHARDS

Born into the Boleyn family in rural Norfolk, obscurity looms, but when Anne's father, Thomas, moves the family to Hever Castle, in Kent, to further his own interests, the family's fortunes take a turn for the better. Thomas secures a place for Anne's sister, Mary, at the prestigious court of Margaret of Austria, but fate has other plans, and Anne ends up taking her place.

At thirteen, Anne yearns for adventure. However, unused to curbing her outspoken tongue and youthful curiosity, she discovers that life at Margaret's court is not quite how she'd imagined. Experiencing love, loss, jealousy and fear, she soon realises that her future happiness lies in her own hands - and that she must shape her own destiny...

Historical Fiction

The Sebastian Foxley Series – **Toni Mount**
The Death Collector – **Toni Mount**
Struck With the Dart of Love – **Sandra Vasoli**
Truth Endures – **Sandra Vasoli**
Cor Rotto – **Adrienne Dillard**
The Raven's Widow – **Adrienne Dillard**

Historical Colouring Books

The Mary, Queen of Scots Colouring Book – **Roland Hui**
The Life of Anne Boleyn Colouring Book – **Claire Ridgway**
The Wars of the Roses Colouring Book – **Debra Bayani**
The Tudor Colouring Book – **Ainhoa Modenes**

Non Fiction History

The Turbulent Crown – **Roland Hui**
Anne Boleyn's Letter from the Tower – **Sandra Vasoli**
Tudor Places of Great Britain – **Claire Ridgway**
Illustrated Kings and Queens of England – **Claire Ridgway**
A History of the English Monarchy – **Gareth Russell**
The Fall of Anne Boleyn – **Claire Ridgway**
George Boleyn – **Ridgway & Cherry**
The Anne Boleyn Collection I, II & III – **Claire Ridgway**

PLEASE LEAVE A REVIEW

If you enjoyed this book, *please* leave
a review at the book seller where you
purchased it. There is no better way to thank
the author and it really does make a huge
difference! *Thank you in advance.*